BREATHE
with me

MICHELLE B.

ISBN: 978-0-9991786-2-1

Editor: Sabrina Capriotti
Cover Designer: Pink Ink Designs
Interior Design and Formatting: Pink Ink Designs

Proofreader: Kara Hildebrand

BREATHE *with me*

Dedication

To the man who let me be free, to be me.
I love you
M.

What is Beautiful?

Beautiful is the sun shining on your face.
The ocean crashing on the shore.
The laughter from a loved one.
But, my kind of beautiful, is the little girl with
expressive green eyes I played with as a child.
She's the same little girl who became a teenager
and filled every one of my dreams.
She's the teenager who blossomed into a
woman that fuels my heart.
My woman.
My woman is a green-eyed goddess and
her name is Sofia Rose Heart.
That's what is beautiful to me.

Caelan O'Reily

one

Ouch!! Oh, that hurts. Damn, my head is killing me.

What in the hell happened to me? Why do I feel so foggy? Clear the cobwebs girl, clear the cobwebs…

Realization's setting in. Something just does not feel right. My body does not feel right. This is not just the alcohol we consumed last night.

Think, Sofia. Think.

I did not get THAT drunk last night… I mean, hell, we were drinking, and we may have been drunk-but we definitely were not trashed. At least, I wasn't. I have been trashed many nights, but last night… was not one of them.

Something's not right. I can't move. Why is it so dark in here? Where am I?

Wait, wait, wait! Holy hell, something's really wrong here. Where am I? Why can't I see anything? Why can't I move? Why do I feel like a ton of bricks fell on me and I'm still stuck under the rubble? I feel like I am moving, but I'm not moving... at least… I don't think I am anyway. What is that smell? It smells like urine. Why do I smell urine?

WHAM!!

The memories... they come barreling back to me. Like a shotgun to the chest, panic starts to set in.

Sofia Rose Heart get your shit together! And-and-and... Jesus get your shit together and figure out what the fuck is going on. Damn that smell! That goddamn smell.

My heart is pounding. Darkness is all around me.

Shit! What was that? Did I hear something? No, that had to just be my heart pounding in my ears from the panic that's starting to work its way into my body...

Move, Sof! MOVE! GODDAMN IT! MOVE! Ugh... why is my cheek so cold? And why is it that all I can smell is piss? Panic! That smell. God that smell... That smell makes me think of him. That nasty vile piece of shi- Wait... I heard it again. What was that?

That smell-the smell of dirty, nasty, stagnant piss. That smell is tattooed in my nostrils. It will never go away. Panic! That smell brings me right back to that horrible night, the night I went through hell, the night that was supposed to be one of the best nights. That night is one that will be engraved into my brain forever. My twenty-first birthday party. That smell brings me right back to the pain-the pain, pure panic, and pure hatred for that sick, vile, monster who abducted me.

Breathe, Sof. Breathe.

Panic is setting in, overtaking my body. I can't move. I want to, I want to get the hell out of here, but something is stopping me.

PANIC!

Oh, God. No. Am I handcuffed again? Is that why I can't move? I don't hear the clanging of the cuffs against the cold steel.

Breathe, Sofia. Breathe.

I feel like my arm is a hundred pounds. I really cannot move! *OH, NO, NO, NO!!!! THIS CAN'T BE HAPPENING AGAIN!!! OH, GOD NO! NOT AGAIN! LIFE CANNOT BE THIS CRUEL, NOT AGAIN!*

Shit, what was that?

Someone's here. Please help me. Wait, is that him? Please, no...please let it be someone that can help me. They're getting closer, Closer, CLOSER. OH, GOD PLEASE!

BREATHE! BREATHE! BREATHE!

I hear the footsteps not far away. The fighter in me is kicking in. It's fight or flight time, but I can't move. I hear a door. The handle? I think so. Now, footsteps and a male voice. Confusion wracks my brain. Yes, definitely a male voice. What did he say?

Everything sounds so far away. I'm so confused, so disoriented. How did I let this happen to myself again? I'm always so careful now. I always watch my surroundings. I always make sure *he* is not following me.

Ever since that dreadful night when he abducted me, only for him to let me go a day later. Now, I always watch my back. Caelan always watches my back. He would never let anything happen to me. We were together last night. He would destroy anyone who would try and hurt me. How did this happen again, especially with both of us being so cautious? How did he get to me again without us knowing he was coming?

Caelan… my protector, my bodyguard, and my best friend. I have known him since I was ten years old. He would never let anything happen to me. Never! Why can't I remember?

How can this happen again?

I'm just like he said I was… Flashes of my father yelling at me fill my groggy, dazed head. He's the man I adored growing up. The man I thought hung the moon. I can still remember his hurtful words that night when I told him what happened to me, the night I was abducted. They hurt me more than anyone ever could. Pain. That's what I felt hearing him say those things to me. Pain as his words ripped my heart out. If you can't believe in your father, then who can you believe in? If your father can't believe in you, then who will believe in you? His words, those words, I never want to hear them again.

Whore.

You're just like he said you were, Sofia: Irresponsible. How could you let this happen to you again? He was right. You let this happen to you again. Whore. A word I'll never forget.

"*Sofia Rose Heart, you are the most stubborn, most irresponsible girl. Your lies, I told you, your lies were going to catch up with you. No daughter of mine will be a whore, a whore like her mother! You bear her name for Christ's sake! Like mother like daughter! You think you can spend a night away with someone? And then come back in here? After my men have been out looking for you! And then you give me a wild excuse like that? That someone abducted you? Like I would believe that. What, then they just let you go? Try again, Angel Face. Tell me, how is it I am supposed to claim you as one of mine and be proud of the woman you have grown into, when the last few years have been nothing but trouble? One of mine would never behave the way you do with your wild, partying ways. You think I don't hear things about my children? You have shamed this family. I have eyes everywhere, Sofia. You know that! I have to in order to make sure you're all safe. That's my JOB! You are the only child of mine that pushes my limits. If you keep going the way you are, you'll be dead by twenty-five. I raised you better than this. What am I supposed to do with you now? You know the type of man I am, Sofia. Tell me how it looked when I had my guards looking for you? My daughter: the whore! You have shamed this family more than once."*

Just thinking about my father that night tears my heart out. That man was my everything. He didn't believe me...

I feel some of the fog lifting. My brain feels less cloudy. Wait, what is that smell? That's a smell I cherish. I know that smell! CAELAN! It's him! He has the best smell. He smells like home, my home.

Scream for him, Sof! Scream!

Caelan, please help me! Where are we? Get us out of here before he comes back!

Why is he not answering me? He's here. He's here to save me. I hear moaning. Why is Caelan moaning? Please no! He can't be hurt. He can't be hurt! I won't survive without him.

"Hey, beautiful. How are you feeling this fine, fucking morning?"

HELP ME, CAELAN! HELP ME! I hear him chuckle. Wait, chuckle? Why is he chuckling? This isn't fucking funny! We need to get out of here!

HURRY UP CAELAN BEFORE HE GETS BACK! HELP ME! PLEASE DON'T LET HIM DO THIS TO ME AGAIN! HE SAID HE WOULD NEVER LET ME GO. HE SAID HE WOULD ALWAYS BE WATCHING, SAID HE WOULD COME BACK FOR ME. PLEASE HURRY UP BEFORE HE GETS BACK!

Oh God, I can't breathe! Breathe Sofia! Fucking breathe! Help me breathe, Caelan. You always help me breathe through this.

"Beautiful, you gonna wake up and get into bed instead of sleeping on the bathroom floor? I mean I know last night went down in the history books as one hell-of-a-friggin'-night, but, shit girl, get that fantastic ass of yours up and back in bed! I can't believe you're passed out on the bathroom floor."

PASSED OUT ON THE BATHROOM FLOOR? WAKE UP? WHAT THE FUCK IS HE TALKING ABOUT?

I'm screaming at him. Why isn't he answering me? Can't he hear me? Why can't he hear me?

"Sofia? Hey, Sofia, you okay? Hey, baby, seriously this isn't funny, open your eyes for me, beautiful. Sofia, you're scaring the shit out of me. Are you okay?" I feel his hands touching me. Shaking me.

"Sofia, Wake Up! No… no. NOOO!" he roars harshly through the cold bathroom. "SOFIA, PLEASE OPEN YOUR EYES, BABY."

Open my eyes? What is he saying? My eyes? Are they closed? Moaning. More Moaning. Why is he moaning?

"Beautiful, please say something. What hurts? You're moaning. Tell me what hurts, sweetheart." I feel air under me now, surrounding me. He's picking me up. I feel his arms wrapping around me. His arms are like a warm blanket that's fresh out of the dryer on a cold, winter morning. I can hear his heart beating fast. His arms are just like my security blanket from when I was a child. Yes, Caelan, get me out of here!

WAIT, NO. DON'T STOP! GO! RUN, RUN, RUN! WHAT ARE YOU DOING? DON'T STOP! PLEASE DON'T STOP!

Why is he putting me down? Something soft touches my almost numb, very cold skin. A blanket? Is he covering me up?

"Beautiful, open your eyes for me. Sweetheart, please open your eyes! Let me see those stunning, emerald greens. FUCK! I'm calling for help. I've got to call for help. You're going to be okay. *OPEN YOUR EYES! PLEASE!* Open them and tell me to go fuck myself. That you're hung over, and just want to sleep. Oh God, please open your fucking eyes!"

I can hear the rambling desperation in his voice. This is not Caelan. He's always so smooth. He's Mr. Calm, Mr. In Control. All 6'2" of pure muscle of him. I know something is really wrong with me because he's panicking just as badly as I am.

"911 WHAT'S YOUR emergency?"

"YES! YES! HURRY!"

"Sir calm down and tell what the emergency is."

"She unconscious. Please, HURRY!"

"Sir, what's your address?"

"230 Washington Ave. PLEASE HURRY! SOFIA, m-my friend, she won't open her eyes! I found her on the bathroom floor covered in urine. She's unconscious!"

"Is she breathing, sir?"

"YES! YES, SHE'S BREATHING! She's moaning. Something's really wrong! SOMETHING'S REALLY, REALLY, FUCKING WRONG!"

"Please, sir, calm down I can't understand you."

"I CAN'T LOSE HER! SHE'S ALL I HAVE! MA'AM PLEASE, PLEASE HELP HER!!"

"Sir, the ambulance is on the way."

"Please, please, please open your eyes, beautiful. Wake up and tell me I'm an asshole for getting us drunk last night. This is all my fault. You didn't even want to go out. I'm so sorry. Please forgive me."

I feel wetness on my cheek. Caelan's crying?

KNOCK, KNOCK.

"Sir, this is the NYPD. Open the door."

"They're here, beautiful. I told you, you're going to be okay. I'll be right back."

I feel him pull away from me. "Caelan, please don't leave me," I cry. Feeling like I'm shouting, but it's coming out a whisper.

"SOFIA?" I feel him come back to me. "Oh, thank God!"

BANG! BANG!

"SIR OPEN THE DOOR!" I hear the forceful order from somewhere that sounds far away.

"Sofia, I've got to unlock the door for them. I swear I'll be right back. I'll never leave you. You know that! It's only you and I remember? I'll be right back."

"NO! CAELAN, NO!"

"It's okay. I'll be right back."

"CAELAN, PLEASE," I shout.

"I'll be right back, beautiful. I promise."

"CAELAN HE'LL KILL YOU! DON'T GO!!"

BANG! BANG!

"SIR. OPEN. THE. DOOR. NOW!"

"I promise I'll be right back."

Silence.

two

"No, Mr. Heart, I don't know what happened. We went out to dinner, then to Club 9 for a few hours. Then came home."

Dad? Is he here? Where's here? Where am I? Beep, Beep, Beep. What is that noise?

"Yes, Mr. Heart we took a cab. Sir, with all due respect I'm twenty-seven years old, I'm pretty sure I know how to look out for myself and your daughter, sir. Yes, Sir, I told you once before, I would never let anything happen to her. I meant it when I said it the first time. She means too much to me. Yes, Sir, I know, but I'm telling you when we left Club 9 she was okay. I don't know. I'm still trying to figure that out myself. I'm still waiting for the doctors to tell me what's going on. They took a bunch of tests when she got here. No, she's still asleep. Wait, what? You're coming here? Sir, I'm not so sure that's a goo-. Yes, sir, I know you're worried, but I don't think she-. Sir... Okay, Mr. Heart. I'll see you when you get here."

My dad, is coming here? Where is "here"?

Beep, Beep, Beep.

"Beautiful, please wake up."

"Here's your coffee."

"Thanks, Nikki."

My sister's here?

"Nothing yet?"

"No. Come on, Sofia, open your damn eyes."

Why can't I open my eyes? They feel like bricks cemented to my lower lashes.

"Caelan, I heard your conversation with my father. What happened is not your fault."

"Thanks, Nikki. Honestly, though, how can this not be my fault? It's my job to protect her. I told him I would always protect her. Even if he never asked me to protect her, I would have anyway."

"Caelan we don't even know what happened yet. How could you blame yourself? You can't."

"I know, Nikki, but we were partying pretty damn hard. We were celebrating my new contract."

This is not Caelan's fault. Why is he blaming himself? I don't know what happened to me, but I know he would never let anything happen to me.

"Open your damn eyes, Sofia! Christ, she's been in and out of it for hours now," he huffs, dropping is head down onto the side of the hospital bed.

"Well, when my father gets here, just know that whatever he says to you... well, just know that this is not your fault. Okay? Seriously, don't take it to heart. He loves his children very much. You know that, and he's very overprotective of his children, especially, Sofia. I don't know why, but just keep that in mind."

"Ya, Nikki, I know. I also know in his mind I fucked up. That's not something you want that man thinking."

Caelan's been talking to my father?

Blink. Blink.

"Ugh, those lights are killing my eyes."

Blink. Blink. Blink.

Why would he be talking to my father? I haven't spoken to him since he and I had that terrible fight and he called me a whore.

"She's waking up! Caelan, she's awake!"

"Hey, beautiful." He smiles leaning down closer to me. "You have no idea how happy I am right now to see those stunning emerald greens."

"C, what happened to me?"

"Sof, I really don't know," he says, holding my hand tightly.

"My throat feels like razor blades are in there."

"Hold on let me get you some water."

"Here take this," Nikki says handing him a glass of water.

"Hey, sis. I'm so glad you're awake." She sheds silent tears. "I'm so happy you're awake," she repeats.

"Why are you here? Where am I?"

"Take a sip, drink slowly."

"My throat feels like it's on fire," I whisper taking a few sips. "Thank you. What happened to me, C?"

"You're in the emergency room. We're not sure what happened to you. The doctors ran some tests. We're waiting for the results."

Looking around, I notice I'm in a private room, not the emergency room. I'm not staying here. "This is not the ER. Why am I in a private room?"

"I'm not too sure." His unsure answer matches the pain filling his handsome features. "They came in about an hour ago, moved you from the ER to this private room."

"I don't remember anything. I feel so out of it." I close my eyes trying to get some kind of perspective as to what happened.

"I don't really know, beautiful. We went to Mr. Wong's for sushi, had our usual for dinner, then went to Club 9 and met up with Chris, Luke, and Jessica. Even Antonio showed up for a little bit, but he left early. We hung out for a few hours. Danced our asses off and left around 2:00 a.m. Do you remember any of that?"

"No. Well, yea. I remember the whole night 'til right before we left. I remember getting into the taxi. It's a little foggy from there."

Knock, Knock.

"Oh good. You're awake."

"Dr. Nolan," Caelan greets. "Sof, this is the doctor that's been taking care of you," he says while shaking his hand.

"Dr. Nolan, do you know what's wrong with me?"

"How do you feel, young lady?"

"Tired-exhausted actually, and foggy. My thoughts are clouded. My head's not clear."

"Well, that makes sense," he says with sympathy in his voice.

"How long have I been asleep?"

"You were admitted into the ER at seven this morning."

"What time is it now?" I ask, looking at the three of them.

"It's 4:15 in the afternoon," Dr. Nolan says after glancing at his watch.

"WHAT? 4:15 in the afternoon? What the hell?"

"That's exactly what I would like to know!"

Daddy! Oh, holy hell. What's he doing here? I've barely spoken to my father in three years.

"Daddy, what are you doing here?" I nervously ask while I watch Caelan stand to shake my father's hand.

"Sir, how are you?"

"How am I?" my father gruffly asks. "How am I?" he repeats his question again raising his eyebrows, piercing Caelan with eyes like he wants to kill him. "Let me see, my daughter was brought to the ER first thing this morning by ambulance. From what I hear, she has been pretty much unconscious most of the day. How do you think I'm doing when I only just found out about it an hour ago, by my son who heard it from his sister?" he yells drilling his very scary eyes through Nikki.

"I'm sorry, daddy. I just..."

"Save it, Nicole, we will talk about this later!" he says. In that tone he uses that means, 'don't fuck with me.' I have heard him use it many times with his "employees." Everyone knows not to fuck with my father and no one does. If they know what's good for them, that is.

"Excuse me, sir. Am I to assume you're Mr. Heart? Sofia's father?" Dr. Nolan asked.

"Yes. Now tell me what's wrong with my daughter."

Dr. Nolan looks at me with sympathetic eyes. "Sofia, what do you remember about last night?"

"Well, Caelan and I went to dinner, our usual spot. Then went over to Club 9." I stopped for a second to collect my thoughts. "We were celebrating the big new contract he just signed. We danced. We had some drinks. We left somewhere around 2:00-2:30. Why doctor? I pretty much remember everything that happened last night. Well, until we got home. That's when it starts to get fuzzy."

When I see the doctor look at me with concern in his eyes I know what he's about to say is not going to be good. He glances at my father. Recognition registers on his face. Maybe. Or knowing that he's someone not to mess with in general. My father does have that air about him. Or does he know my father? Do they know each other? No, couldn't be. But then again, he pretty much has everyone in his pocket. This situation is why I don't trust anyone except for the people closest to me.

"Sofia, I'm sorry to tell you this... you had a significant amount of Rohypnol in your system."

"Ummm... wait, Rohypnol? Like you mean-" Before I can say anymore, C yells.

"*Motherfucker!* Are you serious, doc?"

I look at C, then to Nikki. Her eyes are huge, her mouth hanging wide open. Then I look at my father. Disgust in his eyes. He wants blood. I can see it in his facial features that just turned stone cold. My father may have done, and may still do many very bad things in his life, but taking advantage of a woman is not one of them. He treats my mother like she's glass. Well, he still does now, but there was a time, not too long ago, that my father was emotionally very cruel to my mother. I don't know exactly why, but I do know for a few months he was not the nicest man to her. He definitely was not the husband and man I witnessed as I grew up. He became... a hard man in our home and towards our mother. A home that was always so warm and loving. Sunday family dinners, meals at six o'clock every night during the week. My father always made sure he was home at that time to make sure his family was okay, to see how his children's day went, and to make sure their day was a good day.

I snap out of those thoughts and look at Dr. Nolan. As I start to say something I hear commotion by the door, my brother Antonio is rushing through. Geez, can we get any more people in this room? I look back to Dr. Nolan again. "Are you saying that someone drugged me? Someone gave me the date rape drug?"

"Yes, I'm afraid so, Sofia."

Oh, holy hell! "But... but, I was fine all night!"

"Well, I'm assuming you ingested the drug right before you left the club being that it didn't take effect on you 'til you got home. This would be the reason that no one knew anything was wrong. What do you remember when you left the club, or rather, right before you left the club?"

I recall the night in my head. "Nothing out of the ordinary. I remember us leaving. C waving down a cab. I remember getting in it. I remember getting sleepy, so I put my head on C's shoulder." Caelan nodded his head when I looked up at him. "Then I remember him carrying me through the house and upstairs to the bedroom, but by that point, I felt out of it. I just thought it was the alcohol combined with me being tired."

"Ya," he nods, confirming what I said was correct. "I put her in bed and crashed next to her. She said goodnight to me, although it was a sleepy good night. I never gave it a thought. We passed out." He looks over at my father who's staring at him with a raised eyebrow. "Next thing I know it's six thirty in the morning. I got up to use the bathroom and saw her lying on the floor. I thought at first that maybe she had gone in there over the course of the night to get sick and just decided to stay in there and passed out on the floor." I hear a growl come from deep in my father's chest. "When I started to talk to her, and she wasn't responding..." He trails off for a few seconds looking like his heart was being ripped out. "Well, that's when I realized something was very wrong. I picked her up, carried her to her bed then covered her up with a blanket," he says, being quiet for a moment before muttering, "she was so cold." He swallowed. "Then I called 911."

"Well, Sofia," Dr. Nolan says, "with your consent we would like to do a rape test on you."

"WHAT?" I screech. "NO! OH, HOLY HELL! NO! ABSOLUTELY NOT!! NOT AGAIN! NO! NO! NO!"

"Now, Sofia-" my father tries to intervene.

"NO, DADDY! NO!" I look to Nikki for some kind of help with our father. Tears stabbing the back of my eyes. Then I look at C and at his hand holding mine. It tightens in reassurance. He hasn't let go of my hand since I woke up and I'm sure he held it the whole time I've been asleep, too. His eyes are glued to mine. On his face is a look of fear because of the whole situation, but yet, also the look of clarity because he knows nothing happened to me.

I hear my brother by the door mumble under his breath. "I'm gonna fuckin' kill someone!"

"NO! NOO! NOOO! I'M NOT DOING IT!" I shout. "Dr. Nolan the answer is NO!" I know nothing happened. "I was with Caelan all night. No one touched me." My heart is pounding! The forming tears stabbing the back of my eyes feel like butcher knives. My throat is closing up. The feeling of not being able to breathe is starting to get the best of me. I look at C in panic. He knows the darkness I'm headed into right now. A full-blown panic attack. He's been there since the very first one. It was the night the abductor let me go free, three and a half years ago.

He snuck into my room because my father wouldn't let him see me. It's the feeling of being out of control. Not having control of myself or what others can inflict on me. The feeling of someone taking or doing whatever they want. Not having the choice. That is by far the worst feeling. Panic. Caelan has helped me through pretty much every one of my panic attacks. He's always there for me. I look into his beautiful blue eyes, and he sees the signs in mine. He knows if he doesn't do something I'm going to have a panic attack in front of my father. He also knows that would be the worst thing for me. To let my father see that I have no control over myself, that I'm weak. No, I can't let him see that. I see the flicker in C's eyes. The realization of what's about to occur. He squeezes my hand in a soft touch letting me know he understands and he will take care of me.

He stands, looks around the room, and broadens his shoulders. "Everyone get the fuck out!" His demand is met with a rush of gasps. Only because my father's in the room and no one ever talks to him that way. The only one who didn't gasp was him, and that's because he's always so calm, cool, and collected. He looks at Caelan like he's lost his damn mind for even thinking about talking to him like that. Dr. Nolan just looks at him confused. Then looks to my father. Nikki looks at C confused and then to me, and realizes that I'm starting to panic. C looks at my brother, giving him the 'what the fuck eyes.' "Get him the fuck out of this room!"

"Well," Dr. Nolan says, "if you refuse, Sofia, there's really nothing more I can do."

Breathe, Sofia. Breathe. Breathe deeply. You got this. Don't do this in front him.

"Oh, there's something I'm gonna do!" I hear my brother say. His words seem so far away thanks to the ringing in my ears.

"Tonio not now!" I barely hear my father say. My sister stands up, looking from him to Antonio.

"A," she starts to say, warning him, but Antonio cuts in.

"Dad I need to talk to you for a minute."

My father's eyes slightly squint at him in question. I look at C, who lets out an exhausted and frustrated exhale. He looks like beautiful death. Bags under his sad sunken eyes and his dirty blond hair is everywhere. I know those gentle, but strong hands have been running through it all day.

My father looks at me and softly says, "Angel Face, maybe you should... just take the test."

"Christ!" I hear C harshly mutter. He looks to my brother.

"Dad, please I need to talk to you, now!" Antonio demands.

"For the love of God just shut up! You didn't believe me three and half years ago, so please believe me today when I say I know nothing happened to me! I was with Caelan all night. Even Antonio was there for a while. He saw me before he left! I. Was. Fine!" My brother nods his head to confirm. "GOD DAMN IT, JUST LEAVE IT ALONE!" I shout.

Deep breath. Deep breath.

"Listen, sir," Caelan says. "I know you want answers. So, do I. So, do all of us, but I'm telling you, I was with her all-night long. When we left the bar, she was alright. Like she said, she fell asleep on my shoulder in the cab. I took her up to bed, and she said good night to me. It was nothing out of the ordinary. Nothing to make me think anything was wrong with her except for her being tired."

"Okay," Dr. Nolan interrupted. "All your other test results came back normal, except for the Rohypnol in your system. Which, will leave your system over time. You can go home once your discharge papers are ready. I'll get them started. Drink plenty of fluids today and get rest when you get home."

Breathe, Sof. Breathe.

A round of thanks went to the doctor by everyone in the room, except for me. Everyone needs to get out. Everyone except for the one person that gives me the air I need to breathe.

"Caelan, I need a word with you. Alone," my father orders. I glance over at A. "The hallway, now," he demands.

What? Shit! Do I say something to my father? I want him out of here so I can calm down. "No, dad! What you have to say, you can say in front of me. C did nothing wrong!"

"It's okay, beautiful. Your father and I will just be a few minutes," he says looking down at me with emotion flooding his eyes. He gently runs his knuckles down my cheek then leans in close to my ear. "Breathe for me, beautiful. Take deep breaths. Believe that you'll be okay. Keep saying it to yourself, Sof. Nikki will be right here if you need her," he comforts, winking as he straightens himself with that crooked grin on his handsome face. "I'll be right back," he says turning towards my father who's giving him a questioning look. When he walks towards the door, my father follows him out. I look at my brother, Antonio. He knows exactly what I'm asking of him.

"On it," he says. "I'll be right back, Sof. You okay?"

I nod as he follows behind my father into the hallway.

three

Caelan

I'M STANDING IN THE HALLWAY WAITING for Mr. Heart to say something to me. He's looking at me with those eyes that kill people. I can't take the silence anymore.

"Mr. Heart list-"

"No! Caelan, you listen to me, and listen to me good son, because right now... right now..." He gets nose to nose with me. "Right fucking now I am not a happy fucking father!"

"I know, sir, but-"

"No! Shut your mouth. I talk. You listen. Do not interrupt me again! You hear me?" I stand there vibrating with anger, waiting for his next words. "First I want to know what the hell is going on between you and my daughter?!"

My eyebrows shooting north at his question. "What do you mean?"

"Do not play games with me."

"Sir, I'm not sure what you're asking. You know how I feel about your daughter."

"You know exactly what I'm asking. I just watched a grown man admire my daughter with love in his eyes. Does she know you're in love with her?"

"Sir, we're just really close."

"Bullshit!" he snaps, as his eyes flick back and forth over mine. I stand there, not knowing what else to say and not wanting to say anything else. It's none of his business what happens between her and I. "When Sofia told me she was moving out of my house and moving into yours, I called you into my office to discuss the safety of my daughter," he says staring at me hard, threat clearly exuding from his demeanor.

Just shoot me now because I know this man is going to murder me.

"I specifically told you to watch over my daughter. I meant what I said to you that day."

I interject, knowing he ordered me not to speak, but fuck this! I can't keep my mouth shut. This situation is just as baffling to me as it is to him. "Sir, she was with me the whole night. I don't know how this could have happened, but my gut is telling me something is not right and that this wasn't a random incident. My gut instinct is telling me someone had to be watching her, like seriously watching her." He looks at me. His eyes are searching mine for answers.

"Are you trying to tell me that you think someone purposely set out to do this to her?"

"Yes, sir, that's what I'm saying! There's no way someone could have gotten that close to her. She was with the group of us the whole night. Some amateur just looking to take advantage of a woman would never take that risk. She was with too many people. I feel like someone had to have been watching her for a while." He stands there, showing all the power that he possesses while assessing what I'm saying to him. "Sir, this is a place we frequent a lot. We know the staff. Christ, we know most of the people in there. I mean I know it's a club, but seriously someone had to have been real close to her to be able to do this without attracting any attention. Plus, whoever it was they had to have spiked her drink right before we left. I think it was done purposely so that when we left everything would look normal. I don't feel good about this at all." I stare at him for a minute thinking about whether or not I should ask this next question, but fuck it, I'm asking anyway. Very quietly I say, "Sir, are you sure we don't have to worry about..."

His eyes become beady looking me over for a few seconds. "He was taken care of! End of it! Got it!"

"Sir, I understand…... I just... this just... something's off, it just doesn't feel right."

"For fuck's sake, how could this fucking feel right? My daughter was drugged last night for Christ's sakes!"

I'm quiet because he's right. What can I say to that? She was with me. I was responsible for her, and I let this happen to her. I let her down.

"Listen to me," he says. "I want to take her home with me, and I want your help. You will help me make her understand that this is what is best for her, Mr. O'Reily. Under my roof and my care, I know she will be safe."

I hear A shuffle his feet and snort out a breath. He knows she'll never go back home. The only reason she used to go there is for Sunday dinners and only because of her mother, brother, and sister. She doesn't even talk with her father while she's there. Antonio doesn't say anything because, well, he knows better and he's not even supposed to be out here with us. Mr. Heart said he wanted to speak to me alone, and A just followed us out into the hallway. So, I guess it's up to me to say something. "Mr. Heart there is no way she is ever going to agree to that. Even if I tried to talk her into it, she still wouldn't do it."

"Besides the point that she's twenty-four years old and stubborn as an ox, pop," A states, just before walking away to answer his ringing cell phone.

"Listen, she's my best friend, we've known each other since I was twelve years old. I promise, I will not let anything happen to her."

With a cold hard stare, he crosses his arms over his still very large chest for a middle-aged man, with one brow raised, the look of death in his eyes. He takes one step towards the door. "Son, it's little fucking late for that. Don't you think? She was already in your care, and she was hurt."

I stand there. Not knowing what to say or do as he walks back into Sofia's room. This man's rep, the stories I've heard from A, Sof, and Nikki...

Hell, I have heard stuff with my own ears, had seen it with my own eyes when I was at the house hanging out when we were all younger. This man is going to put a hit out on my head. Granted, I have known him since I was a scrawny, little kid. A little kid and scrawny I am no more at six foot two and well built, but for men like him, that means nothing. I turn, take a deep breath, and step towards her room when I hear my name.

"Hey, C wait up, don't go back in there yet."

I turn back to see A walking towards me. He and I have been best friends since we were all kids. As a matter of fact, the moment my family moved next door to their estate we all became very close. A and I are best friends. More like brothers. We've been inseparable since the first time we met. Sofia, Antonio, Nikki, my brother Christopher and I were like the five musketeers.

As we got older and started college, we began different paths in our lives, but we stayed very close through it all. Shit, we hang out with each other pretty much every day. When Antonio graduated high school, he started working for his father, not that he had a choice. We all knew that was coming. It's the family business, so there was no choice. He started out small, and now, well now we don't talk much about his work. My business, yes, but his, no. I like it better that way. I started a small construction company building homes with the help of my father before he passed two years ago from a terrible car accident. My father would be proud of what I have accomplished with the company. It has grown into a very successful business. Building vast estates homes.

Sofia, Nikki, and Chris, all one year apart in age, went to college. Sofia being the youngest in the group at twenty-four and Antonio being the oldest at twenty-eight. The three of them all went to the same college. Chris dropped out after two semesters and now works for me. School just wasn't for him. Nikki got her Associates and now works as my PA.

Sofia, well, my beautiful girl decided to leave school. With my help with funding, she owns her own very successful high-end boutique called "Hearts Desire." After she had been kidnaped three years ago, she decided to leave school. Knowing that some lunatic was stalking her for more than a year has changed her, rightfully so. From the bits and pieces that she could remember from that drugged up, horrible night, the police finally went to question a suspect after two weeks of investigations. It wound up being some addict that she passed every morning and afternoon on her way to the coffee shop. He had become infatuated with her. When they searched his place, all of his belongings were there, but from what the landlord and his neighbors stated, the guy had just vanished a few weeks prior. What they did find in the apartment, however, was disturbing as hell.

Pictures of Sofia hung all over his walls like a collage. Pictures of her everywhere she went. My front steps letting herself into my house, now our house. The coffee shop, the drug store, school, hell, just walking down the damn street. He was everywhere. Even had pictures of her at the bowling alley one night with all of us. There was even one of her at the food store picking up tampons. She works at a massive club called Club Ice, and he had pictures of her there, too. The worst ones were of her undressing in her dorm room. Those pictures, for me... well those were hard for me to swallow. It was unbearable to know this guy knew everything about her. Every place she went to and none of us knew it. It was one of the most difficult things that has ever happened to me in my life. To know that someone as close to me as she is, was being followed to that extent and I didn't even know it. I can only imagine the true depth of insecurity she feels on a day to day basis.

I do have my suspicions of what happened to him, though. Of course, I do. I just asked the man that I think-no, that I know, 'took care of him,' but in this world, in their world, that I know all too well, I live by their rules. Keep my head down, eyes closed, and mouth shut. And personally, I'm glad that fucker got what was coming to him.

Turning, I look at the six foot two replica of myself. The well-built, jet black hair and blue-eyed man standing in front of me. I have more muscle on me than he does, but that doesn't make a difference. Antonio is not a man you want to piss off.

"C? You okay man?" I look down shaking my head trying to rid the terrible thoughts infiltrating my mind right now about finding Sofia that horrible morning after she was abducted. Her cold, trembling, small hands reaching out for me. Wailing with tears unable to speak.

"C? Hey, C you okay man?" I feel A grabbing my shoulder.

"Yea, I'm good. What's up, A?"

"Dude, who you tryin' to fuckin' kid? Where's your mind at right now? I just had a whole conversation with you. Did you hear anything I said?"

"Nothing man, sorry. I'm just-I'm just all worked up over this thing, like I told your father. Something is not sitting right with me on this, A. I don't know, maybe, maybe I'm just overreacting. Maybe it was just some random scumbag. Which is still disturbing in itself, but I just feel like this is not random. I don't know, man. It's Sofia. You know how I feel about her. Maybe I'm just overthinking this."

"C, listen, man," he says grabbing my shoulder again. "I know what you're thinking, but it's not him." I watch his pupils dilate as he looks me in my eyes. "It's not him, C. Trust me. He can never hurt her again."

"Yeah. Yeah, you're right man, I know. It's just me over thinking this. This situation has brought back so many feelings from when I found her on my doorstep that morning. You're right it's probably just some other sick fuck out there victimizing women. Just… FUCK… just thank God she's alright man, and that this didn't go any further. I know she's your sister, but I-"

"I know man. I do," he cuts me off, "out of all of us, I know."

"I just feel like I've got to do something, A."

"I know how you feel. I know how close you two are." He slaps my shoulder twice. "Come on we've all been telling you guys for years you two should be together. Listen, I'm already on it," he says. "Giovanni's already on his way down to the club to get the security footage from last night. That's who I was on the phone with just now. Whoever did this, I promise you I will find him, and he will pay for what he did to my sister. No one fucks with my family; that goes for you and Chris too. We're family." He cups the back of my neck resting his forehead to mind. "You got that?"

"Yeah, dude, I got it. I also know if you find anything out, you better fucking tell me."

"I'll tell you as much as I can like usual, C," he says taking a step towards Sofia's room. "Come on, Giovanni is on his way down to the club. He'll get the film, and we'll find out who this piece of shit is."

Giovanni is one of the main bodyguards; He's just under Lorenzo. Lorenzo is Mr. H's personal bodyguard. The guy never leaves Mr. H's side. As a matter of fact, he's sitting down at the end of the hallway pretending like he's reading the paper as we speak, waiting for Mr. Heart right now. Honestly, he doesn't know a thing about what those articles say because he's doing nothing but scanning the hallways with his well-trained eyes looking for threats. He's never more than a few steps away from Mr. Heart, at all times. We both stop talking when we hear yelling coming from Sofia's room. I can hear her getting upset. Mr. Heart has a way of doing that to her.

"Come on man, let's get in there and save them both before they kill each other. You know how those two battle it out."

"Well, we are close to the morgue in case one of them doesn't come out of this alive." I grin.

"Haha, funny dude." Antonio laughs.

I step back into the hospital room when I see my beautiful girl ready to lose her shit with her father. I see the look in those beautiful, stubborn as fuck, emerald green eyes, and I know this is going to become a major battle between the two of them. "My money's on, Sof!" I say turning my head back to A.

"Oh shit!" I hear Antonio mumble from behind me.

"This is going to get ugly," I confirm as I look over my shoulder again. "My money's on Sof."

"A C-note on my father."

"Make it two hundred, and you're fucking on!" I mouth back to him walking farther into her room.

"Hey, Sofia, calm down," I say trying to defuse the situation. "This isn't good for you."

"OH OKAY! REALLY? Soooo why don't you tell my dear ol' dad that! He's insisting that I go home and stay with him," she says calmly but there is a hint of nervousness behind it that only I can hear. "Ya know to the big ol' castle with the guards, and ohhh wait, don't forget the fucking moat around the house so that no one can get to me!" she shouts throwing her hands around.

"Angel face, calm down," Mr. Heart commands with a calm, stern, voice.

"CALM DOWN DADDY! REALLY? CALM DOWN? You're demanding that I go home with you. Like I'm ten years old and you're telling me to clean my room. I'm twenty-four years old, father, almost twenty-five and you're demanding I go home with you like I don't know how to take care of myself. Are you kidding me? This is why I moved out years ago. This is so not happening, daddy dearest. Plus, mommy would agree with me and by the way, where is mommy?" she screams even louder.

"I haven't told your mother what has happened yet, Sofia. I was trying to save her from the pain of rehashing the past."

"Oh, well, see that's another reason I'm not coming to live with you," she shouts again. "I don't want to upset mommy. What she doesn't know won't hurt her, right daddy?" she roars with a snide look and a raised eyebrow like she's holding something against him.

What the hell is that about I wonder to myself. I glance over to Antonio, and he gives me the 'oh shit look.'

"Angel face, listen to me. I only want to make sure you're safe, and no one gets close enough to hurt you. That's all."

She pins her father with beady squinting eyes as she says, "A little late for that don't you think, Daddy?"

Damn, I just heard those same words from him out in the hallway. Looking at him I see nothing but pure anger, hurt and regret on his face. Regret? I question myself. Yes, that's hurt I see in his eyes.

"Fine, Sofia, you win. I will tell you this though as of right now, Giovanni will be your bodyguard for a few weeks until I see that things are okay."

"Giovanni?" she shouts. "Giovanni?" she screams even louder. "OH HELL! Daddy he's a pure meathead. I don't want him following me around. It's not like his big ass can be inconspicuous."

Over my shoulder, I look at Antonio and mouth, pay up bitch! I won! His "fuck you" smile lets me know that he knows, I got him.

"Giovanni? Really? No, dad! I'm not having him or any other guard," she mumbles ranting on.

Oh shit, here we go again. I look at Mr. H, and he's looking dead at me. SHIT! I better say something or I might lose some limbs shortly. Awwww hell! Here goes, she's going to rip my balls off when we get home, but she will be going home with me. "Sof listen," I say reaching down to grab her hand, "your dad's right. We don't know who did this to you and honestly, I'm really uncomfortable with someone getting that close to you. None of us noticed it. If you had a guard, he would have been paying better attention to who was approaching you from every angle."

"OH, MY GOD!" she shouts slapping her hands against her blanket covered thighs. "Caelan are you serious?" she screams.

"Hey! Hey! Hey! What the hell is going on in here?" I look over my shoulder seeing Nikki standing at the door. "I can hear you guys screaming at each other all the way down the hallway! What the hell? This is worse than a Sunday dinner!"

"Where the hell have you been Nicole?"

"I was in the bathroom, father. Is that okay with you?" After giving her a stern twice over, he turns his head back to, Sofia. He starts to say something when she promptly cuts him off.

Very calmly she says, "Dad listen, I know you love me, I do. I know you want to protect me too. I get it, but you have got to cool your jets ol' man. I'll be fine. I have C to watch over me. I appreciate that you worry about me, but seriously, I'll be fine."

I look over to him. He's pissed. Maybe it was because she just called him an ol' man. I don't know but he is furious.

With a very commanding lethal voice he says, "Angel face, I know you will be fine because Giovanni will be guarding you and that is final." I watch her as she goes to say something else, but he gives her 'the stare.' "That's fucking enough, don't say another word, young lady!" he sternly orders as he puts his hand up in a stop gesture.

And she doesn't.

four

"**C**, WILL YOU BRING ME A BOTTLE OF water please?"

"Give me a second. I'll be right up."

A few minutes later I hear his footsteps by my bedroom door. "How you feelin'?"

I look up to see him leaning against the door frame with his arms crossed and head tilted. "I'm okay. Just tired. I'm so glad to be home, though." I take in his amazing body. Strong broad masculine shoulders that narrow as you go down to his waist then flare out again into solid strong hips and legs. His medium length, dirty blond, hair has a slight wave to it. His blue eyes are like brilliant crystal gems that have just been unearthed. I melt when I look into them, every time. They sparkle with deep dark blue and lighter blue shades. I would say they look like the Caribbean ocean, but honestly, it wouldn't do them justice. Behind those eyes is the boy I grew up with and then became the gorgeous, soulful, man I now know.

As he strides over to my bedside, I take in the royal blue t-shirt he has on which only makes his eyes bluer. His dark jeans hug his body as he sits down next to me. "I still can't believe this happened, Sof."

"I know," I sigh dropping my shoulders. "It's crazy, C. I mean, just think about it, one minute we're partying our asses off, having a great time... then heading home, thinking we had a great night with friends and then... shit, I still can't believe it."

His sad concerned eyes watch me. "It's going to be okay. I promise you, beautiful."

"I know," I murmur dropping my eyes down towards my hands laying in my lap.

"No, look at me," he orders with a stern voice.

"I promise I will not let anyone hurt you again."

"C, do you think, no..." I trail off. "Forget it," I whisper.

"Hey," he sighs cupping my chin gently in the palm of his large callused hand. "Hey, look at me." He shakes his head. "No, I do not think, I know. Do you hear me? I know, Sofia. He's gone. He's never coming back. He can never hurt you again."

I sigh with sadness looming deep in my chest. "This just felt like the same thing to me as last time, that's all. It just... it's just that this, the whole thing freaks me out."

He wraps his warm arms around me. "I know, beautiful, I know." He kisses my forehead with a gentle lingering kiss.

"We'll get through this. Now call Alex, it's Friday-you're supposed to work tonight. You're not going in."

He's not asking. He's telling me I'm not going into work.

"Nah, I already called in sick. I told him what happened. He was shocked, couldn't believe it. Told me to take the rest of the week off. I'm not going to though. I'll just take the weekend off and go back in for my Tuesday shift."

"You sure?"

"Ya, I'm sure."

"So, you wanna hang out and watch a movie?" He adjusts himself on my bed. Uncurling his long, impressive frame to get comfortable.

"Sure, but it's Friday night. Don't you have a date tonight? I remember the blonde from last night hanging all over you. I thought you asked her to go out tonight?"

With a heavy brow and a harsh tone, he says, "Beautiful, I'm not going anywhere this weekend. It's me, you, movies, junk food, and a few beers."

I laugh. "Uggggh, you're tryin' to make my ass fatter! I haven't been to kickboxing in four days."

He tilts his head to the side giving me his cocky, sexy, grin; the grin that I love. The one all girls love. He's a very sexy man. Sex exudes from him like rippling waves in a stormy ocean. He knows it too. How could he not? Women throw themselves at him. Literally! I love him dearly, but he's got more women falling all over him and subsequently, one nighters, that sometimes I feel like our home is a supermarket, with some organic and some very overly processed foods walking the floors in the morning!

I love him, though.

It does, however, make morning coffee a little uncomfortable at times though. Especially when they thought his roommate was a guy. Then they see me, a five foot six, curvy, chestnut haired, emerald green eyed, girl standing at the kitchen counter with her giant coffee mug that says, "Don't talk to me until I'm fucking finished with this coffee!" in a tank top and boy shorts.

Ahh, good times. I chuckle to myself.

Some of their faces are priceless. It's helped him get them out the door quicker, especially when we pretend that I'm the not-so-happy, surprised, girlfriend.

"Never!" he says smirking. "I've already told you many times, your ass is fine as hell! I'm an ass man, I know! Along with those-"

"Caelan O'Reily!" `

"What? I was going to say eyes! Along with those beautiful eyes!"

"Ya, ya, ya, I'm sure." I roll my eyes. "Because my beautiful eyes are on my tits, where your eyes were just glued to!" We both laugh. "You're a jerk!" I shove him.

"Ya, but you love me anyway, beautiful."

"That I do, C. I really do," I admit with a solemn tone. Because I really do. I don't know what I would ever do without him, and the fact that his nickname for me is, 'beautiful.' I mean for someone like me, who at times doesn't feel quite so beautiful, it's uplifting to hear a lot.

"Okay, so, what are we going to watch?" he asks as he's now looking through the DVDs.

"How about my favorite?"

He whips his head around. "Ummm no!"

"Okay, how 'bout-"

He cuts me off before I can even say the second movie. "Ya, that's a no again, beautiful." I giggle. His back is facing me while he roots around in the DVD drawer. I take the opportunity to examine his fine, round, sexy, manly, totally squeezable, ass. Hmmmm. Hot damn he needs to stop bending over like that. "Come on, after everything that just happened last night you wouldn't watch-"

"No!" He cuts me off again.

"A chick flick with me?" I finish my sentence.

Turning his body completely around, standing to his full six foot two masculine stature, he smirks, "Sofia, I would do anything for you. I hope you know that, but I am not watching a chick flick!"

I give him the saddest eyes I could and drop my shoulders. I look up at him through my lashes.

"Don't do it Sof!" He points at me. "Don't you dare put that li-" He runs his hand through his hair. "Awwww fucking hell, there it is, that plump pouting lip."

I chuckle because it works every time.

"It's not fair. You know I will do anything for you if you give me that pouting bottom lip. Damn!" He throws his action-packed movies back into the drawer. "Okay, which one do you want to watch?"

I laugh holding my stomach.

"You think this is funny that I have to be subjected to a hooker and a millionaire love story? AGAIN! Really?" Ahh... look at her. Look at that smile on her beautiful face. The sparkle in her eyes. Ya, that's beautiful. That right there... that is worth every bit of the hour and a half of pure agony I'm going to have to endure through this movie. I hold my hands up with a movie in each hand. She points to my left hand with a cat just ate the canary look on her face. "Christ, I was right." Okay, let's do this. The hooker it is. "But, Sof when we are done with this one you have to watch one of mine."

She shoots me the, 'are serious look?' Her left brow's cocked. "Caelan O'Reily, I am not watching porn with you!" she chastises sliding off her bed. I watch her sashay her ass as she starts walking towards the bathroom.

Seriously? She kills me. Like I would watch porn with her. Well, shit we have watched porn together, but, hello-we were teenagers! I don't think I could handle watching porn with her now. "Oh, sweetheart, if you want porn, I'll give you porn, but there will be no TV on!" I say slapping her ass as she walks by. She squeals, arches her back throwing her hands behind her to cover her ass. "Now take that fine ass of yours to the bathroom and do what you gotta do so we can get this movie of your choice over with! Then we can move on to watching something educational like Trixie Goes Wild!" She shoots me a look. I laugh. "I'm just kidding! Go!" I point, shooing her away.

"I love you," she cheerfully yells as I hear her peeing.

"I love to hear you pee," I laugh, yelling back.

It's HOT. THE room is still dark. I must have fallen asleep while watching the movie. What the hell time is it? I reach for my cell phone. Really? We slept through the whole night. I can't believe we slept through the night. I feel something heavy draped across me. I open my eyes wider to see and feel that familiar feeling of C's arms and legs curled around me.

Such a good feeling.

Well, I guess he fell asleep too. I chuckle just thinking about how I conned him into watching it. What guy wouldn't fall asleep during a chick flick? If people didn't know us and saw us together, they would think we were lovers. We're not. That's just how Caelan and I are. We have much love and respect for one another, but not "that kind" of love. He's a damn good looking man too, always has been. Even when we were kids, girls would be falling all over him. With his two-day old beard, short to medium length wavy, dirty blond hair and sparkling blue bedroom eyes. Bedroom eyes that will make your panties feel like they just came out of the washer, with no spin cycle! He's six foot two of pure gorgeous, panty-melting muscle, shoulders and arms as strong and muscular as his lower body with legs like well-sculpted tree trunks. His narrow waist and washboard abs are to die for. To go along very nicely with those abs is that damn little curly happy trail that will make a girl's clit throb like she's a set of drums being banged on at a rock concert.

Damn! Is it getting hotter in here?

We joke with each other. Make comments about each other's, and hell, at times have seen each other's, bits and pieces. Yes, hmmm yes... he has some nice bits and a really good looking piece too.

DAMN!

I need to get laid. I chuckle to myself. I know it's been a while, but dang girl, get C's very, very magnificent bits and pieces out of your head. Oh hell, I need a distraction. I should just give Jake a call. Ya, good ol' Jake. Poor guy. I must be really desperate right now. I'm grabbing at straws here. Jake was good looking enough and had a nice smile, but he wasn't... he was okay, but... ya... maybe not so much. Nice guy, but he wasn't that good. Thought he was a stallion he did but... I'll give him credit for that. He thought he was the mac daddy. Kudos to him for his self-esteem. Shaking my head. Hell, I wish I had half of his self-esteem. He was okay though. Nice guy and all, got the job done, that's all that matters, right? I just wasn't seeing the stars and all, but well, hell who am I kidding there were no friggin' stars. Not even a spark, but he was there and available and well, yea... a means to a very much needed end. It may have been a couple of months of a means to an end, but plain and simple I needed some and he was willing. More than willing.

I'm no whore, that's for sure. I've only been with four people and I'm twenty-four years old. With a birthday coming soon. I'm as picky as they come. I'm, 'that girl' even though my tough exterior doesn't show it. Inside I'm a soft romantic girl. I want the dream: the dream guy, the passion, the stars-hell, I want shooting stars, but I'll settle for just some stars, and that guy can be the perfect guy. You know that guy. The one that has all the check marks next to the list every girl makes when she's a teenager with big dreams and a big overflowing heart and puppy dog eyes. That guy... yea, the guy who's going to show me the world. Is that too much to ask? I want the damn stars that I had once before. It was a long time ago. I don't know... maybe, it wasn't even there, but I thought it was. I really thought it was. I take a deep breath thinking about those memories from so long ago. I inhale C's masculine unique smell. A fresh, clean crisp sent. One that smells like he's fresh from a shower. That added with sandalwood from his delicious cologne.

Damn, he smells good!

Okay, Sofia, get up and get out from under him. I go to move. His Celtic shield of armor tattoo across his shoulder and down most of his arm is draped across me. It's like he's protecting me even while he's sleeping. He grips my side tighter. I wait a few minutes to make sure he stays asleep. I become fully aware that something enormous is poking my thigh.

Awww hell! Really?

Okay, I really got to get up. I can do this. I stop asking myself the question I already know the answer to. Is that really what I think it is? Yea it is! He's hard as a rock, and it's on my thigh. It's one thing to have the memories floating around in my now screwed up head, but to have the memories and have him hard as a rock pressed against my thigh and combined with being horny as hell... "Fuckin' A," I mumble. I have got to move and get out from under him before the rock band starts to show up! I go to shimmy again and this time, he doesn't move.

Phew!

I slide out from under him. Start tip toeing towards the bathroom to take a much needed-shower when I hear his rough, sleepy, sexy as fuck, voice.

"Ahhhh, beautiful, you should have stayed in bed we could have had some fun this morning."

I freeze not looking back at him. Then crack a smile while I slightly shake my head. I start to walk towards the bathroom again. Turn slightly when I hit the threshold and look over my shoulder. "Ya, ya, ya, lover boy, you couldn't handle this kind of fun!" I tease smacking my ass as I'm walking into the bathroom and close the door.

"Oh, you think so, beautiful? I'll rock your fucking world, sweetheart. You won't be able to walk the rest of the day without thinking of me!" I hear him yell in a very awake deep male voice. I close my eyes sagging my back against the bathroom door. My head hangs. My body tingles. Goosebumps invade my skin. That fucker was totally awake the whole time. I giggle.

Shit, I just giggled.

"Ya, C, you would rock my world. You already have," I whisper.

five

Yummm, I smell something good. I head out my bedroom door following the delicious smells wafting through the loft. I look towards C's room which is two doors away from mine. I hit the top of the stairs and look down to see Caelan cooking. The overhead speakers are playing Jason Aldean's *"Just Getting Started,"* one of C's favorite songs. We've been to see him in concert more times than I can count.

I stand there for a minute just watching him work in this space that he created. This place is beautiful. Stunning really. He did a fantastic job. Well, hell, he didn't just remodel this place, he rebuilt this place from scratch. Gutted this place to the bare bones. All except the poles that they would slide down. This place was an old abandoned firehouse that was going to be torn down. He incorporated the poles into the design to leave some history and character. He bought this property when he started his business. It took him almost a year to finish it, but this place turned out stunning.

He has such vision for things. For as long as I can remember, he has always loved the construction and architecture of buildings. That's why his business has become so successful. His workhorse ethic, keen eye for detail, and his passion to build and construct is why this place, and everything else he touches, comes to life. He has his nose in every aspect of his company too. Everything from the purchase of the right size nails and screws, to the ledger books that need to be rectified down to the very last penny every week. If it has to do with his business, he knows about it and makes sure that every aspect is top notch.

I hit the top of the stairs and look down to the wide-open space. Everything is open downstairs. You can see from one side to the other. There's a gorgeous massive see-through Gray Ledgestone fireplace with a hand carved wood mantel that he got from an old French farmhouse just outside the city. It was a timeworn farm house that was being torn down. The fireplace was built between the living room and game room. He put it there to separate the two, but still have an open room. I can see the pool table from where I stand so, all in all, the whole downstairs is still an open concept. The upstairs is more private, all four bedrooms and the bathrooms are private. Off his and my bedroom he put French doors in, they open to a large balcony. Nice touch being that this place is on the outskirts of the city, but still has no yard. At least we can still get some fresh air if we want to. Plus, the balconies are private with the potted arborvitaes that enclose the space.

The kitchen though, it's the hub of the home downstairs. There's a giant island in the middle of the kitchen. The traditional black cabinets give the kitchen a modern look, but not so much that the place feels cold. On the contrary, this place gives off the feeling of upscale-warmth. The white Carrara marble counter tops against the black cabinets and the gray and white chevron backsplash all pop. The whole home has a sophisticated look and feel to it. There's tile flooring in the kitchen area, but the rest of the place including the upstairs, has very dark, almost black, hand-scrapped hardwood floors. There's a white, shag, area rug in the living room and big, soft, oversized, dark chocolate leather couches with oversized, fluffy, white, pillows. It gives the whole place a feeling of cozy, sophisticated, comfort. A place you just want to pop a squat with a glass of wine, watching the blue and yellow flames dance in the fireplace.

"YOU GOING TO come down and eat or are you just going to stay up there and admire my hot body some more?"

Smiling, I shake my head, snapping myself out of my day dreaming. I start walking down the stairs noticing the black cotton pajama pants that are hanging low on his hips. He's smiling at me with a cocky ass grin. "Something smells delicious, what did you make?"

"Your favorite, french toast with glazed bananas and bacon. Scrambled eggs too."

"Ahhh yum, I can't wait to eat. I'm starving," I tell him, sliding onto one of the stools at the island.

"I know, I heard your stomach growling this morning. You want orange juice or just coffee?"

"Just coffee for now, thanks." He makes me a plate and slides it over to me. Then makes himself a plate and sits across from me. We're quiet for a bit while we eat, but I can tell he wants to talk. I can always tell when he intends on talking to me about something, especially something that he thinks will make me upset.

"Well, what is it? You might as well just spit it out." He smiles at me. "And please do not tell me it's about your cute little manhood being on my leg this morning and how I will think about it, and you, all day because, quite honestly, I have already forgotten about it!"

His eyes widen in shock. "Cute *little* manhood?" he asks. His eyebrows raised to his hairline in shock. "I can assure you that my "manhood" is *not* cute! If you like, I can whip it out and-"

"C!" I yell in a half-hearted warning.

He smirks at me, eyes shining with that cocky-ass look, narrowing down on mine. "If you forgot about it and it didn't leave an impression on you, Sofia, tell me why are you talking about my cock right now, beautiful?"

Shit, he's got me!

I shake my head from side to side. "Get on with it, C!" I sneer at him rolling my hand in the air with a smile.

"Get on with it? Well hell, beautiful, you want me to show you that I can and will handle that fine ass of yours? We aren't eighteen and twenty anymore. I'm a lot more experienced now. You sure you can handle what I'll give you?" I'm speechless, can't say a single word, totally tongue tied. "Okay Sofia, the shit talker. I thought we could have a nice breakfast, but now... now you'll need to eat, you'll need your energy for what I have in mind. If you want me to demonstrate how *not cute* the beast is, right now, I'll be glad-"

"C!" I yell, because I do not need him to elaborate anymore. I can feel the band starting to warm up. Hell, who am I kidding, the band's warmed up and starting the opening song. Any more and I will have to be performing a solo.

"What?" he says cocking his head to the side with a gleam in his eye.

"Move on now lover boy!" I say with a wave of my hand.

Laughing a belly holding, mouth open, head tossed back, laugh, he teases me. "Getting a little hot under the collar there, Sofia?"

My cheeks could start a fire right now. "Just say what you have to say!"

"Damn girl, I know you so well!" He smirks in a devious knowing way. "Okay, here goes. I know you don't want to talk about the elephant in the room, but we need to talk about Thursday night. We need to try and figure out what the fuck happened and who did this to you. If it was just some random jerk off or someone who was targeting you."

"Damn!" I drop my fork to my plate. The atmosphere in the room has now totally just changed now. "You couldn't wait 'til I was at least done eating my friggin' breakfast?"

His sympathetic eyes accompany his soft voice. "Sorry, beautiful, but we have to talk about this."

"I know. I just... damn C. I just want to forget it even happened. Although, I know I can't."

He tosses his head over his shoulder towards the front door where the entrance hall is. "Giovanni's been sitting out there since last night." Oh, damn.

I forgot about him. "I'm sure you would rather talk about this situation and try to figure out who it was than ignore it all together and have him following you around for months."

Sighing, resigning myself to this conversation. "Yeah, well now I have to figure out a plan to lose him too." I smile sheepishly wiggling my brows at him.

"Sof, don't do it," he admonishes. "He's here for your protection, I for one, would feel better with him tailing you then no one being around at all. Plus, I just signed this new contract, I won't have as much time on my hands for a few weeks. So, at least if he's with you, I know you're not alone. Please don't do anything to hinder that."

I see the pleading in his eyes. Damn. I feel terrible now. Taking a deep breath and exhaling, I sternly say, "I won't, but if he starts hovering over me, I'm telling you right now, he's getting the bounce," I inform him with a smile.

"Seriously, you crack me up. I'll talk to him. Tell him to stay back a little. Not that he's going to take orders from me, but I'll try," he huffs with a soft chuckle. "Now finish eating your French toast. I slaved over the stove making that for you!" He winks. "Now let's start from the beginning," he says starting the dreaded conversation. "Dinner, everything was fine while we were there. Nothing unusual. We'll get the security footage from there too. Just in case. Maybe if this wasn't some random act then maybe whoever it is was at the restaurant too."

Goosebumps rise on my skin. "Ugggh just the thought that someone could be following my every step again freaks me the hell out."

"We don't know for sure that someone is following you just yet. Seriously, this could have been just some random low life targeting a pretty girl."

"I know," I say sighing. "So, I'm thinking this all happened at the club. Though, not that I would tell my father this, but we were pretty banged up- but not really bad."

"Yeah, we were, but I wasn't so banged up that I didn't know what was going on around you or me. Neither one of us was. Had someone been close enough to you or your drink, I would have noticed."

"I really don't know then, C. The only times I was away from you was when I went to the bathroom. I didn't carry my drink with me. I left it on the table with all of you. Maybe Chris remembers something?"

"No, I already called him this morning. He said nothing out of the ordinary that he can remember. Call Jessica today, see if she saw anything unusual. I'll talk to Luke in a bit. He's stopping by later to drop off some paperwork from the office. We can ask him then. Antonio said he didn't see anything unusual either, you know your brother, he's got eyes everywhere. His own and others as well. Although, he did leave about an hour before we did with Carmine. I guess Carmine was picking him up because he came to the table looking for him while you were in the bathroom."

A flash of my uncle flickers in my brain. "I think I saw him. You sure it was while I was in the bathroom?"

"Ya, it was right after you walked away."

"Well, it doesn't matter anyway that's not unusual either. Uncle Carmine and Antonio are always partnered up when they have to deal with business for my father."

Uncle Carmine is one of my father's longest employees. When my brother started working for him, my father made sure Antonio was partnered with Uncle Carmine to keep him safe out in the field. If I had to put them in order of how long they have worked for my father, it would be Uncle Carmine, Lorenzo then Giovanni. Giovanni being the youngest. I'm assuming he's somewhere in his early-thirties. Very good looking guy. Short dark hair, green eyes, nice olive skin, nice, full lips, too. Yeah, I'm sure there's no shortage of warm sheets for him to lie on at night! Hell, what am I even saying those sheets are probably hot as hell! That much I can say for sure. He's very built. He's the only one bigger than C. Where Caelan is broad and built, Giovanni is bigger in a meathead kind of way. Laughing to myself. I shouldn't pick on him. He really is a nice guy and at times... especially one time in particular, a long time ago when I asked him for his help, he did without question and without telling my father. And just for that one time, I shouldn't even be thinking about giving him a hard time. Well, as far as I know, he hasn't told my father. Just for that one time when I really needed someone in a desperate way, he was there for me without any judgment. And just because of that time I feel like we have some sort of a connection. Damn, now I do feel bad for even thinking about bouncing his ass and giving him a hard time.

Shit, I should just think of it this way... he's much better to have than Uncle Carmine. That's for sure. He's is the oldest of all three men. I would assume he's in his early fifties. No family. Never been married. He has worked for my father the longest but instead of being the number one guard to my father, Lorenzo is. He is the number one field soldier and Lorenzo is the number one guard protecting my father. He's my father's driver and everything else in between. He's in his early forties; a nice guy. Has always treated me with respect. He's tall at six feet, blond hair, hazel eyes, built, definitely cut up. I saw him with no shirt on one time in my father's office. He has muscles on top of muscles, but his body is more on the athletic lean side then the meathead side. He's an ex-Marine, Special Forces. That man is scary just for the fact that his trained eyes see everything that goes on, but he acts like nothing is going on at all. If there is a problem, you would never know it. He takes care of it with precise and swift movements. Most of the time, before the problem has even become one.

He has a beautiful wife and two children. My father let him have their wedding reception on our estate's property, and what a stunning reception it was. He's always with my father. I don't know how his wife does it without him being around. My father demands a lot of his time, and Lorenzo's always there for him.

Uncle Carmine is the oldest of them all. He has dark eyes, almost black. His black hair has some grey sprinkled through it, making him look distinguished. I would say he's around five foot ten. A small pouch for a belly that most middle age men get. It's small though, and all in all, he's in great shape for his age. He's always well dressed and clean shaven, always looking put together.

It feels like he's always been around. He works mostly in the fields now; fields being code for night time work that needs the utmost caution and confidentiality. There's never been a time in my life when I can't remember him being around. Even pictures of our family holidays and birthday parties from when I was just a baby, he's always in the pictures. My mother always told my sister, Antonio, and I, that if we ever needed something and she and my father weren't around that we should go to Carmine. The three of us call him Uncle Carmine, even though he's not really an uncle by blood. So, in a nut shell, if I had to have someone following me around all the time, I wouldn't want it to be Uncle Carmine. Just for the simple fact that he's way too close to my dad and I don't need him all up in my business, telling my father every single step I make. At least I know Giovanni won't report back to my dad with every single, little, mundane, thing I do, like me going to the coffee shop to get a coffee. Ha! I laugh to myself. He probably already knows.

"Sof? You still with me?"

I snap out of my daze. "Yeah, I was just thinking. It had to have happened after Antonio left and right before we left. So basically, the last half hour we were there. So, between 2:00-2:30 am. We need to get our hands on that video footage. I'm sure A has it by now. He probably gave it to my father already."

"Speaking of, he called me this morning too, while you were in the shower."

"What did he say?" I ask cautiously, taking a sip of my coffee.

"He wanted to know why you weren't still in bed with me taking care of the raging hard on I had!" I snort and throw my head back cracking up laughing. He totally caught me off guard with that. "Well, I'm happy to see that you can laugh at my 'cute' dick. Thanks!"

"Shut the hell up!" I yell still laughing pretty hard. "You take care of your own cute little dick, big guy. Or better yet, call one of your girlies."

He smirks at me, and we laugh together for a few more minutes. "No seriously though, Sof. He wanted to know why you weren't answering your phone and if you were okay," he says raising his eyebrows at me. "You have to call him. Blowing your father off will only infuriate him, which will then make the meathead out there," he says tossing his head back again towards where Giovanni is sitting in the entrance hall, "stick to you closer. Call him. Talk to him. Got it?"

Damn. I hate when he's right. "I'll call him when we're done, okay?" I sarcastically say.

"Good girl." He grins.

six

"So, we all agree? We need to watch the surveillance video before anything else. I want to watch this video from start to finish," I say as I sit there thinking about the events of the night. I gasp at the thought that has just popped into my head. "Oh fuckin' A, Caelan! Damn It!" I just stare at him in shock.

"What? What? Sof, tell me!"

"My father! Oh no... he's going to see me on the surveillance tapes, dancing. He's going to... Christ, C, he's going to freak the fuck out on me! When he sees me doing the bump and grind with you and whoever else I was dancing with last night. He's going to go ballistic," I yell then hang my head looking at my now trembling hands.

"Hey, look at me." My eyes latch onto his concerned, angry sparkling blue eyes. "It's just dancing, Sofia. That's all. Friend's having a good time together. There's nothing wrong with it."

"You know that. I know that. But my father, he will look at it very differently. He always does when it comes to me, especially when it comes to me. Never my sister. Why? He always calls me a..." I stop before saying the word that hurt me terribly. Dropping my head into my hands in despair. "I don't know why it's okay for him to chea-"

Shit, just stop talking Sof.

I can't say anything. It's something I have kept to myself for years, out of respect for one person and only one person. No one else needs to know.

"It's okay for him to what, Sof?"

"Nothing. Just leave it be."

"Ahhh, no! Sofia, you said something in the hospital too. Something to your father about 'what she doesn't know won't hurt her.'"

"C, please leave it alone."

His questioning eyes are piercing me right now. He's quiet. Too quiet, 'til he finally agrees. "For now… for now, I'll leave it alone, but I know something's bothering you and I will find out what it is."

"What? My father calling me a whore every chance he gets isn't something that should bother me?" I question in anger.

He abruptly shoves himself off the stool, standing to his intimidating, full height of six foot two with a look of sheer determination in his eyes. "That's not what I'm talking about, and you know it!" he boomed pointing at me. "And you're not a damn whore! I don't ever want to hear you say it again, Sofia!" he reprimands. "Do you hear me? I don't fucking give a shit what he thinks! You're not a whore! I know you better than anyone. I will not sit here and let your self-esteem go down the fucking toilet again because your father is now back in your life at the moment!" He's silent for a moment collecting himself and his thoughts. "It took too long to build you back up. When you moved out of his house and into here with me, you were a mess. I won't let that happen again. Part of it was my fault. I know that, Sofia, but I swear to you, I will never let you get hurt again."

His determination was the forefront of his words, but the torment radiating from his captivating, sapphire eyes is what annihilates my heart. Standing up, I walk over to him with tears overwhelming my eyes. I slide my arms around his bare stomach, leaning into his naked chest. I tilt my head back to hold our eye contact. Breathing rapidly, he wraps his warm, safe, strong, arms around me tightly, his anger radiating heat from his body. He leans down and kisses my forehead, holding his full, warm, soft lips there for a few seconds.

When he pulls back a little, he inhales deeply, and releases a long exhale. "I'm sorry for yelling at you, beautiful. I just can't-" He stops talking while he shakes his head. "I won't have you putting yourself down, Sofia. I care way too much about you," he declares with a shaky breath. His large, strong hands come around and cup my face. His thumbs running delicately over my cheeks. His fingers tenderly holding the base of my head. "You. Are. A. Beautiful. Strong. Intelligent. Woman," he proclaims. His gorgeous, unwavering sad eyes holding mine captive as he assertively demands. "Don't you ever forget that, beautiful! Mistakes are just that, Sofia, mistakes. Every human being on this earth has made them." Closing his eyes for a second. "Hell, I've made plenty." I see the pain as he reopens them and it rips me apart inside. My lip trembles along with my quivering chin. Tears slowly stream down my face, flowing over his thumbs. He gently brushes them away. Overwhelming sadness lurks deep in my chest. I'm not sure I can handle the conversation that I know is coming.

"You... you, Sofia, were never a mistake," he clarifies. "Please, don't cry, beautiful. It destroys me inside to see you cry. You were never one of my mistakes. I failed you that night. You have no idea how much I regret letting you down. We were young, yes, but I knew better. You were inexperienced. I was not. I screwed up. We can't change those decisions we made back then, and, honestly, Sofia, except for one tragic part of it, I wouldn't change it for anything in this world. It was the best night and morning of my life." I squeeze him tighter. I'm the luckiest girl to have this courageous, strong, loving, man in my life.

Yeah, I'm a damn lucky girl.

MY HEAD'S STILL resting on his broad chest. Enjoying the silence before I bare my soul.

Just say it! I chastise myself. He deserves to hear it. He deserved to hear it a long, long time ago.

"Caelan..." I cry barely hearing my own words. "I'm sorry." I feel him stiffen. His instincts kicking in. "I'm sorry I lost our baby. I'm sorry for the way I handled the whole situation." I weep. "I never told you I was sorry. I hurt you more by not talking to you about it. I'm so sorry," I apologize again while tears rapidly flow freely down my cheeks. My words are broken by the knot in the back of my throat. It's so hard to talk about this. He hugs me tighter then releases me to cradle the back of my head. His fingers weaving through my hair. His eyes are intimately searching mine, but I have no more words at the moment.

His devastating loving eyes hold mine captive. "I wouldn't change a thing either. I wish that things could have been different, but God had different plans for us, beautiful."

This conversation is the only conversation I have had about me losing our baby. I have never talked to him about it. Ever. I just couldn't do it. It hurt too much. I've only ever spoken to Kathrine, my therapist. "Even though I lost the baby. I would do it all over again. Except for the part of me losing the baby." I look up into his warm, loving teary eyes. "I couldn't have asked for a more perfect first time with a more perfect guy to lose my virginity to. Most girls say their first time is not what they dreamed of, but with you, Caelan, it was everything I had dreamed of and more. It was a dream come true, and I thank you for giving me those memories." He starts to say something, but I gently place my finger over his soft lips to stop him. "Please let me finish. If I stop now, I may never get the courage to say it again." He nods slightly never losing eye contact with me.

"When I lost the baby, I was so mad at myself. At first, when I found out I was pregnant, I sat there on my bathroom floor crying, sobbing, gut wrenching sobs praying that God would take it away. I was just so young, and shocked," I incredulity admit, sighing. "I was so shocked," I say in a deeper slower tone. "Honestly, I know it's stupid, but I don't know how I could have been so shocked being that you and I both made the decision not to use protection. I was so furious at myself for making that decision. I mean how stupid is an eighteen-year-old girl for thinking she can't get pregnant if you pull out. It's pretty damn stupid, and I blamed myself. Then I became angry with you. Ohh, Caelan, I was soooo angry at you. I knew for weeks I was pregnant before I told you. I was so mad at you for getting me pregnant. But, in reality, it was both our faults. Yes, you may have been two years older than me, but we both knew better. We're both smarter than that." I close my eyes for a few seconds as the memories and emotions come to the surface inside me.

He kisses my forehead. "It's okay, beautiful, take your time."

I blow out a heavy remorseful breath. "After weeks went by I became so afraid that you would be mad at me when I finally told you. Then, I thought when you found out how far along I was and how long I knew, and I still didn't tell you, that you would be even angrier at me. The stress... oh, Caelan the pressure I felt. It was unbearable. You asked me every day what was wrong. I just couldn't bring myself to tell you. I felt so guilty. I knew if I told you, I just knew I would lose you."

"You will never lose me, Sofia. We may get off track sometimes, but you will never lose me."

I hug him tighter. "Then I started thinking about my father and what he already thought about me. I started to believe him. I got myself knocked up, so I must be a whore, right? And that on top of the fact that I thought I was going to lose my best friend, I couldn't bear it. I was going to chicken out and tell my mother first. This way she could tell him, but I knew that wouldn't have been the right thing to do either, and I had already messed up so bad. Even then I couldn't do anything right in my father's eyes. It was an emotional overload for me. I was so sick. I was throwing up every day, all day. I didn't know if it was from the pregnancy or the stress. When I finally told you, you were so happy. Shocked yes, but you were so happy. Your words that day... 'Sofia I know I'm only twenty years old, but I will do everything I can to make sure you and this baby are taken care of and happy. I will always be there for both of you.' those words changed everything for me." I beamed at him remembering how I felt when he made that statement. "Those words changed my life. I didn't care about what my father thought anymore. As long as you and I were okay, I was okay. We had created a life together, you and me. A life that was made during such a special moment. I was so full of overwhelming love I finally felt like I could do it. We could do it." I blink my eyes a few times trying to remove the long overdue tears. "Then..." I look down, shaking my head in disbelief.

"Hey, look at me. You don't have to go back there," he sadly expresses.

"I do, though, C. I really do," I say looking up at him. "I've cried so many tears over this, but never tears with the one person I should have cried with. I'm sorry," I apologized. "It was all my fault we lost that baby. When I started bleeding, I was in shock. I thought, why would God give us this and then take it away? First, I begged for him to take the baby away. Then, when I wanted the baby more than anything, it was ripped away.

"That morning, when I woke up with cramps, I just thought it was normal. They weren't that bad. I tried to go back to sleep. As I laid there and some more time passed, they started getting worse. I knew then something was wrong. When I got up and went into the bathroom... when I saw the blood... I knew. I just knew. I panicked, Caelan. I just couldn't believe I was four and a half months pregnant and bleeding. I couldn't believe that I finally got the courage to tell you and working up the courage to tell my mother and father to that very moment of sitting on my bathroom floor covered in blood, now losing my baby. The pain became excruciating within minutes. I laid there on that floor all alone curled up in a ball. I didn't know what to do, but I knew I had to do something. I wanted you, C," I confess. "I wanted you with me," I stutter through broken words mixed with my tears. "I just couldn't face you and tell you I was losing our baby. I couldn't even do that right." I watch as heart breaking tears flow from his shimmering eyes. "I knew that me losing our baby would change things between us. I just knew in my heart, and it did... for a while," I confessed mourning the time we lost together.

"I was mad, Sofia. I was so mad at you. I wanted to be there for you, and you kept pushing me away."

"I know. I know you were, and I don't blame you. I should have told you when I found out I was pregnant. I should have called you that morning when I realized I was miscarrying our baby. I'm sorry," I apologize again then take a deep cleansing breath to try and get through the rest. "As I sat there weeping, I knew I should call you. I just couldn't. Everything in me told me to call you, but I couldn't bring myself to do it. I was such a coward. I knew I had to get to the hospital, but how was I supposed to do that with my father being home. So, I made a decision. I was going to climb out my bedroom window and down the trellis. Then drive myself to the hospital."

He looks at me with shocked, furious, incredulous eyes. "Are you serious?" he admonishes.

"I couldn't though. The pain was so bad, C. It was so bad." I crinkle my eyes thinking of the pain I felt that day. I took a deep, shaky breath. My body trembling, and if it weren't for Caelan holding me up right now, I would drop to the floor. "I could barely walk. I wanted you, C. I wanted you to come and wrap your arms around me and make it all go away." I weep. "I decided to go downstairs to find my mother. I had to stop on the staircase three times before I got to the bottom because the pain was so bad. That's where Giovanni found me, at the bottom of the stairs."

"Giovanni?" Confusion crossing his face. "What do you mean Giovanni?"

"I was doubled over in pain. I couldn't move anymore. My jeans were saturated in blood, Caelan. Our baby's life was leaving my body, the protected nest where I was supposed to nourish and flourish and grow our baby. My body betrayed me." I start jerking with gut wrenching sobs. I wipe my face with my shoulder and sucked in the snot escaping my nostrils. The ugly cry has taken over my body. I stumble through my words. "M-m-my father was in his office on the phone. G-Giovanni was j-just walking out of the office to l-leave. When he saw me, he knew something was terribly wrong. He went to yell for my father, but I grabbed his arm pulling him down to me. I begged, and I pleaded with him to help me and not tell my father." I swipe my nose and face with my sleeve. Everything is breaking loose inside me. "I'm so sorry. Oh God, I'm so, so sorry," I wailed while my knees begin to wobble.

I feel Caelan's arms loosen around me then his strong arm come around my back and the other one under the back of my knees. He cradles me to his body as he carries me over to the couch. He places me softly in the corner of the huge L-shaped couch. He picks up my legs laying them across his strong thighs as he slides in closer to me. He reaches over and grabs a white cashmere throw blanket from the back of the couch, laying it over me. He twists his body towards me. Stroking my hair gently, his desperate eyes looking deep into my soul. He wants to hear the rest of the story, and I need to tell it. So, I continue.

"That's when Giovanni picked me up. He started to carry me towards my father office. I freaked out. Begged him to not tell my father. Told him I was pregnant and that I was losing the baby to please bring me to the hospital." When I see his tears slowly roll down his cheeks, I apologize again, "I'm sorry." I hold his face in my palms. I take a deep stuttering breath and continued again. "Giovanni got this look on his face when I told him I was pregnant and losing the baby. He turned and walked straight out the front door. Carried me to his car and laid me down on the back seat. He had a jacket or something in the front seat. He propped it under my head. The whole time I was so scared one of the guards would see him and I. Then he drove off the property very calmly. All I could think was if my father finds out he helped me, he will kill him. As I laid there sobbing, screaming from the pain, all I could think was how much I wanted you." His breathing becoming rapid pants. "I wanted you to hold me, C. I wanted you to make it better. I just wanted you! You always made things better," I implore. "I wanted you to tell me it would all be okay! I knew deep down inside it wasn't going to be, though. I was crying out your name. Saying it repeatedly telling you how sorry I was when Giovanni reached back, grabbing my hand. He held my hand the whole way to the hospital, Caelan. Whispering that everything would be fine." I become silent reflecting back to the time. The memories pouring into me like unrelenting, unforgiving, crashing waves.

He's caressing my face trying to sooth me. "Calm down, Sof. Take a deep breath. Breathe with me, baby. Ready?" He inhales a deep breath. I mirror him a few times. Breathing as one. Calming myself enough to continue.

"When we reached the doors to the ER, he carried me through the automatic doors demanding that the doctors and nurses help me. He laid me down on the bed and wouldn't leave my side. He held my hand even then, even when they ordered him to leave the room, he refused. Finally, security came to remove him. I guess he thought instead of being arrested and having to explain that to my dad he better just wait for me in the waiting room. The reluctance in his eyes was... God, Caelan, he did not want to leave my side. After... after everything was over, they let him back into the room. The look on his face." I shake my head in disbelief, hiccupping. "It was pure devastation, sadness, anger. He asked me how far I was. When I told him, he was so shocked. He just stared at me with confusion in his eyes. I begged him again not to tell my father. He promised me he wouldn't. He asked me who the father was. Which I guess he just wanted confirmation because in the car I kept screaming your name. He asked me if you knew. I told him I had just told you a few weeks prior, that we were going to tell my parents that upcoming weekend. He just looked at me with sympathetic eyes. Like he knew exactly what I was going through.

"It made sense when he then told me a story. A story about how he had a beautiful girlfriend when he was younger. He said she was his heart and soul. He had gotten her pregnant when they were nineteen, and she too, had lost the baby. I guess he was telling me his story to try and alleviate my pain, but in doing that I could see his own pain in his eyes, pain that he's never gotten over. All I could think about was you feeling that pain. I guess it was a selfless act letting me know he knew how and what I was feeling and I knew just by looking at him, he wasn't telling me some story to make me feel better. I laid there in that hospital bed mourning the loss of our baby while Giovanni held me. Trying to comfort me, but all I wanted was you."

"You should have called me, Sofia. That was my baby," he roared.

"I know. I'm so sorry. Giovanni was going to. He pulled his phone out to make a call, and when I looked at him, I knew he was going to call you. I asked him not to. I told him I wanted to be the one to tell you. I just needed a few days to do it." I look up at him warily. He wrapped his arms around me. We held onto each other for comfort for a few quiet moments. Something we have never done over this situation and should have done a long time ago.

I pull back from him a little. He wipes my tears away. "After everything was over, I just couldn't bring myself to talk about it. I wanted to pretend that nothing happened. I wanted it all, everything to go back to the same way it was before. After I told you, I fell into a deep depression. You tried to talk to me about it. You asked me to talk to you so many times; I just couldn't. I became a shell of myself. You deserved to know what happened Caelan. I know that. I just couldn't bring myself to tell you. I felt like the biggest failure. I knew you were pissed at me. After some time passed, we didn't talk at all. I fell into an even deeper depression. I checked out. The next thing I knew, a few months later, you started dating Kate."

I watch him drop his head back against the couch to look up to the ceiling. He mumbles something then shook his head shamefully.

"I thought, at first, she was just some girl you were banging. Someone to pass the time with. I mean I know we weren't together. I knew that when we slept together. Everything I went through, us losing the baby, I don't know… it just tore me apart knowing you were with her. You were moving on, and I was still stuck on the day of losing our baby. I had no right to be upset. I knew that, but it… hurt in here," I whisper touching my chest. "I was so sad that our once closer-than-close relationship was now nonexistent. I was alone, hurt, and scared of the feelings I was having. I felt like a huge failure. You, you of all people," I say shaking my head back and forth, "I just didn't want you to look at me like I was a failure too. I wouldn't have been able to handle that. As the weeks, and then months passed, I dropped deeper and deeper into depression. I overheard Antonio and Nikki talking one day, saying that you and Kate were serious. That was it for me. I had trouble sleeping, eating, and caring about anything at all. I lost so much weight. My family kept asking me what was wrong. My father kept demanding to know what was going on.

I wouldn't tell him. I just kept telling him to give me time. The only people that knew then, and still know now, are you and Giovanni. No one else." I reach out to hold his hand.

"Then one day, I was sitting in the library, Giovanni walked by to go to my father's office. When he passed the library doorway, he saw me sitting on the couch staring out the window at the rose garden. I knew he was standing in the doorway looking at me, but I didn't say anything. I didn't care. I hadn't showered in days. I was a zombie. A shell of myself. My father was ready to admit me, and my mother kept telling him to give me time. That day, though, Giovanni walked into that room and knelt in front of me. He laid his hand on the back of my head, leaned in and whispered in my ear, 'you will be okay, sweetheart. I will make sure if it.' He kissed my forehead and walked out. I never even moved. Just kept staring at the roses. I sat there like a statue for hours upon hours. The next day there was a business card sitting on my night stand with a women's name and phone number on it. Handwritten at the bottom was a note."

Life can rip away something we never thought we wanted,
but it can also give you something you have dreamt about.
Keep dreaming...

"I didn't know what to think. I knew the card had to have been from Giovanni. When I called the number, a woman answered. She knew exactly who I was. She was so nice. I set up an appointment with her and have been meeting with her ever since. In the beginning, it was three times a week. Then it went to two a week; now I go once a month. I have never paid for any of the appointments. When I asked her about it, she just blows it off telling me that sometimes in life, things are free. I know deep down that Giovanni is paying for them. Until this day, I still don't pay for them. I asked him about it one day, and he just pretended like he didn't know what I was talking about... but I knew he did."

"That's because he does know, but it wasn't him paying for it."

"What?" I ask, not believing what I was hearing.

"It was, and still is, me who pays for it, beautiful. I will continue to do so for however long you need to go." His thumb softly grazes over my jaw.

Gasping I throw my hand over my mouth. Hesitation fills my words. "Wh... Why? Why would you do that? How did you even know?" I'm so confused. "I thought... I thought it was Giovanni this whole time."

"It now makes sense to me, why he came to me. I didn't know how he knew about the baby, but now I do. He called me the same night he saw you on the couch in the library. I hesitated when I heard it was him. He asked me to meet him down at the park on Cross Street. He must have heard my hesitation because he told me he meant no harm. That he really needed to speak to me about you."

"So, I met with him later that night. He was angry, but not at me. Just in general. I could see the agitation radiating all over him. He wouldn't give me any information. He just said that you needed professional help, that I should be the one to help you get that. I asked so many questions, but he wouldn't tell me anything except that I needed to man up and make sure you got the help you needed. I had no problem manning up, but because we hadn't talked in so long, I didn't know exactly what I was manning up for." His voice wary. "Even though... in my heart, I knew why you needed help."

Slightly tilting his head back, closing his eyes. "Fuck!" He turns towards me. "I'm sorry, I fucked up. I fucked up bad. If I had just..."

"C this wasn't your fault." I reached out and grabbed his arm. "I pushed you away. I couldn't take the pain of seeing you, knowing I let you down and hurt you. Plus, for me, after a few months went by and you and Kate got more serious, I just thought... damn, I just thought you moved on and didn't want me around anyway and forgot about me."

"Hurt me? Want you around? Forget about you? Sofia, you didn't hurt me until... you didn't hurt me 'til you pushed me the fuck away! That's what fucking hurt me! Not want you around? Are you kidding me? I would have dropped everything if you had called me or texted me. Fuck! Sofia, I would have dropped everything and everyone!"

"I'm sorry, Caelan. We lost a whole year because of me."

"Let me finish! Let me just say what I have to say. I need you to know the whole story." I nodded. He continued, "I asked Giovanni why it had to be me to be the one to man up. Really, it was just to see what he would say. He stared me down like a stone-cold killer. He fucking snarled when he roared 'You fucking know why!' He just kept staring at me. We both stared at each other saying a lot without saying anything at all. I just knew he knew what happened with the baby, I just didn't know how he knew. I wanted to know everything. He wouldn't give me any information. Fuck, Sof!" Rubbing his hands on the back of his neck. "Fuck, Sof!" he says again. "So, there I was, the father of that baby, not really knowing if he knew I was the father of that baby and there I was, a man in front of another man who knew what happened to my baby and I knew nothing, but yet he knew everything! That's fucked up, Sofia! That... that fucking hurts!" he admonishes.

"Caela-" I reach for him. He pulls away removing my legs from his lap so he could sit on the edge of the couch.

"NO! Let me finish!" he snapped. "Giovanni wouldn't say anything else to me except that he had a good friend that was a therapist. He already called her, that I would be the one paying for the sessions. I agreed, told him I would do anything for you. Told him I tried talking to you, and you just kept pushing me away. After we had parted, I called Nikki and Antonio. I asked them about you. All they would say was that you weren't feeling good, to just give you time. I tried to reach out to you again. You wouldn't return my calls or texts. I was so lost, Sofia. I didn't know what else to do. So, two days later I pretended to be at the house for Antonio, but really I was looking for you."

"I remember that day," I say recalling the moment I saw whim.

"So do I, beautiful, so do I." He hangs his head. Elbows resting on his knees now. Knuckles turning white because his fists are curled up into a ball. Whispering gruffly, "When I saw you"- he groaned with painful frustration- "man I could not believe my fucking eyes. I couldn't believe I was looking at the same girl. You were always so vibrant, feisty and full of life." I laid my hand on his back for reassurance. "When you saw me standing in the doorway looking at you, you just stared at me. Your eyes were so empty. Then after a minute, shock registered on your face, but then came the hatred, shame, and guilt. I saw it alright there on your beautiful, tired face. All those emotions right there and then they disappeared just as quickly as they came; going back to being vacant. My heart broke. I was staring once again at my beautiful girl's empty eyes. I was angry! Fuck, I was so angry. I was mad at myself. I was mad at you! Christ, I was so angry at everything and everyone. I couldn't believe how bad you were. When you screamed at me to get out, I was so taken aback. That's why I just stood there. I couldn't believe that was my girl screaming at me like that. The anger that emanated from your frail body could be felt from miles away. I couldn't move. I just couldn't believe that was you. I knew if I left I wouldn't see you again for a long time and I... I was right. I thought, I did this to her. I did this, and at least, I know I can help to fix this. Well, at least pay for you to get the help to fix what I'd broken in you. So, I left. I walked out. I did what you asked and left." He turns his head towards me with a jerk. "But, Sofia, it was the hardest fucking thing to turn my back on you and walk out. I did what I thought was right for you. I thought if the problem wasn't in the picture you could get better. I was a fool for thinking that. I needed you!" He points at me. "And you needed me! Fuck!" he yells, dropping his head. "We needed each other, Sofia! You were broken, and I was lost. We needed each other." He lifts his head again, turns and grabs me by the waist pulling me onto his lap. We wrapped our arms around each other. Sitting there for a long time. The only sound is the beautiful soft musical sounds of *Broken* by Lifehouse playing on the overhead speakers. I hugged him tighter listening to the lyrics. We sat there holding each other, letting our long overdue physically exhausting emotions ebb and flow, and finally... let go.

seven

"Sof? I'm gonna order the pizzas. You want the usual?" I hear from the doorway of my room.

"Yeah, everything's good. Just make sure you tell them-"

"Ya, ya I know, well done."

"C, can you get me a piece of cheesecake too, for later."

"Cheesecake huh? You never get dessert."

"With a scoop of vanilla ice cream too." I give him a cheesy smile.

"Wow, you're going all out."

"Ha, ha. I'm just in the mood for something creamy and sweet." I snap my mouth shut because as soon as I said it, I knew exactly where his brain was going with that statement.

"I'll give you something creamy and sweet, sweetheart! No calories either!" he says with the cockiest grin on his face.

I throw a sassy grin at him. "That's salty, not sweet. Get it straight, stud!" I smile at him while I look at him in the mirror. All the while I'm leaning over the countertop putting my mascara on.

"And how would you know that, Sofia?" he questions smirking with a raised brow but there is also a hint of anger in his tone while he stares at my protruding ass.

"Out!" I laugh. "Out!" I say pointing to the door.

"Oh, come on, Sof, I wanna know how you know that," he chortles.

"Caelan O'Reily! Go!" I point again. My cheeks are getting redder by the second.

"Aww, beautiful don't get embarrassed." He smirks masking what I think is jealousy.

"You know one of these days I'm going to shock you." I point at him "You think it's funny, Mr. I-sleep-with-anything-that-walks!"

"Oh, come on, Sofia. I'm not that bad," he states incredulity.

"No, you're not that bad." I roll my eyes. "Just in case you forgot, Trojan called and left a message, their stock is getting low. They wanted to know if you could cut back. They can't keep up with the demands of making mini condoms."

His eyebrows shoot to his hairline in shock. "Oh, it's like that huh?" His bottom lip pushes up crinkling his chin. "Okay, I get it, but Sofia... whether it's big or small, which I need to clarify, It. Is. Not. Small! It's A Fucking Beast!" he brags. "But, my question to you, Sofia, is why are you still talking about my cock? You must be thinking about it an awful lot."

I twist fast to look at him. Mouth hanging open. "I'm not! You started it with the creamy sweet shit!" I accuse.

"Ahhh, but you went directly to my cock size which means you must be thinking about it. All I was talking about was giving you something sweet to eat."

"My ass! C, get the hell out!" I yell exasperated.

As he turns to walk out of the room I hear. "And a fine ass it is, beautiful!"

"Ugggh." I grab my hair brush and throw it at him. Hitting the door frame!

He ducks out of the way. "Fuck, you really are frustrated! Just let me know and I'll take care of that for you anytime, beautiful." he barks with laughter as he's walking out the door.

"In your dreams, C!" I yelled.

"Always in my dreams, baby!" he murmured, but I heard it. "Everyone's on their way over now. A's picking up the pizzas."

I HEAR THE front door open and close.

"Hey, anybody home? I got pizza and beer!" I hear Antonio yell.

"And my three hundred bucks, right?" I hear C yell from his office.

"Three hundred? Nice try buddy."

"Wait, A why do you owe him three hundred bucks?" I ask as Bob Marley's *One Love* carries me down the stairs.

"Get the fuck out of here, fucker, it's two hundred!" Antonio reiterates loudly throwing two bills on the kitchen island.

"Pay up loser," C says as he's walking out of his office slapping his hands together.

"Wait, what the hell?" I say. "Why do you owe two hundred bucks?"

"Well, you see your brother-"

"Hey, hey, hey!" I hear Nikki say from the front door. "My brother what?" she says as a round of hellos and heys are tossed her way.

"Yeah, that's what I wanna know," I say.

"Well," C says again. "Your brother bet me-"

"What's going on! Something smells awesome up in here!" Chris noisily states walking through the door

"What's up dude?" both guys greet him.

"Hey, Chris." I hug and kiss him.

He leans back from the hug. "How are you?"

"I'm okay. Just creeped out by it all." I can see C from the corner of my eye listening to our conversation.

"You need anything you let me know. You know that, right? I'll be right there for you if you need me."

"I know, Chris. Thanks."

"What the hell? I don't get a hug?" Nikki laughs holding her arms up.

"Damn, girl get in here! I got love for everyone!"

I shake my head. "Yup, you and C are definitely brothers! You two should be twins with all the love you two spread around!" I look over at C and smile to share the joke with him, but instead of his big, beautiful smile that I would usually receive back from him, he just raises his eyebrows and one slight corner of his mouth.

Hmmm, what was that about?

I thought we were okay after us talking yesterday. Maybe not, maybe I was wrong. I tilt my head a little, looking at him with questioning eyes. He slightly shakes his head and turns away.

What the hell?

"What's this I hear, someone owes someone two hundred bucks? What's the deal? Who lost a bet?" Chris asked.

"Yeah, that's what we wanna know," Nikki says, pointing back and forth between her and me.

"So basically, A and I made a bet Friday while Sof was in the hospital."

"You two have no shame. Seriously? While I was lying in a hospital bed?" I shoot them both the 'are you fucking serious look.'

"No listen," A says. "You and Daddy were fighting. C and I could hear it from the hallway. Before we walked back into the room we bet who would win the fight. He chose you. I went with daddy. He won!"

"Nice bro! I would always go for Sofia! She's feisty as hell," Chris says, giving his brother a fist pound.

Caolan just smiles and glances my way. "I will always pick Sof," he says assessing me.

What the hell is going on with him? My belly does a flip. *I thought we were okay.*

"Hey, Sof can you help me?" Nikki yells from the oversized Carrara marble kitchen island. "Coming!" I yell, but my eyes are still on locked on his. We gaze at each other for a few more seconds before he turns away. What the hell did I do? We were just fine joking around upstairs. What happened between that time and this moment? I give my hair a toss over my shoulder to shake myself of the unease settling in my stomach and walk over to help my sister.

I hear the doorbell ring. In walks Jessica, Luke and Sage. Jessica's my best friend. We met freshman year in college. I'll never forget meeting her for the first time. She's tall, five foot ten, gorgeous, and blonde. Great body and a great personality to go with it. Me, I'm the short, curvy girl. Men fall all over her. Trust me, she has her pick. She had a crush on Caelan a long time ago. I don't know why he never took what she so clearly had offered him, but as far as I'm aware, he hasn't. She's so his type too. He loves the tall blondes. She and I are absolute total opposites. I have tits, ass, and hips, and she looks like a runway supermodel. We get along great, though, and she and I are just as close as my sister and I are.

Luke works for Caelan. He hired him a year after C started his business. They have been good friends ever since. Luke is C's, right-hand man. No doubt they are as thick as thieves. The two of them alone are chick magnets, but together, forget about it! It's ridiculous! Seeing them work their magic at the bar should become a 'how to' show in Vegas. Seriously they're that good. Luke is a sexy man. Smooth operator. Just a little bit shorter than C with dark brown wavy hair and deep brown soulful eyes that have seen a lot in his short life. They're so expressive, they'll make any girl melt. Funny as hell at times, too. I know for a fact the two of them have had threesomes. I know because I've been here when they come back from trolling the bars. This place is built well, but when some chick is screaming like a banshee well... now that's hard not to hear.

Then you bring Sage into this crazy close group of friends, and that gives you a full house of craziness. Although, Sage would rather sleep with C or Luke, not the chicks they bring home. He's a straight up gay man, and I love him! A gay man is the best friend a girl could ever have. He's sexy in his own right. Just as tall, but a thinner build than the rest of the guys, but not by much. He hits the gym five times a week, and it shows all over his fine ass.

Blond hair, blue-green eyes, full luscious lips, and a great ass. Oh, and he can dance, too. The man can move! I love dancing with him. Jessica and Sage work for me at Hearts Desire. Sage applied when I first opened the boutique and the three of us have been glued together ever since. They both help me so much because of my schedule at Club Ice, which everyone keeps telling me to quit. I can't quit just yet, though. Caelan loaned me the money to start up HD, and I am determined to pay him back fast. The boutique is doing well, really well actually. But, I still can't bring myself to quit Club Ice just yet. I started working there as a shot girl when I was eighteen. Moved up to bartending when I was twenty-one. It's great money so why would I leave. I'm young. Besides I like the nightlife, and like I said I want to pay off Caelan as soon as I can. He was nice enough to loan me the money to start up the boutique, so my gratitude to him would be to pay him back faster than we agreed.

"Heyyyyyyy, gorgeous!" I hear a deep voice heading towards me. The hard slap on my ass makes me yelp.

"Woo!" I jump up to the tips of my toes. "What the hell Luke, that was hard!" I laugh as I chastise him.

"Sorry girl just had to get my hand on that fine ass of yours!" he jokes as he wraps his arms around me pulling me into a tight hug.

"Hey there, sexy man."

"How are you doing, sexy girl? This shit... this shit that happened is fucked up. Us five guys find out who the hell this is that did this to you... yeah well, I feel sorry for that motherfucker!"

"You slap her on her ass like that again, and I'm not gonna feel sorry for what happens to you either, fucker!" C threatens from behind me. I turn my head to glance at him. Luke just laughs and with his cocky smile tightening his hold on me.

"Come on, dude, look at this ass!" he compliments as he cops a feel squeezing both cheeks with both of his hands. Giving my stinging, hot, ass cheeks a firm squeeze. "She's got an awesome ass. I just had to!"

My hands that were resting on his shoulders now give him a firm but friendly shove. I nervously laugh glancing at C again. His eyes are still glued to Luke. Something passes between the two of them in their guy code. Not too sure what that was all about, but hell, let me break the tension I think is starting to settle around us. I take a step back and look back to Luke.

"I'm good, Luke. I just can't wait to watch the videotape from the club that night." Caelan's walking away but his body stiffens at my comment. Sage catches my eye. He and Jessica are both staring at me. I ask them both through my eyes if they just saw that whole situation.

Sage raises his brows at me and mouths, "Oh ya honey, I saw it!"

I look over to Antonio. Figuring I can get past the whole uncomfortable situation that just happened. Not that I even really know what just happened. "A? Did you get the video from the club?" I ask from across the kitchen.

"Nope, not yet. We'll have it by tomorrow, though."

I look to Nikki and C standing there. Then back to Antonio as Nikki hands me a bunch of plates for the pizza. I take them and start to walk toward the island to set them down. My eyes are questioning both of them with A's statement. I mean it's been three days. He didn't get it yet? No, I don't believe him for a second.

"A, when you get it bring it straight here to me. Okay?"

"You got it, sis," he agrees looking at Caelan.

"Everyone dig in!" Nikki yells.

"Who wants a beer?" Chris yells from inside the state of the art refrigerator where his head is buried grabbing bottles as a round of mes went around.

C walks over and tilts my Mexican beer towards me.

"Thank you," I say looking up into his eyes. His eyes linger on mine before he taps the top of my bottle with his and winks at me then turns to grab another slice of pizza.

It's quiet for a little bit while everyone's digging into the pizza. Caelan must have his iPod set to the well-known Bob Marley and The Wailers because *Is This Love* is now playing from the overhead speakers. Italian food, Mexican beer, and Reggae Music. Can't beat it. Enjoying the music and food, I'm quiet for a bit. I love music, it relaxes me and helps me express my feelings. I sit here thinking about the last three days. I look at all the people standing around me and can't help but think to myself how lucky I am to have such great friends. All of us are from all different walks of life, but we all fit together like a well-oiled machine. There's not one of us here that wouldn't help the other one. As I sit here gazing around the kitchen, listening to the conversations, ball busting, and laughter from these incredible human beings, I close my eyes and say my thanks for having these amazing people in my life.

"So, tell me the truth, sis. How are you really doing?" Antonio asks pulling me out of my sappy thoughts. I didn't even know he walked up next to me. "I can see somethings going on, and by the looks of it, it's more than just what happened Thursday night." I glance up at him just as he's wrapping his arm around me. "You want to talk?"

"Ya, I do," I say as I put my plate down. His eyes flick back and forth over mine trying to figure out what's going on.

"In private. Okay?"

"Come on, we'll go into the game room. That's far enough away from everyone here." He grabs my beer from the counter and leads us towards the game room.

"Hey, A? Where are you going?" I hear Christopher yell. "We getting a game of pool going?"

"No pool. Need to talk to my sister," he yells over his shoulder. "I'll be back in a few minutes." I turn to look at Chris and standing next to him is Caelan watching us with squinted eyes as we walk towards the game room. He smiles at me, but it's a small smile, and there's definitely questions in his eyes.

"Here," A says, handing me my beer.

"Thanks," I say, jumping up onto the pool table to sit.

"What's going on, Sof?"

"I just need some quiet time with my older brother, A."

He sighs. "Start talking, little sis."

"A, just don't lie to me. Please don't lie to me, okay?"

"Sof, I would never lie to you, but you know I can only tell you so much."

"You already lied to me A, and you just did it again. You're my brother I can't have my brother lying to me."

He looks at me. "What? What are you talking about?"

"Please, A. Honesty is the only way with me. I have to be able to trust the people closest to me."

He resigns hanging his head. "Ask me."

"Who has the tape?"

"Daddy."

"Did you watch it?"

He looks at me for a second before releasing a breath. "Yes."

"With daddy? Did you watch it with, daddy?"

"Yes."

"How bad?"

His head drops again. He palms the back of his neck rubbing it back and forth for a few seconds before he confirms my suspicions. "Bad, Sof. Be prepared the next time you see him."

"Shit!"

"I tried to talk to him. I did. He just wouldn't listen to me. Honestly, Sofia, I don't know why he freaks about you. I just don't get it. He doesn't freak out on Nikki and he sure as hell doesn't flip out on me."

"Seriously? You're a guy! It's entirely different for you, Antonio." I shake my head. I'm quiet for a few seconds while I look around the beautiful, elegant game room Caelan has created. Trying to think of which question to ask next. It's either about the tape or the even harder one I want to ask him, but I'm afraid to hear the answer. The question being, what was the look between him and C when I asked about the tape. The dim light from above the pool table is throwing off a soft glow on the burgundy pool table cloth that I'm sitting on, but even though it's dark in here, I can still see my brother perfectly clear. Antonio's hip is leaning against the table next to me. He's waiting for my question. The question I know needs to be asked, but not sure I want the answer to. I'll go with the easier one first. "A, what did you see on the tape? Anything?" I ask shaking my head at him willing him to say no. "Do you know who it was? Can you see who did it?"

"No, Sof. We watched it over and over, and we didn't see anything."

"Why lie to me? Why tell me you didn't have the tape yet?"

"I didn't want to bring it up in front of everyone."

"Liar! Please stop lying to me, A!"

"I'm sorry. Caelan and I talked, we didn't want you to see the tape. Watching yourself on the tape and knowing our father the way he is, you're only going to get yourself upset over it, Sof. We just thought it would be better if you didn't see it. There's nothing wrong with what you did, but knowing daddy, the way he is, how he already freaked out, we just thought it would be better that you didn't see the tape. We thought we could alleviate that stress for you. It's going to be hard enough when you see him, Sof. I was bringing it over tomorrow so C and I could watch it together with you."

Bastards! I take a deep breath. Realization just hit me. Now for the hard question that I already know the answer to. Something I know I don't want, but I have to ask it just to make sure.

"So, C knew about this?" He glances at me when I ask the question then drops his head back to look at the ceiling. He's stuck in the middle between his sister and his best friend. I don't care. "A, don't lie to me again. I can't have you and Caelan hiding things from me. It will make me feel alienated, and I don't need that from the two people I care and trust the most." The tears I held at bay slowly start to trickle down my cheeks. They're tears caused by hurt, the hurt is from the trust that was broken and along with that... I'm pissed off!

"Yeah." I barely hear him reluctantly confirm.

"And he also saw the tape too? When?"

He turns towards me laying his hand on my arm. "Last night."

"So, last night when he told me he had to run to his office for paperwork he went to watch the surveillance video with you and daddy?" I murmur it more to myself than to him.

"Sof, he's only trying to protect you."

"Yeah? Well... I don't need that kind of protection. You know, from the people who say they love me, but then lie to me."

"Sof?" I hear coming from the archway to the room. He's leaning against the grey stone archway. Our eyes connect and lock. I'm not backing down from this. He was wrong. He is wrong, and I am pissed. More than pissed. I'm hurt.

"Uhhh, I'm gonna go," my brother uncomfortably mumbles throwing his thumb over his shoulder. "Don't cry, Sis," he tries to console as he leans down to kiss my cheek. "We're just trying to protect you." I won't even look at him or acknowledge his words because my eyes are still glued to Caelan's. As my brother starts to walk towards him he smiles. "Look when it comes down to it, and I do not wanna know about it, but you two need to get it on or something. Fuck man, the sexual energy between you two is frustrating as hell!"

Caelan squints his eyes, glancing at him with a twist of his head.

Well, that pissed him off.

As Antonio gets closer, Caelan's eyes turn back to mine. They're unwavering on mine when Antonio puts his hand on his shoulder and stops to say, "Sorry dude. I had to tell her." He glances back at me and winks. "Besides, she's a smart girl she already figured it out." Caelan doesn't move a muscle when Antonio gives him a hard bro slap on the shoulder. "Good luck, man." He gives him encouragement as he looks back at me again. "I love you, Sof. Go easy on him," he says as he walks out.

eight

O UR EYES ARE STILL LOCKED ONTO EACH other's. Deep, sapphire blue gems to my emerald green. His hands are tucked into the pockets of his low-riding jeans, letting his black boxer briefs peek out from behind the denim.

Damn, he's sexy.

I notice the music on the speaker system is no longer playing the great Bob Marley, but instead the beautiful lyrics of James Bay, *Hold Back the River*. His eyes are still holding mine with a soft and tender gaze, like when a man cradles a newborn baby in his arms.

"I'm sorry," he apologizes, shoving himself off the stone archway. He frees his hands from his confinement of pockets while he walks towards me. His muscles flex through his white t-shirt with each strong movement he makes. He stops in front of my swinging spread legs. His strong thighs are now between mine. "I'm sorry," he muttered again.

I can hear everyone's laughter from the kitchen. Everyone's so happy, but I'm... not. A tear slides down my hot, flushed cheek. I'm mad as hell at him right now, so much so that I can't bring myself to say something to him. He knows how I'm feeling. We know each other like we know ourselves.

"Say something, beautiful. Rip me a new ass. Tell me how much of an asshole I am. Kick me in the balls." He stops to think for a second. "Well, wait, don't do that. I need those." He grins. I roll my eyes. "Say something, Sof."

Our eye contact hasn't broken yet. Well, except for the eye rolling. "You lied to me," I utter slowly and quietly with trembling hands in my lap.

He lays his hands over mine trying to calm the irritation causing the tremble. "I did. I didn't want you to hurt anymore. After what happened Thursday, then yesterday…" he breaks off. "The two of us finally talking about the baby, I know that was hard for you, Sofia. Shit, for both of us. I'm still…" he shakes his head, but he doesn't finish his sentence. "I just wanted to give you some peace. I knew if you saw the video it would cause you stress. I thought… fuck, beautiful, I was only trying to protect you."

Protect me, he says. And why didn't he finish his sentence. He's still what?

He didn't want me to hurt, but who hurt me? The man standing in front of me, telling me he didn't want me to hurt. Who lied to me? The same man. Oh, the anger I'm feeling is making my insides vibrate. I am so pissed at him, but I still can't bring myself to say something. I think it's because I am so full of anger right now, I'm not sure what I'll say. Unlike him, I don't want to hurt him by saying or doing something I'll regret. So, I just stare into his eyes trying to figure it out. I see something flicker through his eyes. Then it's gone. What was that? All day he's been giving me confusing looks. This is C so why is it so hard for me to figure him out?

He lifts his hands to my face, cupping my cheeks, wiping away my leftover tears. "Beautiful, say something."

"Fuck you," I bite glaring at him. I grab his warm hands. The ones that are still cradling my face. I don't know where inside me that came from, but… well, it's out there now. His head jerks back a little in shock. His brows furrowing in confusion while his eyes are darting back and forth over mine. "Fuck You!" I repeat with even more force. His eyes become dangerously sexual. I see the flash in them again. Like a switch has just been turned on.

Crash!

His lips are on mine with such a rush of want and need it baffles me. He's kissing me like it's his last breath. The passion unfurling from his body into mine is explosive.

What the fuck?

I'm holding back, shocked at what's happening between us right now. His warm tongue slowly grazes my lower lip tempting me to open for him. Feelings and emotions start unraveling inside me. The tears that were slowly streaming down my face from hurt and sadness have now halted.

Cue the drum roll.

Desire explodes inside of me. My body is humming at a rapid pace, but I still hold back for one more second. Then... I let go. I open my mouth for him and give him everything I have. My hands that were grabbing his hands cradling my face tightly, now move to the front of his shirt. I grab at his t-shirt pulling him closer to me. He leans into me even more intimately spreading my thighs even further apart with his hips. His right hand drops from my face and grabs onto my hip pulling me forcibly into him causing a whoosh as the air leaves my lungs. My hands fall to the bottom of his shirt. I slide them under, feeling the ripple of his hard stomach. The faint line of curly hair from his happy trail are at my fingertips. I run my fingers through the tightly knitted hairs. Up and down, up and down. His stomach muscles expanding and contracting with his heavy breathing. His hand that's on my hip slides, slowly, under my shirt, tenderly grazing my tingling skin until he reaches my ribs. My nipples are at full attention, longing for his warm touch. My skins on fire, tingling and hot. He slowly glides his hand up, closer to my breast rubbing the pad of his thumb to the underside of my full aching breast. Our tongues are in a slow, intense, sexual dance. Slow, sexy... hot. I have never been kissed or felt like this with anyone I have ever been with in my life. This is passion. This is ecstasy. The music, the laughter and all the sounds from the other room fade away. All I hear now is our sounds. Our breathing. Our moans. Our sighs. He releases my lips dropping his lips to my neck, slowly kissing, nipping, sucking, and licking my collarbone. Making love to my over-sensitized skin. His left hand slides around to the back of my neck. His fingers weaving through the strands of my hair. Gripping it tightly he pulls my head back holding me in place exposing more of my neck. His right hand now fully encases my breast with a squeeze and a husky moan. He caresses and pinches my nipple through the fabric of my lace bra while he slowly licks from the deep hollow between my collarbone to the bottom of my chin making me shiver with excitement. He lowers my head moving back to my now swollen lips. Our teeth clash while our tongues battle each other. I run my hands around to his back pulling him down into me. I can feel his strong back muscles flexing under my trembling fingers and it's the sexiest damn thing. I caress my way around to the front again, dropping my hands to the top of his jeans. He's slowly pushing me back to lay me down on the pool table while he's lifting my shirt. I slide my fingers into the front of his jeans. With my thumbs and trembling fingers, I unbutton his jeans. I want to touch him. I need to touch him. With my right hand, I slip lower feeling my way down lower, lower, lower...

"Oh Shit! That's Fuckin' Hot!"

I PULL AWAY quickly gasping for breath. Throwing my hand over my mouth, I see Sage abruptly turning and apologizing. "Sorry, sorry, SO sorry, girlfriend! Carry on! Pretend like I didn't just burn my retina's out with that hot as hell scene I just saw!" he exclaims with a wave of his hands walking away at a fast pace. I quickly look up at Caelan. Reality setting in. My hand still over my mouth. Oh, No! My stomach flips. What did I just do? Tears flood my eyes. The lump in my throat is growing bigger by the second. What did we just do? Oh God, I gotta get out of here. I jump down from the pool table shoving Caelan as I pass.

"Sofia, wait." He grabs for my wrist. "Wait!" he yells as I pull my arm away darting for and through the living room to the stairs! "FUCK!" I hear him thunder from the game room.

"Sofia, what's wrong?" Antonio yells as I'm running up the stairs with Caelan right behind me! "Sof what's... dude what the fuck, C? What the fuck just happened?"

"Leave it alone, A," Caelan demands. "Sofia, wait!" he begs from right behind me still grabbing at my wrist. I hit the entry way to my bedroom. "Let me-"

Slam!

I slam my bedroom door shut and lock it. I fall against the closed door. My legs give out and I slide down to the floor. My head drops to on my knees sobbing.

Bang! Bang! Bang!

"Sofia open the door!" I hear the handle jiggle. "Shit! She locked me out?" The disbelief in his voice clearly heard.

"What the fuck dude! What did you say to my sister?"

"A, leave it alone. Go back downstairs. This is between her and I."

"Beautiful, open the door. We need to talk."

"Fuck You! I'm not leaving 'til she tells me she's okay," Antonio barks.

"What the fuck is going on?" I hear Nikki yelling at them.

"I know what's going on! Move out of the way bitchesssss," Sage sings.

Knock Knock.

"Honey, open the door it's me, Sage. Girl open the door so we can talk."

"NO!" I yell through the door! "Oh, honey open the damn door. Let me in, girlfriend." He laughs.

"I don't wanna talk right now, Sage."

"Oh honey, I'm a gay man remember? You tell me all the time a gay man is the best friend any girl can have. Now open the friggin' door, hot pants!" he rejoices in a happy tone.

It makes me chuckle. He's right I do always say that, and he always makes me feel better. Then I hear C's agitated voice. "Move out of the way! She's not gonna open the door for you, Sage."

"Umm hello hot pants number two. I'm not the one who made her go running her curvy, voluptuous, sexy ass up the stairs! You did. Did you forget that because quite honestly if you forgot about it already, you need Jesus, 'cause that shit was hawt!" he sings again.

"What the fuck is he talking about?" A interrogates. "What was hot?"

"Nothing, A. Sage, shut the fuck up."

"What was hot?" Jessica chimes in asking.

Great now every one of them is up here!

"Oh, honey if you could have seen-"

"Sage! Shut. The. Fuck. Up!" Caelan demanded.

"Dude, what the hell is going on?"

Are you kidding me right now? Luke is up here too? This is getting out of hand. I think the only one not up here is-

"C you need a shot and a beer right about now man? Or maybe just a cold shower?" I hear Christopher laughing.

Oh, okay, nope, that's great! Even Chris is up here too. So yea every single one of them is up here right now waiting for me to open the door. This is ridiculous! I feel like I'm five, and all my friends are picking on me.

Hell, I'm acting like I'm five by locking myself in my room. I just can't face him right now.

"No, I don't want a fucking beer," Caelan yells. "What I want is for Sofia to open the fucking door!"

BANG!

"Sofia, please open the door so we can talk."

"Oh? Is that what they're calling it these days, big boy, talking?"

"SAGE! Seriously, shut the fuck up! You're pissing me off."

"Oh, Caelan honey, your scary, deep-voiced, manhood only makes me hot and horny. And by the looks of what I just saw downstairs you're pretty good at-"

"SAGE! FUCKIN A' MAN!"

"Oh, just where you were headed to honey!" Sage chuckles.

"That's fucking it! Move out of the way!"

I hear scuffling.

"NO!" I hear Jessica worried yell.

"C, don't do it!" A warns.

"You sure you don't need that beer, brother?" Chris jokes his hysterics.

I hear a high-pitched yell.

"Ahhh! Don't you dare Caelan O'Reily! I might be a gay man, but I will kick your fucking ass!"

Oh, what the fuck seriously? He's going after Sage? I stand, grabbing for the door handle.

"Everyone go the fuck back downstairs!" Caelan bellows as I'm opening the door. He stops in his tracks. His broad shoulders expanding to almost the whole width of the door frame.

"Sofia, baby. We need to talk."

"Sofia, baby?" A questioned in confused anger. "What's with the 'baby' bullshit right now?" my brother inquirers as he stares at Caelan. "Something already going on that I don't know about?"

He drops his head into his hands. Running his hands up and down over his face exhaling a large breath. Frustration at the forefront of his emotions. My eyes dart to the right, and see everyone stopped at the top of the stairs looking at the three of us.

"You got to be fucking kidding me right now," he says shaking his head.

"A, go downstairs," I tell him. "Sage get your gay ass in here! I need my bestie."

"Seriously?" I hear Nikki and Jessica say simultaneously with annoyance.

"Girls, he knows what happened. Please just give me a few minutes."

"Why does he know what's going on?" Nikki whines as Sage struts his shit into my room.

"Oh honey, this gay bestie is coming right on in! I want details, details, details!" he sings as his hands are flying everywhere in the air walking at a rapid pace into my bedroom.

Caelan steps to the side for him to pass, reluctantly. When I go to close the door, his look of hurt and confusion twist my heart strings. He puts his hand on the door and his work boot in the way so I can't close it. "You shutting me out, beautiful?" he whispers with hurt in his eyes.

"No, just give me some time, alright?" I sigh.

His eyes darting back and forth over mine. "I'll give you some time, but it will be tonight. You got that beautiful? Tonight, we will be talking about this," he states matter-of-factly, then drops his hand from the door.

I quickly glance over towards the stairs again and every single one of our friends is watching the quiet exchange between us. When I go to shut the door his work boot is still in the way. I look up at him and raise my eyebrows in question.

"Tonight, Sofia," he dictated, nodding his head. Then turns and walking towards his room. Before I shut my door, I see Luke walking towards Caelan's room. I close my door softly but the pang of guilt hitting my heart, is hard.

"Girl, Spill It! Right now!" he orders with eyes as big as saucers. "Spill it, spill it, spill it! I want deets from you! Details! Details! Details!" he demands with flying hands. Hands that could take flight if he's not careful. "That shit was hawt!" he sings.

"You're crazy." I laugh, plopping myself down on my bed against the headboard. Pulling my knees up to my chest. He sits in front of me. It's so funny to see him this way. He is such a strong, powerful human being. Sexy as all hell! His muscular body is to die for and his short, light blond hair and crystal blue eyes are like gazing into a watercolor painting.

"No! That was crazy! So hot! Like burn the sheets up hot! Rip the panties right off your body, hot! Crazy hoooot! Girl, I walked in and couldn't move. That shit was so hot, it stopped me in my tracks! I got me a nice woody, real quick over that. If I had watched anymore, I think this gay man would have lost his load, that shit was that hot!"

"Ewww Sage Stop! I don't need the visual!"

"Oh honey, you almost got more than that." He laughs.

"Sage. What did I do?" I groan.

"Oh, honey if you don't know-"

"Sage! I'm serious. What the hell did I just do?"

He looks at me with confusion written all over his face. He's turning into the more serious man I know, instead of the flaming gay man that I love. There are two sides to Sage. The one that everyone sees is the serious, very masculine, man. You wouldn't even know he was gay. The over exaggerated flamer gay man is the guy that only comes out around his friends, and when he does come out, it's hysterical.

"What do you mean, Sofia?"

"I just messed up, big time! Why did I do that? Why did I let that happen?"

His eyebrows raise as his very serious voice blurts, "Uhhhh maybe because he's hot as hell and you're totally in love with him!"

"What? I am not!" I say very sternly deny.

"Oh, Sofia, you are so in love with him you can't even see straight! Actually, you don't want to see it, but we all see it. You can try to deny it, but deep down inside, where you stuff it all, you know you're in love with him too. And as far as I know, you have been in love with him since you were a teenager."

"You all gossip too much," I chide. Other than that, I have nothing to say because he is right-deep down, I am in love with him. I know I'm in love with him. I am so in love with him to the point that I can't be. I can't do it. I can't let it happen. I lost him once. I can't... no, I won't lose him again because of my feelings for him. I messed it up the last time. We didn't talk for over a year. That can't happen again, friends can't be lovers. When friends become lovers and it doesn't work out. You lose both, the friend and the lover. I refuse to let that happen

"Sage, I can't. I can't do it. If I let it happen and it doesn't work out, I will lose my lover, and more importantly, my best friend."

"Sof, you won't ever lose him. He's not going to go anywhere," he assures, pulling me into his arms.

"I can't do it." I shake my head. "I can't take the chance, Sage." The ugly cry is brewing its ugly head. "I won't let it happen, Sage," I sobbed with broken words. "I can't lose him again. I won't get through it this time."

nine

Caelan

"**F**uck! What did I just do? Fuck me, man! I'm a fucking idiot!" I yell, talking to myself, throwing my hands through my hair and down the back of my neck. I'm so pissed off at myself right now. "Fuck! Why couldn't you wait just a little longer?" I chastise myself.

Pacing back and forth in my room, I hear a heavy hand knock on my door. I know it's Luke. Luke or Chris or both. Or... shit, it could be Antonio wanting to beat my ass! "Not now!" I yell. The door's already opening as I shout it. "Luke, dude not now man. Not now!" I ramble and rant as I pace.

"What the hell happened?"

"What the fuck don't you understand about Not. Right. Now!"

"Listen, man. You wanna hit something? By the looks of it, you do. I don't know what happened, but instead of hitting a wall and breaking your hand, hit me instead. Not the face, though," he stipulates pointing at me. "I need that to pick up the ladies."

"I'm not fucking hitting you, asshole!"

"It got you to look at me, didn't it?"

"You're an asshole, man! Seriously. You know that, right? I was looking right at you through the reflection of the mirror." I point.

"Yeah whatever, now tell me, what the fuck is going on?"

"I kissed her, man. I fucking kissed her."

"Awesome! It's about fucking time!"

I shake my head at him. "You don't understand I went all-in, man! It wasn't just a kiss. I couldn't pull myself back. I was full steam ahead. I want her so bad. Why couldn't I just hold on a little bit longer…"

"Hold on? Dude, you've been holding back for years. I think that's called strength, dude, because I don't know if I could do it. As a matter of fact, I know I wouldn't be able to. Especially growing up the way I did. Pussy was everywhere."

"You could if you felt the same way I do about, Sofia," I mumble.

"Then tell her man!"

"I can't! She'll run, and I can't have that. I lost her once, and I won't do it again."

When I turn, Chris is walking through the door with three shots, three beers, and a cheesy-ass smile on his face. "Thought you could use these. But, dude! It's. About. Fucking. Time!" he cheers.

"What?"

"You two, it's about time!"

I just look at him not sure how he even knows what's going on. Then it dawns on me. "Fuck." I hiss tilting my head back to look at the ceiling. "Fucking Sage! That guy has the biggest mouth!"

Chris and Luke just smile at me because they know I'm right.

"Well from what was said downstairs, that shit between you two was pretty intense! Well, wait if I quote Sage, it was 'Fucking Hawt!'"

"Seriously?" Luke shoots his eyes over at me. "I mean you said you went all in, but damn dude to be that hot she must have been all in too."

I stop pacing to think about that for a second. With my hands on my hips looking down at the hardwood floors, realization dawns on me. "She was. She was all in. She was pulling me into her. She let go. She undid my jeans herself. She wanted me. She finally let go. It's because of yesterday. She finally let go," I say more to myself than to them, but they heard every word!

"What happened yesterday, man?"

"Nothing, Chris. Seriously that's between her and I. Don't go digging and do not go saying anything to Sage for fuck's sake. He would be like a dog trying to find a buried bone trying to find out." I look at them both. "That doesn't leave this room you both understand me? Seriously I'm not fuckin' around. It's very personal."

"Understood, dude." Luke replies thoughtfully.

"Yup, got it. Are you going to tell us, though?"

"No! Chris, what the fuck? It's personal, really personal. It would hurt the both of us. It's not something you just throw out there. Leave it alone."

"Got it, bro. Won't breathe a word of it," he responds seriously.

I look at both of them. "FUCK! I fucked this up bad. I don't know how to fix this besides just giving her time."

Chris hands Luke and I our shots of tequila.

Luke raises his shot glass and toasts, "To time-it heals all wounds."

I look at him because he just nailed it right on the head. I hope he's right, I think to myself. But, in the back of my head, all I can think is, it's been a long time already. If I have to wait longer, I don't know if I can do it. I throw the shot back, drop the glass on the dresser, look at Luke and say, "By the way"- I point at him- "slap her on the ass and grab her like that again, and you're going to need a doctor! Got It?" I threaten.

"Got It! But, it got your blood boiling, though right? Just trying to get a reaction out of you."

I raise my eyebrows at him. "Don't fucking do it again," I warn him as I look him dead in the eyes.

Laying on my bed thinking about tonight, I hear the beep of my phone lying next to me. I grab at it hoping it's from Sofia. It's not.

> **Luke: Hey, dude. Just making sure your walls are still standing and your hands aren't broken!**

I laugh. It's been a few hours since I kicked everyone out. I have been lying here listening to music ever since. I'm trying to give Sofia some time before I go into her room, but I'm finding it real hard to stay here in my room and not go to her.

> **Me: I'm good, dude. No ER visits necessary. See you in the morning.**

> **Luke: Yup. See you in the morning. If you need anything, call me.**

A minute later.

> **Luke: Give her time. I know it's not what you want, but if you really want her, and I know you do, just give her a little bit more time and it will be worth it in the end. You've opened the door.**

I didn't text him back. Instead, I stare at the ceiling for another two minutes. Fuck this! I can't wait anymore. I jump out of bed and cross the hallway to her door. It's closed. I knock lightly. No answer. I slowly open the door. I see her small curvy frame in bed.

Damn, she's sexy.

I walk over to the side of the bed and look down at her beautiful face. She's asleep. How can she be sleeping? I'm freaking out, and she's sleeping. Then I see her eye move. I take a deep breath. She's not sleeping. She just wants me to think she is.

Wow, okay that hurts.

Two can play this game. She wants to avoid this, and I'm going to make sure she knows how I feel. I'm not playing games anymore. I want her! I bend down, reaching over and caress her face with the back of my knuckles. "I'm sorry if I hurt you, beautiful," I whisper. She doesn't move. I know she heard me. I know she's awake. I kiss her on the forehead, softly. Lingering there for just a few long seconds. Then I walk out. I go back to my room, grab my phone and send her a text with a song from a great band letting her know exactly how I feel.

Me: Red-Not Alone.

ten

MY ALARM'S BEEPING AWAY. I FEEL LIKE I just went to sleep, probably because I did just go to sleep. Three hours ago. It's going to be a long day for me. I roll over and shut off my alarm, rubbing my eyes. I'm exhausted. I think I finally fell asleep around four. Between no sleep and my eyes being swollen from the tears I shed over this situation, I look like someone beat me up. I better get out of bed and shower, then see what kind of makeup job I can do to cover up the bags I know I will have. I've cried more in the last three days than I have in three months. I'm a sensitive girl, but I'm a strong girl too. But these last couple of days have been hard. I mean, seriously, I was drugged, I finally talked to Caelan about me losing our baby, then the kiss last night. To top that all off, I made him feel bad about it by running away from it all.

Deep breath, Sofia. Today is a new day. Wipe the slate clean and start your week off fresh. Well, as clean as you can.

After he had come into my room last night, I knew I wouldn't be able to go to sleep. It pretty much became a night of me listening to music, tossing, turning, and thinking about that kiss. That kiss... the kiss that blew my socks off! His words tore me apart, though. I felt so bad pretending I was sleeping. I just couldn't bring myself to talk at that moment. It was all just too much for me. I thought if I just could pretend that I was asleep, then maybe we could talk today before we both went to work. A new day. One with some sleep behind us both so we could think clearly. Well, that's what I thought, but I got no sleep, and I can't stop thinking about that kiss!

What I didn't expect were the words that came from him. That in itself threw me for a head spin. He thinks he hurt me. When he said it, I almost threw open my eyes to stare at him in shock. I know we have always flirted with each other, but for him to think he hurt me, only upsets me. He would never hurt me purposely. That tore me up inside.

Sage was right in saying I had feelings for him. I've had feelings for him since I was fourteen years old. The sad part is nothing ever came of it. So, I just kept pushing my feelings away. Then when I lost the baby, and I lost him as well, I just couldn't bear it. When I finally got him back, it was like the universe was lined up right again. I can't lose him again. So, therefore, my feelings for him, the ones I've had for him for years, and still deeply have, need to be stuffed way down and locked away. I can't chance it again.

I love my sister and brother, even my friends, but, Caelan is my home. He's like your favorite, fuzzy slippers, sweat pants, and t-shirt all mixed up into one. The one you can't wait to change into at the end of the day when you get home. He's that warm fuzzy blanket that keeps me warm on a cold night when he wraps his strong warm arms around me.

No, these feelings I have, they need to be checked and put away. That kiss last night, even though he's a damn good kisser, that kiss for me… ya, I have never been kissed like that before in my life. Well, we did kiss once before, but that was long ago, and we were just kids. Now that I think about it, those kisses were sweet and innocent. Last night's kiss… that… that was a different kiss altogether. That kiss was a grown man kissing me with the most passionate kiss that has ever been laid upon me. I rub my arms to calm the chills I just got. Ahhh… stop thinking about it, Sofia. It was… it was just a moment between two close friends. That happens between two people as close as we are. Right? We have a history together. Plus, with us finally talking about me losing the baby, I'm sure that's what sparked the high emotions between us. Just the intimacy of the situation brought two people together for a brief moment. A moment I will never forget, that's for sure.

Damn, the girls he's with are lucky. If that kiss says anything about how he makes love, then, damn skippy, whoever he's with is one lucky bitch, even if it is just for a night. Then I think about the girls he has brought home and my stomach flips, and I feel myself getting angry. Even though he has every right to be with other people, it does make me jealous. Jealous that they get to spend that kind of time with him. Who am I kidding? It pisses me right the fuck off!

Get over it, Sofia. Move on. He doesn't see you like that.

"Uggggh, get your ass out of bed and face your day." Today isn't going to be easy. I grab my phone, so I can listen to music while I'm in the shower. I see the song he sent me last night. I listened to it repeatedly last night. I was going to send him one back, but I decided my emotions were running high and that maybe it wasn't such a good idea.

I take a quick shower, throw on some makeup and blow dry my hair. I decide that it's the best I'm going to get today. Bags are there, but the dark circles are covered up with some really good cover up. I throw on a cute maxi dress I just brought home from the boutique on Wednesday before all this craziness started. I give myself a once over in the beautiful ornate custom carved wood floor standing mirror he created for me. The dark red strapless maxi dress looks awesome with the chunky necklace I paired with it. All I need now is some dressy sandals, and I'm ready to go for the day. One more look to make sure I'm good and then I head for my bedroom door. I may look good on the outside, but on the inside... I feel like I'm slowly dying. I stop. Take a deep breath, grab the door knob and head downstairs.

As I walk down the stairs, I give myself a pep talk, telling myself to apologize for acting like a baby and let him know he didn't hurt me. That it was just everything that has happened over the last couple of days all coming together at once. I hit the top of the steps and see C sitting at the kitchen island. I give myself the 'pull up your big girl panties you can do this' talk and head down the stairs.

eleven

"**G**OOD MORNING," I CHIRP WITH A SMILE.

His head snaps up from his phone. "Hey," he replies cautiously watching me. "I didn't hear you come down the stairs."

He looks tired.

Yeah, well, that makes two of us, buddy.

I guess he didn't get any sleep either. That's okay because I'm going to fix this right now and put us back on track. I put my clutch and phone down on the counter top. He's giving me a slow once over. Hmmm, I guess he likes the dress. I walk over to the coffee pot and pour myself a cup. I throw some sugar in along with some cream. Well, extra sugar, really because I need the boost today. I stir slowly trying to get my thoughts together so I can start this apology. I hear Start Again by Conrad Sewell playing softly through the overhead speakers. This is going to be hard. Today is going to be hard. If I could throw extra caffeine in my coffee, I would. Maybe today when I stop for my mid-morning coffee, I'll get some extra shots.

Stop stalling, Sofia. Let's do this.

I take a well needed deep breath. "Caelan," I blurt as I turn around with my mug of coffee at my lips. Noticing that his eyes were lingering in the area of my ass.

"Sofia?" he answers saying my name as a question with a smirk.

I smile, shake my head, take a sip of my coffee and start. "Listen, about yesterday-"

"No. Sofia, let me say something first," he says cutting me off.

I cut him off, holding my hand in the air. Hoping the hand gesture will help make my point. "No. Listen, I'm sorry about how I reacted. You did nothing wrong. It was just everything all coming to a head. Between what happened Thursday night, then Saturday, you and I finally talking about the baby." I sigh at that. Then quickly start again before he could get a word in. "You and Antonio lying to me about the surveillance tape yesterday, it just became all too much for me, and I became overwhelmed. The kiss was just that... a kiss. It only happened because of the high emotion between us from talking about the baby. It's okay. I'm just sorry I didn't handle it better. I apologize. I hope that we can just put these last few days behind us and start the new week fresh." I smile at him with a smile that is so fake, it's starting to hurt my cheeks. My stomach is flip flopping around while he stares at me. Shock, I think that's what I see on his face. "Sofia, about that kiss."

I cut him off again. "It's okay. We're okay. No need to rehash it." He goes to say something again and stops. His squinting eyes are dancing back and forth over mine. He takes a sip of his coffee, contemplating what he's going to say. I can see it on his face. He's not sure if he should say more about the kiss or move on. Move on, please move on. I plead holding my breath. Please, move on.

His full luscious lips start to move again then stop. "Listen, about the tape," he starts to explain. My held breath is now released in a slow, steady relieving whoosh, washing away the conversation about the kiss. "I'm sorry I should have never kept it from you," he says. "I was trying to protect you. It was wrong of me to keep it from you. Plus, when I lied to you, telling you I was going to the office, and really went to your dads to watch the tape without you knowing, that was wrong too. I apologize. Antonio's bringing the tape over tonight so we can all go over it again to see if we missed anything."

Phew! I let out the last little bit of breath I was holding. I didn't think he was going to let it go. I wasn't too sure I could keep talking about that kiss. What I didn't need to hear him say was that he regretted it. Regretting it would mean he didn't think it was that good. Hell, I don't know how he could think that because that kiss was like fireworks on the Fourth of July. Geezzz! I'm getting hot.

Sofia, stop thinking about that damn kiss.

Great now I'm talking to myself. You're almost in the clear. So, I move on. "What time is he coming over tonight?"

"Not sure. He said he would let me know."

"Okay, just text me later when you find out." His head slightly nods. Sofia, that's your cue. Move on. Move, Move, Move. Leave for work so we can just get back to normal. I walk over to the sink dumping the small bit of coffee I had left in my cup. I put it in the dishwasher and turn around to walk over to the island where my clutch and cell are. I grab them both, give him a smile and say goodbye as I head for the door. Just as I grab the handle, his deep, sexy, panty-dropping voice calls for me.

DAMN! I thought I was in the clear.

"Yeah?" I open the door and turn back to look at him.

His head is tilted to one side. Both his dimples are on display. His strong as steal, sexy forearm and large muscular hand are at a forty-five-degree angle resting on the counter top. He's pointing to the area behind me with a slick Rick smile on his face. "Don't forget you have a bodyguard."

I whip my head around. Giovanni is standing right there ready to go.

BALLS!

I totally forgot! I've been stuck in the house for days and days. I forgot he's been on guard out there in the vestibule, for days! I whip my head back around to look at the cocky bastard sitting at the kitchen island.

He smiles at me with one brow raised and a big shit eatin' grin on his face. "Have a nice day, beautiful!"

Damn! He knows I was trying to get out of here as fast as I could. He's like a pig in shit right now! Happy as can be!

twelve

GIOVANNI IS GLUED TO ME. HE INSISTED that he drive his SUV. No, let me clarify, he demanded he was driving. There was no questioning about it. I was going to be chauffeured around whether I liked it or not. I'm so independent, so for me to have someone follow my every move is going to drive me crazy, but, because it's Giovanni, I'll try not to make his life as miserable as mine is going to be over the next couple weeks.

We finally make it to my boutique in Soho. It felt like it took forever today, but really, it was only fifteen minutes from our home in East Village. The ride was kind of quiet. Not much to say really. We need to have a chat he and I. Quite honestly driving with no music on is just not acceptable for me. When we pull up, I go to jump out the back of the SUV but stopping short when he yells at me.

"Stay!" he abruptly commands. I jump back and look at him. "Stay inside the vehicle until I open the door for you. I need to check the surroundings first before you get out."

Two minutes later he's opening my door. I step down, look up into his green eyes and point my finger up at his huge, six foot five body. I'm two inches away from his nose when I say, "You ever scare the shit out of me like that again, and I'll beat your ass!"

He tried not cracking a smile, but the corner of his mouth lifted, slightly betraying him. Yea I know buddy, you could crush me with one hand. I think to myself as he walks me to the back door.

I'm the first one here today, so I pull out my keys and look at him. "You want to go in first? Make sure there isn't a crazy man waiting for me inside?"

He steps around me as I open the door and walk inside. He proceeded to check the whole place out. Office, bathroom, storage and front shop before coming back. "All clear," he confirms as he walks back towards me standing in front of my desk.

I look up at him. Eyebrows raised. "Did you really think someone was going to be in here?"

"It's my job to make sure there isn't and you're safe. That is exactly what I will do."

"Okay then," I comply nodding my head once.

It's going to be a long day.

I grab the cash bag sitting on the front counter, and the drawer for the register and head over to the front doors to unlock them, then head back to the office to get the register ready for the day. A few minutes later I'm walking back up front with the cash drawer in hand when I hear the door chime and him... my flaming gay bestie.

"Ohhhh hot pants where are you?" he calls in his sing-song voice.

"Oh geezzzzz, I can't do this with him today." I look over at Giovanni shaking my head at the same time not answering Sage. I don't have to. I know he'll find me.

"Sunshine, where are you? Tell me how your morning breakfast went with stud muffin!"

I roll my eyes at him as he turns the corner.

"Oh hey, and you are?" he questions in his now normal voice extending his hand for them to shake.

"Sage, this is Giovanni as you already know. You have already met him being he was posted at my front door for the last three days. You had to get through him to get into the house yesterday. He will be my bodyguard for the next few weeks 'til we find out who did this to me last Thursday."

Sage's eyes lit up. "Oh! I'm excited! I get a beautiful piece of man meat to look at for the next couple of weeks."

"Down boy. He's straight and has a job to do, and doesn't need you drooling all over him while he does it," I chide, shooting Giovanni an apologetic look. He just cracks a small smile.

"Oh, I'll work on his straightness. See if we can't bring him over to Sagie's side," he flirts twirling his finger at himself. "Now spill it, Sugar britches! How was morning breakfast with stud muffin after last night? Tell me was breakfast just as hot or did we cool off some? Did the kitchen island get a workout like the pool table did?"

"SAGE!" I yell throwing my hands in the air. "You're making the situation bigger than what it was."

"Ummm. Nooooo, hot pants," he corrects with big eyes, circling his index finger at me with a giant smile. "You forget I saw it all, and it was HOT!"

Giovanni is trying to be polite. Pretending that he's not paying any attention, but Sage's overdramatic ways are making it hard for him. His eyes dart to me then back to Sage.

"Oh, G. Honey you should have seen the two of them! It was like two cats in heat going at it on top of a hot griddle!"

"SAGE! Seriously," I desperately yell.

Giovanni's eyebrows are reaching maximum height.

"Oh, sugar. I'm as serious as they come! Speaking of coming! G honey, if I would have kept watching the delicious pool table porn I walked in on between the two of them I would have-"

"SAGE! DAMN IT! SHUT THE HELL UP!"

"What's this I hear about coming? Did more happen last night after we all left? Fill me in! FILL ME IN!" Jessica cheers with flying hands as she walks towards us.

"I didn't even hear the door chime."

"That's because Sage is flapping away at the jaws!" She laughs.

"Ohhhhh my God you guys! I just can't do this with you two today. Nothing happened! You two knock it off! I'm serious!"

"Ohhh, Sofia. From what I hear it was that serious, and something definitely happened!" she says as she looks at Sage.

"Oh, girl you have no idea," he confirms dramatically. "They were all over each other! It was straight up porn candy! But, classy porn candy! Hands were everywhere and when she grabbed that delectable ass of his... WOOOO I thought I was going to just faint!" He throws the back of his hand against his forehead. I drop my head into my hands that are resting on the front counter. "Oh, but it wasn't 'til those hands of hers reached around to the front and went down and grabbed at his-"

"SAGE!" I growl in warning. "You two are not going to stop, are you?" I look back up to see Giovanni looking at all three of us. He's totally amused and not shocked! "Okay, that's it!" I say clapping my hands moving them along. "Both of you get to work! Sage go get the white cashmere sweaters that were delivered on Friday. Put them up front. Jessica, can you please straighten up the sale racks." When they both turn to go do what I asked, I feel like I'm in the clear. I turn to take care of the cash drawer when I hear Sage.

"Seriously you have to tell us did you at least touch the tip? That boy is well hung. You had to have touched at least the tip!"

"YOU'RE FIRED!" I laugh pointing in the direction of the sweaters. "GO!" Out of the corner of my eye, I see Giovanni smiling at me. "What?" I snap.

"Nothing. Nothing at all," he calmly replies shaking his head while he shrugs his shoulder. "Just say it. I mean those two already have."

His brows raise slightly. "Nothing. I'm just here to make sure you're safe."

"Ya, Ya, okay!"

"Oooh, hot Pants? The back-door alarm isn't working."

Giovanni stands and starts walking towards the back. I follow.

"I just went out back to throw the boxes in the dumpsters, and it didn't go off."

"You sure, Sage?"

"Honey, I think I know when alarms go off. Especially when it's a five-alarm fire burning like the one my eyes got to experience last night!"

"Sage! Don't start again!" I body check him with my small frame as we follow behind Giovanni.

"No seriously, sugar. The back-door alarm really isn't working."

"It went off this morning when we came in," I say to Giovanni's back. "No big deal, maybe it's just some wiring. I'll call today and have someone fix it."

He pulls a chair over to get closer to the alarm. He starts playing with some wiring that was underneath the bells. "You ever have a problem with this before?"

"No, never."

Hmfp, he grunts.

"What?"

"These wires seem a little stretched out."

"What does that mean?"

"It looks like they were pulled down. Some were so stretched they were barely attached."

"… Oh… well, like what does that mean really? I never paid any attention to the alarm. I mean it's always worked. I've never had a problem. It's probably just stretched and worn out from time. Right?"

"I'll fix it for you now. You guys go do what you have to do, no need to watch me fix it."

"Thanks." I walk back up front to see Jessica taking care of a customer. I stop for a second and take in my surroundings. The business I have built over the last few years has flourished tremendously. This place is beautiful inside. Caelan helped me every bit of the way. There were many sweaty late nights in here for the both of us. I would dream it all up in my head, and he would make it happen. The walls are a deep dark majestic plum colored Venetian plaster. With one large accent wall in the same Venetian plaster only jet black. The Venetian plaster gives the whole boutique an elegant, upscale look. There are several seven-foot floor length mirrors all over the boutique that Caelan custom made for me. But the most beautiful ones he made are the three largest mirrors that stand in front of the black accent wall. When Caelan built them for me, he replicated a picture of a Venetian style mirror I had found online. He did an amazing job. They truly are stunning. Especially reflecting the black floors throughout the whole store along with the three large, off white, French tufted couches and large old looking whitewashed coffee table that sits in front of it. Underneath the large coffee table are layered rugs. An extra-large white one, with a black and white fake animal hide zebra print on top. It's a great seating area for customers to sit while their friends or their loved ones are trying on clothes. With the thick crown molding, along with the crystal chandeliers that flicker and sparkle throughout the boutique the whole place feels like being transported back to a turn of the century home but with a modern French twist.

This space is the one thing I am proud of. Yes, I had help from C in all aspects of it, financially and manual labor. What I'm most proud of is that I had a vision, and the vision came to life with the help of him. He helped me financially, with no strings attached. What I'm prouder of is the fact that I was determined to stay working at Club Ice even while working long hours here so that I could pay him back as fast as I could. I almost have him all paid off. He tells me all the time not to worry about it. To quit Club Ice because I work too much, but that's who I am. Once something gets into my head I work hard to get it. I want to be independent. I want to make my own money. I want to be able to buy the things in life that I want, whether they're expensive or not. I want to able to have children one day and still be able to take care of them while I'm at work. By having my own business, I can do all that and not have to answer to anyone, but myself. In time, I want to open another boutique. I have given it a lot of thought. Before I can do that though I want to make sure this one is paid off, and I can afford to open the new store with my own money.

"Sofia, do you know? Sofia?"

I snap out of my daydream. "Oh... I'm so sorry I was totally daydreaming. What do you need Jessica?"

"Mrs. Radcliff would like to know if we will be getting these cashmere sweaters in black?"

I smile. "They're beautiful, aren't they? Yes, we will be getting some in towards the end of the week. Leave your name and number with Jessica, when they come in she will give you a call and set something up with you for delivery."

"Oh, that's lovely dear. The customer service is why I love coming to this place. It's impeccable."

"Thank you, Mrs. Radcliff."

At that, I see Giovanni come out from the back. "Did you fix it?"

"Yes. Sofia, you have never had a problem with the alarm before?"

"Nope. Why are you asking like that?"

"Something just seemed a little off to me, but it's fixed now."

THE DAY DRAGGED on. I needed my afternoon coffee. That extra caffeine I needed this morning, I definitely need right now. Giovanni escorted me to my favorite coffee shop. He refused to let me go by myself. I begged and pleaded and then fought for it. He didn't budge. Not even a slight lean.

"Seriously Giovanni it's just two blocks down. No one's going to get me! I'll be back before you know it. I walk there every day," I argue, but in the end, he won, and I really didn't want to give him too much of a hard time. He's just doing his job. I know this. On the walk over my phone buzzed in my pocket. I pulled it out to see the text.

C: How's everything going? Is Giovanni getting on your nerves yet?

Me: Uggggh he's walking to the coffee shop with me as we speak! He

wouldn't let me go alone! All's good though except there was a problem with the back door alarm this morning, but Giovanni fixed it.

C: GOOD! You shouldn't be walking alone! Don't try and ditch him Sof he's there to keep you safe. Backdoor alarm huh? Is that code for something else? Lol. What do you mean there was something wrong with the alarm? What was wrong with it?

Me: Don't be fresh! That was not a code for 'the back door,' there's no back door for me. The alarm went off this morning when Giovanni and I came in and even Sage a few minutes later but I didn't hear it go off when Jessica came in about fifteen minutes later. I don't really know. Giovanni looked at it though. It's all fixed now.

C: Oh, beautiful there's a backdoor, and it's mighty fine to look at! ;) I'm glad he was there to fix it. Oh btw, A will be over around six can you make it home by then? I'll pick up dinner on the way home from work. Chinese good?

Me: Stop looking at my backdoor! :O It's closed! It's in the export business, not import! I'll see you at six. Get me some egg foo young and an egg roll, please.

C: Are you sure? The import business is very lucrative which is very pleasurable!
Soo you at six! Lol.

Me: Uggggggggggh!!!!!!

The walk to and from the coffee shop was uneventful. It's a gorgeous day out. Sunny with a light breeze. The walk was nice except for the small conversation Giovanni and I had.

"So, you and C huh?"

I look up at him. My cheeks getting redder and redder by the passing second. Oh, hell. Really? Now I have to talk to him about it too. Damn! "No. There's nothing going on between us."

"Really? Didn't sound like that to me." He smirks.

Do I tell him or no? That's the question I'm asking myself over and over as we walk down the busy street. I look into his honest green eyes. "C, and I finally talked Saturday." He looks down at me confused. "The baby," I say quietly looking up at him. "We finally talked about the baby. We have never talked about it before. Six years later and we finally talked. He's tried to talk to me. A few times. I just couldn't do it, it was too hard for me."

His demeanor changed from a happy one to a somber one. He stopped scanning the streets with his trained eye and stopped walking. He turned his attention directly to me. "I'm sorry, Sofia. I know how hard that was for you. At least you two finally talked about it. That's good."

"Ya I'm glad we did too, but I think because our emotions were running so high from the talk that's why the kiss happened."

"You think that's the only reason it happened?" he asked with skepticism.

"Ya, why?"

He raises his brow and makes a straight line with his lips. "Just asking."

I thought about it for a second, and instead of questioning him, I let it go. I mean it's not like Giovanni, and I are close. We do share a few hard-emotional moments in my life, and he has been there for me more than he ever should have been, but I'm just not comfortable having this conversation with him, at all. Especially about last night's kiss.

That damn kiss! Shit, that was more than a kiss! That was sex with clothes on! Nope! Nope! Nope! Sofia, get it out of your head!

THE REST OF the afternoon was busy. We got a lot of shipments in so we had a lot of inventory to go through. Giovanni helped with boxes but mostly he watched every customer that came through the boutique's doors. At five-thirty I said goodbye to Sage and Jessica. Unscathed by Sage's lust for information about the night before. As I got into the SUV my phone buzzed repeatedly.

The Best Sister Ever: Hey you on your way to the house?

C: Just checking in on your back door. Making sure there wasn't a B&E today after we talked. Lmao Nahh, just letting you know A and your sister are here. See you soon!

Uggh he's killing me! He's such an ass! I'm so glad we're back to being normal, though. This morning was hard for me. Okay, he wants to play games? I'll play. Just wait, Mr. O'Reily. Little does he know his evening is going to be very difficult. I text my sister back first. Just letting her know I'm on my way. Then text C back.

Me: Okay... Mr. Ass man, for your information there have been no B&E's on this ass, and there will be none in the future. However, since you like asses so much I could always have a chat with Sage. I'm sure he would love to explore yours!

C: Real funny! No need, HIS is hairy! I like smooth, plump, supple, sexy aoooo!

Me: OH? Well, shit you're in luck I hear Sage waxes! Tootles! ;)

thirteen

I WALKED INTO THE HOUSE SMELLING Chinese food and hearing laughter wafting through the air. Then I see the best sight ever. My best friend, brother, and sister are all sitting around the kitchen island laughing. Too bad we're all here to watch the surveillance tapes from Club 9.

"Well, hello, sexy girl! That halter dress is gorgeous!"

"Thanks, Nik! I love it. We just got them in the boutique last week. We have it in yellow too. You would look great in that color. If you want one let me know, I'll grab it tomorrow," I tell her walking over and laying down my cell phone and purse.

"Your tatas look damn good in it too. How many eyes were on your boobs today?" She laughs. "Them girls are up there," she compliments ending in a higher voice than when she started.

"Ahhhh hellooo? Her brother is sitting right here!" A points at himself. "He doesn't want to hear about how many guys are staring at her girly parts!"

Laughing I look over at C and see him staring at my boobs with a panty dropping sexy as sin grin on his face. "Ahem!" I clear my throat.

"You okay?" Antonio asks as he follows my line of sight to C and notices the same thing. "What the fuck, dude? Seriously? I'm sitting right here, fucker!" He throws a kitchen towel at C, breaking him out of his ogling.

He drops his head with a smile on his lips then gets up and walks toward the refrigerator. "Come on let's eat before it gets cold," he mumbles, grabbing beers from the fridge.

"No worries, Antonio," I pacify, smirking. "He likes the back doors of soft, supple, sexy waxed asses." Confusion crosses Antonio's face. Caelan whips his head around. His eyes are big. His mouth drops open wide with shock. "Yup, stud muffin," I say mimicking Sage's pointed twirling finger at his gaping mouth. "Keep that mouth open just like that big guy," I tease very slowly. "That's about the perfect size for what you'll need when you're with Sage!" Antonio cracks up, but is still confused! Nikki's crying she's laughing so hard, and my handsome best friend is just looking at me with a raised brow and a cocky glimmer in his dreamy blue eyes. I smile trying to hold back the hysterics I want to fall into. I got him, and he knows it! I turn the sexy up, pop my hip out to the side put my hand on my hip, lift my shoulders back so that my boobs are even more pronounced, give him the sexiest face I can, lick my index finger on my right hand slowly and then close my moist lips around it. Push it in my mouth as far as I can go and pull it out even slower. All the while seductively locked onto Caelan's mesmerizing eyes. When I pull my finger out to the very tip, I swirl my tongue around it. There's still some lingering spit attached when I pull it out. It breaks off on my lip, so I lick my bottom lip slowly. All the while still locked onto his gorgeous sexy eyes. I point my finger towards the sky and whip it down and wink! "Ha! One for me stud!"

He's transfixed on my face right now. He snaps out of it after a long moment and cracks up laughing! "Okay! Okay!" He throws his hands up in surrender. "You win! No more talking about Sage's ass! I can't take it! No More! Please, no more! I can't do it! You won! You totally won this round!"

DINNER WAS GOOD, but I dreaded the ending knowing I was going to have to watch the video.

"Oh, by the way, I got the surveillance tape from Mr. Wongs, too. I stopped by there on the way home from the office. He was more than happy to help. Said if we need anything else just let him know. You ready to do this, beautiful?"

"Ya, I'm ready." I nod at him. "A?" I call turning towards him.

"Ya?"

"Do you think this was a random thing?"

He doesn't say anything for a few seconds. Then glances over at Caelan. "I don't know, but my gut is telling me it's not. So that's where we need to start, with our gut instincts. C and I already watched the tape as you know, so basically your fresh eyes will hopefully be able to see something we missed."

I stay quiet. Just thinking that someone is after me again scares the living shit out of me. "You okay, Sof?"

"… Ya… let's go do this."

"We'll go into my office and watch them. I'll put it up on the flat screen, so it's easier to see," Caelan tells us walking towards his office.

Nikki and Antonio are chatting away about different things while we wait for Caelan to set up the video. I start to drift off. Looking out the window watching the sun starting to set, I can feel my anxiety starting to rise. I try to push it away and calm myself. I take a deep cleansing breath. Images from the night I was abducted unexpectedly flash before my eyes.

Another deep breath.

The feelings are always there, but I'm pretty good at making sure it stays buried deep. I release the breath trapped in my lungs. I have talked to my therapist about this extensively. I know what happened to me was not my fault, but there's still that feeling of dirtiness, embarrassment and shame that muddy my thoughts at times. I can hear the chatter between the three of them getting further and further away. I start to panic more thinking they're leaving me and I'll be alone. It's ridiculous to feel that way because I know they're standing just three feet in front of me.

Another deep breath.

This one quickly released. I feel myself starting to tense up. Why the hell is this happening right now? I'm going to have a panic attack? I can feel the relaxed, loose feel of my muscles, now becoming rods of steel. My breathing is starting to pick up to a short, rapid pace. "Ohhhh, don't do this to me now. Please don't do this now." Small bits and pieces of that horrific night are penetrating my brain. Infiltrating my mind from every possible angle. "Go away, go away."

Breathe Sofia breathe.

It's been a long time since I've gone back there. My hands rise to my nose and mouth covering them. The musty smelling urine soaked dreadful black basement is seeping into my now flared nostrils.

"Breathe, Sofia. Just breathe." I hear deep mummers.

Why is this happening right now?

FLASH... a snapshot of chains.

Inhale.

FLASH... a bed.

Exhale.

FLASH... the blood.

Inhale.

FLASH... the darkness.

Inhale.

"Breathe, Sofia."

Inhale.

FLASH... nasty smells. Menthol cigarettes, and whiskey and something else I still can't figure out.

"Breathe with me, Sofia."

Exhale.

FLASH... 'Little Ms. Perfect.'

Inhale.

FLASH... black painted walls.

Inhale. I gasp for air.

FLASH... a mirror on the ceiling above the bed.

My chest is burning from my held breath.

FLASH... blindfolded and gagged

FLASH, FLASH, FLASH... images flashing before my eyes, 'til it all comes crashing around me, on me, into me.

"Sofia, look at me." I feel gentle but firm hands touching me, shaking me.

FLASH... tick. Tick. Tick. It looks like black and white old videos clicking away before my eyes. Every picture changing from one horrific scene to the next. One of me shackled to a mattress,

FLASH... me spread by the cold heavy metal chains on my wrists and ankles flash through my hazy mind. My visions are now looking down at my cold, naked, captive body.

FLASH... filthy, dirty, nasty, vicious hands on my upper thighs, gripping tighter and tighter. Ripping my soft tender skin with his filthy jagged nails leaving trails of blood-soaked scratches behind, dripping down to a nasty, stained mattress which my body is shackled to.

I gasp, slam my legs closed and grip the chair harder. I can feel the weight of those torturous hands on my cold skin.

"Sofia, baby, please look at me. Breathe with me, baby. You can get through this."

I cringe and tuck my ear into my shoulder. I can smell his tobacco ridden, repulsive breath on my neck. I can hear his snarling, angry voice.

'Oh, the things I'm going to do to you little Ms. Perfect. Daddy's precious, little girl. You won't be so innocent when I'm through with you,' he snarls in my ear, hostility evident in his tone. I can feel myself getting tenser. I whimper at the feel of his hot breath penetrating each layer of my dirty skin. I realize my fingers are starting to hurt, and that they're gripping and piercing through the arms on the leather club chair I'm sitting in.

Details of that night are becoming like a flash flood in my brain, coming to me faster and faster. They're quick snapshots of pictures that seem to just linger in my mind, set on repeat, like the clicking sound of an automatic camera just endlessly snapping away. I can't get it out of my head. Flashes over and over and over again. I start shaking my head. "Stop! Stop! Turn it off! Stop! Don't do this. Please stop!"

"Baby, it's me. Look at me." I feel a firm shake of my body. "Focus on me, baby. You're safe. I promise you're safe." I feel the shake of my shoulder again. It's not hard, and the hands, they're not rough or malicious. They're soft and warm.

FLASH... the crippling fear begins, I feel it working its way through my veins like the rush of a tidal wave snapping everything in its way. *NO! NO! NO!*

My body starts convulsing.

I'm going to die!

These images are pure torture. "God, No!"

Then my mind suddenly switches, what if someone takes me again? I feel like I'm stuck in-between then and now. What if he doesn't let me go this time?

I will always be watching you, 'little Ms. Perfect.'

I gasp, begging for the air I need.

"I'm going to die."

'I'm going to rip your world apart,' he sneers against my ear.

Throwing my hands over my ears to cover them from his rancid words.

'I'm going to rip you apart Little Ms. Perfect. You will never be fucking perfect again after I'm done with you!'

Trembling, I think what if I never see the people I love again? I can see all of them talking to me right now through my haze-Nikki, Caelan, Antonio, all with worry on their faces. The thought of losing these amazing human beings that I cherish dearly hurts me deeply. Thoughts of all my loved ones are what got me through that night. I only survived that night because of them. I don't think I could do it again-the emotional scars and mental footprints of memories. The deep lacerations through my heart, all from that one night, will forever be tattooed on my soul. I will never be able to let go of the filth and shame I feel inside. I will never be able to let go of the horrible things that happened to me. Those are here. I feel my cold hand rest on my chest. My heart beats desperately, pounding at a rapid pace.

Those memories are kept deep, deep inside me. I never have and will never be able to let them go. Those will stay buried and locked away in the vault I have inside me. If he knew everything that happened to me that night, if anyone knew what happened to me that night… "Oh, God No!" If anyone knew, it would destroy me, but if he knew, I would never survive. He would never look at me the same.

"Beautiful look at me," he orders shaking me. "*LOOK. AT. ME!*" I hear him demand with a harder shake to my shoulders. I feel a heavy hand touch my arm. My head snaps to the spot his hand now holds, and I jerk my arm away. My eyes connect with his very scared, stormy blue eyes. The intense, heartfelt sadness in his eyes overwhelms even me. With a very soft understanding voice, he reassures me, "You're safe." He lifts his hand. With his eyes, he asks for permission to touch my arm again. I slightly nod. He lays his large, strong, safe hand on my arm, rubbing my cold skin gently. "Come back to me, Sofia. Breathe. Just look at me and breathe. You're not back there. Look around you. You're right here in my office, safe. You're safe. I promise no one will hurt you. Take a deep breath with me." My eyes lock with his. I breathe in his exhaled air, slowly in, and even slower out. He nods his head at me. "Good, good, baby. One more time." We breathe in together and then again slowly out. I start coming out of the hazy memories. Reality is slowly setting in. I glance around the room. Caelan is crouching down in front of me. Antonio is hunched down on my right, and my sister is on her knees to my left now holding my hand. It hits me all at once, the three of them just witnessed my meltdown.

"Oh God! Oh God! Oh God! No! No! No!" I shake my head frantically. The impact is fully hitting me now like a sledgehammer. I just had a major, major meltdown in front of them. The only person who has ever witnessed my panic attacks is Caelan. "NO!" I scream flinging Caelan's hand off my arm, and forcefully pushing myself out of the chair, shoving between him and my sister.

"SOFIA!" he calls after me as he's grabbing for my arm.

I pull away.

"SOFIA, WAIT!"

"GIVE ME A MINUTE!" I yell. "I just need a FUCKING minute!" I scream as I run out of his office.

fourteen

Feeling the pain of shame and humiliation, I run through the house, up the stairs to my bathroom, and slam the door shut, locking myself in. Then I sink to the floor and sob. Still trying to catch my breath through the buckets of tears flowing from my tired, weary body.

Breathe, Sofia. He's not here, he can't hurt you.

I tell myself over and over.

Don't let anyone see you break.

If they see you break, they'll know more happened than what you've told them. I rapidly strip myself of my clothes. I take the hottest shower my skin can stand. I scrub at my thighs with excruciating strokes to wash away the degradation and pain.

I hear a faint knock on my bathroom door.

"JUST GIVE ME A MINUTE! I'LL BE DOWN IN A MINUTE!" I yell.

I sit at the bottom of the shower with my knees curled into my chest. My arms wrapped around them in a protective form. While my head's resting on my knees the water rushing over my trembling body from the large rain shower faucet above my head. The white and blue-green glass shower tiles have now taken on heat from the hot water endlessly rushing over them. I look down at my pruned fingers. I don't have a clue how long I've been in the shower, but by the looks of my fingers it's been a long time.

I stand, turn off all the shower heads. Grab a warm white towel from the towel warmer and wrap my body in the soft, fluffy security. I take a deep cleansing breath and open the bathroom door slowly, hoping no one is in my room waiting for me to come out.

The room is empty. I walk over to my bed and sit down along the edge. I look around my all white room in a daze, thinking how ironic it is that it's so clean and fresh looking and I feel so dirty.

My eyes wonder to the hand carved mirror directly in front of me. Caelan made it for me. It's beautiful. I stare at myself in the mirror, mesmerized at the sight I see reflecting back at me. The girl that reflects back isn't beautiful though. A few hours ago, yes, she was strong, confident and beautiful, but now... no. Now she feels weak and ugly. I've worked so hard on myself. I was doing so well. I'm a beautiful, strong woman, but right now, I feel broken and weak again.

I gasped when I notice the raised broken blood vessels on my thighs through the mirror. I look down between my legs where the white fluffy towel has fallen open. Some are deeper and redder than others. Some bleeding. I can't tear my eyes away from the vicious streaks I left on my own body. Water hits my thighs. My tears. I swipe my cheeks as more tears fall to my thighs. I slowly wipe away the tears that are there, but more just keep falling one right after another and another and another.

"Oh. My. God!" I hear a quiet deep, and very distressed voice say. I robotically look up through the haze of my tears to see the most handsome, caring, considerate man I have ever known, standing there looking down at my inner thighs. I don't move one bit. My eyes lock on his like two magnets. The force of which I cannot physically pull myself to look away from his warm, safe haven that he holds in his eyes.

He slowly kneels in front of me, laying his hand on the bed beside my thighs. Making sure he doesn't touch me. "Beautiful what did you do? Why did you do this?"

Sighing, I think about the word beautiful. If only he knew his nickname for me burned me to my soul right now. I reach for his face with a trembling hand. Cupping his stubbled cheek, I tilt my head to the right a little, staring at him with such reverence in my eyes. I give him a small smile. "I did this," I whisper. "I did this to myself, to wash away the pain and filth he left in me."

His eyes shutter over with thunderous force. I can see the pain, the hurt, the rage, the need for revenge behind them. It's the same rage I feel inside me. His eyes search mine. Moisture pooling in the corners of his. I've only seen Caelan cry twice. Once when I told him I lost our baby. Then again just a few days ago, when we finally talked about the day I miscarried our baby.

"Stay here, baby. I'm going to go get stuff to take care of you."

He leaves me sitting on the side of the bed in a daze still staring at myself in the mirror. Looking at the shell of a person I was just two short hours ago. Two hours ago, I was in the kitchen laughing, seductively flirting, confidently flirting and playing around with him. Now I can't bear to even look at myself in a mirror.

I hear him in my bathroom. "Okay, baby," he says with a tremor to his voice as he kneels down in front of me between my thighs. He has a washcloth in his hand. He lifts his hand slowly stopping mid-air to looking at me. Seeking permission to touch me. I nod slightly. Opening my legs further. My towel has now fallen open more. I know he can see way more than just my thighs, but I can't seem to move myself from this spot. My eyes never leave his handsome face. When the sting from the warm wash cloth catches me off guard, I look down, slightly closing my thighs. He stops, jerking his hand back.

"I'm sorry."

"It's okay," I whisper.

He grabs a tube of something off the floor and again looks at me for permission. I nod again, spreading my thighs more for him. Gently he rubs the cream on my thighs. It feels good. I feel safe. I feel peace when he touches me. I have always felt safe and at peace with him. A tear rolls down my cheek to the curve of my lip and slips from my lip to the top of his hand placed on my inner thigh where he is now gently putting bandages. He looks back up to me with soft, caring eyes. I reach out, cradling his tense jaw and wipe the lonely tear that trails down his cheek.

His hand cradles my face. His thumb meets my lower lip wiping off the tears that are falling softly and freely. "Baby, tell me what happened to you."

WHAM!

The tender moment is over. That's when the rod crashed back through my spine. Reality hits me hard with a forceful smack! My brain starts registering that I just let him see me bare, emotionally and physically. He can never know what happened to me. *NEVER!* I drop my hand, my body becoming tenser. I shove myself up from the bed to stand. Caelan stands with me, taking a step back waiting for what's to come. "Can you please just give me a few minutes alone. I'll come down as soon as I'm done getting dressed. I'm sorry I made you guys wait."

"Beautiful?" He sighs softly, confused at the change in my demeanor.

"No. Just please give me a few minutes to get dressed. I'll be down when I'm done."

"Baby, look at me."

"*NO!*" I snap because now the embarrassment and humiliation are creeping its way back in. "NO! Please just go!" I point towards the door. "Let me get dressed!" I secure my towel with both my hands, turning away from him, and walk into my closet. Once inside I hear his footsteps walking towards me. I feel his hands softly fall on my shoulders. I stiffen at the unwanted touch.

"There's nothing you can't talk to me about, beautiful, just know that. I'll always be here for you, no matter what you tell me. You are the most beautiful woman I have ever met Sofia Rose Heart, inside and out, and nothing will ever change that," he whispers into my ear.

The pricking of tears stabs the back of my eyes. My throat is starting to choke up. I'm trying so hard to hold them back. I feel a soft, warm, lingering kiss on my shoulder. Then his safe hands and warm lips leave my tingling, overwhelmed body. Holding my breath, I hear his soft, unsure footsteps walking towards the door. When I hear my bedroom door softly close, I exhale.

He's gone...

"Oh Caelan, If I ever told you, you would never look at me the same..." I say with a whispered breath.

My legs start to tingle, giving way. I collapse to the floor, sobbing once again.

SOME TIME HAS passed. I'm not sure how long. I'm actually surprised no one has come up here to check on me. I unravel myself from the child-like ball I'm still currently in, inside my closet. I look around to find my favorite black sweats. Pulling them on over my sore bandaged thighs. Then pull the elastic bottom legs up to my knees. My black spaghetti strap tank top is laying on top of my dresser, so I grab that too and throw it on. No underwear, no bra. Just can't deal with them right now. I walk into my bedroom from my closet and see Caelan's black zip-up hoodie laying on my chair. I pick it up and I cradle it in my hands, bringing it to my nose. It smells just like him, the best smell in the world. I notice the business logo on the back and smile. I'm so proud of what he has accomplished. I smell it one more time then pull the sweatshirt over my shoulders. The swoosh of the air from the sweatshirt hitting my shoulders makes me feel like home has just wrapped its warm arms around me. This man's scent is exquisite. It's clean, sandalwood and Caelan all wrapped up into one unforgettable delicious smell. It's replacing the wretched, lingering smell, still lingering in my nostrils from before. On him, this sweatshirt fits perfectly. But on me, it's huge. It amazes me how much bigger he is than me. This man could crush me with just one touch. Yet, I think to myself how soft and caring his touch is and how it makes me feel so safe. Studying myself in the mirror, I grab a hair tie and throw my hair into a messy knot on top of my head. I walk to the bathroom, throw water on my face, and brush my teeth. I picture Caelan's face reflecting back at me in the mirror, telling me to take a deep breath with him. So, I do just that.

Him breathing
for me,
with me,
as one.
Tomorrow will be a better day.

I take another deep breath and head downstairs. My feet pad softly across the hardwood floors to the top of the steps, to what I know will be a firing squad of questions. My brother, sister, and I'm sure even Caelan will have more question about my meltdown. I'm sure of it. I reach the top of the steps. Darkness has fallen outside and inside is just as dark. The only light is coming from the dimmed, kitchen island lights that are barely on. I hear *Still* by Luke Sital-Singh playing all around me, wrapping me in his truthful lyrics.

I notice something move to my right. Sitting in the dark, in front of the fireplace, Caelan sits, shirtless. With his elbows on his knees, head hanging, hands strapped across the back of his strong, thick neck, rubbing up and down through his dirty blond, wavy hair, making it even sexier and unrulier.

I stand there watching his perfection quietly. The ripples of his back muscles move his full-back tattoo to the point where it almost becomes animated art on his skin. He has many tattoos but this one has meaning. Although, even though I've asked him, I still don't know what the meaning is because he won't tell me.

The intricate Celtic cross tattoo covers his whole back, running the length of his spine to just below mid back and from left shoulder to right. There are majestic, shaded angel wings that flank each side of the cross. The wings look like they're holding the cross in protective, soft arms. With Caelan's strong, broad, back muscles, the wings look like they're gliding across his body. The whole tattoo is predominantly black-black lines and black shading-except for a few detailed spots. The intricate Celtic love knot basically looks like four connecting hearts that connect all four corners in the middle of the cross. Written down the length of the cross is the word 'alainn' that is encased and weaved into the Celtic knots of the cross. The word 'alainn' and the love knot are colored in, in a stunning, emerald green. There are three other words on his back written in Gaelic as well, two of the words flank the outside length of the cross on each side from mid cross to the bottom. The words look like they're tucked away under the majestic angel wings. 'Dioltas' and 'bhfeice.' 'Dioltas' is colored in blood red ink and 'bhfeice' is colorless just outlined in black. Underneath the two words at the base of the cross written from left to right across his back is the word 'maithiunas' that as well is also colored in the same emerald green to match the love knot and word 'alainn.' The whole tattoo, in general, is a work of art on a beautiful soul.

I see his pain radiate from his body. It unfolds before my eyes. He must sense I'm here. He picks his head up and looks directly at me on the stairs where I am still cemented to the first step. He stands, quickly wiping his right eye with his shoulder and then looks back to me. Our eyes lock as he slowly walks towards the stairs. Step by hesitant step, I reach him at the bottom step at the same time he reaches it. Where almost eye to eye now because of the height difference from the step to the floor but I still have to look up to him. He smiles sadly at me, but it leaves his face just as fast as it came. Now just sadness lingers in his facial expressions. I cup his jaw with my palm while still locked with his eyes. He puts his arms up to wrap around me but hesitates, waiting for my approval. He embraces me with such strong, warm, loving, protective arms that I wrap my arms around him and melt into his body.

"Caelan?"

"Ya, baby?" he whispers into my ear while his hand cradles the back of my head.

"You never have to ask permission to touch me. It is you and only you that I am never afraid of. You make me feel safe, warm, and protected, always. Never ever think I am afraid of you or your touch."

He holds me tighter. I can hear the tears caught in his throat. "You okay?" he asks, slowly exhaling.

I had to think about it for a minute before I could answer.

Am I okay?

I just had one of the worst flash memories flood through my body, ripping me to shreds. My inner thighs are still sore from the intense scrubbing I gave them. It's something I haven't done in years.

Am I okay?

"No." His body tenses. "No, I'm not okay, but with your arms around me, I'm better."

He softens. Leaning back from me he cradles my face in his large rough hands. His thumbs runs gently over my jaw. His sad eyes flicker over mine. "Do you wanna talk?"

I shake my head. My lip starts to tremble because to see him hurting only hurts me. "No. No, I'm sorry, I can't."

He nods with understanding in his eyes. They flicker back and forth over mine again. "You know you can talk to me, right? You know no matter what you tell me, I will never think differently of you, right?"

A tear slides down from the corner of my right eye. His thumb catches it. "I wish that were true, Caelan. I wish that were true," I say again whispering. "But I just can't take the chance of you looking at me differently and losing you. So no, I'm sorry, I can't talk to you about what happened." I drop my eyes to his muscular naked chest.

"Sofia. Beautiful, look at me." I do. "There is nothing, and I mean absolutely nothing, on this earth that you can tell me that will ever change my mind about what I think of you or how I feel about you. I promise you that. With every fiber of my being, I promise you that. I will always be here for you. Always! Do you understand me?"

I nod slightly. My eyes drop to his mouth. I inhale his masculine scent as I close my eyes. Licking my lips as I exhale. Before I can even finish exhaling

Caelan's soft lips are touching mine, reverently. The kiss deepens slowly. My hands are now on his chest caressing his smooth skin. He kisses me deeply, but tenderly like I'm breakable.

Too bad I'm already broken.

This kiss is nothing like the kiss from the other night. That kiss was passionate, hot and lust driven. This kiss is sweet and loving. I want this man. I deepen the kiss. Moving my hands lower to his strong rippled abs. I caress him across his stomach to his hips, dropping my hands lower to where his jeans are hanging low on his hips. I feel the elastic band of his black boxer briefs. My heart starts to race.

I. Want. Him.

He drops one hand. Gently grabs my hand to stop it from going any lower. His other hand is still cradling my face when he pulls away from my lips. My eyes spring open, shocked. He's looking at me with... what? What is that I see in his eyes? Pity? I feel the sting of rejection hitting me square in my chest. A melon has lodged itself in my throat.

"Don't do that," I bitterly snap shaking my head and dropping my hands, pulling my body away from his. "Don't do that to me. If you don't want me, just tell me. I understand. What I can't do is... just" My chin trembles. "Don't... don't look at me with pity. Don't treat me like I'm a victim, Caelan."

He reaches for my hand, but I pull away before he can grab it.

"Baby, that's not why I stopped you. That's not what I'm doing. You are a victim. You are, a victim of one of the most violating, demeaning crimes, but you are by far not a victim at heart. You are the strongest person I know. I just... I just know that today was really hard for you and as much as I would kill to be with you. I can't. It has nothing to do with you and everything to do with me."

I stand there not knowing what to say. Of all people, him. I never thought he would hurt me this bad. I need to take my bruised ego and go. I can't stand here another minute with him looking at me the way he is.

"Yeah, I know. I know, why you can't be with me. It's okay, and I get it." I step down from the steps I'm still standing on and push past him heading straight towards the kitchen.

"Baby, it's not like that at all," he says grabbing at my wrist. "I promise you it's-"

I whip myself around, throwing my finger in the air at him. "Don't! Don't call me that!" I forcefully say pulling my arm away. "I'm not your baby!" Shock burns deep in his eyes. "You can't be with someone like me. I get it! I do! I wouldn't want me either, but don't try and make it about you when really, it's about me."

"Beautiful, let me fucking tell you something," he growls grinding his teeth, glaring at me. "You have always been mine. You just can't see it yet."

I'm on overload, physically and emotionally spent. I just can't do this with him. I turn and walk into the kitchen. I hear his footsteps follow behind me. I grab the biggest wine glass I know we have. Fill it with my favorite Pinot Grigio with the total acknowledgment I'm going to get plastered. This isn't an oh just let me have a nice glass of wine. No, this is a, fill the bitch to the top of the glass, let the alcohol numb the pain and take it all away kind of glass of wine. On second thought, one glass isn't going to cut it. I turn back around. "Fuck this," I say reaching back and grabbing the bottle too.

Yup, I'm getting wasted!

When I turn back, I see his cautious eyes looking at me. "Sofia, let's just talk. You don't need that. Put the wine back and let's just talk."

I see the desperation in his eyes. I do, but right now... I just can't. I start walking towards the stairs again, and when I get shoulder to shoulder with him, I look up and him. "This is not your fault, I should have known better. I shouldn't have tried for anything more. It was stupid of me. I'm sorry. I just needed to feel..." I shake my head slightly. "I thought I could do that with you. I'm very sorry. I need to be alone. Don't follow me." With that, I walk past him, up the stairs to my room with my glass and the bottle in hand.

fifteen

Caelan

"**H**OW THE FUCK CAN SHE THINK I don't want her? It just took everything I had inside me to stop the progress of what was happening between us." I'm the one that started kissing her. I couldn't help myself. The electricity between us is like nothing I have ever felt before in my fucking life. I will never feel this with anyone else. It's not possible. Only Sofia can do this to me. Only Sofia has done this to me," I rant pacing back and forth.

"F.U.C.K!"

I take a long, needed draw from my bottle of beer. "I just hurt her again." It guts me just to think that. Fuck me, man! What the fuck am I doing? Why do I keep fucking this up? Last night I went too fast. Tonight... I stopped her from advancing the situation further because I didn't want to hurt her any more than she was already hurting from today.

I knew she was emotionally and physically raw. I knew the memories that came to her today were worse than what she has remembered in the past. It was written all over her trembling body. I've helped her through all her panic attacks but today was different. I didn't think I was going to be able to pull her out.

Jesus Christ, her fucking thighs… they were raw. That fucking tears me up inside. Just knowing that motherfucker hurt her like that. I might not know the details of what happened to her, but I know. In my heart, I know. If that piece of shit were still alive, I would kill him myself all over again.

"I'm such an asshole." On top of all of her pain I go and hurt her again. Fuck! I just didn't want her to regret it in the morning. She was doing it for all the wrong reasons. I did the right thing. I know I did. I can't win. Christ, I think tonight hurt her even worse than last night. For Christ's sake, she thinks I wouldn't want her because of what that sick fuck did to her. FUCK NO! I wish I were the person that destroyed that fucker! I would have enjoyed every fucking minute of ending his pathetic life.

"I hurt her." My insides twist with the thought. For fuck's sake, how could she think I wouldn't want her. I've wanted her since I was sixteen years old. Nothing will ever change that. Nothing!

I swipe my phone off the counter. I text Jess and Sage because I know Sofia won't be in any shape tomorrow morning to go to work.

Me: Sofia won't be in tomorrow until noon. Make sure one of you are there to open the store. Just wanted to give you guys a heads-up.

My phone goes off quickly with a few consecutive dings.

Jess: Okay I'll be there to open on time. Is she alright?

Sage: O.M.G Puh-leazzzzz tell me you hit that fine ass of hers, and she won't be able to walk in the morning?!!!!!!!!!!

Jess: Sage really?

Sage: What? A man can hope his two besties bonk it out finally, can't he? Fuck buddy tear that boootaaay up if she's finally giving it up!

The guy is pretty damn funny, but right now I'm just not in the fucking mood.

Me: She's okay. She'll see you both tomorrow. Thanks.

Jess: Dumb ass!

Sage: What? I'm just sayin'.

A Side text from Jessica comes through.

Jess: Is she really okay? Today she looked a little off. I'm worried about her.

Me: She's fine. Just not feeling too good. She's sleeping now. Thought it would be nice for her to sleep in.

Jess: Good. Tell her not to worry about tomorrow. See you this weekend. Have a good night.

Me: You too.

I walk up the stairs to check on her again. Before when I checked in on her, she was on the balcony lying in one of the lounge chairs. She was crying softly, drinking her wine, and listening to Rob Thomas~ *Pieces* playing on repeat. Half the bottle of wine was gone. I felt like my fucking heart was being ripped out seeing her like that. Listening to a song like that, on repeat.

I just wanted to hold her in my arms and tell her it would all be okay. I wanted to go to her, but I know Sofia better than anyone. She needed to be alone. As much as it kills me, I will give her that needed space. It's the reason I sent Antonio and Nikki home earlier. Antonio wanted to kill someone seeing Sofia like that. Nikki was so scared for her sister she was freaking out. I was afraid she would make it worse for Sof. I huffed and snorted at myself.

Really asshole? Nikki would make it worse for her? You dumb fuck, you made it ten times worse for her.

I have to back off. I have to create some distance between us. My beautiful girl isn't ready for what's between her and I. I fucking want her, there's no doubt in that, but it's time I back off, let it happen on its own. I need to bring us back to what we were. Let her come to me. All I seem to be doing is hurting her. She's been hurt enough in her lifetime. Her happiness means more to me than anything else and if that happiness is with someone else, even though it will gut me, then so be it. I will take that pain if I have to for her to be happy.

Looking into the room, I see she's still on the balcony. The bottle of wine drained of its contents, tipped onto its side on the patio floor. Walking into her room farther, knowing at this point if the wine is gone, she's probably passed out.

My God, she's so beautiful.

Even passed out she takes my breath away. While I'm watching her chest rise and fall my phone chimes with a text. I reach into my jeans pocket quickly, so it doesn't wake her. Honestly, nothing is going to wake her. She's passed out cold. I look down quick and swipe the screen.

Luke: Everything okay?

Fuck man! Word travels fast in this group.

Me: Sage?

Luke: Ahh let's just say word travels fast in this group.

Me: Ya, no shit. Everything's fine.

Luke: No, it's not, but I'm here if you need me, man. She alright?

Me: If you call a big bottle of Pinot by herself being okay... I guess she's fucking great then.

Luke: Ouch! No wonder why you told them she would be in late.

Luke: You coming to the job in the morning or no?

Me: I'll be there. See you tomorrow.

Luke: Later

A few minutes later.

Me: Hey Luke...

Luke: Yea buddy?

Me: Be ready to party this weekend.

Luke: Christopher's birthday?

Me: Yup. Fucking need to let loose man!

Luke: You got it. See you in the A.M.

I gently pick her up from the lounge chair, cradling her soft curvy body against mine. Damn she feels good in my arms. Her skin on mine, there's no other feeling like it. I carry her into her room, laying her down on her white fluffy bed. I wish I could just hold her in my arms all night. Instead, I grab the blankets and cover her up. I lean down and kiss her forehead with a lingering kiss. When I lift my lips from her soft skin, I gaze at her angelic face. "I love you, beautiful. But if my loving you hurts you, then it's time for me to back off. I'll always be there for you. Always. I hope you know that," I whisper against her soft brown waves. I inhale her scent. Her unique smell that I hold in my vault of a heart. It's all in there. Every memory of her, of us, is in there. She smells of crisp, fresh, delicate flowers and her own natural sweet sent. I go to stand and feel her small hand barely graze my arm.

"I love you too," she whispers.

I could barely hear her, but I know what she said. I look down at her again, but she's still asleep. I close and lock the balcony doors. Walk over and grab a throw blanket from the end of her bed then crash on the chair for the night so I can keep an eye on her. Usually, I would just climb into bed with her, but tonight, somehow it just doesn't feel like the right thing to do and by morning, I'll be gone.

sixteen

MY EYES SLOWLY OPEN. AM I DEAD? "Ohhhhh." Nope, not dead. My head is bangin' too much to be dead. What the hell time is it? I groan as I reach over and grab my phone off my mirrored nightstand. Wait, how did my phone get plugged in? I don't remember doing that. "*SHIT!*" I yell as I jump up throwing the white feather down comforter off me. "Ten o'clock! Are you kidding me? Damn!" I was supposed to be at work an hour ago.

I jump out of bed. "Owww!" With my head spinning, I sit right back down and lean against my white tufted headboard. Ugh, my hand drops to my stomach because it's doing cart wheels in there. I hold one hand on my head and the other on my stomach. Damn! I'm sure I look like a steaming pile of dog shit right about now. I sit there for a minute and make sure I'm not going to yack all over the bed and the hardwoods. I notice the note laying on my night stand next to some aspirin, water and a glass of juice. I grab the note, trying to get my bearings together. Oh hell, why did I drink so much? Wait, oh yeah that's right because you had a fucking terrible day yesterday! Then made an ass out of yourself with Caelan when he turned you down.

Okay, great! Son of a bitch! Just friggin great! I really didn't need to relive all that. Shit, my head hurts worse now. I focus my eyes on the note he left.

Texted Sage and Jess last night.
Told them you wouldn't be in 'til noon.
Thought you could use the sleep.
There's water, two aspirin and OJ for your head.
C

I'm still holding my throbbing head in my right hand, and staring at his note left in my left hand. This note is not Caelan. I can feel the distance between us in just four sentences. Yesterday was an emotionally draining day for me. One I haven't had in a very long time. I need to get this under control. I know where all this is coming from, it's because of Thursday night. It's been a long time since I've had a flashback, and a flashback as bad as that one was. It was definitely the worst I have ever had.

I lay the note down in my lap, scooch forward to the side of the bed and prop my feet up onto the frame of the bed. I rest my elbows on my still sore thighs and drop my head into both my hands. "I'm exhausted," I mutter to myself. Knowing I have to text Sage and Jessica I pick up my phone because there's no way I am going in today at all. I need some time to myself. Some... sober time, to myself. I also need to call Katherine, my therapist. The last six days have just been too much for me.

Me: Hey, I just woke up. Not feeling too good. Gonna take the day off. You guys going to be alright without me?

Sage: Not feeling good? Hehe is that code for... I can't walk this morning?

Jess: Sage! Stop!

What the hell is he talking about?

Jess: Are you okay, Sof? I'll come by if you need me to.

Me: I'm good. Just a little hung over.

Jess: Aahh, get rest. If you need me, let me know, I'll swing by. You going to make it to work tonight? It's your first night back at Ice since last week, right?

Oh hell! My stomach flips again. I totally forgot I have to work tonight at Club Ice. There is no way I could call out tonight. Not after taking off this past weekend. Mentally and physically exhausted I throw myself back on my bed. "Ouch!" I grab my head to stop the throbbing. "Asshole!" That was dumb. Now my brain hurts, again! Just the thought of having to go in tonight and throw a smile on my face for nine hours is enough to make me run to the porcelain god!

Me: Aww hell!!! I totally forgot I had work tonight!! Well, I guess it's a good thing I'm taking today off. Thanks for the offer and thanks for the reminder. lol. I'm good though just going to rest up as much as I can today.

Me: Sage, what the hell are you talking about?

Jess: Sof?

Me: Ya

Jess: I love you girl, you know that, right?

I sigh. My girl knows me. Shit everyone in this small group of friends knows each other so well. We all know when something's wrong, but we don't butt in 'til we have to or until we're let in, and on top of that we all have each other's back. That's what makes this group so tight.

Me: I do. ;) xoxo See you tomorrow afternoon.

Jess: Or tonight. I might check up on you at work. Mwahhhh! Don't be mad.

Me: Never. Will be good to see you there.

Sage: Oh honey, I was praying for you and that fine slice of heaven finally knocked some boots! Oh, forget the boots... bumped the uglies... Oh forget that too 'cause I know his is definitely not ugly (well only in my dreams) and even though I'm a gay man, yours is pretty nice to look at too, And I've seen all of your kibbles and bits, sugar!

Cracking up, I grab my sore head yet again! "Ow!" I grab the aspirin and OJ he left for me and swallow. Thoughts of yesterday start filtering back to me. I answer Sage back. I love this guy. He's so damn funny, but just thinking about yesterday is making me more and more sad. We are never going to happen. Caelan doesn't see me that way. I know last night he was just trying to let me down easy. As for the lust driven passionate kiss the night before... I'll just blame that on alcohol, emotions, and hormones. It's been awhile for me. Honestly, now that I think about it, I haven't seen Caelan with anyone in a while either. So, I'm sure it was just hormones racing between the both of us. I have to move on. I have to open my eyes to new things. I have to let people in. I have to learn how to trust again. I have to stop being afraid. I was doing so good. So good and this one thing flips my world upside down.

Me: Sage...

Sage: What? A gay man can dream, can't he? They're big ones, I know, with rainbows and unicorns, but good Lord it's a glorious dream, honey! Gezzz why does everyone have to kick a gay man for dreaming about his two gorgeous besties getting it on? I love you guys.

Shaking my head at my phone even though he can't see me. I can just see him now with his hands flying everywhere drawing out unicorns and rainbows.

Me: Not gonna happen, Sage. He doesn't feel that way about me. We're just too close.

I can't tell him the real reason. It's too hard, and that conversation would just lead down a road I am not willing to go down with anyone except Katherine. I can't tell him that I tried last night, and Caelan pushed me away. If I did... I just don't want to get into it all. I'm too exhausted. He would demand a blow by friggin' blow of what happened last night and that, that I just won't go through again. No way... it was hard enough the first time. It would be like getting rejected all over again.

Our whole group knows that I was abducted, but they don't know the extent of what happened to me while being held captive. I don't want anyone to know either. These feelings I have, those memories I have... they're mine. They will stay mine.

Ding.

Sage: Oh honey you're close that's for sure. You're closer than most married couples if only you two would get your heads out of your fabulous, delectable asses!!!!

Me: Please let it go.

It just hurts too much to even think about it. Let alone sit here and talk to Sage about it. Besides, he's a guy. I mean ya, ya, I know he's a gay man and my best friend, but he's still a damn man and don't all humans that have a penis stick together? No, I need to change this subject.

Sage: Never!

Me: Sage can you do me a favor? Pull the purple cashmere sweaters from the front window and put the red slip dresses there.

Sage: Nice! Real smooth on the change of subject, sugar britches! I'll let this go, for now, honey, but in the future, we will be chit chatting about this.

Me: Thank You~

Sage: Okay, the blonde Attila the Hun over here is bitching at me! I have to go to work now! My job is never done! Xoxo love ya, sugar~

Me: love you both~

Me: {with a side text to Jess} Thank you~

Jess: anytime, 'sugar britches' ;) You need to talk, you call me. Got it! xoxo

Me: Yup. xo

SLOWLY STANDING, I make sure my legs, head, and stomach are all on the same page. Tentatively I walk towards the bathroom, when I notice the throw blanket that's usually at the end of my bed is now on the wing back chair. Hmmm, I don't remember getting into bed last night or plugging in my phone. I look over at the French doors; they're locked. Caelan...

He must have carried me to bed. The blanket on the chair, though... did he sleep in the chair? No, he didn't. Why would he sleep there? He crashes in my bed all the time. Then realization dawns on me. It's because of last night. I'm so stupid. I pushed it that far that he didn't even feel comfortable sleeping in my bed with me.

I make it to my bathroom without any mad dashes to the toilet. I brush my teeth, wash my face, take a pee and then do the inevitable and check on my inner thighs. After carefully taking off the small bandages, I'm surprised at what I see. For the most part, it's nothing. Just some redness. I thought for sure my thighs would look like chopped meat. The bad ones, the broken blood vessels are very high on my upper thighs. At least, makeup will cover the redness, and I don't have to worry about anyone seeing them tonight at work. I look at the thin white scars left as a painful reminder of the torture he put me through. Small thin lines, high on my upper thighs from the razors and knife he used. I look at the few that are lower, but those are very faint, and really only my eyes can see them. Our uniforms at Ice are very short, so thank the Lord most of the damage is on my upper thighs.

The aspirin and OJ are working already. I'm starting to feel much better. I grab the water, guzzle it down and throw the bottle in the trash that is currently next to my bed. I start to head downstairs. I stop at the top of the long stairs, to inhale the morning goodness of coffee like I always do. Then realize I don't smell the delicious morning wake me up wafting through the air. Humph. He didn't make coffee? He always makes coffee. In fact, I can't remember a time when there was ever a morning it wasn't made. As a matter of fact, usually the coffee is brewed, my favorite mug is sitting on the counter next to the coffee machine, and sitting next to my mug is the sugar and a big spoon. Double Humph! He's usually sitting at the island reading work reports and drinking his coffee waiting for me. This morning there is nothing. Nothing! No coffee, no mug, no sugar, and no... Caelan. I can understand him not being here. It's mid-morning, and he usually leaves for work at 8:00 am, but the no coffee and no mug is kind of throwing me off. I stand there for a minute taken aback a little.

I walk over to the coffee machine and hit the brew switch. Open the cupboard, grab my mug and lean over the counter and hit the switch for the overhead speaker system. I grab a spoon and throw that on the counter then reach for a butter knife for the English muffin I threw in the toaster.

Adele is singing about *Love in the Dark* and moving forward. It's one of my favorite songs. It's sweet, sad and truthful to some. I listen to the lyrics and think to myself... I have to do the same. There's a part in the song that makes me realize the huge distance lingering between C and I right now. Leaning against the countertop waiting for the coffee to brew I drift off thinking about last night. As Adele's incredibly talented beautiful voice bellows out heartfelt words, I take the deepest breath my lungs can stand and just think about how I want to live my life.

I exhale and feel the weight getting lighter and lighter. It's not gone, but it's not drowning me either. I drift off again thinking about the flashes from yesterday. Fragments of memories I've hidden. As I stand here, snapshots of pictures filter through my mind, realizing at that moment that I've subconsciously hidden those memories. Small particles coming together, making a picture. I remembered more of what happened during that time. More vivid details than what I have ever remembered are wildly coming to the forefront of my thoughts. The mirrors... I remember my hazy sight looking up at the ceiling and seeing the reflective material capturing the vile scene below. It's shocking to me that I can see this so clearly now. It's like it's happening to me right before my eyes. My knees become weak, so I grab the counter and hold on. I can see my wrists and ankles handcuffed to the four corners of the footboard and headboard. I feel sad, terrified eyes staring blankly back at me. Gasping, I sit down on the tile floor and lean against the cabinets. Those are my sad, terrified eyes looking back at me. It's me. I'm watching myself!"I can't do this." It's like watching a movie in high definition being played out before me. I hear his heavy breathing and grunting in my ear. My right ear. I see my body being rocked back and forth on the dirty mattress. I can hear the chains clanking as my body is jilted. I feel his hot, heavy breath on my now dirty skin. And the whole time, sad, terrified eyes were watching over me. My sad, terrified eyes. He was some sick, twisted, fuck. He wanted me to watch what he was doing to me. This feels almost persona-

"Sofia?"

I feel a hand on my shoulder. I snap my head up to the voice and swing my fist. Jessica jumps back from her crouched position next to me.

"It's me! It's me!" she yells with distressed concern standing there with my favorite green and white venti coffee cup. "Giovanni let me in. Honey, put the knife down."

I can't say anything to her right now. Hell, I forgot Giovanni was even sitting out there

on guard. She's now hesitantly walking towards me with her hands up.

"Sof?" she cajoles softly.

I still can't bring myself to speak. The rising anger holds me captive to the video playing before me. "Those were my eyes watching me," I mumble in disdain to myself. "He wanted me to watch."

"Sof? You're scaring me, honey. Put down the knife and tell me who was watching you?"

A burning smell starts to bring me out of my thoughts. Put the knife down? I shaking my head snapping myself out of my haze. "I'm sorry. Nothing. I was just daydreaming," I mutter and then realize I'm now sitting there with a butter knife in my hand.

Great, I guess I didn't say it to myself.

I throw the knife on the counter while Jess takes the burnt toast out of the toaster. "What are you doing here?" I asked with some bite in my tone.

"Sof you're trembling. Honey, whose eyes were watching you?"

"Yeah, yeah, I'm good," I tell her waving my hand like it's nothing. "I'm sorry. I have the worst hangover." I make an excuse. "Ahhhh am I happy to see that coffee cup!" I say trying to forestall her questioning as I walk towards the island where she quickly placed it when I almost stabbed her.

Giving me a questioning once over, she throws a new English muffin in the toaster. "Looked a little bit more than just a hangover to me. You almost stabbed me. Tell me what's going on."

"I'm good. Really, I'm sorry. You just startled me. I didn't hear you come in.""For now," she says sitting down on the stool at the counter I can tell she doesn't believe me one bit. She's just being my girlfriend right now.

"I wasn't going to stay long. I told Sage I would be right back. You know Sage, he wanted to close up shop, call in the hangover reinforcements and make it a girl's day watching movies in Pj's pigging out. But, I talked him off the ledge saying I was just bringing you a cup of coffee and would be back within the hour."

I chuckle thinking about Sage and his girly PJ's. "Thank you for this," I say lifting my coffee. "I needed it, badly!"

She laughs. "Hangovers... you'd think, after all this time, you and I wouldn't get them anymore," she says pretty much laughing through the whole sentence.

She is right, though.

"Right! Hell, this one is bad, Jess. Haven't had one this bad for a long time." I'm pretty sure I'm just physically drained from yesterday, and it's not all hangover, but I'm not going to say that to her.

"I'll stay. Let's talk about what made you drink so much last night."

I drop my head shaking it back and forth softly. "Do I have to?" I look up at her with tears stinging my eyes. "I made a fool of myself last night, Jess. I feel so stupid."

She reaches out and grabs my hand. "What happened?"

"I kissed him. I know we cuddle all the time, sleep in the same bed at times, flirt, and joke around, but I took it too far. I started to kiss him. Actually, he started to kiss me, but then I started to take it further than a kiss, and he pulled away. I'm so, so stupid Jess. I feel like such an idiot. I made a fool of myself. It just hurts that's all. I'm just feeling sorry for myself." I give her a half-assed smile. "I'll get over it."

"Oh honey, maybe he pulled away for a reason."

"Ummm yeah, 'cause he doesn't see me like that Jess. I mean seriously what was I even thinking? You see the girls he's with, hell, Jess, they're gorgeous. Tall, skinny, legs that can wrap around him five times over and usually blonde. Shit!" I outright laugh and snort. "I just described you to a T." I smile at her. "Look at me, Jess. I'm the total opposite of what he likes. I'm short, I have curves, I have an ass, and my boobs are borderline too big for my body. I don't know what I was thinking. I'm so embarrassed and feel so stupid. I'm such a fool."

"Listen to me, Sofia Rose Heart. You are a gorgeous woman. No matter where we go, men are admiring you. Damn, let it be said I'm pretty good looking too! We're damn good looking chicks!" She flicks her hand up with a huge smile to give me a high-five.

I laugh because that sounded so damn conceited coming from her, but she is so the opposite of that. I know she's just trying to make me laugh.

"Yes, you and Caelan have a close relationship. Yes, you two are most definitely closer than most married couples, but please do not think he isn't attracted to you or doesn't want you or that he never has been because I've seen the way he looks at you. I have seen his protective, dominant side over you. I mean shit, even Antonio takes a step back to Caelan when it comes to you. Even though A busts his balls all the time, he even knows that Caelan has feelings for you and is extremely protective of you so, please do not think he doesn't want you. That's just not someone protecting 'a friend,' honey," she says with her fingers up in air quotes. "There has to be another reason he stopped."

Well, he may have, at one time, wanted me, but clearly, after seeing me last night, with my thighs torn to shreds by my own hands, he put two and two together after I told him I was trying to wash away the dirtiness. He was disgusted by me. Why would I think he would want me after that? What he finally saw was the pure ugliness of the shame I hold. The shame, the guilt, and the anger.

Move on, Sof. Get it together. Call Kathrine and make an emergency appointment. You are not a victim. Never a victim. 'You are a strong, beautiful woman!' The mantra I've told myself every morning in the bathroom mirror for three years straight.

I sigh. Yeah, this strong woman is feeling a little weak at the moment. Well, at the very least, I can be honest with myself, right? One day at a time.

"Sof?" she whispers.

"Hmm? Spaced out there for a minute. My head's starting to hurt again."

"I'm gonna go, you rest."

"Yup, I'm going to crash on that big comfortable couch as soon as you walk out and I close that door on your ass." I smile.

"Sofia?" She looks at me with a sad frown. "I know this is more than just a hangover. I know last night was hard with Caelan and everything, and I know that you want space, but know this my bestie, I am always here for you. Hell, you almost just stabbed me. I know you have never actually talked to any of us about the horrendous things that happened to you three years ago, but with everything that has happened on Thursday, I'm sure it's bringing back some memories and insecurities. Just know that I am here for you. Never doubt that. Whatever you tell me will never leave my lips. I promise. I pinky promise and where I come from that means the world!" She puts up her perfectly manicured French pinky tip with a reassuring smile.

I'm shocked for a minute. No one's really ever just came out and said something to me about what happened three years ago. I look at her pinky and get the biggest smile on my face. It takes me a minute, but I wrap my finger around hers and nod my head looking straight into her eyes. "Not today. But... but maybe one day."

She wraps me in a big hug. "I love you girl, and so does he. We all do. Don't forget that. We're the elite eight. Nothing gets better than us."

I FINISH MY COFFEE Jess brought me. Actually, it's a shame we just call it coffee. It's a delicious dessert in a cup, with coffee added. I throw the container in the trash. Walk over and hit the warmer button for my English muffins in the toaster, then pour myself another cup of the freshly brewed coffee that has finally stopping brewing. I fix my cup of coffee, butter up my English muffins, then grab my cell phone and sit at the island to call Kathrine. I catch her in-between clients. Instead of going into the office I ask if we can just have a phone session. We talk for thirty minutes. I tell her everything that has gone down within the last six days. We discussed some things through and agreed that I should go into the office tomorrow.

I finish my muffin and coffee. Clean up the kitchen and wander over to the front door. I open it to see Giovanni sitting there in the vestibule talking on his phone. Dressed in all black. Black V-neck tee, black jeans, and boots. He really is a good-looking man. I say, 'a man' like he's so much older than me, but really, he's only six or seven years older than me. With his hair being dark and him wearing all black clothes the two things standing out are his green eyes and his gold chain that's adorned with two charms. The charms are two letters. K and A. I wonder what the meaning is behind them.

"Morning," I greet him in a weary voice when I realize I am staring at him just a little too long.

"Morning, Sofia," he responds giving me a once over. "How are you feeling?" he inquires in a calm concerned tone.

"Caelan told you?" I sputter with disbelief.

"Told me not to expect you 'til noon. Said you weren't feeling well."

Ahhh. Well, at least C didn't tell him I passed out last night. That would just be something more for my father to freak out about. Well, that is if Giovanni went back and told him. Which, I don't know if he would but... "Well, I'm better, but I took the whole day off. You don't have to sit here all day. You can go. I'm not leaving until tonight. I have work at Ice soooo..."

"Sofia, first off it is my job to sit here and make sure you're safe. Second if you think you're going to go to work tonight, without me, you're dead wrong. I will be there, all night, making sure you're protected. After I bring you home at three am, Carmine is coming to relieve me so I can get some sleep. I will be back to take you to the boutique tomorrow at noon."

I exhale loudly. "I... I... you can't go to work with me, Giovanni. Alex will never allow that."

"Sofia, if you think we would let you go to a club like Ice and not think someone would be there to watch over you, you are sadly mistaken. I can assure you, Alex has already been informed of the situation and was quite accommodating."

"Oh, I'm sure he was," I sarcastically say tilting my head to look up at him. Man, this guy is enormous. If I didn't know him, he would scare the piss out of me. "If you say so." I give in, because honestly, I know nothing I say will stop him coming to work with me. "Well, there's freshly brewed coffee on the counter, help yourself. At some point, I'm sure you're going to need a bathroom so feel free. You're more than welcome to hang out inside. You don't have to sit in the vestibule."

"Thank you. I might take you up on the coffee in a little bit."

seventeen

CLOSING THE DOOR ON GIOVANNI, I find myself wandering into Caelan's office. I stand there for a few minutes taking in the room and yesterday's events. I feel myself drifting off into territories I know not to go to. My breathing starts to pick up when it dawns on me, I never watched the tapes. I quickly walk over to his desk looking for them. One is still in the disk drive. It must be the one we were going to watch last night.

Do you really want to watch this by yourself? Can I handle watching them by myself?

I should call Jess and tell her to get back here to watch it with me. No, I quickly think. I need to do this all by myself. I have to do this on my own. I pop the monitor on, then sit in Caelan's oversized manly black leather chair. I take a deep breath and hit play. My eyes are glued to the computer monitor. I watch for a few minutes then realize I need to fast forward because we are not even in the club yet. So, I fast forward until I see all of us walk in the front doors of Club 9.

I feel my breathing starting to pick up. I try to calm myself down. At the moment, it's not working. I'm just so afraid of what I will see. What I do see is nothing, but all of us standing around by the bar ordering our drinks. I watch Chris leave the bar, walk over and claim us a table, while Jess and I run to the dance floor. I take a deep breath and start to calm down, realizing that at this point in the night nothing has happened to me yet. All this is, is me watching my night unfold in front of me. Nothing happens to me while we're at the club so for right now my shaken nerves calm down.

I watch Luke and Caelan get our drinks from the bar and walk over to the table where Chris is sitting. They hand him his drink, then put the rest down on the table. I see the three of them laughing and kidding around with each other. Pounding each other's fist and doing their guy thing. Chris leans over and says something to both Caelan and Luke then all their heads turned towards Jess and me on the dance floor. Caelan's leaning one elbow on the bar height table. His long legs crossed at the ankles in a relaxed, casual, sexy stance. He's now watching me dance when Luke says something to him. They both smile when Luke punches him on the shoulder. When Caelan says something back to him, Luke gets an even bigger smile on his face. Hmmmm, wonder what that was about?

Caelan then walks away from the table, directly to me on the dance floor. He pushes the front of his body up against my back. His broad chest, shoulders and iron clad abs engulf my small frame. His large, strong hands circle my waist pulling me into him. My body just molds into his like hot lava. I watch as we move our bodies as one in sync to the magnetic upbeat music that's pounding through the system. For him being such a big man he can move really well. I catch myself smiling at the computer screen while I watch us dance together. My heart swells watching us together. Then sadness sets in when I think back to last night. I shake my head to clear my thoughts and focus my attention back on the video.

I concentrate on the table. I see Luke staring at Jessica with a cocksure smile on his face. "Hmmm, what's that about?" Luke then walks to Jessica, now dancing by herself. When he reaches her, she looks up and smiles at him. This is nothing out of the ordinary. We all dance with each other but that smile she just gave him made me raise my brow in curiosity. We all may dance with each other, but no one dances with me quite like the way C does. I chuckle to myself. I watch for a while, and nothing really out of the ordinary stands out to me. I start scanning the people that are dancing around us. I see nothing, but people having a good time. I see Chris at the table talking to some girl. Then I see us all go back to the table when the song changes. We're laughing, joking, and drinking. In general, it's the same ol' same ol'. Just us having a fun time celebrating Caelan's new contracts. "Nothing! Nothing stands out," I mutter in frustration. It's the same thing over and over.

Antonio finally walks in. He looks around for our group. When he sees Chris, he walks to the table giving him a bro hug and a back slap, interrupting the conversation Chris was having with the girl he was talking to. They talk for a minute when Chris nods his head towards the dance floor. Antonio's gaze follows his. He looks back to Chris and says something. Chris shakes his head no. Then A heads for the bar to get a drink. I watch Jimmy pour three fingers of his favorite scotch. He looks like he's doing a once over of the club. He takes a few sips of his scotch and heads back to the table with Chris and the girl he's still talking to.

It's around twelve thirty in the morning when Jess, Antonio and I head to the bathroom. Luke, Caelan, and Chris stayed hanging out by the table. While we were gone, Uncle Carmine shows up. He walks over to the table and talks with Caelan for a minute. I watch as Uncle Carmine cups his ear and leans over to hear him better. I remember the music being so loud that night. C lifts his chin jerking it in the direction of the bathrooms. Uncle Carmine turns and walks in that direction. I look over to the side of the screens where the bathrooms are located. I see Antonio leaning against the wall waiting for Jess and me to come out. He's talking to some blonde I remember quickly talking to inside the bathroom. I watch us walk out of the restroom and stand there for a minute while A introduces us to the blonde. I remember giving her a once over. I smile to myself because it's kind of funny how protective we all are of each other. The funny part is these guys pick up girls all the time, but God forbid one of us girls do it. They send the guys packing before they can even get close enough to ask us our names. Why I gave her a once over I have no idea because I knew she wouldn't be around in a few hours. Which was good anyway, because I remember catching bad vibes off her.

The three of us, plus the blonde still tagging along, head back to the table. Before we get back to the table, Jess and I decided to hit the dance floor one more time being that the night was coming to an end. Back at the table, I see A grab his phone. He hangs up and says something to Caelan. A few minutes later A leaves with the blonde in tow. Luke and Caelan walk away from the table and head straight to the dance floor to dance with us again. I smile when I watch them side stepping the girls who were provocatively throwing themselves at the guys on their way to us. They pay them no mind and keep heading straight for us. We danced for a little while enjoying one another's bodies. I'm captivated watching him, and I dance together. I lose myself within his arms. As I watch, I realize how sexy we look together. "Damn! We look hot together! He's so flippin' sexy," I say out loud but to myself chuckling.

Okay, okay Sof get it together.

We head back to the table deciding to call it a night. I grab my drink and finish it. I remember it being warm but I still guzzled it. I chat with Chris and the girl he's been talking to all night. I watch myself look over at C, who is trying to politely get rid of the blonde who has attached herself to his side on our way back to the table. He leans down and says something to me. I see my hand lift holding up my index finger.

I watch myself look around for Jessica, but she's not there. I figure she and Luke are still on the dance floor. I head to the bathroom by myself for one last quick trip before we head home. Going to the bathroom alone is not something we typically do. Us girls always go together and usually one of the guys goes too and wait outside the bathroom for us. I see myself scan the bar to see if they're getting another drink, but knowing in my head, it was too late. I then scanned the dance floor and didn't see him or her. Hmmm, I start scanning the crowd again. Then I see it! I see them! The two of them coming out from one of the upstairs back private rooms. "Oh hell! That little vixen!"

Luke stops and grabs her arm pulling her back to him. He gives her a quick kiss on the cheek then lets her go. She walks back to the table while Luke heads to the bathroom. A few minutes later he's walking out of the bathroom back to the table with everyone like they didn't just have something going on upstairs! "Oh, you and I will be talking," I say to the computer screen like she can talk back to me. She's been holding out on me!

I focus back on the screen. I watch myself go into the bathroom. When I come back out, I head straight for the bar. I walk to the back of the bar to the service station where Jimmy the bartender, who we all know so well has my drink waiting for me. I smile. He's, I'm guessing, in his early thirties. Good looking, not over the top good looking, but charming and cute all wrapped up into one nice little package. He's been bartending here for years. Sometimes on his nights off, he comes into Ice to hang out. I look over at him as I'm walking towards the service station pointing to the glass asking if it's mine just to make sure. He nods with a smile and a wink. I don't expect him to come over to me because he seriously has his flirt on with a beautiful redhead right now. Go, Jimmy! I remember thinking to myself! She was gorgeous. Maybe too gorgeous. I watch myself grab the glass and guzzle it down. Throw him a thank you wave and head back to the table.

The group is back at the table now, sans the two blondes. When I reach the table, C puts his arm around me and leans down to ask if I'm ready to go. I watch myself as I smile up at him nodding my head. I guess it's about ten minutes later I watch as we head out the door. "What the hell? Nothing! Absolutely Nothing!" Wait, I didn't feel anything until we left. That glass of water. It had to have been the glass of water Jimmy left for me.

I rewind the tape and start to watch from the point of me walking to the bar for my water. This time I watch the bar instead of watching me walk from the bathroom to the bar. I wait to see if anyone goes by my glass of water. I watch at it again, closely. My eyes are glued to the monitor I'm totally entranced by the footage. But there's... nothing.

eighteen

"**A**HEM."

I jump out of my skin, whipping my head to the doorway. "What the fuck?" Giovanni's standing in the door. "Holy shit balls, you scared the piss out of me!"

"I apologize. I called your name, but you didn't answer."

"I didn't hear you. Damn! My heart is pounding!"

"You were pretty glued to that screen."

"Yeah, it's the footage from Thursday night at Club Nine."

"Didn't you watch it last night? You didn't see anything?"

"O," I stammer, "I-yeah we were supposed to watch it, but... never got around to it."

He looks at me questionably. "Never got around to it, huh?"

That was stupid of me to say. I made it sound like we were going to watching a comedy movie or something. Change the subject Sof.

"Yeah, umm I thought maybe it was my glass of water at the end of the night that was drugged."

"What do you mean?"

"Come here, watch this with me. Wait, why are you inside? Everything alright?"

"Yeah, yeah everything's fine." He waves his hand. "I was going to make a cup of coffee and use the restroom," he answers stepping into the office.

I turn the monitor towards him. "I'll get you a cup."

He holds his hand up. Leans over the desk to watch the video footage. "The coffee can wait, hit play."

I explain to him that at the end of every night we go out I always go to the bar for a glass of ice water before we leave.

He looks at me. "You do this every time?" he asks with concern on his face.

"Yeah, helps the hangover." I smirk. "I do it every single time. Jimmy usually has it sitting there waiting for me."

"Jimmy?"

"Yeah, he's the bartender at Nine. He's been there a long time. Not sure how long, but for as long as we've been going there, he's been working there."

We proceed to watch the tape, quietly. The buzz of the bar unfolds in front of our eyes. My eyes are watching the screen like it's going to do magic tricks. I point to the screen and show him Jimmy, grabbing the glass. He fills it with ice, then water, and then placed it on the bar by the service station for me. No one goes by it except for me. Nothing! I look over to Giovanni. "See? Nothing. I would think that would have been the perfect time for someone to have slipped something into my drink. If it were random, they would just wait to see who drank it and waited for the drug to take effect. Right?"

"Ya, but if it wasn't random and someone is watching you, they would know about the water and wouldn't do it then. It would be too obvious."

"So when could this have happened? I just watched the whole tape. I didn't see anything. Caelan, Antonio, and my father watched it the other night, and they didn't see anything either."

"I don't know, but clearly no one was by your water. So, it wasn't that." He points out, frowning. "So that means it had to have happened within thirty minutes of leaving, Sofia."

"I just watched this whole tape, Giovanni. I didn't see anything. Did you watch it with my dad, brother, and Caelan the other night?"

"No. No, I didn't." He shakes his head.

"Will you watch it with me now?"

"Absolutely," he says dropping his extra-large frame in the chair.

"I'll put it up on the flat screen so we can see it more clearly. Maybe that will help."

I start the tape, fast forward to the time frame when we all walk in. We both watch closely. We don't say anything until Giovanni calmly tells me to pause the tape.

"What?"

"There's a guy in the corner that's been watching you."

"Seriously? Where?"

"Right there." He points to the guy on the screen. "He's been watching you for a while. Do you know him?"

"No." I squint to see the screen better, but it's still blurry. "No."

"He doesn't look familiar? Someone you might have passed on the streets in the past."

"No," I say shaking my head, "but it's hard to see. This tape isn't the best quality. We are at a bar though maybe he was just checking me out."

"Rewind it. This is more than checking you out. Watch it." He points to the screen "He's glued to you and Caelan on the dance floor."

I rewind it again. "Well, I mean we do dance pretty provocatively together. Maybe he was just watching us because of that."

"Yes, you do, but that's precisely my point."

I kind of shrink a little at the 'yes, you do' part.

He must notice the change in my demeanor. "Sofia, I don't care how you dance with Caelan. I don't care how you dance with anyone. That's your choice and your right to do. I'm not your father," he says, with a raised brow and half smile half frown on his face. He points at the screen again and says, "My point being that a man will check out a female if she's good looking or he's attracted to her. He'll even hawk on her a bit if she's alone, but you're not alone, you're with Caelan, and you look like a couple by the way you're dancing together. Plus, the fact that Caelan sends off the signal of 'don't get within fifty feet of my girl.' So, the question is, why is this guy watching you so much? Most smart guys know to move on, but some don't, they see it as a challenge. This guy doesn't take his eyes off you. Watch," he orders, pointing to the screen again.

I follow the man for a few minutes. He's right. This guy doesn't take his eyes off me for an extended period of time. We rewind the tape and start again. The guy is following me the whole time we're there. He doesn't take his eyes off me. When I get up and go to the bathroom the guy nods his head. "Did you see that?" I burst and look at Giovanni pointing at the screen.

"I did. Rewind it again," he orders.

I do, we watch it again. The guy nods his head at someone across the room. It looks to be directed to someone standing by the bathrooms. We can't see the person he nodded to, though. The video is too fuzzy from this angle, and the camera was too far away. You can see me walking to the bathroom, but you wouldn't know it was me had you not known it was me. "BALLS!" I grit out in frustration, slamming my hand down on the desk. I'm pissed we can't see who it is. Giovanni looks at me shocked. "G-Man do you think this is the guy?"

His brows shoot up. "G-Man?" He smirks holding back a laugh.

I laugh right along with him. "Yea, yea." I wave a hand in the air like it's nothing. "Everyone around here gets a nickname. Well, no, that's not true either, but I just gave you one," I say cracking up.

He smiles at me. "Don't let your father hear you call me that."

"Ugh, my father. Really? You just had to bring him up?"

He smiles, but then his face turns solemn. "He loves you, Sofia. I know it's not my place to say it, but he does."

I'm taken aback when he says it, but honestly, because of what he has helped me through, I feel very comfortable with him. "Well, G-Man, I think with our history," I say flipping my index finger back and forth between us. "You and I are probably a little past the point of not being able to say something to each other. Don't you think?"

"I guess you're right. I just don't want to overstep my boundaries."

"You haven't. I appreciate your honesty," I truthfully admit.

With a slight nod he asks, "You ready to watch this again so we can catch this son of a bitch?"

"Absolutely." Wow, I thought watching this tape would have been really hard for me, but it wasn't bad watching it by myself and now with Giovanni here to help me watch it actually helped me to relax. "How far do you want to go back?"

"To the beginning."

I rewind it again, and we watch it from the start. I see the same stuff I saw before. Giovanni points out that I need to be watching the background, not just my own movements.

"It wasn't yourself who drugged you. It was someone else, so keep an eye on the background." So, I do what he says and start watching all the people around me. "Was Antonio drinking?" he questions.

"Yea, he had," I say, letting the words lingers while I rolled my eyes thinking. "I think three glasses of scotch. Why?"

"I thought he had a job that night. That's all. He doesn't drink if he has a job."

"Oh," I say distracted. My eyes are glued to the screen now watching for the creepy guy. "Wait, look!" I point at the screen. "That guy is by the bathroom now where Antonio is waiting for me and Jess to come out. Jesus, that's creepy. To not even know this guy was watching me most of the night, then to see it on tape... man, that's flippin' creepy."

"I see him, I also saw him walk closer to you when you went back to the table, but the fact of the matter is that this guy, even though he's hawking you down most of the night, hasn't been by your drink at all."

"No, he hasn't. The only people that have been by my drink are the two girls. Chris was talking to one all night, and Caelan had one clinging to him towards the end of the night."

"Rewind it again, Sofia. Go back again. Let's watch these girls better. We are going to find out who did this to you."

I smile at him. "I'm glad you're here watching this with me G-Man."

"Why didn't you watch this last night with everyone? Did they watch it?"

I scan his face for a minute contemplating if I should tell him or not. I know I can trust him with my life, but can I trust him not to say anything to my father? "G? If I tell you something will go you back and tell my father?"

HE GIVES ME a once over. Taking the time to think his answer over. Which doesn't make me feel too good.

"Let me start by saying this. I know how you feel about your father knowing your business. I have to tell you; I do understand why you feel the way you do. I don't know why he behaves the way he does with you and not your sister, but I never have and will never say a word to him or anyone about what happened six years ago. That's your business. Now to answer your question... if the situation is life-threatening, then yes, I will say something if I can't take care of it myself. And know this, Sofia, anything you need help with now or in the future, all you have to do is ask me. Other than that, anything you tell me stays with me. I have worked for your father since you were a young teen. Your father is good to me. I see your family as my family. I protect family." He smiles. "So, if you want to talk to me about something, and you're comfortable with telling me, then Sofia, I'm here for you. Like I said what you tell me, stays with me."

I nod my head in acceptance of his answer. "Last night I had a meltdown." I take a minute to think and see his reaction. Nothing. He is just sitting there like a statue waiting for me to finish. "The four of us came in here last night after dinner to watch the tapes." I hesitate. "I... I have panic attacks from time to time. They used to be a lot, but the past two years they have become few and far between. Caelan helps me through them." I sigh thinking of him.

"They started after the night I was abducted." I stop to look at him. He gives me a reassuring face, but his eyes flicker, I can see the anger in them, he wants blood. Yep, he's fucking scary when he gets pissed. Note to self... don't fuck with Giovanni when he's mad. He gives me an encouraging head nod to continue. "Last night was the worst one I have ever had. It was a panic attack with the combination of new memories." I take a deep breath trying to calm my shaky nerves.

"I sat down to watch the tape... memories just started bombarding me, hitting me like an automatic flashing camera. Bright, vivid memories. I- I remembered some sick, twisted things that were done to me-things things I've never remembered before, things I wouldn't wish on my worst enemy, G. No, that's not right either. He is my enemy, and I wish I could do worse to him. To do to him what that sick, twisted fuck did to me, but worse!" I stop to take a deep breath. He sits there patiently waiting for my next words. I see the tension in his jaw line. "G, no one knows. I have never told anyone. None of them. The whole group of us. All seven of them. The eight of us are all so close, but I have never told any of them. I can't talk to them about it. The only person I've ever talked to about that night is my therapist. Caelan... God Giovanni, so many times he tried to talk to me about it, I just can't tell him. I can't! He won't look at me the same way." I take a minute and think about last night. How I felt when he turned me away. "Last night... last night he saw the worst of me," I say slowly. "After I had snapped out of my memories, I ran to the shower... scrubbed my thighs to a bloody mess trying to wash away the filth I felt. He saw me after I came out of the shower, saw my raw thighs. I just broke down, G. The memories were too much to bear. Those memories of being chained to that bed in that dark basement..." His forehead crinkled. "The mirrors that that sick, twisted fuck put on the ceiling so I could watch everything he was doing to me," I murmur shaking my head trying to rid myself of the memory. "I want to murder him. I want to kill him with my bare hands. I want to take razor blades to his inner thighs like he did to mine. Then I want to make it even worse for him by pouring salt on the open raw bleeding skin and watch him suffer. I want to take his life, Giovanni."

His head twists to the side a little. His jaw is clenched, and his face is red.

"Sofia he is dead. He will never hurt you again." He tries to console me with complete assertion.

"Ahhh," I disbelievingly say lifting my head with a slight snort and sniffle. I look him dead in his eyes with clenched teeth. "That's where you're wrong. That's where you're all wrong. He's alive. He's alive, and I know he is. I can feel him. I feel it in my bones. He's alive, Giovanni." He sucks in a shocked breath at my vehement statement. "I know what you all told me. I know you all think he's dead, but I know he's alive, G. Someday he will come back to get me. He told me he would. Those were his last words to me before he let me go."

"Sofia, look at me," he says, forcefully demanding my attention as he rounds Caelan's desk and crouches down in front of me still sitting in C's black leather chair. He gently grabs hold of one of my hands. A contradiction to his commanding voice. His other hand reaches up and wipes away my tears in a silent moment before he makes me a promise I don't want him to keep. "I promise you, even if he were alive I would never let him get to you again. I will kill him with my very own hands before I let him get to you."

"No," I shout. "You have to make me a promise." He nods slightly. "When he does come for me, 'cause he will come for me, promise me this... that if you get to him first, you will save him for me."

He sighs with reluctance. "Sofia, I don't kno-"

"Promise me, Giovanni." I force his words.

He wipes another falling tear away, then reluctantly nods again before giving me his word. "I promise you. I promise, I'll do that for you."

"What is it you're promising her exactly?" A deep, husky, angry voice to my right asks.

I jump and snap my head towards the door.

"What is it that you're making a fucking promise to her for, G?" he sarcastically asks emphasizing the G.

I squirm nervously in my seat. Giovanni never moves. I'm startled to hear someone's voice. Caelan's powerful force is standing in the doorway to his office with a scowling face. His large muscular arms are crossed over his black t-shirt clad swollen chest. His blue jean covered legs are set a foot apart in a stance that definitely says don't fuck with me. Giovanni nor I say anything. He's pinning Giovanni to his spot with his fierce malevolent eyes.

"Someone wanna fucking say something? I asked a question."

Giovanni looks back to me, tightening his hands around mine for reassurance. I hear C growl at his actions. Giovanni gives me a soft smile, pats my hand, and slowly stands to his full height of six foot three maybe even six foot four. I'm not sure how tall he really is, but his big ass is intimidating as all hell.

"Caelan we were-" I nervously start to try and explain.

Giovanni cuts me off. Squaring his shoulders up to Caelan. In a very control dark voice, he says, "We were having a private conversation that you walked in on and interrupted. I would appreciate if you would give us a few minutes to finish that conversation, *in private*. If Sofia chooses to tell you, that's up to her. If she chooses not to tell you then I would expect you to give her that right and respect her privacy."

Oh, fuck! Oh shit! This is not going to be okay.

The transformation of C's face lets me know he's ready to blow and I'm ready to throw up when his eyes flicker to mine.

"Is that what you want, beautiful?"

Oh shit!

I nod my head slowly as I stare at him. Then I glance to Giovanni quickly before looking back to Caelan. "Yes, please."

He becomes tenser and stands there for a few more seconds looking at us both then turns to walk out.

"Close the door, please," Giovanni orders Caelan as he's walking out.

The scowl on C's face when he turns back to look at Giovanni was so fierce I think he could actually kill someone with it. With one last look at me, he slams the door closed.

My stomach twists and the bile rises. I want to throw up. "Oh Fuck. That was not good. He's so mad."

"He'll get over it," he says trying to comfort me by crouching in front of me again. "That was just a man claiming what he believes is his. Basically, he just pissed on your leg, letting me know you're his and to back off."

With eyebrows raised, I look at Giovanni with an incredulous look on my face because there is no way he thinks I'm his. Not after last night. "Giovanni, he doesn't look at me that way. Trust me, I know. I- I kissed him last night. He pulled away, turned me down."

"You think maybe he turned you down for another reason?"

"Ummm yeah because he saw me. *The real me.* The messed up in the head me. He saw what I did to myself."

"The situation of last night might have been why he stopped, but trust me, seeing you like that is not what stopped him. I'm sure it was more out of concern and respect for you, Sofia. It's something maybe you two should talk about because by the looks of it there's some tension between you two."

"Ha. You saw that, huh?" I laugh. "Was it that obvious?" I now nervously laugh.

He snickers at me trying to lighten up the intensity in the room. "Just a little bit." He holds his thumb and index finger up an inch apart.

"I'm sorry about what just happened."

"No worries, Sof. Seriously, he'll get over it."

"Umm, I don't know there may be a rabid dog out there ready to rip off your legs when you open that door."

He taps the top on my hand he's holding. "Trust me, sweetheart, I can handle Caelan."

I chuckle. "Okay."

"Now, let me ask you something. This might be hard."

Damn. "Go ahead," I tell him because I'm the one that opened this door between us.

"Well, first off let me just tell you how truly very sorry I am for what you've been through. If you ever need to talk more or just need me, you call me. You have my number, right?" I nod. "I will be there for you faster than you can count to ten, Sofia. Now, here comes the hard part, sweetheart. When you were telling me about your memories, you said 'the dark basement.' Was that correct? Were you in a basement?"

I take a deep breath, closing my eyes to think. "Yes," I rush to say when I open them. "It was a basement, I'm positive. It had small basement windows that were spray painted over with black spray paint. I remember when he was releasing me, he literally dragged me up a long flight of stairs because my legs were so weak from the drugs he gave me they kept giving out."

He stiffens. "Do you remember anything else? Do you remember what he looks like?"

I look off to the side trying to remember. "Things are fuzzy, but the memories that came to me last night is what made me remember the mirrors on the ceiling above the bed. When I saw myself in those mirrors, that is what made me remember the other things." I start to shake.

"You're okay. You're right here with me. You're safe. I won't let anything happen to you," he assures me. "Can you remember anything else about him? Hair color, moles, tattoos, piercings, scars?"

He believes me. He believes me when I say he's still alive!

"Giovanni?"

"Ya?"

"You believe me? You believe me, don't you? When I said I know he's still alive?"

He takes a deep breath and is quiet for a minute. "I'm not saying I don't believe you. I'm saying that things you just said don't add up. The guy we... *found*, lived in an apartment. So, you saying you were in a basement with blacked out windows doesn't work with living in an apartment. However, he could've brought you somewhere else."

"Black hair."

"What?"

"The guy-the guy you... you know. Did he have black hair? Because this guy had black hair."

He's speechless for at least a full minute. "I'm not sure."

"Please don't lie to me. Please, Giovanni. I just told you something I have never told anyone. Not even my closest friends. I never even told my sister for God's sake. Please, don't lie to me."

He tilts his head back and looks at the ceiling. "The man that was extinguished had blond hair."

Gasping, grabbing my chest. "I knew it! I knew he wasn't the right one! I knew it!"

"Sofia, listen to me very carefully. He could have dyed his hair. This doesn't mean it wasn't him. Promise me you're not going to freak out over this. Let me do some digging around and see what I can come up with." He nods his head coaxing me along. "For now, we keep this between us. You can tell Caelan if you want, but if you do tell him, tell him to keep his mouth shut. Can you do that?"

"Yes. Yes, I can do that." I frantically nod my head.

"Good. You okay?"

"Yes. No. I'm not okay! But, I actually feel better than I have in a long time. Does that make sense?"

"Good. Enough for today. You should rest, you have work tonight. You need to be alert while you're at Ice. I'll be there to watch over you, but I need you to pay attention to your surroundings while you're there. Not just there, though, Sofia. From now on, everywhere you go, you need you to pay attention to your surroundings. You understand? Everywhere."

nineteen

I OPENED THE DOOR TO THE OFFICE AND walked out with Giovanni right
behind me. Caelan's sitting at the kitchen island with a beer to his lips
and a deep scowl on his face. His dark blond wavy locks look disheveled like
his hands have run through the strands a thousand times. Realizing when I
look down at my watch that it's one-thirty in the afternoon, all I can think
is- why is he home? When I look back up from my watch, his stone-cold face
is drilling Giovanni with a death glare.

Shit! This is not good.

I've seen Caelan pissed off. I watched him destroy a guy one night in a
club for touching me. This, though... is beyond that. I don't really know what
to say *or* do. I know I should go to him, calm him down because I always do,
but the anger coming from him right now is making me uncomfortable. I
look back to Giovanni. For what? I don't know.

With a reassuring smile and a hand on my shoulder he says, "It'll be fine.
Go upstairs for a few minutes so I can speak with him."

Yep! No problem! I'm outta here. See ya later. Goodbye!

I look back to C giving him a soft smile. The glare he gives me, not only disappoints me, but hurts me. I feel an overwhelming sensation of sadness because of it. My shoulders drop, and I let out a held breath as I turn my body to go upstairs, but my eyes stay on his for a few seconds longer hoping we can connect, but it doesn't happen. There's nothing but anger in his beautiful, blue eyes, so I turn fully around, and run up the stairs to my room. These two guys can handle it between themselves.

THIRTY MINUTES LATER after a nice, hot, needed shower, I head downstairs to grab something to eat. I only have a few more hours left before I have to leave for work. I figure I'll grab something to eat first then get dressed. Maybe talk to C if he's calmed down.

When I get to the bottom of the steps, I look around in hopes to see him, but I don't. Again, I wonder why he was home at one o'clock in the afternoon when he should be working. Especially since he just got this new contract. By the looks of it, he already left. So, I'm assuming he went back to work. We really need to talk, though. I have to find out why he was so angry so we can fix this... *fix us*.

I head to the refrigerator grabbing some lunch meat and sandwich fixings. I grab a butter knife out of the draw before leaning over and flip the switch to the speaker system. Lifehouse's *Blind* comes alive around me. I start to sing softly. It's been a long damn day, and I need some food and music. My hangover is gone, but mentally, physically, and emotionally I'm beat up. Food will help. It's going to be a long night at work. I sigh just thinking about it. Then I hear it. Words that shock and hurt me to my core.

"You fuckin' him?"

It startles me so much I twist around quickly. C's standing four feet behind me in the same stance as before. Arms crossed and legs shoulder width apart. Damn, he's sexy, but I'll be dipped in shit before I let him talk to me like that, in that tone.

"Excuse me?" I indignantly question scowling at him.

"You fuckin' heard me, Sofia. Answer me!" he yells glaring at me. "Are. You. Fucking. Him?" he grounds out slowly like he's giving a two-year-old instructions.

I'm so astounded I just stand there for a minute, trying to grasp the fact that he just asked me that. Oh, fuck him! My anger spikes. *No!* This is going to go down in a hard way because there is no goddamn way I'm letting him get away with this. "What's it any of your business?" I yell right back at him. He's got me pissed off! His face twist with more anger. I didn't deny or confirm, so now his mind is really working overtime.

Good!

"You are my fucking business!" he roars, so loud it hurts my ears. Pointing at me, he roars again, "And you were in my fucking office!"

Oh, hell no! I may be his business on an everyday level, but on this level, absolutely not! I could have been his business, but he turned me down last night. And not for anything, I have slept with people in the past. He doesn't get worked up over them so what the hell is going on right now? Time to hurt him just as much as he's hurting me.

"Well, you didn't want me last night, so maybe I had to go looking somewhere else." I raise my brows. "A girl has her needs. I needed yo..." I stumble quickly changing that statement. "I needed some last night, and *you* turned me down. Plain and simple." I shrug my shoulders poking myself in the chest. "He was here. Hell, he's a damn good-looking guy. Plus, he's big." I quickly raise my brows twice with a cocky smirk. "I thought- what the hell, his dick might be big, too." I quickly toss my head left and right. "Turns out, I was right." I wink at him. Then just because he pissed me off so bad, I add the cherry on top. "And he was pretty damn good too. Took care of my needs *real* good, that's for sure. The man can move for as big as he is." I winked again just for good measure, rubbing it in just a little bit more. I'm playing with fire here; I damn well know it. Hell, I shouldn't be egging this on, but he pissed me off talking to me like that, and a pissed off Sofia, is not a pretty one. Poor G-man is going to catch the wrath of Caelan over this. I'm sure of it. I might want to let Giovanni know I just put some serious fuel on an open burning fire when I see him later. I watch C flinch like he just took a bullet to the stomach, but he's still standing there like a brick shit house. Good, that stung! I watch him cross his arms and then uncross them again. Like if he crossed them he wouldn't be able to breathe. His chest, if at all possible, just swelled even bigger, and his breathing has picked up to a rapid pace. Oh, man. Fuck. Caelan would never lay a hand on me. I know that, but right now his big, pissed off, scary ass is starting to make my knees shake. Okay, maybe, just maybe, I shouldn't have said that. Hell, no! He shouldn't have talked to me like that. Who the hell did he think he was talking to. Fuck him!

"Let me get this straight... because I wouldn't fuck you last night, you just decide that fucking the bodyguard was alright?"

"Seriously? He's not 'just a bodyguard,' and you know it!" I shout pointing at him while I stare him dead in his blazing eyes. I'm blown away right now with what has just transpired in the last five minutes. Where's the guy that was afraid to touch me last night? The caring man who bandaged up my thighs, and had tears in his eyes while doing it. The guy who handled me like I was a piece of glass and always treats me with so much respect... that guy has never talked to me this way.

At this point, I'm just standing there not knowing what the hell else to say. I know I have to be the rational one here because clearly, he is not. Something's going on with him that's obvious, but he has totally pissed me the fuck off! I'm not sure if I can be the rational one. I'm ready to explode. This argument has to end before it gets worse. I need to stop this. "Well, at least the bodyguard didn't talk to me the way my best friend just did," I say to him with sarcasm dripping from words. "Asshole!" I scream with exasperation, throwing the butter knife I had in my hand onto the kitchen counter. I push past him and take the stairs two at a time to my bedroom and slam the door shut as hard as I could. I flick the switch to lock it and walk double time to the switch for the whole house speaker system to play. "Oh, he's going to hear what I have to say!" I rant turning on my iPod and blast Salt-N-Peppers *None of Your Business*. A smile crosses my face when I flip my hair over my shoulder and get ready for work. "Fuck Him!"

"Hᴇʏ G," I greet him when I open the front door to leave for work. "You ready to go?"

"I'm ready whenever you are," he answers with a genuine smile.

He walks me the fifty steps to the back of the blacked-out SUV parked on the street in front of the house and opens the door for me. I slide in grabbing for the handle to close it, but he holds onto the door. I smile at him, but before he closes the door, he gives me a lingering once over. Yes, G-man, I'm in a bad mood, and not for anything, I really don't want to spend nine hours in a club like Ice tonight. I just don't have the energy for it. I snort out a laugh.

You better get the energy because if you don't, you'll never make it through your shift.

Work at Ice is not for the weak. It's one of the most famous and biggest clubs there is in New York. Most nights it's jam packed. With its three floors, if you're not a person that can hustle you won't last working there. I have seen many employees come and go.

I take a deep breath as Giovanni gets into the front seat. When he looks back at me, I smile at him. "Well, G-man you ready for craziness?"

He shakes his head. "Great club to go to on my personal time, but when I'm trying to protect someone's life... not so much."

"Totally agree."

"I wish you would have taken a few weeks off."

"Sorry, G-man, I know this isn't going to be easy for you, but I can't be taking off any more time."

"You work too hard, Sofia. With everything that's going on... you really should reconsider."

"Not gonna happen, G," I adamantly say letting the conversation fade out. The first few minutes of the ride to Ice is quiet. I need music. "Giovanni, can you turn on the radio?"

"Sure, what do you want to hear?"

"Doesn't matter, anything you want is fine." He flipped through the channels and settled on *Long Day* by Matchbox Twenty. "Can I ask you a question?"

"What's up?"

"The conversation you had with Caelan when I went upstairs, what did you talk about?"

He's quiet for a few seconds. "Let's just say we had a man to man."

"That's pretty vague. You're not going to tell me, are you?"

"It is. And no, I'm not."

"Great." I'm quiet for a minute. "Did you tell him what I told you in the office?"

He pulls up to yet another red light and turns in the driver's seat to look at me. "Sofia, I would never tell anyone what you told me. I promised you that." He turns a little more towards me. "Something wrong? You seemed upset when you opened the door to leave for work tonight. You okay?"

"Honestly... no. No, I'm not." I turn and gaze out the tinted window. "Caelan and I..." I trail off look up at the city sky thinking about what to say noticing the faint flashing lights in the distance from Ice's rooftop lighting system.

"You and Caelan what? Did he hurt you?"

I look back at him. Who's now staring at me through the review mirror. "Yeah. Yeah, he did, but not in the way you're thinking," I tell him turning my head back to look out the window. "I'll get through it."

"Sofia?"

"I'll be fine. Just let it go."

Will I be fine? Because right now I don't feel like I will be.

WE PULL UP in front of Ice. It's packed as usual with a line around the building. Bobby, the valet, comes over to open my door. Giovanni opens the window, waving him off he tells him to give us a few minutes. Bobby's not too happy about waiting being there's a line starting to form, but then he sees me sitting in the back. "Hey, Sofia." He looks back at Giovanni "Sure man, take your time," he agrees tapping the top of the truck.

I quickly smile at him letting him know we'll be quick. "We won't be long."

"No problem just let me know when you ready."

Giovanni turns in his leather seat to look at me. "Tell me what happened."

I sigh. "I'm fine. Really, I am."

He studies me for a few seconds. "Tell me what happened," he orders again with a clenched jaw. "Did he put his hands on you?"

I gasp. "What? No! No way! He would never put his hands on me! Never!" I reiterate by shaking my head vigorously.

He nods his head accepting my answer. "Then tell me what happened because clearly, you are not fine. I know something's wrong."

I do not want to tell him what our argument was about, but I guess I have to being that Caelan might go after Giovanni. I mean the least I can do it give the guy a heads up. Right? Maybe not, maybe they already saw each other, and I don't have to tell him. "Did you see him before we left? After you two talked?"

"No, why?"

Damn! I thought maybe if C left after we had our fight he would have seen Giovanni on the way out. If anything were going to happen, it would have been then. Although all C had to do was open the front door if he really wanted to go after Giovanni. He would have been sitting right there if he really wanted to say something to him.

I scrunch my nose up. "We had a fight. The worst one we've ever had," I mummer. "He said some... stuff that shocked and hurt me. More shocked than anything, and it pissed me off." I might have started that sentence whispering, but it sure didn't end that way. Just thinking about it angers me.

"So, I gave it right back to him. We've never had a fight like that before. *Ever!* He hurt me with his words, that's all. It wasn't C talking either. I'm not sure exactly what's going on with him, but he's never been that way with me before." I shrug my shoulder. "I'm a big girl. I'll get over it. No big deal."

His face is red. He's pissed. "It's a big deal to me. You don't need this right now." He pauses. "Did you tell him about the tapes?"

"No, not at all. Trust me, the conversation we had, had nothing to do with the tapes." I snort out a harsh breath holding my hand up. He scowls at me while trying to figure it out. He tilts his head to the side and crinkles one eye a little. "He asked me if I fucked you," I whisper with a disbelieving face.

I watch this stone-cold killer of man as shock registers. His eyes grow wide, and his chin shoots forward, and his eyebrows hit his hairline. "The fuck you say?" he asks in pure shock.

I laugh because of the look on his face, but that kinda hurt. Like it's so unbelievable that he would sleep with me.

What the hell? I hate men today. I swear I do.

"Well, gee Giovanni, thanks for making it seem like you wouldn't touch me even if I were the last girl on this earth. Whatever. But yeah, that's exactly what I said to him when he asked me. It's the way he asked me that pissed me off, so I went back at him, *hard!*" He laugh-snorts, but it's more of an 'are you fucking serious' laugh-snort.

What the fuck? Seriously what is it with men? Fuck him, too. Hell, my already torn up self-esteem is going right down the fuckin' drain with a can of Drano within the last twenty-four hours.

I shrug my shoulders before turning to watch the patrons stand in line for Ice. "I don't know. I really don't know." I have to get this conversation over with quickly. I have to tell him what I told Caelan, but I do not want to tell him what I said while we are face to face in this truck. I already feel vulnerable. "Giovanni, I really need to get inside before I'm late." I go to grab the door handle to open it.

"Wait!" he yells, stopping me. "You don't get out unless I'm there to open the door for you. Got it?"

Ahh, Mr. Bodyguard is back.

"Got it," I say with a nod of my head. He gets out, walks around the truck and opens my door. He waves over Bobby to come get the truck. Ice owns their own parking garage that you can valet in. It costs a fortune, but being the club is in the middle of the city, parking is definitely limited. I step down. He doesn't move. I look up to him because he's blocking my way with his big body while he scopes out the area.

Tell him now before you don't get the chance.

"Giovanni?"

"What's up?"

"Just so you know... C thinks we're fucking." I put my hands on his shoulders, smiling. "Sorry, I had too. Oh, and you're great in bed, with a huge dick, and to top it off, you gave it to me real good!"

He chokes, his eyebrows shoot off his forehead yet again. I don't think they're coming back down they're so far up there this time. I think his eyeballs just about popped out and fell onto his cheeks.

I scrunch up my face. "Sorry, I had to do it. He had me boiling mad! I'll clear it up, but I just wanted him to stew in his own shit for a minute. I wanted to let you know in case he came after you. At least, you would know why."

He bends at the waist bursting with laughter. His shoulders are jumping up and down he's laughing so hard. "Thanks for the heads up," he says shaking his head, still laughing. He's laughing so hard he's making me laugh. "Oh, I'm sure that pissed him off big time," he says wiping the tears from his eyes. "Would have loved to have seen his face when you said that."

"Oh, I saw it," I tell him with big eyes, "and it was flippin' scary. I thought he was going to explode."

"I can't believe you told him that. You take no shit, that's for sure. Don't worry about him coming after me. Let's let him stew for a couple of days. He deserves it. He should know better anyway."

For real? What the hell? He should know better! What the hell is that?

I need to get inside before I actually start to feel like dog shit! Everyone with a penis is an asshole today! So, all I say is- "I agree."

twenty

WALKING INTO A CLUB LIKE THIS is like nothing you have ever experienced before. The place actually has three names: Ice, Fire, and The Devil's Lair. Instead of saying the whole thing all the time we all just call it Ice. It has two and a half floors plus a rooftop. The roof top is just for air and smoking, only allowed for use by the guests in the VIP area. That's also not counting the basement. The basement holds all the offices and locker rooms for the employees. The first-floor entrance is Ice. The second floor is Fire, and a flight of stairs up from Fire is the private Devil's Lair that looks down over Fire.

Each floor has its own individual sexy feeling. When you walk into Ice, it's breathtaking. It's the only way to explain it. Modern, sexy, and sophisticated. You walk in through the outside doors to the comfortable, sexy waiting lounge. If you made it this far, you're doing pretty good. While you're in the lounge waiting to get through the gates into the club, you see them. The massive white iron gates that are flanked with sheer curtains that block you from getting into Ice unless the bouncer gives you the go ahead. Just beyond those gigantic gates is nothing but spectacular. Ice is all white. Every bit of the floors, walls, and bar. The only black in there are the guy's uniforms. When you're granted access into the club the gates open for you, stepping inside, you feel like you entered a whole different world. The place is remarkably contemporary with its sharp lines and walls built strategically to make the place look like an open maze. White, bar-height tables are everywhere the eye can see, plus there's a huge dance floor. The blue and purple LED lights are the only colors that grace the walls and floors of Ice. They change from purple to blue slowly. What is blue at one moment is purple the next.

There are 5 bars on this floor. Six bartenders, both male and female, behind each bar. Every one of us bartenders is in constant motion all night long. If someone calls out sick... forget it, that one person makes all the difference. We get a half hour and two fifteen minute breaks throughout the night. Trust me we need every minute of them. Our uniforms downstairs in Ice for the girls are all white. A white, very low-cut, two finger strap tank top with Ice's logo on the front across our chest in rhinestones. Combined with a pair of white, very short shorts. Very short! Basically, my ass cheeks play peekaboo all night. The guys have it way easier. They get to wear black V-neck tees with tight black pants. Although I'm not complaining, their asses look fantastic in those black pants. Ice's music is more fast, club, happy music. Sexy, but not over the top.

As you look up the flight of stairs from Ice to Fire, you see the black iron gates this time and blood red velvet drapes. The black ceiling in Ice pulls you up into an ominous feeling hovering over you. The music changes as well. It becomes very sexy and seductive strands of music. You just know every step you take you're getting further and further away from the innocence of Ice and closer and closer to the dirty, wicked, fun of Fire. You know everything is about to change when you hit that last step. When the gates are opened for you, and you take that final step through the blood red velvet curtains into Fire, you can feel the change in your bones. It's dark and sensual on the second floor. Your whole mood changes. It's all black and blood red. All the walls, floors, ceiling and bars are black. The LED lights up here are red, and red only. They change from a deep almost muted red to a blood red.

There's ceiling to floor blood red drapes everywhere the eye can see. It's sexy, sophisticated, and private. It gives off the feeling that you're in the devil's lair, but you're not... not yet. That's one more flight of steps up above Fire. The Devil's Lair looks down over Fire.

The guy's uniforms on all three floors are the same black uniform throughout the whole club. The girl uniforms are the same in Ice and Fire just change from white to black. With the black tank tops having red rhinestones across the chest saying Fire. That all changes again when you get upstairs into the VIP rooms of The Devil's Lair.

In the back of Fire, up a flight of stairs is The Devil's Lair. There are blood red gates at the top with a sign that says Welcome to The Devil's Lair. It is flanked by the same blood red curtains that hang from the ceiling to floor throughout Fire. The gates are always left open. Suggesting to come up and play with the devil. The VIP rooms are large, elegant, and private. So private that there are doorbells on the outside of the door, in case the door is closed. If the door is closed, we are not allowed to open it without ringing that bell first. Then we have to wait a minute after ringing it before we can enter. There's a countdown clock above the doorbell that starts once the bell is pressed. There is also one on the inside of the room as well, so the patrons know someone is coming in. Some patrons care, some don't. I have walked in on many sexual acts that don't stop just because I entered the room. Most of the time they ask if I wanna join. *No thanks.* By now I'm used to it. The walls inside the caves are black velvet material, and the seating is black and red velvet.

The girl's uniforms up here are entirely different from the other two floors. The top, if you can call it that, is a fully open back red satin halter top with a deep V-plunge in the front that goes all the way to our belly buttons. Thank God for boob tape! The shorts are gone, now it's a skirt. It's a black satin short skirt. Black garters that hold up black satin stockings that have red rhinestones that line straight up the back. Honestly, there is nothing left to the imagination in these uniforms. You really can't call the skirt a skirt. It's just a scrap of material you put over your hips and upper thighs. Most of us girls wear black lace booty shorts under the garters. Otherwise, all of our bits and pieces would be hanging out, and you would definitely be able to tell if I shaved that day or not.

Bouncers are placed throughout the VIP floor and even before you get to that floor, there are three bouncers standing at the bottom of the steps that separate you from Fire to The Devil's Lair. Enormous, very intimidating men with chips in their ears dressed all in black.

There are only about twenty of us girls that work the VIP rooms. For one, you have to be able to handle yourself up there, at times it's rough. Two, you need to go by the old saying of 'keep your eyes and ears shut.' You have to work in Ice for a year then Fire another before you get the privilege of working in The Devil's Lair VIP rooms.

A lot of the new girls try to get up there because of the celebrities and wealth that surround the Lair, but trust me if you don't belong up there, you will not be granted access. Even as an employee, if the bouncers know you and know you're one of the girls that work the VIP all the time, you still won't get up there unless you're scheduled to work the VIP rooms that night and have the required uniform on plus your security bracelet.

Before you even start your shift for the night you first you have to go to Alex's office so he can inspect you and make sure you look presentable in your uniform. Once approved you get the mandatory wristband. It has your name, date and code on it that says you're working the VIP rooms that night. The only people that know the code are Alex and the bouncers. Once you pass the gates to start your shift, you don't come back down until your shift is over. If someone approaches the bouncers and they belong to a party in the VIP area, one bouncer walks them to the group to confirm they belong there. While the other two bouncers stay at the bottom of the steps to make sure no one else gets past. It's extremely private back in the caves of the VIP rooms, and although The Devil's Lair looks over Fire, the people in Fire cannot see up into The Devil's Lair. Because of that, pretty much anything goes. There are four bars in Fire and then a private bar upstairs in the Devil's Lair VIP area. I love working up there because the money is unbelievable.

There're only four bartenders that work the bar in The Devil's Lair. Usually two girls and two guys.

Mostly high-powered businessmen and celebrities rent out the private rooms. As long as our service is on point, the alcohol keeps flowing, and we hear and see nothing, the tips are phenomenal at the end of the night. And that is where I am working tonight.

twenty-one

GIOVANNI FOLLOWS ME DOWNSTAIRS INTO THE locker rooms. Before I can walk inside, he makes me stand by the door so he can check the whole room out. Usually, I just change right there in front of my locker, but being that he's with me tonight, I figured I'd go change in the changing room. "I'll be right back." I grab my stuff and start walking towards the bathroom stalls and changing room. "I have to go change. That is unless you're going to leave the locker room, which I highly doubt you will. So, unless you wanna stand here and watch me change, G-man," I say wiggling my brows at him with a slight tilt of my head, "then I need to go to the back."

"Go." He points. "I already checked the stalls and changing room. It's secure."

I change pretty quickly. The changing room is big. Lots of mirrors and vanities for the girls to put on their makeup or freshen up during the night. My phone dings with a text. I hear Giovanni giving someone, who I think is one of my coworkers, Travis, a hard time. I start getting butterflies in my stomach when I grab my phone to see who it is.

C: The Killers~ Mr. Brightside

I gasp, sputtering, "Son of a bitch!" I'm floored as I stare at the illuminated screen for a second trying to wrap my thoughts around the meaning of this song. We always send songs back and forth to each other. We've been doing it since we were kids. It's *our* thing. We let each other know how we're feeling at the moment or whenever we hear a new song and want to pass it along. I know this song... well. It's a slap to my face, pissing me right the fuck off. He's saying I slept with someone else and he's angry, feeling betrayed. Which baffles me because we're not together. So what the hell is he saying? I can sleep with whomever I want. Why is he being like this? The curtain flies open startling me. "What the hell?"

"What's the matter? What happened? I heard you gasp," Giovanni interrogates while his eyes scan the room.

I look down at my phone. Then back up to him. "Nothing. I'm fine." He frowns letting me know he doesn't believe me. I look back down at my phone, shocked. I text back the first song that comes to mind.

Me: Blow Me ~ Pink.

Because that is exactly how I friggin' feel right now. He can go to hell!

C: Did you...? Blow him, that is?

Oh. Hell. No! He did not just say that! Oh, I need a really good song, but at the moment my brain is short circuiting, so I can't think of one. So, I do the next best thing.

Me: Yeah and I swallowed too! Oh, wait... a little did get on my lip, so I licked that up with my tongue. He loved it! :0

Then I thought of the perfect song.

Me: Fuck You ~ CeeLo Green.

I shove my phone into the waist band of my skirt as I side-step my overzealous bodyguard. His eyes follow the placement of my phone with a deploring look. I shrug because it's the only place it will fit in these uniforms. Not for anything, I would like to stick it in my shirt but between the boob tape and my ample size rack, there's no way. I take a step out from the dressing room, noticing that he was in fact giving Travis a hard time. Poor guy, he's been here longer than I have.

"Hey! Giovanni stop," I yell at him when takes his eye off me and whirls back to say something to my co-worker. "He's okay, that's Travis."

He turns back to me, with a very displeasing face he gives my uniform a once over again. His lips mimic the words 'what the fuck' then continues. "I don't care who he is. No one is safe. Remember that, Sofia. And can't you wear a sweater or something!"

"Oh geezzz!" I roll my eyes. I grab my co-workers shoulder. "I'm so sorry, Travis, this is Giovanni, my bodyguard. You'll be seeing him around for the next few weeks. You can go now," I say pushing him towards his locker. I glance back to the big man glaring at me.

"Sofia let's get a couple things straight. First: everyone is a threat. You will take that seriously. I do not care who they are or how long you have known them. Got that?" He points at me. "Second: that goddamn uniform should be illegal and banned!"

I crack up. "Yes, I agree, but I guess they want to keep the whole illegal thing going upstairs being that half the stuff that goes on up there *is* illegal." He rolls his eyes.

Hold the phone. The stone-cold killer just rolled his eyes! Crack me up.

"This night is only going to get more interesting, I can see it now," he mumbles.

"I have to go into the office and get my ID tag for tonight," I tell him as I walk out of the locker rooms towards Alex's office. His door is closed so I knock.

"Who is it?"

"Sof," I yell. "I'm getting ready to head up to VIP I need my ID bracelet."

"Come in."

Alex is sitting at his desk wrapping up a conversation with a new girl. I look back at Giovanni and murmur, "Another one bites the dust." I smile, feeling bad that she just lost her job. She gets up, says goodbye and gives G-man here not a once over, but a twice over with fuck me eyes as he and I stand by the door. I look at him with an 'oh, okay stud' look, but his facial expression is stoic.

"Hey, Sof," Alex greets handing me my ID bracelet and gives Giovanni a quick nod.

"Thanks. This is Giovanni," I introduce gesturing toward the big man.

"We've met," Giovanni informs me.

Hmph. Well, hello that's not a shocker to me, but I was trying to be polite by introducing them because this situation is just awkward.

Alex looks at Giovanni then to me. He's a good-looking man, my boss. I'm guessing he's in his late thirties early forties. He's single as far as I know, with a tall, well-built body. He's always dressed well and with his dark hair, hazel eyes and alluring smile, there's no shortage of women chasing him.

He wraps his arms around me in a soft hug. "Sofia, I can't tell you how sorry I am about what happened to you. How you feelin'? You sure you'll have the strength to make it through the night?"

"Thank You. Yes, yes I'm alright," I answer taking a step back from him.

"I was hoping you caught the son of a bitch who did this to her by now, but I'm guessing that's not the case being you're here with her," he expresses, looking at Giovanni. "Anything you need, anything at all, you let me know." He hands Giovanni a wristband too. "This is just so the guards know who you are. They have their instructions. You can come and go as you please. Anyone of them gives you a hard time you call me."

Hmph! What the hell? He gets to roam around, but the rest of us who work here can't even come down from the top floor until our shift is over. I shouldn't be complaining because it's for my safety, but again, what the hell?

Plus... call me? Umm since when does G have my boss' personal number?

"Sofia if anyone bothers you beyond the typical bullshit and you feel uncomfortable you let us know. Whoever did this to you, hopefully, is long gone, but if he is still around well... let's just say"- he glances at Giovanni-"he won't be around for long."

Giovanni doesn't say anything. He's just standing there like a statue with his hands crossed and cupped in front of him. "Thanks, Alex. Whoever this was or is, would be stupid to try something while I'm here. There's too much security."

He pats and gives my shoulder a soft reassuring rub. "Go make some money, sweetheart. You have another boutique to open."

I smile. He knows I own my own boutique. He also knows I keep working here to make money to open another one. As a matter of fact, at times, he's called me to personally attend to his "friends" when they need a last-minute dress or something to wear. Over the years, we have become friends. He's my boss, yes, but when the night ends and the club closes and the regular house lights come on we're friends that have an end of the evening drink together.

WE HEAD UPSTAIRS, stopping at the wall of security guards. We all say our hellos. No one says anything to Giovanni. Just the quick nod of acknowledgment. When we get to the top of the stairs, he grabs my elbow and leans down close to ear. "How long have you and Alex been more than employee-boss?"

I stiffen pulling my arm away.

Here we go again. Someone else accusing me of sleeping with someone I'm not.

"Excuse me?"

His facial expression changes. "You're more than just boss-employee. You're friends, I didn't mean it the way you took it."

"Or maybe the way you phrased it."

"I apologize. It wasn't meant to be phrased that way."

I relax. "Sorry, long day." I inhale and exhale deeply. "I don't really know. Years I guess. I mean, I've been working here since I was eighteen, so gradually over the years I guess. He brings some of his girls into HD sometimes to get dresses and stuff. Why?"

"Alright, now answer this…" He takes a second as his eyes flicker over mine. "No judgment, Sofia, I don't really care what the answer is, I'm just trying to figure things out to keep you safe. Have you been with him?"

Now I'm pissed, but I keep that to myself as best I can, because quite honestly his original question wasn't phrased wrong. He just didn't realize how harsh it came out. "No. Never," I say turning away not letting him get another question in, but not before throwing him a dirty look as I walk away.

I flip the bar top open, saying hi to everyone. I start setting up my top bar. Making sure all my mats are on my rail and all my garnishes are set up. Then I check the underbar making sure my speed racks are stocked. The bar is set up for all four bartenders to have our own section, unless you're a runner bartender, which I am tonight along with Sara. Runner bartenders get more of a percentage at the end of the night being that all night long when drink orders come in from a VIP room we have to run them to the rooms if the floor runner girls are backed up. The two guys here tonight, Jake and Cory will make sure the drinks keep flowing at the bar.

The night starts off slow. It's quiet. Well, quiet for the VIP floor. As the night goes on a large party comes in. Someone's bachelor party. Great! Why anyone would throw a bachelor party on a Tuesday night, I have no idea. Maybe the wives thought it would be safer and wouldn't be as wild. Ha! Well, thank God they're not here to see what's going on behind those closed doors.

The party gets larger as the night goes on. The floor is packed at this point and I'm running my ass off. The music is thumping into my core with deep sexy, sultry music. The dance floor is packed as well. Regardless of everything that has happened today, I'm in a good mood. It's one of the reasons I love working here. Between the music pumping, being busy, and the energy from the people, the night flies by and it takes your mind off everything else. Even if it's only just a few hours of escape.

The night starts to wind down. I notice someone sitting down at the end of my section of the bar. Good looking guy. Dark jet-black hair. I noticed him in one of the caves while the groom was getting more than just a lap dance. When I walked into the cave, I saw him in the back of the room talking to another guy when we shared a quick glance at each other. I look down the bar at him again and he gives me a sinful, sexy smile.

Oh hell! This is nothing but trouble on a barstool.

I politely smile back while walking towards him. First thing I notice, are his eyes. They're green like mine, but way darker with some lighter green reflecting. The outer rim is outlined with a darker greenish black ring. They're mesmerizing. They sucked me right in. I can't help but lose myself in them for a minute.

"Like what you see?" A deep sultry voice asks.

I unwillingly snap out of my gaze. "Uhhhh sorry," I mumble shaking my head to clear my fog. "I'm sorry, your eyes are... are just... *wow.*"

He smiles. "So are yours. I feel like I'm looking into tropical waters."

I blush. "Thank you."

Okay, Sofia get it together before you look like a fool.

"What would you like?" His smile becomes bigger, sinfully sexy, totally dripping with innuendos.

Lord give me strength; his lips look delicious. I wonder what it would be like if he... Oh hell, the band might be coming out to play.

"To drink." I stumble out of my day dream laughing. "What would you like to drink?"

His smile becomes even bigger, cocky. "Ya, ya, I'm sure that's what you were asking." He glances down at my name tag. "Sofia."

Oh, Lord, the deep tone of his voice drips with pure sex.

"Well, that's unfair, isn't it?" I tilt my head a little to the right in a flirty way.

"What's that?"

"Well, you know my name, but I don't know yours."

"Ahhh…" He shakes his head back and forth with a laugh. "I guess it is, now isn't it. But, Sofia, when I see a beautiful woman I make it a point to know what her name is."

Bam! There it is! Annnd the band just called it a night! The drummer just died. He's a cocky bastard.

"Okay there, big guy, you're one of those huh?"

"What's that?" he asks with some confusion.

"A womanizer." I raise my brow. "Damn." I point at him, then wink. "You were good 'til you just said that. Now, what can I get you to drink Mr. I-don't-care-what-your-name-is-anymore." Flirty Sofia has all but left The Lair.

"Johnathan."

"I'm sorry?"

"My name, it's Johnathan Reznor."

"What can I get you to drink Mr. Reznor? As you can see, I have a bar full of customers waiting for drinks." I wave my hand in the air.

"I would like a do-over. Rewind back to where I didn't just piss you off."

"Well, Mr. Reznor, you can start by telling me what you would like to drink. The do-over, yeah probably not gonna happen for you."

"Macallan. Three fingers, neat."

"So, a womanizer *and* a man with expensive taste. Hmmm." I turn grabbing a rocks glass, then throw a cocktail napkin down on the bar in front of him placing his glass down then filling it with three fingers of very expensive scotch. "There you go, Mr. Reznor. Enjoy. I hope it keeps you warm tonight." The sauciness in my voice makes him smile as I walk away.

"Fuck me." I hear as I'm walking away smiling to myself.

Good. Cocky bastard.

I go about my business filling drink orders, helping the girls out with the VIP rooms and start straightening the bar area. I notice Giovanni has moved from his post between the bar and the VIP rooms to standing closer to Mr. Sexy. As. Sin. Womanizer. With. The. Delicious. Lips! I give G-man a quick smile even though I'm supposed to pretend he's not here. It's pretty late in the night, though and things are settling down. The crowd has thinned out tremendously. Cory and Jake are starting to clean up, while Sara and I keep filling drink orders.

"Hey, Sofia." I feel someone touch my lower back with the words. When I turn to see who it is, Jake is standing there behind me. He's a good-looking guy. Tall, thin, not too thin, not the muscular kind of man I like, but all in all, his bright blond locks, hazel eyes, and great personality works for him. He started working here a few years after me. We work together a lot and innocently flirt with each other all the time.

"What's up? You need me to do something?" I smile, looking up at him.

"Nahh." He jerks his head to the left. "The guy at the end of the bar is asking for you. I offered to fill his drink for him, but he said he was waiting for the beautiful woman he pissed off. Then pointed at you."

I look down to where Mr. Luscious Lips is sitting. He grins. I look back to Jake rolling my eyes. "Thanks, Jake."

"He bothering you? If he is, I'll take care of him. Or even call the new security guy over to bounce his ass. That guy hasn't taken his eyes off you all night long."

New security guy? Ahh, Giovanni. He thinks Giovanni is new security for the club. I glance at Giovanni. His eyes flicker questioning if I need his help. I shake my head subtly. I look back to Jake, resting my hand on his chest in a reassuring gesture. "Thank you, but no, I'm good. Mr. Three Fingers Macallan over there just needed to be put in his place before."

Jake cracks up. "Oh, he messed with the wrong woman. You're just the woman to do it, too."

I saunter down to Mr. Macallan swaying my hips with a smile on my face. "Well, Mr. Reznor, I see you stuck around my bar. Would you like another drink or just another kick in the ass?"

"Well, beautiful, how about an apology, another drink, and your phone number?" I suck in a breath when I hear him call me beautiful. There's only one man that calls me beautiful. Caelan... shit. I've been so busy I haven't thought about our argument all night. As a matter of fact, he hasn't texted me all night either. He always texts me during my shifts to see how I'm doing.

"I'm sorry, Sofia. I didn't mean to insult you before."

I barely hear his apology. I snap out of my thoughts. "You didn't insult me. A man that drinks expensive scotch and has to make it a point to find out 'every beautiful women's name' is not my thing anyway."

"You know many?" he inquires, slightly taken aback with a disbelieving smirk.

"I know a few," I confess, giving him a wink. Namely my father and brother. My brother being the womanizer. My father just the arrogant scotch drinker.

"Well, I guess those men did me a disservice then. I was just trying to flirt with a beautiful woman."

I smile at him with the cockiest smile I can conjure up. "They didn't do you a disservice, Mr. Reznor. You did that all by your cocky self. Word of advice to you, on your future bed endeavors," I retort leaning forward over the bar resting my chin on my fisted hand. With my other, I pick up his drink swirling the amber color around. Then I get so very close to his damn luscious lips and mesmerizing eyes. "Never ever tell a woman you're flirting with that you make it your job to know the name of every woman you find beautiful. That was cocky. I have enough cocky men in my life." I drink the last of what he had left in his glass staring him directly in his eyes. I set the glass down, turn and grab the bottle of Macallan again and refill his glass with his preferred three fingers. Then turn and stretch my body out purposely putting the bottle back on the upper shelf. Just enough so he would get a good view of my ass and stretched out body. A body he'll never lay a hand on.

"Christ!" I hear coming from Mr. Juicy Lips behind me. I smile to myself walking to the other end of the bar.

Serves you right!

Jake and Cory call last call. There are a few stragglers left, there always are. They're either the ones who don't want to stop drinking or the ones who just don't want to go home to their wives.

Jake comes over and puts his arm around me. "Well, I watched the whole thing. That was pretty damn impressive, gorgeous! If I were him, I would be going home with that vision of you stretching in my spank bank."

I crack up, wrap my arm around him, lowering my head to his chest. "Eww totally could have done without knowing that Jake!"

"Well, just an FYI scotch man is staring us down."

I look from the corner of my eye noticing Jake is in fact, correct. Mr. Luscious Lips is still down at the end of the bar looking our way. "Great! Hasn't he taken enough abuse tonight?" He still has half his drink left.

Well, hell, not an alcoholic I guess. Must have a wife.

I release Jake and saunter down to Mr. Lips again. "Well, Mr. Reznor, I would think the amount of money you're paying for that glass of amber liquid savoring it is a respectable, but being that we're getting ready to close up shop, you shouldn't let expensive scotch like that go to waste," I tease him with a sparkle in my eye as quirk my brows with a smirk.

"Well, on top of a cocky, asshole, bastard, womanizer, I didn't want you to think I was an alcoholic, too," he taunts but with a very serious tone.

"Damn that would have just rounded it all out so nicely wouldn't it?" I laugh a genuine laugh.

"I am sorry about before, Sofia. I ahhh, I noticed you in one of the back rooms, you're a beautiful woman. I was..." He chuckles slightly in a disbelieving chuckle. "I ahh…" He clears his throat. "I actually was nervous to come up here and approach you. And because I was nervous, I came across as a pompous jerk. I'm sorry for that. I'm really not that guy."

I snort out a laugh. "Nervous? Why would you be nervous? You're a very attractive man. I'm sure you have women falling all over you, all the time."

"That's the point. No cockiness, I swear." He smirks raising his hands in surrender. "I really don't have to do much flirting with other women. You, on the other hand, didn't give me a second glance when we noticed each other in the cave. I knew you wouldn't be like most women, and it made me hesitant because... well, because I really want to take you out to dinner. I was pretty sure you would shoot me down when I asked."

Well, holy catfish! I see vulnerability on his face. That sets me back a step.

Wait, is he flippin' messin' with me? I assess him for a minute. *No, I really don't think he is messin' with me. Wife, Sof. Wife. Does he have one? Probably does. Some long-legged blonde goddess he has in hiding somewhere.*

"Are you married?" I blurt at the same time I look down at his ring finger. No band, no indentations, no tan lines.

"No. No, I'm not married." He smiles softly.

So, not married, not an alcoholic, not so much of a cocky bastard either. Dinner? Hmmm... should I even be thinking about this right now with everything that's going on? I guess he can feel my hesitancy.

"Okay, how about you give me your number? We'll talk for a few days. I'll ask you again, and then you can make your decision."

I shake my head back and forth. "How about you give me your number, if I decide I want to go to dinner with you I'll give you a call," I inform him with a saccharine smile.

Not happy with that, but settling for it. He nods his head. "Sounds fair. You have a pen?"

I grab the pen from the bar down by the service station. As I'm walking back to him, he grabs a cocktail napkin. He writes out his name and cell number then hands it to me. He grabs his unfinished scotch and polishes it off before standing and grinning at me. "Hope to hear from you soon, Sofia. It's been a pleasure getting my ass handed to me tonight." He nods.

"It's been a pleasure kicking your ass, Mr. Reznor." I chuckle with pride. He stares at me for a minute with a serene smile on his face and something else I can't figure out.

"You alright to drive?" I flick my hand toward the empty glass when he doesn't look away.

"I have a driver." He pulls his cell out and texts someone. I'm assuming his driver. He looks back up to me, taking a step closer to the bar. "I really do hope I hear from you." I nod slightly. He winks at me, then strides away. I watch him walk to the gates and disappear.

Damn, he has a nice ass. Hate to see him go, but that view is worth it.

Well, holy hot damn! I know I won't call him, but he sure was fun to look at. Hot, sexy, funny, and hello the drummer came out of hiding and started to at least tune up to play. *DAMN!*

I shake it off and start getting ready to leave for the night. Grabbing my purse and saying goodbye to the other bartenders, I look over to Giovanni, who is still standing there watching me. He looks pissed. I'm assuming it's because of my flirting. Well, too bad, I don't care. I just got hit on by a gorgeous man who at first was an asshole, but then turned out to be... sweet. Even though I won't call him, G-man is not going to ruin my high right now.

twenty-two

GIOVANNI HELPS ME INTO THE SUV, closing the door rather hard behind me. I settle myself in while waiting for him to get in the driver's seat. Once in, he turns to me.

"Who's the guy at the bar?" he harshly questions.

Annoyed at the brash interrogation, my eyes widen as I scowl, not saying a word.

"I'm just trying to make sure you're safe, Sofia," he clarifies when I don't answer.

"Well, may I suggest in the future, if you want information from me, you ask me with a different tone to your voice."

He exhales. "I'm sorry."

"That's twice today you've apologized to me for the way you have spoken to me. Not your usual demeanor around me. What's up? Something going on I should know about?"

After a minute and another exhale, he explains, "I take my job very seriously, Sofia. When the person I'm trying to protect is flirting with a customer, the way you were tonight with Mr. Reznor, it kinda puts me on edge."

I'm instantly enraged. How does he know Johnathan's name? "First off, how the fuck do you know his name? Was this a joke? Do you know him? Was this... was this some kind of a game between you and him? A test?"

He points to his ear with a tension-filled finger. "Chip with an extra amplifier in it. Lets me hear what you're saying and what is being said to you. And no, I do not know him that's why I'm asking you who he is."

That infuriates me. "What? You just heard everything he said to me and everything I said to him? And every other customer I talked to tonight? What the fuck?" My hands are flying everywhere. I'm pissed. I feel violated. I had no privacy all night and didn't even know it. I'm so mad I'm trembling. I swallow. *Twice.* Then look out the window to the now clearly seen flashing crisscross lights from Ice's rooftop that you can see because of nightfall. I feel exposed. I feel... vulnerable. I trusted him.

I hear him groan and mutter the words, 'fuck me.' "Sofia, look at me," he commands in a soft voice. I don't. I can't. "Sofia. Look. At. Me."

I still don't look at him. I have chills racing up and down my body. My eyes flood with tears, and I'm uncomfortable being confined in this vehicle with him right now. So, I keep staring out the window at the flashing lights and ignore his order. Wishing I could be them, the flashing lights, because they're... so far, far away. You know when you're a little kid, and you see them in the sky, flashing back and forth? You wonder where they are and how far away they really are. I wish it were me that was that far away right now. "You should have told me," I fume without looking at him. "You should have told me I had no privacy. Do you know what that feels like to someone with my history?" I don't give him a chance to say anything before I explode. "No, you don't! You should have told me!" I yell through gritted teeth. "Now take me home, Giovanni!" I demand. He's silent and the forward motion of the vehicle gives me some relief and the radio he turned on makes me more at ease as he drives me home.

I just want to get into bed. It's been a long day of ups and downs. I'm exhausted. I'm more than exhausted. I can't wait to just fall into bed. Usually, I shower when I get home from work, but tonight I'm just dropping onto my soft, warm, comfortable mattress.

Tomorrow is a new day. Tomorrow will be a better day.

We pull up in front of my house. The front porch light is off. Caelan always leaves it on for me... maybe he hasn't even come home yet. I open the back door of the SUV letting myself out before Giovanni can come around the car to open it for me. I walk right past him and head for the front door. He's pissed I didn't wait for him. Oh, well. I can hear him mumbling under his breath, but I don't care. How am I supposed to have consideration for him when he didn't have any for me? He should have told me he could hear everything I was saying tonight. It's such a terrible feeling. I grab the door handle to the front door, but before I can open it, Giovanni lightly grabs my elbow. I snap my head up to his hand touching my arm in indignation and then to his face. "Take your hand off me right now." I order with a growl.

He releases me immediately. "Damn," he murmurs.

"What do you want, Giovanni?"

"I should have told you. I didn't even give it a thought. I should have taken your past into consideration. If I had, I would have realized you would have felt violated. For that, I am sorry, Sofia."

Anger and exhaustion are steamrolling through my body. "We'll talk tomorrow. Right now, I just want to curl up in my bed. I'm exhausted. I just want my bed," I repeat with dejection.

"Tomorrow," he concedes with a nod. "I'll walk you in. It looks like Caelan's not here, I want to make sure the house is secure before I leave. Remember, Carmine's relieving me. He should be here in a few minutes." I nod back, confirming that I heard what he said. "I'll be back tomorrow to take you to work." I nod again, opening the front door to a scene that scares the shit out of me at first, then just devastates me to the very core of my soul. Just like a movie it happens in slow motion. Never in a million years did I think I could get hurt this badly by someone I love and trust.

I TURN THE door handle, pushing the front door open. I see something scattered all over the hardwood floor by the wall next to the door. I stop. Taking a hesitant step forward, I realize the pieces on the floor are a cell phone, Caelan's cell phone. It's smashed to pieces. I gasp, holding my hand on my heart.

Someone hurt him.

"Oh, My God! No!" I stammer. Giovanni pushes my trembling body to the side, hearing the desperation in my voice. He shoves me behind him when he sees the cell phone and pulls his gun.

I then notice *him. Them...* him and *her.* Caelan and... whoever she is, on the couch. A direct view of the back of his head and his bare muscular shoulders and back, and the front view of a pretty blonde with the worst fake tits I've ever seen, bouncing in his face. With her head thrown back, she rides him like her life depends on it. When I see his hands on her small hips, I gasp even louder, throwing my hand over my mouth as my reality starts really sinking in, becoming my nightmare. Giovanni grabs me harder, pulling me behind him to block my view while he holsters his gun. I jerk away, refusing to budge. My lungs expand from the air I sucked in until the point my ribs expand and burn. It feels like cement has found its way down through my veins and into my bone marrow, slowly seeping into my soul, suffocating me. I can't move. My throat feels like a grapefruit has been lodged in it, being squeezed causing the burn. My eyes sting like someone's poured gasoline in them, then set fire. My nostrils burn from the forbidden unshed tears I'm trying so desperately to hold back. Between the loud music infiltrating the space, the blonde's loud groans and screams and Caelan's own noises they don't even know we're standing in the same room watching this unfold. Giovanni's strong, deep, angry voice vibrates through my body as he roars at Caelan.

"Yes! Yes! Baby, fuck me!" The blonde whines in a high-pitched, breathy voice.

I grab my ears like a two-year-old hoping to block the desperate, pleading, sexual screams coming from her.

"You're so good, baby! Yeah! Oh, God! *YES!* More, baby!"

"*Caelan!*" Giovanni thunders stepping towards him.

My eyes just can't believe what is unfolding in front of me. The realization that my best friend, the closest person to me, the person I trusted with my life, the same person I have loved since I was a young girl, just purposely tried to hurt me.

Yes, Caelan and I have both been with other people, but we've never blatantly put it in each other's faces, nor have we *ever* disrespected each other like this. Yes, I have heard them from time to time through the walls of this house, but he always brings them to his room, and the door is always closed. This act was to hurt me because he thinks Giovanni and I slept together. He knows what time I come home from work, he's usually waiting up for me. He knew all too well what time I would be here. This was planned. *He* planned this. Well, his plan worked. Mission accomplished... he just hurt me. No, who I am kidding...

He. Just. Destroyed. Me.

The blonde's eyes snap open hearing Giovanni's thunderous voice. Caelan immediately whips his head around.

Giovanni yells again in a deep, robust, infuriated voice. "*Take. That. Fucking. Shit. Upstairs!*"

I jerk my arm away from Giovanni. He hastily jerks his head toward me, but I can't take my eyes off Caelan.

"Are you okay?" he asks tenderly.

I can't answer him. My head is like a bullwhip reacting to the movement to my left. Caelan's throwing the naked blonde off of him. Jumping up off the couch he turns towards me haphazardly pulling his pants up. Time stands still. The second hand's stuck in this very moment with us as we stand there staring at one another. He cautiously watches me with remorse as disdain drips from my eyes. He's totally exposed to me. I don't think he even realizes it. I take the deepest breath I can when more tears pool in my eyes. Then I see it... regret. The emotion floods his facial features. His shoulders drop. He knows he fucked up. I slightly shake my head.

Yes, C. Yes, you did fuck up. Real bad.

"Hey, baby." The blonde purrs, rubbing herself up against his arm. "They wanna join in? It will be fun. Hey, you guys you wanna joins us?" She giggles.

"Shut the fuck up!" Caelan harshly growls at her, but his sorrowful eyes never leave mine.

She's so sexually ramped up, she doesn't even realize the magnitude of the situation.

"Come on, baby," she whines. "He's damn fine, and she's real cute. I wanna get my hand on her."

I snort a disgusted breath, rolling my eyes.

He breaks our eye contact. "*SHUT THE FUCK UP! GET YOUR SHIT! GET OUT!*" He shoves her hands off him as I turn and walk over to shut off the music. When I turn back, Giovanni is just a few steps behind me. Caelan then takes a few steps towards me.

"Sofia," he pleads with his hands out, realization now hitting him that his pants are wide open, hanging low, exposing his neatly groomed nest of hair and base of his very impressive dick.

"Well, at least you were smart enough to wear a condom," I hiss, shrugging my shoulders heedlessly. He glances down to where my eyes are settled and starts to tuck himself into his jeans better. He zips up his pants, but doesn't button them. His broad, naked chest and abs are glistening with sweat, and his pants are now hanging low on his narrow waist. The distinctive V disappearing under his old, worn, tattered jeans holds my attention. I can't help it, even in a situation like this, to admire his beautiful body, but my gazing is interrupted by his pleading.

"Sofia. Sofia, please let me explain. Will you please let me explain?"

My hot, pooling tears start to fall at the same time that my lip and chin start to tremble. I throw my hand up, barely able to talk. "D-don't you f-fucking dare take one more step towards me. There's nothing to explain," I say with broken words. I feel Giovanni put his hand on my back to comfort me. Slowly, I turn my head towards him and try to hide the pain I'm feeling. The hard, outer shell I'm trying so desperately to hold onto is starting to crack. The dam is getting ready to rupture and flood with turbulent rushing waters. "Plea-," I clear my throat and lift my quivering chin. "Please w-wait here. I... I'm going to go upstairs, p- pack some things. Will you wait for me? G-give me a ride? I can- can't stay here tonight."

"Oh, Jesus Christ! Sofia, please don't go," he begs, stepping towards me as he runs his hands through his disheveled hair.

I take a step back, not wanting to be too close to him. Giovanni protectively steps in front of me.

"Oh, what the fuck? You think I'm going to hurt her?" C yells throwing his arms out to the side. "Seriously? I would never fucking hurt her. She's my life," he declares, gripping at his dirty blond locks.

"Looks like you already did that," Giovanni responds before turning towards me. "Sweetheart, go upstairs, get your stuff together. I'll wait right here for you."

"Baby, is that your wife?" I hear the blonde grumble as I'm walking up the stairs.

I hear Giovanni growl. "*OUT! CAELAN, NOW!*" I look back to see Giovanni pointing at the chick telling Caelan to get bad-fake-tits out.

"*GET THE FUCK OUT! NOW! RIGHT FUCKING NOW!*" Caelan bellows at bad fake tits. "*SOFIA!*" he cries yelling up the stairs to me. "*DON'T LEAVE!*"

Yeah, fat chance I'm staying here. No way. I can't. I can't believe my best friend, the boy I grew up with, the man I love and have always trusted, just purposely tried to hurt me. No, he didn't just try, *he succeeded.* I sit down on the edge of my bed, thinking about that for a minute. I just said… the man I love. The man I love? I say again letting the words roll around in my head.

Sofia, you love him, and you have for a long time. That's why this hurts so much. You love him. You have loved him since you were fourteen years old. Most likely even before that. You fell in love with him that summer at the cabin. Right there, sitting by the lake. I remember every second of it. You're such a fool.

"That was a long, long time ago," I mumble to myself. "It's a shame it takes a situation like this to admit your feelings to yourself." *Damn!* I have loved him for so long. It may have started at fourteen as puppy love, but over the years it has grown into full-blown being *in love* with this beautiful man. I have denied my feelings for him for so long, in fear I'd lose him as a friend.

You lost him anyway, Sofia.

Shouting I can't understand filters up the stairs.

"You're wrong!" I hear Giovanni holler as I get closer to the door. "You're so fucking dead wrong!"

It makes me get my ass in gear packing my things. I don't want the two of them getting into a fight. I walk to the top of the stairs. Giovanni is standing guard at the bottom of the steps refusing to let Caelan up. He's pacing back and forth like a wild, caged animal. His head snaps to me when he hears the creak of the top step. He turns charging for the steps, but Giovanni steps up forcefully putting his hands on his chest.

"Caelan, don't do this. Give it a few days. Talk tomorrow, but not now, dude. You don't want to do this now."

"The fuck I don't! I have to explain to her!" he screams pointing up at me. "I can't let her leave!" he yells. "Sofia, talk to me. Please, let me explain." His chest is rapidly rising and falling, making his broad shoulders look even broader.

"There's nothing to explain, Caelan," I say calmly. Taking each step down getting closer and closer to him. "You chose her," I say pointing at the door because, well, fake tits is now nowhere around, so I'm assuming she got the hint and finally left. I point to myself. "I chose you the other night. In a moment, I was so… vulnerable. I needed you. I needed your love. I wanted you to hold me. I wanted to be with you. I needed your touch. You saw me… you saw me, Caelan. No one has ever seen me like that," I murmur. Then anger hits me. "*I Needed You!*" I grind out through gritted teeth. My chin starts to quiver, and my bottom lip, tremble. "You turned me down. I was open, raw and exposed. I let you see me. I chose you and you made your choice, Caelan!" I hiss. "It just wasn't me," I say flapping my hand towards the couch. "Clearly, it wasn't me. I wasn't good enough for you," I sob. "So, there's nothing for us to talk about." I reach the bottom of the steps right behind where Giovanni is standing. He steps to the side blocking Caelan and flanking my side as we head for the door.

"Beautiful, please don't go! Please stay! Please stay and talk to me."

"*Don't!*" I scream at him with a broken breath, whipping my body around, taking two steps towards him, and pointing. "Don't you dare call me that! You don't have the right to call me that! You lost that privilege the moment you decided to purposely set out to hurt me!"

He stands there, stock still. Hands hanging at his sides in defeat. I think he's in shock because I just screamed at him.

"I fucking love you," he whispers with desperation.

"I love you with everything I have inside me!" he reaffirms louder.

"You're mine!" he thunders.

"You've always been mine!" he booms.

"No one else's!" he growls.

"I've loved you since I was sixteen years old, Sofia," he confesses. "Please, I'm sorry. Please, please don't leave. Please stay and talk to me," he begs, running his fingers through his hair with frustration.

I close my eyes because the pain is becoming too much for me. "You don't love me." I whimper opening my eyes, to look him dead in his. "When you love someone, you don't try to hurt them, Caelan," I state, sobbing. "I would never hurt you purposely. You did this because you thought we slept together," I remind him, flipping my finger back and forth between Giovanni and me. "Do you know how crazy that is?" I look up at Giovanni, who is just standing there in-between the two of us with a somber look on his face. I feel sorry for him actually, to be stuck between the two of us.

"*DON'T TELL ME I DON'T LOVE YOU! MY BACK IS A FUCKING SHRINE TO YOU!*" he roars thrusting his thumb over his shoulder.

What the hell is he talking about? I have to get out of here.

"Giovanni, can we please..."

"Yeah." He puts his hand on my lower back as I turn away from Caelan.

"Sofia, please. Please, baby," he begs with a ragged plea with even more anguish owning his voice.

I reach for the knob and turn back to look at him. He's standing there, looking utterly lost with tears in his eyes and his hands cupped on the back of his neck. "I never thought in a million years it would be you." He tilts his head up slightly, confusion clearly written on his face. So, I say it again. "I never, in a million years thought it would be you, Caelan O'Reily, who would hurt me. Not you, Caelan. Not you." Turning I dropped my head and walk out with Giovanni right behind me.

WHEN WE HIT THE sidewalk, I look up to see Carmine getting out of his black SUV. I twist around quickly looking at Giovanni. "Please no. Please, I beg you. Tell him anything, I don't care, but please don't tell him what just happened. He'll tell my father. I can't deal with him, too. Can you please just drive me somewhere. I'll be okay for the night. Please, G. Please!"

He stares at me for a second. "Hey, Carmine. What are you doing here? I shot you a text earlier saying I didn't need you to come out tonight."

A look crosses my Uncle's face that unsettles me. "Why? I didn't get a text from you," he accuses.

"I don't know man, sent it about two hours ago," Giovanni nonchalantly tells him.

Carmine stares at him for a few seconds accessing the words coming from his colleague. Then looks to me, noticing my bag. "You goin' somewhere?"

"I'm dropping her off at a friend's house. We just stopped by the house so she could grab some stuff. I'm gonna crash on the couch where she's staying. I'll get some sleep there. She'll be safe."

I drop my head because Carmine's eyes have landed on me again. He will not stop examining me while Giovanni is talking to him. I'm unsure why, but it's kinda creeping me out. I just feel so raw right now. Maybe he can tell I've been crying. That's all. I'm sure he can tell I was crying. I know it's dark out here, but I'm certain he knows something's wrong. I have to pretend everything's fine. I walk up to him giving him a hug and a kiss. "Hey, Unc. Sorry you came all the way out here."

"You okay, honey?"

I take a step back. "Yeah, thanks. I'm just exhausted. It's been a long week. Plus, you know how hard it is to work at Ice. I'm regretting not taking tonight off."

"Maybe you should take off the next few days. Get some rest," he says smiling at me.

"Yeah, you're probably right, but you know I won't. I'm too stubborn. Plus, I need the money," I lie, faking a smile, then kiss him on the cheek before taking a step back.

"Honey, if you need money you know all you have to do is ask."

"No, it's alright. I would never ask, you know that," I remind him taking a step towards the open back door Giovanni is holding for me. After a minute he agrees, telling us to keep safe. He gives Giovanni a head nod, then gets back into his vehicle.

We pull out of the parking spot and into traffic. Once we're on the road a minute, he looks back at me through the rearview mirror.

"I'm so sorry. I just didn't want him to know. If he figured it out or started asking questions... my father would have been hunting me down first thing in the morning. I just can't handle that right now. I'm barely hanging on by a thread," I whisper. "I'm sorry."

"It's okay," he consoles me. We stop at the traffic light not too far from my house. The light feels like it takes forever to change. I want to get as far away from here as possible. He's still looking at me through the rearview mirror when he asks where I want to go.

"I haven't thought that far." I see his frown. Then slight confusion crosses his facial features. I can't call my sister because she still lives with my parents. "Let me call, Jess. Give me a second." I called her three times, but it keeps going straight to voicemail. I mean, it is three thirty in the morning. "She's not answering. I'll call Sage." I sigh deeply wiping fresh tears from my cheeks. "I don't know how I am going to get through this. Sage is not going to leave me alone," I murmur taking a deep breath and start dialing the number of my best friend who is going to be relentless with questions.

"Hang up, Sofia. You can stay with me tonight."

My eyes snap to his. "Are you sure? You just looked a little mad when I said I didn't know where to go. I don't want to put you out. You can just bring to me to a hotel." I try to pacify looking up at him from my cell phone. I didn't even notice he moved, but he's now twisted in the driver seat looking out the back window. The squinting of his eyes tells me he's watching something, but before I can turn to see what he's observing his eyes flicker to me.

"Yeah. It's not a problem," he says like it's an afterthought.

"You sure? I don't-"

"I'm positive. You think I would subject you to Sage for the night?" he uncharacteristically snorts with a laugh.

"Thank you."

The light finally changes, and we take off. We drive in silence for a bit 'til we pull up in front of a stunning, contemporary building. I'm not quite sure what's going on because this is an expensive building to live in, especially being in the middle of the city. He pulls the Cadillac SUV up to the valet. He gets out, walks around and opens my door. He holds his hand out to me. "Come on, before Freddy here has a heart attack." I look at him with confusion. "I've never brought a female to this place with me." I look at him, then to... I guess it's Freddy, and smile.

Freddy nods with a return smile and what I think is recognition in his eyes. Quickly he shuts the back door and turns unsure eyes on Giovanni. "Have a nice night, Mr. Moretti."

"You too, Freddy. I'm sleeping in tomorrow, have the truck waiting by eleven. If anything changes, I'll shoot you a text."

"You got it, sir."

I'm quiet while Giovanni's hand on my lower back guides me inside. With my bag over his shoulder, he greets the doorman with a nod as we walk to the back of the building to a private elevator. He slides a card into the slot opening the elevator doors. With a soft nudge, he guides me inside. When we get to the top, the elevator door swooshes open right into an enormous, spectacular living room. I turn to look at him with questioning eyes.

"You live in the penthouse?"

"I do."

"How long have you lived here?"

"Few years."

"Wow," I babble, "my father must pay really well. This place is stunning."

"You could say that." He smirks.

I walk over to the floor to ceiling windows. "Wow, this view is breath taking. I can guess why you bought this place."

"It is. But it's not why I purchased the place. It's safe here. The building is private, secure, and the employees are loyal and respectful of the tenants' privacy."

I turn to look at him. "Sorry, I'm intruding on your space."

"Sofia, if I didn't want you here, you wouldn't be here. You'll be safe here. No one will be able to find you here unless you want to be found. You and I will both be able to get a good night's sleep without worrying about your safety." I nod slightly. "Come on. I'll show you where you can get some sleep." I follow him to a gorgeous room. I'm kinda stunned at how beautiful his home is. He explains the room has room darkening curtains, then shows me the en-suite bathroom. Just before walking out of the room, he tells me the kitchen is fully stocked if I need a drink, or get hungry. "Don't leave the apartment without me," he orders. I nod in compliance. We say good night to each other, and as I turn to sit on the bed, he calls my name.

"Yea?"

"I'm really sorry you had to go through that tonight."

Instantly my eyes fill with tears. "Yea, me too," I whisper.

He gets a somber, but also angry look on his face. He places both his hands on my biceps looking into my eyes. "If anyone deserves happiness it's you, sweetheart. Sometimes people make stupid choices out of anger. Caelan knows he fucked up, trust me. I'm only a couple years older than him. Sometimes us men are real stupid when it comes to women. I'm not saying you should forgive him, but trust me, he knows he fucked up bad. I know if I were him right now I would hate myself for hurting you that much." I drop my head shaking it. I can't talk at the moment. He kisses the top of my head. "Good night, sweetheart. Try and get some sleep. If you need me, I'm two doors down on the left."

When the door closes behind him, I sigh deeply. I desperately long for the bed to lie my throbbing head on. I walk over to the curtains pulling them closed. I want darkness. I want to shut the world out. I drop all my stuff to the floor. Stripping off my clothes while grabbing and throwing on a white ribbed tank top. Then climb into the bed I swear was made in heaven. I lie there in the pitch black while tears fill my eyes. My stomach twists with the memories of what I saw tonight. I wish I could just stay in this dark room for weeks.

My cell phone chimes with a text message. I roll over searching for the glow of the phone's screen. Grabbing it I see a text from C. I hesitate for a minute because I'm not sure I want to see what he has to say. But, my heart won the fight, and my finger swipes the screen to open the app. I hesitate again, laying the phone on my stomach, not sure I want to read it but, again, my hesitation is short lived. I want to read what he wrote, of course I do. There's no way I cannot not read it. The message pops up, and it kills me.

C: The National~About Today. (4:15 am) I'm sorry. I'm so, so sorry, beautiful. You'll never know how sorry I am. What I did was stupidly done out of jealous anger. Will you please just talk to me?

His words become blurry as tears flood my eyes again. I click on the link to play the song he sent me. I lay my phone down on my pillow by my head. I listen to the heartfelt, sad words of the song for a few minutes. The singer's raw words fill my ears and my soul. He wants to know how close he is to losing me? That's what the song is asking. That is what he is asking me. I curl myself up into a ball. My body racked with sobs. I feel so alone. I'm afraid it's too late and he's already lost me. Trust... trust is a huge thing for me, in the life that I've been dealt. He broke that trust. The song ends. I wipe the tears from my eyes, hitting play again. I have no right to be mad at him for sleeping with someone, but because he slept with someone else to purposely hurt me after he turned me down… yeah, that's what hurts the most, and that's what makes me mad. And honestly who am I kidding, the vision of him nailing bad-fake-tits kills me. It's one thing when it's not put in your face, but when you see it with your own eyes… ya, that hurts. He's the only person in this world that could hurt me this badly.

That's because you're in love with him, Sofia.

I quickly text him back letting him know exactly how I feel at the moment with a pretty powerful song. One letting him know he has ripped my heart out. Nothing more needs to be said.

Me: Eminem (feat. Sia)~ Beautiful Pain

Then I cry myself into a restless sleep…

twenty-three

I WAKE WITH A RACING HEART. The room is pitch black. I have no idea what time it is, so I fumble for my phone. It's dead. I left it on repeat last night while I cried myself to sleep. I jump out of bed, stumbling, feeling my way on the walls to what I hope is the bathroom. Reaching for where I remember the light switch being, the bathroom illuminates. I run my hands over my face in a desperate attempt to wake myself up more. I walk back to the bed and search for my phone. When I finally find it, I plug it in and wait for life to come to the screen. When the screen illuminates, I see that I've only been asleep for two hours.

I'm dying of thirst, so I grab the soft white throw blanket sitting on the chair, and wrap it around myself. I open the bedroom door as slowly as I can, trying to make the least bit of noise as possible. Just because I can't sleep doesn't mean Giovanni should be awake too. I head towards the kitchen in the dark. I grab a bottle of water out of the refrigerator and start to head back to the room when the wall to ceiling windows draw me in. It's such a beautiful view. I feel so far away from everything and everyone up here. I wrap the blanket around me tighter. Then lean against the window.

Thoughts of yesterday filter through my head. The blonde, Caelan, the way she screamed for him, the way his pants hung open, the look on his face when it finally hit him that he hurt me, him begging me to stay, him... telling me that he... loves me.

He told me he loves me.

My knees become weak. I slowly slide down the window to the floor. My head resting on the cold window feels good. Looking down upon the city that never sleeps, the city that I love; the one I love living in, but sometimes I just want to go away, far, far away. From everyone and everything, I drift off thinking in a sleepy state.

I feel myself levitating in the air in a dreamy-like state. When I start to open my eyes, I hear a soft masculine voice shushing against my ear telling me to close my eyes and sleep. I feel the warmth of safety and protection wrapped around me. When I wake again, I'm in a soft bed. Realizing I'm in the room Giovanni gave me to sleep in. Searching for my phone once again to check the time, I notice I have multiple missed calls and forty-two missed text messages. I can't even begin to process that. I glance at the time, ten-thirty. Wow. Dropping my phone in my lap, I sit up to get my bearings. I'm supposed to be at HD in ninety minutes. "Yeah, that's not happening today," I murmur.

That's why I have two excellent employees. I pick up my phone.

Me: Hey, not coming in today. Only call me if the place is burning down.

Jess: OMG! Honey call me! What's going on? Where are you? Are you okay?

Two seconds later my phone is vibrating in my hand. Jess... damn. I inhale deeply preparing myself for the million questions I'm going to endure right now. "Jess?" I answer.

"OMG! Honey, are you okay? Please, tell me you're okay? Where are you? What happened last night?"

"Jess, please. One question at a time. I'm okay."

Not at all.

"No, you're not okay! My best friend doesn't call me three times in a row at three-thirty in the morning and then tell me she's okay. Then I can't get in touch with you when I try to call you back. Then Caelan called me a half hour after you called. Demanding I put you on the phone. When I asked what happened, he screamed at me to put you on the phone. He was beside himself, Sofia. I told him you weren't with me. I guess he didn't believe me because my neighbor called me thirty minutes after that saying someone was banging on my apartment door. She described Caelan to a tee. Then Luke's phone started blowing up and..." She gets real quiet.

"Jess?"

"Yea?"

"I already know. No need to hide it."

"How?"

"Surveillance tape from the club. The back room."

"Shit."

"Jess, I'm happy for you. Your secret's safe with me, honey."

"We'll talk later about that. Right now, though... tell me what the hell happened?"

"Is Luke with you?"

"No, shower."

"Please don't tell him anything I'm about to say to you."

"Babe, I won't say a word. Scouts honor and if you were in front of me, I would pinky swear you."

I chuckle because I can picture her with her perfectly French manicured pinky up in the air. "He broke my heart, Jess." I sniffle." I walked in on some chic riding him on the couch in our living room. Jess... he did it on purpose. He wanted me to see them together, to hurt me."

"That son of a bitch! Honey, I am so sorry. He called Luke yesterday afternoon freaking out about you being with someone else. I asked Luke what was going on and he refused to tell me."

"Jess..."

"Yea, honey."

"He told me he loved me." I snort-sniffle. She gasps. "He told me he loved me after he realized how bad he hurt me. I was walking out the front door, and he screamed it at the top of his lungs that he loved me."

"Oh, honey... Where are you?"

"I'm safe. I just want some peace and quiet. I'm going to take off the next few days if you can handle the shop. We have some big orders coming in so..."

"Sage and I will be fine. You take care of yourself. I'm here for you. Call me, text me, anything you need from me, you let me know. I'll be right there. Don't worry about HD."

"I know, thank you. Jess?"

"Yea honey?"

"She had the worst fake tits I have ever seen. She should really sue her doctor."

She busts out laughing. "He's such an asshole!"

"I love you." I chuckle because really, only your bestie can see the humor in that.

"Love you too, sweetie. I'll call you later. Oh, and Nikki's looking for you too, and A. He's freaking out. Call him."

Awesome.

I SHOWER, GET dressed, then wander out into the living room. I smell food coming from the kitchen. When I turn the corner, I see a half-naked man hovering over the stove, flipping some pancakes. He's dressed in a pair of pajama bottoms and a black tank top. Half naked? No, but I have never seen Giovanni like this, so at the moment I am desperately trying not to stare, but it's kinda hard not to because for as big as he is... he's all cut up and looking... Well ya...

"Good morning, Sofia."

"How did you know I was behind you?"

"It's my job, sweetheart," he says turning around to look at me.

"Did you pick me up last night and carry me to bed?"

"Must have been an angel knowing you needed to get a good night's sleep, in a bed." He winks.

"Couldn't sleep. Came out to get a bottle of water. The view pulled me over. It's so peaceful up here. I watched as the city kept moving below while I hid from it all way up here in what felt like another world. I can see why you live here." I give him a small unsure smile. "What are you making over there?"

"Pancakes and egg whites. You good with that?"

"Sounds delicious. I'm not that hungry, though."

"You gotta eat, Sofia," he says turning towards me again. He places a plate down in from of me with a glass of orange juice. "Coffee?"

"Please."

While he's grabbing a mug, I look around his kitchen, thinking to myself, there is no way he is this domesticated. "So, tell me G-man, do you have a house keeper?"

He smirks. "Why do you ask that? I can't be domesticated?"

"Well, I mean your kitchen is fully stocked. Your fridge looks like it came straight out of a magazine ad it's so well organized, and the decorating is definitely not the typical bachelor's touch. No offense."

"None taken." He grins then hesitates for a few seconds. I'm assuming he's contemplating how much he wants to tell me.

"That's alright, you don't have to say anything. I'm sorry for intruding."

"My sister. She stocks this place for me. When I first moved in, she came and decorated for me too."

"That's nice. You two close?"

"We are. Now eat up, we gotta get you to work on time."

I guess that means the conversation's over. "About that. I, uhhh, called in sick." I laugh. "I called Jess this morning, told her that I wouldn't be in for a couple of days. I'm going to work tomorrow night at Ice because it's too late to get coverage, but I'm going to take the rest of the weekend off-if I can get coverage."

He nods his head. "What's the plan for today then?"

"I wanna go see my momma. I need to spend some time with her today." His brow furrows, and his eyes flickering back and forth over mine. I look away.

"Sounds like a plan. I needed to check in with your father sometime today too, so this works out good."

The drive over is quiet. Duran Duran's *Come Undone* is playing over the radio. I hum to the words. I can't wait to see my mom. Nothing like having your mom's arms wrapped around you. Especially when you need it, and right now, I truly need it. I need to thank Giovanni for letting me stay last night. Not sure where I'm going to sleep tonight, but I'm not ready to see Caelan just yet, so it won't be at his place.

"G-man? I just wanna say thank you for letting me stay with you last night. I know that probably wasn't easy for you. Especially since you have never brought anyone up to the ivory towers." I smile. "It means a lot that you let me into your space. I just wanted you to know I appreciate it." He gives a quick head nod but doesn't say anything.

We pull up in front of the fortress of a home I grew up in. Massive iron gates and stone fencing, along with an abundant amount of foliage for security greeting us at the beginning of the long driveway. Giovanni pulls forward punching in the security code for the gates to open. He pulls down the expansive paver driveway parking in front of the main doors. As he opens the back door to the SUV, my mom opens the front door with a huge smile on her face looking elegant and as beautiful as ever.

I love that woman.

She is a pillar of strength. I need her strength right now. We look and act so much alike that everyone says we look and act more like twin sisters than mother-daughter. I run into her wide open, loving arms. "Hey momma," I squeal. "I'm so happy to see you," I say wrapping my arms tightly around her. My father hears the commotion and comes out of his office to see what's going on while Giovanni is standing behind me waiting to enter the house.

My mother embraces me tightly. Then her motherly instinct must kick in. She pulls away slightly to look into my eyes. I give her a slight head shake, telling her now is not the time.

"I'm so happy you took the day off, Fia," she cheerfully calls me by my childhood nickname. "I haven't seen you in... what, two weeks?"

"I know, I'm sorry. I've been so busy." I hug her again.

My father is standing behind her. A smile crosses his handsome face. "Hey, angel face."

"Hey," I mutter back. My mom must notice the strain between us because she quickly hurries me into the house.

"Come on, honey. You want some tea? Let's go to the kitchen, leave these guys to their business. We'll grab some tea and do some well-needed catching up."

twenty-four

"So, Fia, what's going on honey? Tell me why Giovanni is your bodyguard right now and why you look like you lost your best friend?"

I love my momma. She takes no shit, and she cuts right to the point, and her intuition, is usually spot on. Even though she doesn't know what's going on most of the time with my father's business, she still knows what's going on with my father's business. She chooses to turn a blind eye. If she asked my father, he'd tell her, but if she doesn't, he won't say a word because he wants her to live a 'worry free life.' It's kinda funny because my father might run the outside world, but in this house, momma runs everything including my father!

"Ohhh, Mom. Where do I even start?"

"Take a deep breath and start from the beginning, honey."

I take a huge breath and begin, starting with last Thursday night. Only touching on the meltdown I had Monday over the video because I don't want her to know the full details of what happened to me the night I was abducted. Maybe another day, but not today... No, not today. Then, finally I tell her the full details of last night.

"I knew something was going on with you. Your father came home like a bear with a branch up his ass Friday night. I figured I would wait a few days before asking him. He sat most of the evening in his study with his scotch. Although," she says clenching her jaw, "not telling me about my child who's lying in a hospital bed... well, now that I'm going to have to address and make sure he knows it's unacceptable."

Ahh, scotch. Makes me think of Mr. Macallan-Mr. Luscious Lips. I smile. He was the only thing this past week that has made me smile. Well, wait no, he pissed me off first, then made me smile.

"What's that smile for, Fia?"

"You reminded me of someone when you brought up dad's scotch drinking."

"You met someone?"

"Kinda. I don't know. At the bar, he's an incredibly attractive man. He asked me out to dinner, but with everything that's going on, I don't think it's the smartest thing to do right now. Plus, I have Giovanni on my tail."

"Well, Fia he's not so bad to have on your tail. I mean he is sexy as sin. Plus, he's only a couple years older than you. On top of that, what is sexier than having an affair with your bodyguard to work those kinks out."

"MOM!"

"What?" She cracks up laughing "Hell, Fia you act like I'm so old. Honey, you do remember I had your brother at twenty years old, right? And that I'm still in my forties?

Your father and I have a great se-"

"MOM!" I cut her off as she hands me another cup of tea. "I do not want to know my mother has a better sex life than I do!"

"Just make sure you wrap up, Fia. No babies until you're ready."

"MOM!" That makes us both laugh our asses off. "I love you, mom. I don't know what I would do without you," I sincerely tell her.

"Now tell me, Fia, are you going to go to dinner with Mr. Scotch man?"

"No. Honestly mom, I don't know. I thought about it before all this happened with C, but now after everything that happened last night..." I pause. "Mom, C told me he loved me."

She beams with a flawless smile. "Honey, that boy has always been in love with you. The question is, do you love him? And, if you do, are you willing to forgive him for what he did?"

My phone buzzes. *Caelan* flashes across my screen.

"Speaking of the asshole."

"MOM! He's not an asshole!" I feign scowling at her. "Okay, maybe he's an asshole, but still!"

"Well, are you going to answer or do you want your mother to answer for you?"

"No! And No!" I say with a colossal smile on my face because she just cracks me up. "He's repeatedly called me since I left last night. I haven't answered his calls or his texts either."

"Good girl! Make him think."

"For how long? How long do I not answer him?"

"That depends on if you can stand hearing his voice on the phone. If you think you can hear him out without hanging up on him at least five times, then pick it up, but the twenty-four-hour rule works for me," she says cracking a smirk.

"Mom, please don't say anything to Daddy. He always gives C a hard time to begin with. I don't need him getting involved in this too. With everything that's happened over the last week, I feel like I am barely hanging on."

"Your secrets are safe with me, Fia baby." She reaches across the kitchen island to grab my hand. "Your secrets have always been safe with me, baby. I love you. I hate to see you hurting like this, but life kicks us in the teeth at times. You, Sofia Rose Heart, are born to Camilla Rose and Robert Heart." She points at me. "You're a strong woman. You can, and you will, get through anything. Remember that. Now tell me about Mr. Scotch man."

"What secrets are you keeping, my sexy wife?" my father questions scowling as he walked into the kitchen with Giovanni right behind him and a frown on his face.

"Ahhhh, Robert," she says sighing heavily. "You and I need to have a conversation, love."

"Shit. What did I do now?" he mumbles as he walks around the kitchen island, planting a kiss on my mother's cheek. "I have some business to take care of, sweetheart. Can we talk about this later?"

"Oh, honey we will be taking later." She forces a smile.

I glance over to Giovanni standing there like a statue. I'm smiling at the dynamic between my mother and father. He tries not to crack a smile, but I see the corners of his mouth lift. My father knows he's in trouble. And so does everyone else in this room. As powerful as my father is, when it comes to my momma he's a weak man. My mother rules!

"Heyyy, what's this, party time in the Heart kitchen?"

"Shit!" I mumble hearing his voice because I know I am going to get an earful. I turn and see Carmine and Antonio walk into the kitchen.

"Hey, sis," he greets as he bends to give me a kiss on the cheek. "How you doing?" he whispers into my ear as he pulls away, studying my eyes.

Balls! Is he asking me how I'm doing because the last time I saw him, I had a major meltdown or because he knows what happened last night?

"Your phone broken? I tried calling you a couple times this morning," he sarcastically asked as he rounds the island to give my mother a hug and a kiss.

"No. I ahh..." I stumble. "my phone was dead. Forgot to plug it in last night."

"Sofia," Uncle Carmine chimes in, "you have to remember to charge your phone. Especially with what happened last week. You should have plugged it in when you got to your friend's house last night."

Seriously?

I implore looking at my mom for some help. She picks right up on it.

"Robert, don't you have business to talk to Carmine about?" My father looks at my mother confused. She smiles sweetly. "Sweetheart, remember, you and I have to have a talk. The sooner, the better. Go take care of your business so that I can take care of mine."

"Oh fuck dad. What did you do now?"

"Antonio Robert Heart! Mouth! Watch it!" My mother scolds him.

"Sorry, mom," he apologizes putting his arms around her with a cheesy grin on his face. Then looks at me with confusion. "Friend's house? I thought you had work last night?" he leans down to whisper in my ear, but it was still loud enough Giovanni overheard it. He shoots Giovanni an inquiring look. "Sofia, can I talk to you in private for a minute?"

Damn.

"Yea sure," I agree, sliding off the stool, following him out the French doors to the stone patio veranda.

I look around taking in the quiet, peaceful serenity back here. The in-ground pool is an amazing piece of art. It looks more like a lake that is surrounded by lush foliage and man-made rocks. The pool house is wrapped strategically into the design, making it look like it was carved out of a mountain of rocks. The size of it is that of a typical family home. In the rock design around the pool, there are five different spots to dive off into the pool, as well as two slides. With the lush well-manicured foliage and the cabanas, it feels like you're in a tropical resort. I spent a lot of time out here growing up. Caelan and I spent a lot of time out here. My first kiss was with him in the pool house. Best day of my life.

Sof, stop reminiscing. That might have been the best day of your life, but last night was the worst, all held in the palms of one man.

I turn, giving Antonio my full attention. I watch him close the patio door softly, then turns on me abruptly with his hands out to his sides. His piercing blue eyes are simmering with anger, making them strikingly bluer. His jet-black hair only makes them more pronounced. His navy-blue V-neck t-shirt and black jeans only accentuate the power behind him. If I didn't know him at this very moment, he would intimidate the crap out of me.

"What the fuck is going on?" he bellows. "C called me first thing this morning looking for you. He was freaking the fuck out! I asked him what was wrong. He told me it was none of my business, that it was between you and him. You would think that my best friend would tell me, but no he wouldn't, so that only means one thing-that it's real fuckin' bad, Sof! Then Nikki called me looking for you because C called her flipping out looking for you. All of us have been calling you all morning, Sofia! And you're not answering your damn phone! What the fuck, Sof? The only reason I knew you were okay was because I knew Giovanni was with you. And that's only after I called Uncle Carmine to find out where you were because he was supposed to be guarding you last night. So, what the fuck little, sis? Where were you? What's going on? And don't give me the 'it's nothing bullshit!'" He points at me snarling, but he keeps ranting. "I know what time you get home from Ice, so I'm pretty sure you're not going to just decide on a whim at three thirty in the fuckin' morning to pack a bag and go sleep at someone else's house!" He takes a deep breath after his tirade. "Talk. Now!" he commands.

I sigh deeply. "I slept at Jessica's house," I lie. "Caelan and I had a fight when I got home. He pissed me off. I left. That's all."

"Try again, little sis."

Shit, he must know I didn't sleep at Jessica's. "Oh come on, A. Just leave it alone. Please," I plead.

"Don't tell me to leave it alone! The last time I saw my little sister she had a major fucking meltdown and hasn't answered my phone calls since!"

Tears now sting my eyes because I feel bad for making him worry. I just didn't want to talk to him it or anyone else about my meltdown. Guilt has now settled in. "I'm sorry. I just didn't want to talk about it," I tell him with an exhausted breath dropping down heavily onto one of the lounge chairs.

He sits down next to me, grabbing my hand as he does. "Not talking about it is one thing, Sofia, but ignoring my calls just because you don't want to talk about it when I just wanted to make sure my little sister was fine, that's not fucking cool."

"I'm sorry. The last couple of days have been really tough on me, and last night was just..." I cut myself off because I start to break down, and I can't finish what I was going to say.

He grasps my hand tighter. "Yeah, I can see that, but I also know my sister. I know something's going on. I know you have anxiety attacks, but that situation the other night was way more than an anxiety attack. That was a full-blown panic attack. That was serious shit, Sofia. I knew just by the look on Caelan's face it wasn't normal. He was scared shitless for you. He wouldn't even let Nikki or I touch you. On top of that, I called him later that night to check on you, and he could barely talk to tell me you were alright. Now you just told me you two had such a big fight you left your own home in the middle of the night. And the two of you never fight. So, that makes every instinct I have stand on fucking edge. Now, tell me what the fuck is going on!"

I stare out at the luscious scenery, then scrub my face with my hands. "It's personal, A," I stammer with frustration running my fingers through my hair.

"Good try. Not going to work."

I inhale, then exhale deeply. Let's go with the truth. "A, I love you. I know it's killing you right now that you don't know what's going on, but honestly... I'm just not ready to talk about it. I'm barely hanging on. I came here today to talk to mommy about it." He's quiet for a minute, but his eyes, they say a lot.

"How serious is it?"

"Pretty serious. Not sure I'm handling it all that well either. Between my past, Thursday night, my break down, then last night... last night hurt, A. It's a lot of things, but right now I just can't talk about it."

"Did he hurt you?"

"Who?"

"Caelan. Tell me, did he hurt you? Because I will-"

"No," I weakly admit. Then realizing yeah, he did hurt me, why say no? "Ya, A. Ya he did, but not physically. He did something really stupid and selfish, without thinking about the consequences. He deliberately hurt me, but it's between him and me, Antonio. I just need a few days to get my head straight." I repeat it again because I know my brother, "This is between him and me, A. Don't go digging."

"Sofia he's my best friend, but you're my sister. If he hurt you, I will fuc-"

"No! No, you're not going to do anything, A. I will take care of my business. When and if I need your help, I will come to you, okay? Besides, part of this is my fault," I murmur. I wrap my arms around him tightly. "I'll always need my brother, but right now I need you to back off a little. If I need you I will tell you, I promise."

twenty-five

S ITTING IN THE BACK SEAT OF THE SUV, I glance at my phone with the
thought of listening to all the voice and text messages that were sent to
me over the course of last night and today. When I turned on my phone,
it became one continuous vibrating ding. "What the hell?" I disbelievingly
mutter with a racing heart.

"What's the matter?" Giovanni asks turning in the driver's seat.

"My phone is blowing up with all the messages." With a nod of
understanding, he turns back to watch the road. My insides tremble from the
anticipation of what his words will reveal. I'm afraid to read them because I
know they're going to break my heart. One right after the other.

C: I'm so sorry, beautiful. (4:24 am)

C: Please answer your phone. (4:37 am)

C: Buckcherry~ I'm Sorry (4:52 am)

Jess:WTF is going on? CALL ME! (4:54 am)

C: Come back home. (5:01 am)

C: I know I hurt you. I know there's nothing I can say or do that will take away what I did, but please just talk to me. Let me explain. (5:16 am)

Jess: Let me know you're alright. Call me, please. (5:21 am)

C: I was so fucking stupid. I let my jealousy get the best of me. (5:22 am)

C: Please talk to me (5:35 am)

C: Where are you? Are you okay? (5:45 am)

C: Jesus Christ, Sofia, I'm sorry, she meant nothing. (6:15 am)

The Best Sister Ever: What the hell is going on? C is freaking out! Are you okay? Call me! What the hell happened? (6:22 am)

C:Metallica~ Nothing Else Matters (6:52 am)

C: We have to talk. (7:44 am)

Tho Boct Sictor Evor: Sic, I'm gotting roally worriod. Call mo. I'm oalling, A. (7:52 am)

C: Sofia, at least text me back and let me know you're okay. (8:53 am)

The Best Sister Ever: Talked to, A. At least I know you're alive. What did he do? It must have been really bad for you to leave. Call me. (8:55 am)

C: I'm going into work late. Come home so we can talk. I'll take the day off. Please, beautiful. (9:22 am)

C: I'm at work. Call me or text me. I'll leave work. I'll meet you anywhere you want. (11:02am)

The texts and voice message just keep coming. I don't know what to do. Do I text him back? Do I make him wait the Camilla Heart twenty-four-hour rule? What he did was wrong, but I can't help feeling that I caused this myself.

No. No, I didn't start this. His jealousy started this. He's the one that accused me of sleeping with Giovanni. He's the one that went out and found someone to bring home and shove it in my face. I just don't get him. He has slept with so many women over the years, and I've never said anything. It's not my business. He's a grown man. He can do whatever and whoever he wants. We've always been respectful of each other. Why Giovanni? Why did he feel that insecure about him?

My phone vibrates in my hand, and Luke's handsome smiling face lights up across my screen. "Shit," I mutter. Do I answer? I know he's only calling for Caelan. What if it is C calling from Luke's phone? My phone keeps vibrating in my hand. Damn. What do I do?

"Hey."

"Sof?"

"Hey, Luke." I sigh deeply. "What's up?"

"How are you, sweetheart?"

"Been better Luke. What's up?"

"Sof, he's freaking out. He knows he fucked up. You gotta call him. At least let him know you're okay."

"And why should I do that, Luke? Why should I be thinking about him right now? About how he feels? How about how I feel? How do you think I felt walking in seeing his dick inside bad-fake-tits last night? How do you think I feel right now?" I verbally vomit my anger. Then take a deep breath feeling dejected. "The saddest part, Luke, is the fact that I have no right to feel the way I do. We're not together, and that's confusing to me because I hurt. And what hurts the most is that he purposely set out to do it. That's what hurts, Luke. He thought Giovanni and I slept together. He accused me of it before I left for work." The roller coaster of my emotions switching back to me being hostile. "Since when is he concerned with who I sleep with? Tell me, Luke? He's your best friend, I understand you're worried about him, but please do not call me and tell me I owe him anything right now because I damn sure don't!" I berate him.

"First off, sweetheart, you're my friend too. Don't you ever forget that. Second, I agree what he did was fucked up. He loves you Sof. You guys have history together. He was hurt."

"Hurt?" I yell flipping my head back, laughing in anger. "About what exactly, Luke?" He stays quiet. "Seriously? Come on, big man, say something!" When he remains silent, my reaction is to react with even more resentment, only giving a piece of myself away. One that I have buried. "Soooo, it's okay for him to stick his dick in anything he wants? And Luke before you answer... it is okay. He's a grown man. I don't care who he's screwin', but when he thinks I slept with Giovanni, he loses his shit. That's bullshit, and you know it, Luke. Why? Tell me why Luke? I would really like to know." I cry to him. I'm so mad right now I'm shaking. I didn't even realize tears were rolling down my fevered cheeks. I swipe at the tears on my face in anger; I'm angry that my true feelings are barreling through and I can't stop them. What the hell is going on with me?

"I don't know, sweetheart." I hear him faintly answer. "I don't have the answers for you, but he does. You two need to talk. You can only get your answers from him."

My phone beeps through with another call. I pull the phone away from my ear to see who it is. "Jess is calling me. I gotta go."

"Sofia, give him a chance to explain."

"I'll talk to you later."

"Call me if you need me, sweetheart. I'll always be here for you."

"Yea, I can see that." I hang up. Then click over to Jess. "I need you. I need my girls. I need a girls' night. Drinks, food, dancing, fun. You in?"

"I'm always in! Who am I calling?"

"I'll call Nikki. You call Sage. That's it, Jess. Girls' night. No one else."

"You got it! Text me later. Let me know the time and place."

As I'm hanging up, I hear Giovanni. "Sofia, I'll drive you all to the club. Tell everyone to meet you at the restaurant. I'll take you all to the club, then bring everyone home."

"Thanks, G." I swipe the leftover, half-dried, angry tears away. "Can we stop at the coffee shop? I need a cup of java, desperately! Actually, what I need is a shot and a beer, but that can wait until later."

A grin crosses his handsome face. His green eyes sparkle with laughter. "You got it."

I text Jess, Nikki, and Sage letting them know the plans for tonight.

WE PULL UP in front of my favorite coffee shop. My mouth is salivating. I can taste the creamy pick-me-up already. Giovanni comes around to my side, opening the door. As I'm sliding out from the back of the SUV, I catch a glimpse of four women standing under the awning gaping at him, their mouths dropped wide open. Fireworks in their eyes.

"I think you have fans G-man." I smile looking up at him while confusion crosses his strong, handsome features. I jerk my head to the side. He turns noticing all four women ogling him. "So," I chirp with a cocky grin, "would you like some phone numbers or do you wanna play boyfriend-girlfriend?"

He jerks his head towards the coffee shop grinning then looking back to me with a smile. "Sofia they're not going to hit on me. No need to play boyfriend-girlfriend."

With a gleam in my eye, knowing exactly what is going to happen, I say, "Okay, big boy." I smile tapping my palm on his chest twice then start walking toward the door to the coffee shop. Right past 'the pack.' Once inside we order our drinks. I excuse myself to the restroom knowing 'the pack' will make a mad rush to the very handsome man waiting for our coffee. When I come back out, I notice that two of the women from outside are now standing extremely close to him while the other two are sitting at a table not too far away. Both ladies are using every trick in the book to get him to bite. I watch for a few seconds giggling.

Hmmm thought they weren't going to hit on you G-man.

Never off the job, his eyes scan toward the bathrooms looking for me. I wave with a look of amusement on my face. "Need my help?" I mouth. With a minor nod, he confirms. Jealous girlfriend here I come.

"Sofia?" I hear my name being called again as I round the corner. "Sofia? Large caramel white mocha with coconut milk?" Blondie has her hands on his arm now.

Crazy girlfriend, here we go.

"Honey really?" I stop in my tracks looking at him with my hand on my hips. "Seriously? You're standing right here! You couldn't grab my drink?" I rant throwing my hands in the air. "Oh, please, excuse me, I'm so sorry, I can see that you're busy with the two ladies that were eye-fucking you outside!" I stamp my foot into the tile flooring. "Are you serious? Bitch get your hands off my man!" I swivel my head. "You are the worst boyfriend ever!" Totally taken off guard, he just stands there looking at me. Total surprise etched across his face. "You two better get the fuck away from my man!" I fling my hand towards the door. "Before I go bat shit crazy on your asses!" I look at him with raised brows. The mirth behind his eyes almost makes me lose my 'jealous girlfriend' acting skills. He's shocked to all hell. For a guy that's a stone-cold killer, I think I just threw him for a loop. I turn quickly grabbing my drink. As I'm grabbing mine, I hear...

"G-man? Dark roast light and sweet." I grab his drink off the counter and strut my shit towards him handing him his coffee.

The two ladies have now taken two steps back almost breaking their necks on their stilettos. Their faces say it all. 'Crazy ass bitch coming through!'

"Here, baby, at least I got your drink for you! Then I turn my head towards the two women. "Oh, and ladies, his nickname... G-man, yeah he got it 'cause he has a giant cock! Your loss! Have fun tonight playing with your vibrators! Tootles!" I joyfully smile as I flap my hand, flipping my hair over my shoulder, swaying my hips and strutting my shit out the door.

Giovanni is right behind me, speechless. I can see the utter amusement on his face. He opens the back door for me. I look up at him smiling and tap his cheek twice. "Thanks, baby, you're so sweet." I wink with an exaggerated cheek lift.

He closes my door, but as he walks around the front of the SUV, he's examining me through the front windshield. I bust out laughing. Doubled over trying to draw breath when the driver's side door opens.

He gets in the front seat turning his attention to me. "What the fuck was that?" He cracks up with a roar of laughter.

"Ahhhhhhaaaaaahaa G-Man you just met crazy, jealous girlfriend! You like her?" I flap my hands in front of my face trying to catch my breath.

"You are fucking amazing!" he roars. "Those women had no idea what the hell was going on!"

"I told you they were going to hit on you!" I roar back with laughter, pointing at him with one hand and holding my stomach with the other. "Oh, I have lots of different girlfriend personas. I have just the plain girlfriend, then crazy girlfriend, loving girlfriend, heartbroken girlfriend, and then jealous, crazy girlfriend. Ohhhh and we cannot forget scorned wife! She's the worst!" I drag out the word so he knows how bad she really is. "When she comes out to play, the situation is out of control and in dire need of a scorned wifey!" He's laughing so hard he can't even drive. "Damn, I needed that!" I belly laugh. After a few more minutes of hysterics, the both of us start calming down wiping our tears of laughter away.

He gazes at me with a sad smile. "You are an amazing woman, Sofia. Don't ever forget that," he says before starting the SUV and pulling away.

After a few minutes of driving, he looks back to me. "What's the plan? Where are we going?"

Oh, hell, I haven't thought about that. I need to go back to the house to shower and get ready for tonight. When I glance at my watch, I see that it's after two thirty. Which means, C won't be there. "Can you bring me back to my house? I'll shower, get ready for tonight and pack another overnight bag. I'll sleep at Jess's house tonight. I'll go back to my house tomorrow."

"Sofia you're sleeping at my penthouse again if you're not sleeping at home," he states. I'm surprised by his statement, but honestly spending the night at his place again would be nice. No one would know where I am at least for one more night. He must think his demand pissed me off. Which it did, but I wasn't going to put up too much of a fight. His next words are what stopped me from giving him the ass chewing he was going to get. "If you stay at the penthouse again, you and I both can get good sleep, and I'll know you'll be safe. On top of that, no one will know where you are to bother you." I nod in agreement leaving it at that.

twenty-six

I SHOWER AND GET READY QUICKLY. THE LATER on in the day it becomes, the more of a chance I have of running into Caelan. I told everyone to meet at the Irish pub around the corner at seven for a quiet dinner. O'Brien's Pub is a great Irish pub for food, drinks, and fun. The place is all dark wood, stained glass and pub style charm. The tall dark wood booths give you privacy, while the mix of music is everything from blues to R&B to pop. It's a great place to chill out with friends and have a few drinks. Plus, we know Pat, the owner. Caelan and I have been coming here at least once a week for years. It's kind of our spot the nights I'm not working at Ice.

I called ahead, asking for *our* booth in the back so we can have some privacy. If we hang out at O'Brien's all night instead of going to a club after dinner that's okay by me too. I just need my girls... and Sage.

Giovanni and I sit at the bar for a quick drink before everyone gets there. I rushed to get ready and left the house so I wouldn't run into C if he came home early. I guess I left just in time because as I slide my ass onto the bar stool my phone beeps with a text.

C:You came home. I can smell your perfume. I wish you would have stayed until I got home so we could talk. I fucked up. I know that, Sofia. I truly am sorry for the pain I caused you. If there's one person in this world I never wanted to hurt... it's you, but I did, and I would do anything to make that right, beautiful. I'm worried about you. I know I have no right to ask this, but can you just text me and let me know you're okay?

I struggle with myself wanting to text him back, but after a moment I decided not to and slip the phone back into my pocket, putting it off 'til later that night because what I want to text back is, 'I'm not okay,' but I don't want to give him that satisfaction. I know he may be hurting and have regrets right now, but it was his jealousy that wanted to make me jealous and by me telling him I'm not okay only shows him he got to my heart.

Giovanni and I make small talk while waiting for everyone to show up. Jess and Nikki strut their shit through the door twenty minutes later, both looking fabulous. Nikki's in a short, sleeveless, black, lace dress and Jess is wearing a yellow satin shorts romper with some killer heels.

Some of the weight is lifted off me because I'm so happy to see them. We head over to our booth. I asked Giovanni if he wanted to join us, but he declined. I feel bad leaving him by himself at the bar. It's such a weird situation being he's my bodyguard, but yet... we're more than just that.

"Hey, you." Jess gives me a big lingering hug. "How you doing, sexy girl? You look hotter than a she-devil in hell."

I decided I needed to feel fun and flirty tonight so I wore my royal blue, cold shoulder, fringed arm dress with four inch, black, strappy heels that lace almost all the way to my knees. Before I can even answer, Nikki's grabbing me pulling me in for a tight, sisterly hug.

"Please, tell me what the fuck is going on!" she demands.

I love my sister dearly, and I know that between the three of them, I will have to spill my guts soon-very soon, but I just want to finish my first drink and relax with them for a minute before ripping my heart out again. Besides, if I start now, I will only have to start over again when Sage gets here. So, I squeeze into the booth deflecting my sister's question and ask Jess how work was and about the shipment that came in.

Before I know it, I hear Sage busting through the bar. "Sunshine, where are you?"

I laugh because he's right behind us and knows exactly where I am. Pat comes over at the same time asking for our drink order. "A round of tequila shots and a couple of beers will do it, for now. Thanks."

"Spill it, girlfriend!" he orders rolling his wrist with a flap. "This morning was pure craziness! There's nothing sexier than a dominant man hunting down his woman, but sunshine, he was out of his mind looking for you! And by the way, where was your hussy ass? Because you sure as hell weren't with me!"

Taking a deep breath and thinking back to last night, the memories form deeper cuts into my heart and the feelings are so strong and raw that knots are forming in my stomach. I spill my guts to my three best friends. I tell them everything from the moment I walked into the house. From the dread filling me, thinking someone hurt him, to the painful moment I saw them on the couch, to the very moment that he professed his love for me, and then the moment I walked out. Although Jess already knew, the three of them sat there silently in shock.

Sage reaches across the table grabbing my hand. "Sweetheart, I'm sorry you had to go through that. What a cocksucker!" he sneers in a deep manly voice. All signs of happy go lucky Sage have left the building. "I'm gonna beat his fucking ass!" he promises.

"Sage, no!" I see the cold look on his face. I know he means serious business. Sage is a fifth-degree black belt in martial arts. For him to say he's going to beat C's ass scares me. I squeeze his hand back with both of mine. "I have to deal with this." I slightly smile. "Thank you though for trying to protect me, but this is between him and I."

"What are you going to do now? Mom told me you were at the house today. Did you tell her?"

"Sure did. She told me to give him the no contact twenty-four hours rule. Make him sweat."

"Well, I don't agree. You should give him the fuck you, five-day rule!" She smirks with a pissed off grimace.

"Fuck! Well, sweetheart you're not even going to get to the five-minute rule 'cause he just walked in," Sage hissed with anger billowing off his tense shoulders.

"*W-WHAT?*" I stammer.

"Shit!" Jess mutters. "He just spotted Giovanni at the bar. They're staring at each other. Hell. He knows you're here. Oh, shit! He's totally searching for you, Sof." She scoots in closer to Sage trying to hide behind the tall both. "Fuck! Too late, he's walking over here." She gulps. "Shit! Ready? Three, two, one..."

"Hey," he says, determination gleaming from his tired eyes.

I'm at a loss for words. The table is silent. He looks exhausted. His dirty blond hair looks like his hands have run through it dozens of times today giving it one hell-of-a- sexy look. His day-old scruff only makes him sexier, but the dark circles under his eyes show his distress. Hints of his shoulder tattoo peak out by the neck of his black dress shirt. The same shirt that is perfectly stretched over his well-defined muscular upper body. I can't help when my eyes run down the rest of his body. His tight gray dress pants, hugging in all the right places, tells me he worked in the office today. I hurt seeing him this way, but I didn't do this to us. He did this to us.

"Hey," I whisper back.

"How are you?"

"Been better," I mutter.

His eyes flicker with even more sadness. "Can we talk?"

Snorting, Sage glares at him with raised brows. "Maybe you should give her some time."

"This is none of your fucking business, Sage. Fuck off!" The tension is rising, quickly. Jessica reaches over putting her hand on Sage's clenched fist.

"Five minutes, Sofia?" he begs turning his attention back to me.

"You could have had a whole night if you weren't such an asshole," Sage fumes.

"Sage, stop." Jessica and Nikki both demand simultaneously.

"Fuck you, Sage! You wanna go? Then get the fuck up motherfucker!"

"Oh, motherfucker, you do not want to go there with me, Caelan," Sage thunders as he's pushing Jessica out of the booth.

I shove Nikki in haste trying to get her out of our side of the booth as quickly as possible before this escalates any further. I hit the table with my hip trying to get out of the booth sending our drinks sloshing around. As I stand, I see Giovanni standing three feet away.

Glaring up at Caelan I grab his forearm. "Let's go. You have five minutes." I walk with haste toward the buildings rear exits by the bathrooms with Giovanni right on my heels. I stop putting my hands up, pleading. "Please give me five minutes. I'll be fine. I'll stay inside, and he would never hurt me, physically, or let anyone else, you know that." He reluctantly agrees after a few seconds, but he's not happy about it.

When I reach the back of the hallway I can feel his breath on the back of my neck because he's so close. Abruptly, I turn to rip him a new ass for starting with Sage, but before I can even open my mouth his lips crash down on mine. His fingers thrust through my strands twisting in my hair, gripping so tightly it's on the verge of pain. His eyes never close. Instead, they're penetrating deeply into mine as he assaults my soft, tender lips. This kiss is anything, but gentle. This is him laying his claim. He knows Giovanni is standing at the end of the hallway. He wants him to know I'm taken. Which, I'm not. His tongue slides across my lower lip. His eyes pleading for me to open. Hesitantly, I do. He takes advantage of it sliding his warm, seductive tongue into the small opening I give him. His hips slam against mine, pushing me into the wall as he grinds his hardness into my belly. I succumb opening wider, falling into the kiss more. The look in his eyes say nothing more than, I'm sorry. But his actions are laying claim.

Damn, this man can kiss.

His breathing is rapidly escalating to the point that only our breathing can be heard echoing through the long hallway. His right hand pulls from my hair roughly sliding down the contour of my body, stopping on my hip.

He grabs it forcefully, pulling me into him as he thrusts himself into me, grinding his erection into me harder. I involuntarily whimper, which only makes him demand more from the kiss. His eyes blaze like an inferno which ignites fire in my belly. Tingling consumes my clit. The drummer has been cued and started playing the first song with the band. No, screw that, the band is now on its third song, this is so hot. His hand roughly cups my ass, squeezing hard. I moan at the same time he growls. His hand slides down the back of my bare leg grabbing my thigh pulling my leg up to his hip. My dress rides up. His hand slides up my hot tingling flesh to where my dress meets my skin. He groans again through heavy panting. His hand slides under my dress desperately gripping my bare, tender goose flesh prickled skin. I hear the sharp sounds of glass breaking in the distance which snaps me back into reality.

This man hurt you last night.

I break the intense kiss and glare up at him while my hands blast his hard chest with a thud. "What the hell, Caelan?" I shout. "What the hell was that?" I hiss.

"That was me showing you how fucking sorry I am!" he explodes. "That was me needing to connect with you! That was me needing you! I miss you, Sofia," he exclaims. "I fucked up! I know I did! I didn't sleep at all last night! You won't talk to me!" he roars.

"No! That was you laying claim on me. You knew Giovanni would be watching from the end of the hallway and you think I fucked him," I interjected. "You son of a bitch." I slam my hands against his chest again. "I didn't! You selfish son of a bitch! I didn't! You couldn't wait? Give me time? You couldn't wait for me to call or text you? You did this, Caelan. Not me! YOU!" I scream pointing at him. "Goddamn, C. You hurt me! What you did was wrong!" I burst out furiously.

"Give you time, woman?" He closes in on me putting his nose to mine. "Are you fucking serious? I have given you so much fucking time!" he bellows, throwing his palm against the wall next to my head in outrage. Movement from the corner of my eye makes me look to the end of the hallway. Sage and

Giovanni are both standing there. Caelan follows my line of site. "Fucking awesome! Your boyfriends are here!"

"Fuck you, C. Don't you dare!" I glare at him at him with contempt.

He leans down. His lip grazes my lobe and the tip of his tongue grazes over the length of my soft tingling skin. "Fuck me? No, beautiful, you got that all wrong, it's not me you're fucking!" he explodes. Pulling away from me he glares down the hallway at Giovanni before turning back to me with his furious eyes flicking back and forth over mine like seconds ticking away on a clock. He snarls. "Tell me, beautiful, where did you fucking sleep last night? Huh?" His lip curls. "Because you damn sure weren't at any of the houses I went to, looking for *you!*" With that, he takes a hasty step back pushing himself off the wall and walking away from me, but not before shoulder checking both Giovanni and Sage as he walks past.

"What the fuck! Are you okay?" Sage spews barreling down the hallway towards me.

I hold my hand up. "Just give me a minute," I apologize ducking into the ladies bathroom.

"Oh. Hell. No!" he admonishes busting through the bathroom door right behind me.

I stop in shock. His arms wrap around me tightly. "Sunshine, what the fuck was that?"

"I'm... I'm not s-sure."

"Man, he's got it bad for you."

I hear the bathroom door open. Giovanni steps in. "Sofia, you okay?"

"I'm fine." The concern in his eyes tells me he knows I'm lying. I need to calm this whole situation down before it gets any more out of hand. "Ummm, guys? You do realize that you're in the women's bathroom, right?"

Sage chuckles still holding me. "Oh, sunshine, I don't know about G-Man over there, but I'm a gay man, I've been in women's bathrooms before. Sometimes you women do not know how to put yourselves together and need some Sage love."

And the fun-loving Sage is back.

Giovanni smirks. Then his facial features become stone once again as we make eye contact. "I'll be right outside the door if you need me."

"Sunshine, I know this is a category five situation, but honey that shit was even hotter than the pool table. The chubby in my pants can attest to that. Now tell me, what did he say to you?" he questions, taking a step back while he's still holding me prisoner in his arms.

"There was no talking, Sage. None! Nada! Nothing! I turned around, wham he was on me! When I broke the kiss, he said it was his apology."

"Oh, no, I heard all that. I saw the tail end of the bumping and grinding too. Wooooooooo that shit was crazy hawt! Sunshine, seriously when you guys finally get it on, can I watch? I might have to wrap up too. He may just impregnate me just from watching."

"Sage! Seriously?"

"Oh, sunshine it will be fireworks. I'm sure!"

"Sage!"

"Don't Sage me, sunshine. Fireworks, I tell you. That man is all alpha male, even though I'm fucking pissed at him right now, he's a sexy man! You can't deny that, girlfriend."

"No shit! But it's not happening!"

The bathroom door swings open. Pat, the owner comes barreling through giving Sage a three times over before asking, "Sofia, are you alright?"

"Yes. Pat, I'm sorry. I'm not sure... I... I don't even know what to say."

"It's fine, honey, as long as you're good."

"I am, Pat. I'm sorry," I apologize again because I feel bad.

"Come on, sunshine, let's go back to the table," he coaxes hugging me tightly.

After a few minutes at the table I hear Nikki's pissed off voice. "Are you serious?" She gasps with questions for Sage as I space out.

I just want to get off the subject of Caelan and me. "So, I met someone Tuesday night at Ice, and he asked me out," I blurt breaking into their conversation. "I think I'm going to give him a call." I hear nothing. Silence. Crickets. I glance up to see three set of eyes on me.

"What?" Sage falters a few seconds later ending the conversation with Nikki.

"Well, okay. Honey, if that's what you want to do." Jess break the silence.

"Caelan's gonna go nuts!" Nikki burst out. "By the way, he went busting through this restaurant on the way out. Pat tried to stop him, but he wasn't stopping for anyone."

My thoughts wander to Sage because he's unusually quiet. "Well, what do you have to say about it?" I ask, already feeling defeated.

His lip tightens, and a look of doubt passes through his eyes. "Sunshine, I think you need to do what makes you happy, but at the same time, you need to realize that Caelan is in love with you and will not make this easy on you if you start dating." He shakes his head to reiterate what he said. "This thing between you two has more to it than we all know. You can see it. Shit, you can feel it when you two are together. Just make sure that if this is what you want to do, that the repercussion of it will not hurt either of you. By the looks of it, you both have been hurt enough."

He's right, but I have to make myself happy, so I nod, then move on. "Who wants to go dancing? Hey, Pat!" I yell over to her at the bar. "Can we get another round of shots please?" I look back at everyone at the table. "Then we're going dancing!"

As we all pile into the SUV, I pull out my cell phone. "Where we going, Sof?" Giovanni inquires.

I look at everyone. "Wanna go to Ice?" I smile mischievously wiggling my brows.

"Oh boy, hot pants is looking to get naked wasted!" Sage hoots.

Giovanni twists in his seat with a stern look on his face. "Just wasted, no naked." I smirk holding up my palms in white flag surrender. "I won't make your night any harder than it's about to get," I taunt.

I'm going to start tonight by doing something for me.

I grab my purse pulling out Mr. Macallan's phone number.

"Who you calling Sof?"

I turn to Jess and smile. "Mr. Macallan- Mr. Luscious Lips- Mr. Sexy- Mr...

"Reznor," he answers.

"Hello, Mr. Macallan."

"Ahhh, if it isn't the beautiful Sofia. I didn't think I would ever hear from you."

"Well, today's your lucky day I guess."

"Well, I guess a crappy day can turn around when a beautiful woman calls you by the end of the night."

"Ahhhh what happened, Johnathan, last night's conquest didn't want to leave your bed this morning?"

"Nothing like that, beautiful, but I can tell you if it were you in my bed this morning I would still be there."

My words falter for a second. He really needs to stop calling me beautiful. "Is that so? Well, Johnathan, just so you know... if it were me you spent the night with, I would have been gone before you woke this morning."

"That would make me a heartbroken man."

"I'm so sure," I tease. "I was calling to see what you were doing tonight. I know it's last minute, but if you don't have some hot chick on your lap, come meet me at Ice."

"You working?"

"Nope, hanging out with some friends. Need to let loose."

"Oh, I see how it is. Bring me around when the friends are there to keep you safe. I get it, but Sofia?"

"Yeah?"

"Friends or no friends... you're not safe with me, beautiful." His husky voice becomes low, deep and sexy.

Hot damn!

"Goodbye Mr. Macallan." I hang up with a smile on my face. I don't know if this is the smartest thing or even the right thing to do, but honestly, at this very moment, I don't care. I'm surrounded by friends, I have a bodyguard and not for nothing, he's sexy as all hell. This girl's going to have some fun tonight.

"Ummm...Wow!" Nikki chimed. When I jerk my head around to her sitting next to me is when I notice all three of them staring at me.

"I'm letting loose tonight," I declare.

twenty-seven

THE MUSIC IS BLASTING. WE'RE TWO blowjob shots in, and I'm feeling pretty damn phenomenal. Sage is dancing with Jess, while Nikki and I are getting ready to do our third shot. Or, is it the fourth? I lost count. Sage started ordering tequila shots in-between. If you count the two at O'Brien's, then it's... well, I'm not really sure how many I've had so far, but I am feeling no pain. We have now switched from blowjobs back to tequila again and I already know that's going to hurt come morning.

Screw it!

"Wooo! Let's Dance!" I hoot after downing the shot. Grabbing Nikki's arms, I drag her to the dance floor. We attract lots of male attention when we start dancing with each other. We're having a blast together when I see Sage crack up and then his face goes serious as he sees something over my shoulder. Next thing I know Sage is on me.

"Vultures, sunshine, gotta keep them away!" he shouts in my ear. We continue dancing together as Nikki and Jess surround Sage. He is now a lucky man smashed in-between all three of us. We're all are having a good time, but most important of all, I am having a great time. It's a good night. The music is pounding into my body, letting my sad soul slowly forget. If I could I would just want to forget this whole last week, even if it's just for tonight, for a few short hours.

Sage grabs me, wrapping his arms around my waist, he pulls me back into his chest as we sway back and forth with each other. His large body engulfs my small frame. His chin rests on my shoulder with a dazzling smile. I close my eyes and rest my head back against his shoulder and enjoy him and the music.

"You having fun, sunshine?" he asks. I smile up at him and lay my hands on his as we sway to the beat of the song. "I think you have an admirer and he's damn good-looking."

I open my eyes to see the gorgeous Mr. Macallan standing on the outskirts of the dance floor curiously watching Sage and me. I give him a warm smile, while he gives me an annoyed smile back. Oh boy, someone's not a happy camper. "It's okay." I turn my head into Sage's ear letting him know I knew him. Then I noticed Giovanni standing right behind him.

Oh shit. Do something before this guy gets the crap beat out of him.

"Is that Mr. Macallan? 'Cause if it is... you done good girl."

I chuckle. "Yeah, that's him." I pat his hand with mine, so he'll release me.

"Good luck. He doesn't look too happy."

Smiling, I walk over to a smoldering Johnathan. "You made it."

"I did. But, it seems I may be too late." His annoyed grin crosses his handsome facial features again.

Damn, he's good looking.

The navy-blue dress shirt makes his green eyes pop even more. The combination of the two is like looking down into the deepest tropical waters from above. The mysterious black green and blues in deep unsure waters. My belly tingles.

Ya, he's trouble.

His black designer jeans hug him in all the right places and he has the air of a rich bad boy. Maybe he's too good-looking for his own good. He's so the opposite of Caelan. Johnathan is clean bad boy sexy, whereas Caelan is tough, rugged, bad-boy, sexy. Whether he's in a suit or sweatpants, he has that bad boy feel to him. Johnathan has that sexy, rich, bad-boy air about him, one that has a lot of snobby women waiting in the wings ready and available at the push of a button.

Okay, Sofia get your mind off Caelan.

"You're not too late," I reassure him holding my hand out to him. "You're more his type than I am." I smile enlightening him. "He's one of my closest friends. Come on, I'll introduce you," I say glancing over his shoulder to a very unhappy Giovanni. I grab Johnathan's hand tossing my head to the right. "Come on." He relaxes as he follows me over to our table.

"That guy's gay?" he questions with disbelief.

"Yep and he's my bestie," I clarify for him. His eyes narrow like he doesn't believe me. "I swear he is and I wouldn't want him any other way."

When we reach the table, another round of free shots has graced us.

Thank You, Jake!

I look over towards the bar and blow him a kiss before introducing Johnathan. "Everyone this is Johnathan Reznor. Johnathan this is Jess, Sage and my sister Nikki."

"Bottoms up bitches!" Nikki yells grabbing her shot.

Everyone grabs their glass when I realize Johnathan doesn't have one. "Here you can have mine." I smile.

"Nah, I'm good." He grins.

"Oh yeah? Damn, here I was passing out a free blowjob, and you just declined it. I must be losing my touch." I snicker with a gleam in my eye as I throw back the shot not giving him a second chance to reconsider. His shocked expression clearly written all over his face as I hear choking from behind me. I turn and Nikki is slapping Sage on the back. His eyes pierce me with laughter before he could catch his breath.

"Fuckin' A girl, that was a gooooood one!" He busts out laughing. "Damn, dude, you just gave up a free blowjob!" Sage cuts on Johnathan.

Jess and Nikki are hysterical. I turn back to Johnathan not knowing what to expect but it wasn't the sexiest, panty-melting grin crossing his lips that's for sure.

"Well," he says staring down into my eyes as he takes a step closer. His hand lifts to my chin and his thumb brushes my bottom lip as his eyes drop to them as well. "That only goes to show you I am not a selfish man in the bedroom. I. Always. Take. Care. Of. My. Partner. First. Multiple times," he brags with a sexy serious grin.

Oh, holy hell. Get it together, Sofia, you're melting here.

"I can see you're a handful, pretty girl," he says with a twinkle in his eye still stroking my bottom lip.

Okay, nope can't let him one up me.

I grin slowly, brushing my tongue along my lower lip slightly touching his thumb then drop my head so my eyes can flicker down to my now full tingling breasts. "More than a handful," I divulge with a cocky smirk.

Johnathan's eyes follow mine, then shoot over my shoulder to look at Sage. The cockiest brightest smile crosses his face again. "Oh, this is going to be fun."

"You dance?" He nods. "Come on," I pull him towards the dance floor. The soul penetrating music beats into our bodies as we laugh and dance for a few faster songs before the music slows down. *Disarm You* by Kaskade (feat. Ilsey) slower beat hits the speakers. He's an excellent dancer, but I haven't let him get that close to me. I've definitely kept him an arms distance away.

He reaches over, grasping my waist, jerking me into his strong, tan body. He's glistening with sweat and the sexual vibes are vibrating from his body into mine as he moves my body with his to the slow, sexy, beat of the song. As the lyrics croon through the airwaves, I think, well hell, that's exactly what he's doing to me right now. He's smooth, precise and very confident while he slowly and seductively spins me around without missing a beat. My back now to his front. His strong, sturdy frame encompasses me with his arms around my waist. He's rocking our joined hips back and forth with wide, slow circles and short quick ones. His palm spreads across my abdomen, holding me tightly to him. I can definitely feel his erection on my lower back. Our bodies are moving simultaneously back and forth, up and down with such careless effort. He has manipulated my body to wherever he wants, in such a way I don't even care. He has disarmed me. This is a man that gets what he wants and doesn't take no for an answer. Right now, with his scorching hot body moving against my tingling flesh, and his deep dark, mysterious green eyes looking deep into my emerald green eyes, I would do just about anything.

Okay, Sofia, cool this situation down.

The slower song is coming to an end as it mixes into Robin S~ *Show Me Love* and a faster beat hits the airwaves. "You wanna get a drink?" I yell over the music. He nods then leads us back to the table, where Jake has a round of water plus fresh drinks for all of us. There's even a three-finger neat glass of Macallan waiting for Johnathan. When I look down at my drink, I realize there's a folded piece of paper under it. I slide it out from under my drink unfolding it.

> *"Looks like you gave in.*
> *If Mr. Macallan doesn't work out tonight, you*
> *could always show me how that blow kiss tastes."*

I quickly fold it back up hoping no one notices. Of course, Jess does. I try to hand it off to her nonchalantly as I smile looking over at the bar letting Jake know I got his message. An enormous chest suddenly blocks my view. When I look up, Giovanni is glaring down at me.

"Give it to me," he sternly demands holding his hand out.

"It's nothing," I whisper trying to keep the situation quiet.

"Now!" he commands.

"Who the hell is this, Sofia?" Johnathan angry questions comes from behind me.

Damn.

"Listen, I don't know what the fucking is going on right now, but you dude, need to step the fuck back before I take you the fuck out," Johnathan hissed with warning stepping in front of me.

I grab his arm seeing the look of fury on Giovanni's face. "It's okay," I stammer.

"No, it's not," he insists staring Giovanni down.

"Dogfight! Love it!" Sage chuckles.

Johnathan takes another menacing step towards Giovanni.

"Oh hell," Sage muttered. "Shit just got real serious!" He steps forward laying his hand on Johnathan's shoulder to back him off. Jonathan barely moves, but his eyes go to where Sage's hand rest.

"Remove your hand from me. Now," he demands calmly with a lethal tone.

Balls! This is getting out of hand.

"Johnathan this is my bodyguard, Giovanni," I state trying to cool the situation down.

"Bodyguard?" I see his shoulder relax slightly, but he's still tense and on guard.

"Yes, my bodyguard," I reply stepping around Johnathan to give Giovanni the note as I stare him down with a cocked brow. Willing him not to say anything. He reads it, then looks back at me. "See I told you, it was nothing."

Folding the note back up, he puts it in his pocket. "I decide what's nothing, Sofia. We will talk later about this," he barks fuming as he walks back to his position out of sight.

I turn to Johnathan. "I'm sorry."

His tension filled eyes search mine. "Why do you need a bodyguard?"

I glance over to Sage, Jessica, and Nikki. All three are waiting to see what I'm going to say.

Damn. All I wanted was one night.

I deflate. Just one goddamn night where I didn't have to talk or think about my past. My really good buzz is now gone. My night has now been ruined by my past, yet again. Every damn minute of every damn day, something always reminds me of my past. I just wanted to let go tonight and be free... free of the pain, free of the memories, free of it all. Just free...

I look up at Sage. "I just wanted one night," I whispered. "Just one." I drop my head because my emotions are getting the best of me. The now loud music is grating on my nerves. My skin pricks with goose bumps. My breathing starts to pick up. I need to go. I need to get out of here. I faintly hear the question again.

"Why do you need a bodyguard, Sofia?"

I start to tremble. All I can hear is the word, why, why, why echoing in my head. Large arms engulf me. I know it's, Sage.

"Look at me, sunshine." I look down. "No, right here, sweetheart." He points to his eyes when I drop my head even more. "Keep your eyes on mine."

I look up and see his concern. "It's going to be okay. Just take a deep breath."

I shake my head back and forth. "It's never going to be okay, Sage. Please, just take me home," I plead, then turn to Johnathan. "I'm sorry. I have to go." Emotions cross over his face. Confusion, concern, sadness, and pity. The guy doesn't even know me, and he pities me. Such a terrible feeling comes over me. "I'm sorry," I apologize again before Sage whisks me out the door. The SUV is already waiting with its doors open. As I'm getting in the last thing I see is Johnathan standing there watching the scene unfold. Giovanni slams the door, shutting him and the world out. I don't remember dropping everyone off or even the car ride itself. If there were any conversations while driving I didn't hear them. I barely remembered Giovanni carrying me into his building, up the private elevator, and into his penthouse.

I SLOWLY WAKE FROM a pounding headache. Trying to get my bearings together I peek around the room with one open eye. There's a glow coming from the bathroom light that's softly illuminating the room enough to see. I roll to my side and see my cell phone charging on the nightstand. It's silently lights up so I reach for it and see that I have five missed messages.

Sage: Sunshine, I know you're in good hands, but call me in the morning and let me know you're alright. I love you, hot pants. XO Please don't be mad.

Please don't be mad? Why would I be upset with him? Shit, I know I don't remember part of last night, but why would I be mad?

The Best Sister Ever: I love you, sis. Call me in the morning, please. So I can hear your voice and know if you're okay .

Jess: Call me if you need me. I love you girl. Xoxoxoxoxo. I'll call you tomorrow. Don't worry about HD, Sage and I have it under control.

Caelan: Are you okay? Sage called me. Told me what happened. If you need me... I know I pissed you off tonight, but if you need me ... call me, beautiful.

Caelan: Lifehouse~ From Where You Are.

Damn Sage! Why'd you do that?

I throw my phone down in frustration, then roll out of bed. I need water. My tongue feels like the freakin' Sahara Desert. I open the bedroom door to deep angry voices. I hesitate for a second, but then hear Antonio's voice so I start to walk again I hear Giovanni's growl of commitment.

"I will find this motherfucker, and I will kill him myself, A."

He believes me. He thinks he's alive too?

"I'll be right there with you brother. What the fuck happened tonight?"

A knows too?

"You should have seen her tonight, A. She was having a great time. I'm not too sure about the dude she met up with, though."

"What dude?"

"Although, he did defend her when I approached her about the note, not knowing who I was. Actually, now that I think about it, he defended her a little too well. His demeanor was that of someone trained. I want him vetted along with the bartender Jake."

"What dude?"

"Johnathan Reznor."

"I'll talk to Freddy on the way out. Tell him to get me jackets on Johnathan Reznor and Jake Cross by nightfall. Where did she meet this Johnathan?"

Wait, Freddy, the valet guy? What's he got to do with this?

"Ice. Upstairs in the VIP rooms of The Devil's Lair the other night."

"Fuck man. I wish she would give that job up. It's a damn meat market in there. Especially upstairs."

"Yeah, I know," Giovanni agrees. "But you know your sister. She works hard. Too hard. She wants to open another boutique. She makes really good cash there. Plus, I believe she is still paying back Caelan for backing her on the first store."

"Yeah after him telling her many times not worry about it. She's so damn stubborn!"

"Yes, she is."

"Caelan's freaking the fuck out. He's been blowin' up my phone all night. Those two need to work their shit out," A says in frustration.

"I agree, but he was an asshole tonight, too. He's lucky I kept my cool."

"Do you know what happened between them?" he asks Giovanni. "I asked him, he wouldn't say anything, said it was between the two of them. I don't know what's going on with him. The last couple of days he's been on a rampage. He's not just pissed off, he's angry about something. I can see it in his eyes," he discloses.

Time to break this up.

I walk out to the living room. They both fall silent. "Hey, sorry to interrupt I just needed water."

"Come here, you." My brother holds out his arms. After hugging me tightly for a few minutes he asks, "You okay?"

"I'm fine. Just needed a drink," I tell him when I release him, like nothing's wrong. "Why are you here? You're not going to tell anyone I'm here, are you?"

He searches my eyes, but for what I don't know. "No, Sof, but he's worried about you. Make sure you call him. Don't blow him off. He cares about you. I don't know what's going on with you guys, but I do know that you have been friends for too long to let something stupid come in-between you two."

I look over towards Giovanni then back to Antonio. "Who says it's stupid? Do you think I'm being stupid?" I question Giovanni.

Antonio looks confused. "Wait? What the fuck? You know what's going on?" he drills Giovanni pointing at him.

Giovanni exhales heavily. "I do. And no, Sofia, I don't think you're being stupid, but I do agree with your brother, you need to talk to Caelan. And Antonio, for the record I will never betray her trust by telling you or anyone her business. That's her business- their business."

"If he hurt my sister I'll fuckin' kill'em. Someone better tell me what the fuck is going on. Like right fucking now!" Antonio demands.

I look over to Giovanni. *Balls!* "Damn it! My head hurts. I can't do this right now."

"Say something Sof, or I'm showing up at his fuckin' house at three-thirty in the morning to beat his ass!" he barks.

"Why? I'm fine! Look at me! I'm fine!"

"You. Are. Not. Fine! You're barely holding it together, Sofia! Fucking tell me what happened. Now!"

"Take it easy, A," Giovanni stresses.

"Wait, is this what was bothering you this morning at mom and pops?"

"Yes. It's no big deal. Honestly, it's not. He just hurt my feelings, that's all," I say glancing in Giovanni direction.

"Here, Sofia." He points his index and middle finger at his eyes. "Look at me. I asked the question."

Oh yeah, he's getting pissed. I gotta play this down big time. "Geeez, stop freaking yelling. My head is killing me," I snap holding my ears.

"Sofia." His deep tone warning me to hurry up and talk.

"I came home from work the other night, saw Caelan and some chick going at it on the couch. It caught me off guard. He's always been good about keeping it private when he brings girls home. I guess he just forgot or lost track of time. I don't really know, but it shocked me, hurting my feelings when I saw them. That's all, now leave it alone, A." His eyes flick to Giovanni's stone face looking for answers he's not going to get. I walked away towards the kitchen to get that much needed-drink of water. When I walk back out into the living room their whispered conversation comes to a halt.

"I'm going back to bed." I start to walk toward my designated room.

A starts walking towards me. "Come here," he says holding his arms out again. "I'm sorry you had to walk in on that. I know you care for him."

"Just bad timing, that's all." I down play it. He releases me with an expressionless face. "Good night," I say. "I'm going to bed before I have the hangover from hell waiting for me when the sun finally rises."

Climbing into bed, grabbing my phone I send Caelan a song.

Me: Sia~Elastic Heart

twenty-eight

THE SMELL OF FOOD BRINGS ME TO THE land of the living. Although, right now, I feel like I'm dead. I get out of bed slowly feeling out my head and stomach. I'm good. I make my way to the bathroom when I realize that I only have on a long t-shirt. Giovanni's? It must be his. He must have changed me into this last night. Ohhh, man. That's... that's... shit, I don't even remember. Shit. I throw some cold water on my face and go to finger brush my teeth when I realize there is an unopened toothbrush and toothpaste on the counter. Hmmm. Well, I'm not sure they're for me, but I'm using them because my mouth tastes and feels like I ate dog kibble.

Leaving the bathroom, I notice a pair of sweatpants draped over the arm of the chair so I grab them and make my way over to my cell phone to check the time. WOW, it's one o'clock in the afternoon? I throw the sweatpants on, then scroll through my messages. I quickly text Sage, Jess, and Nikki a good afternoon and let them know I'm alive. I don't however, text Caelan back. His text message from last night was long and I need a clear mind when I read it. Right now, the smell of the food permeating my nose will lift the fog, clear my head, and give me the strength to read it.

I make my way through the open living room to the kitchen island where Giovanni is standing pulling food out of a bag. "That smells so good," I eagerly chirp with a watering mouth.

He glances up smiling at me. "Good afternoon. How bad is it?"

"Not too bad. I've definitely had worse hangovers," I declare feeling uncomfortable knowing he changed me last night.

"Good. Sit." He points at the stool. "There are hot and cold subs. Didn't know what you liked so I bought a few. The oil, vinegar, and mayo are on the side. Plus, there's a Fat sandwich right there if you're feeling up to it."

"Oh, my inner fat girl just perked up. Give me that Fat sandwich," I plead with a huge smile on my face.

He laughs. "Take it slow, killer, you had a lot to drink last night."

That I did. I smile. "Giovanni, come on, you know that greasy, cheesy, stuffed with everything fried is the best thing for me right now to soak up all that leftover alcohol and sugar."

He nods with a smile. We're both silent for a while enjoying our food before he turns to the refrigerator grabbing us cold waters. "We need to talk about last night, Sofia. Then you're going to tell me why you came out here feeling uncomfortable."

Wow, he noticed. I thought I hid it pretty well. I guess not. I nod in acceptance. "Go ahead, lay it on me."

Putting his food down, his face becomes severe. "First off, my job is to protect you. That is what I will do, at all costs. You need to live a normal everyday life, I agree with that. That's why I didn't have a problem with you going out last night, but when you deliberately try hiding something from me that could potentially be information or even a clue to whoever is out there, that's where I draw the line. I will not stand for it. I take my job seriously, and you, Sofia, are more than a job. You're not just my boss's daughter. I think at this point we can say we're friends, good friends, but I am still your bodyguard and you will listen to me. Do not do it again."

Well, slap me sideways, I just got reprimanded by G-man! I'm not sure what to say right now except for what needs to be said. "I agree with you. I'm sorry. I just didn't want Johnathan to see the note from Jake. He was already not happy when he saw Sage and I dancing together. I thought hiding the note would make my night easier, but that didn't happen, it only made it worse." I huff to myself. "I'll never see him again. Not after seeing how much of a nut case I am," I acknowledge sadly, shrugging my shoulders in defeat. "Too bad too, 'cause he was hot!" I smile trying to lighten the mood with some humor.

"Apology accepted. Now tell me why you were so uncomfortable coming out here just now," he questioned with a raised brow.

Well, this is going to be awkward.

"D-Did you undress me last night?"

"No."

"I undressed myself?"

"Not exactly. I called my sister when we left the club. She was here waiting for me when we got here. She helped you. The only reason you're wearing my shirt and sweats are because I left your bag in the truck. I figured the faster we got you into some clothes and into bed would be better."

"Ohhhh I don't know what makes me feel worse, knowing that your sister had to take care of me, or you making the poor girl get up in the middle of the night to help."

"Trust me. It's not that big a deal. She doesn't live far."

"Well, thank you for respecting my privacy."

"I will always respect your privacy. I know your history, and I know that me helping you change would have made you uncomfortable. Now finish eating your Fat sub," he orders directing his gaze at my four thousand calorie sandwich.

When I get out of the much-needed shower, I notice my overnight bag sitting on the bed. I change into a strapless yellow and white chevron mid-calf maxi dress. It goes well with my tanned skin and dark hair. I throw a pair of white strappy sandals on, and some bangle bracelets then throw my hair into a messy twist with some light makeup and call it a day. When I reach the living room, Giovanni's on the phone. I walk to the kitchen grabbing another water giving him a few minutes of privacy. When I return, I hear the tail end of his conversation.

"When? When was he there? Why? I'll talk to him. She's fine. I'm not sure. That's up to her. I guess that's up to you now, isn't it? Trust me he's already being checked out. None of your business. Let's get one thing straight, do not take my kindness right now for weakness. I'm being sympathetic because I know you're worried, but in the future, you will watch how you talk to me." He ends the call and turns to see me standing there.

"I wasn't eavesdropping. I came out to get a drink, you were on the phone, so I went to the kitchen to get a water to give you some privacy for a few minutes."

"It's fine."

"Caelan?"

"Yes."

"Does he know I'm staying here?"

"No, but I'm sure he assumes. From what I understand he's been to everyone's house, even Luke's to see if you were there."

"He's acting crazy."

"Yes, he is. One of the worst kinds of crazy. He's in love with you, Sofia. He wants to be there for you, protect you. Both of you have more history than most married couples so you can't blame him for being worried, but you can, however, blame him for being an ass."

"You think I'm being stupid for blowing him off?"

"No. I think you need time."

"What if, we're too close?" I mutter questionably. More to myself then to him. "Sometimes two people can be too close, right? I mean I gave myself to him the other night, he turned me down after he saw what I did to myself." Images of the other night hit me with an overwhelming sadness. "With

Johnathan last night, I felt free. He doesn't know my past. He doesn't know I lost a child. He doesn't know I was abducted, beaten and… r-raped," I falter to say because I have never said it out loud to anyone. "My history to him is a blank canvas. I can be whoever or whatever I want to be with him, or anyone else I meet because quite honestly let's face facts here, I'll never hear from Johnathan Reznor again, that's for sure." I exhale. "I feel like I wanna just run away. Start a whole new life somewhere else and become someone new. Change my name, change my hair. Live a life where I'm not Sofia Rose Heart with a past worse than a lifetime movie," I whisper. "I mean… dammit!" I frustratingly yell, gritting my teeth. "Am I ever going to live a normal life? Get married to a man that loves me unconditionally, have children, own Heart's Desire's boutiques all over the country? Is that too much to ask, Giovanni?"

He pads the floor quickly towards me. "Look at me," he commands lifting my chin so my eyes meet his clear determined ones. "There is no other life. This is your life. There is no running away. You will not run away from this; do you hear me? You're strong, Sofia. If there is someone out there after you, A and I will find him. We will make sure he doesn't hurt you again. Antonio and I are the only ones who know about this. Not even your father knows we're looking into this. We will be the only ones that know about what's going on to keep you safe and trust me, we will keep you safe. You just have to work on you while we protect you. Do you hear me?"

"Ya."

"My best advice, take your time. Think things through. Don't go jumping into something with someone new when you have this hanging between you and Caelan. You can stay here as long as you want or you can go back home. It doesn't matter to me. But, Sofia, you and Caelan need to talk."

"COFFEE FIRST? THAT'S the only thing I couldn't supply you with this morning. That latte you get is pretty serious." He laughs waiting for my answer.

"Absolutely! Hey, maybe the hot chicks will be there again today. Did you change your mind? I could always set you up."

"Yeah, like they would let you get within ten feet of them now! And, no, they weren't my type anyway."

"Really? What is your type? Let me guess. Platinum blonde, legs that don't end and a rack that stands at attention without the help of a bra?"

"You got me all wrong." He laughs as he throws the truck in park.

"So, tell me then, what's your type?" I ask as he holds open the coffee shop door.

Smiling down at me he says, "Average height, curvy, dark hair, easy going personality. Someone that can sit on the couch with beer and pizza watching a movie and think it's a great night."

"Wow, that shocked me. Would have sworn you would have said the opposite." My phone rings as I'm getting back into the SUV. "Hi, Momma."

"How's my girl doing today?"

"I'm better."

"No, you're not, but we'll go with it, for now. Anything interesting happen last night? Your brother came to the house early this morning looking like a bear that hadn't slept with hot shit stuck on his tail."

Hmmm, wonder what that's all about?

"No, mom I'm good. I went out last night with Sage, Nikki and Jess. I'm headed over to Hearts Desire right now to check on the new inventory."

"Have dinner with your momma tomorrow night?"

"Sure, what time?"

"Six-thirty at The Surf?"

"Perfect. See you then. Love you."

"Love you too, Fia baby."

Walking through the back door of HD feels good. It feels like home. With everything going on right now, I need something that feels like home. It doesn't matter how many Hearts Desire's I open I will always cherish this one. As I'm setting Jess' and Sage's coffees down, Jess walks into the back-storage area looking as green as can be, but still throwing her arms around me in a big hug.

"I didn't know you were coming in today. How are you feeling?"

"I'm good. Hangover this morning, but G-man here had me a nice Fat sandwich waiting for me when I woke up."

"Nice!" I hear Sage's tired deep voice. "I should have come to your place this morning. I had the worse hangover. Whose idea was it to switch to tequila shots last night? And not for nothing, but how many shots did we consume?" Sage asks as he's walking into the back room rubbing his head.

Jess starts laughing at him.

"What are you laughing at blondie? You looked like a cat's ass this morning after a bad case of the shits."

I damn near choked on my laughter. "I'm sure I didn't look any better."

"I wasn't that bad, Sage," Jess complains.

Now both Giovanni and I are cracking up.

"Ohhhh, honey, did you really get a good look at yourself in the mirror this morning?"

"Sage, be nice," I jokingly reprimand.

"Oh, sunshine, I am being nice, you should have seen her this morning dragging ass through the door." He pokes. Now we all crack up.

"Well, Sage, you can blame yourself for the shots of tequila, because I'm pretty sure it was *you* that started it." I point at him accusingly.

"Fuck me! Sunshine, my head may feel explosive today, but last night was fun!"

We all nod our heads in agreement.

WHILE MY HEAD is buried in the stack of invoices for the new inventory, I hear the faint knock on my office door. When I look up, I find Giovanni standing there.

"I gotta step out back and make some phone calls. Don't leave the store."

"Got it, boss."

I watch him walk out the back. My cell phone dings with a text.

Mr. Macallan: Have dinner with me tonight?

I jump out of my seat as Jess walks through my office door.

"What? What's going on?" She beams.

I flip my phone towards her. "Johnathan just texted me. Asked me to go to dinner with him tonight. Jess, I didn't think I would hear from him again after last night."

"Well, what are you going to do?" she asks smiling cheerfully at me.

"I can't go."

"Why?"

"I have work tonight. It's my last night for a few weeks."

"Tell him you can't and see if you can switch it to tomorrow."

"I'm having dinner with mom tomorrow, though."

"Sofia Rose Heart, you know your mom, she would cancel on you if she knew. Call her, switch mom to a lunch. Then have dinner with Mr. Sexy."

My phone starts vibrating in my hand. "Shit it's him!" I squeal fumbling my phone.

"Answer!" she yells bouncing on her feet and waving her hands.

"Hello." I try to sound calm cool and collected.

"Hello, pretty girl. It was taking too long for you to answer. I didn't want to give you too much time to think about it." His deep chuckle vibrates in my ear. "Have dinner with me tonight?"

"I'm sorry, I can't."

Silence.

"Did I blow it that bad last night?"

"No, if anyone blew it, it was me. I want to go to dinner with you, but I have work tonight."

"At Ice? In the VIP rooms?"

"Yes. Well, no in Fire."

"So, if not tonight, how about tomorrow night?"

"I'd love to."

"Good, I'll pick you up at seven."

Hesitating for a minute because I know Giovanni will be pissed. "Sure. I'll text you my address."

"How about you just give it to me when you see me. I'll stop by Fire tonight for a drink."

"Sounds good, see you then," I calmly say staring at Jess with a huge smile across my face. Jess is bouncing back and forth from foot to foot.

"Well?" she probes. "Come on, Sof, you're killin' me!"

"I have a date tomorrow night with Mr. Johnathan Reznor!" I squeal. "And he's coming into Fire tonight to see me!"

"Really? Wooo!"

"Why are we woooing? What's going on? And stop woooooing so loud my head still hurts," Sage barks rubbing his temples as he walks through the door. Poor guy, although it is his fault we all have hangovers.

"I have a date tomorrow night with Johnathan," I say beaming. I can't read Sage's expression, but he's not the happy Sage like I expected him to be.

"Good, sunshine, I'm happy for you."

"You don't look happy."

"It's not about me, Sofia. It's about you, being happy, and if this makes you happy, then I'm happy for you."

"What's going on?" Giovanni inquires walking through my now crowded, tension-filled office.

"Nothing. I have a date tomorrow night with Johnathan. He's picking me up at seven." I half smile downplaying it.

"Absolutely not," Giovanni states with a stone face.

My shoulders drop. "Giovanni, I'm going to dinner."

"No, he is not."

"Yes, I am!" I yell. My stubbornness coming out in full effect so I'm not actually listening to what he's saying.

"Give us some privacy," he demands glaring at me without looking at Sage and Jess.

As they walk out Jess throws me a concerned look. "Giovanni, I'm telling you right now, I'm going on a date with Johnathan tomorrow. You're not going to stop me."

"Sofia, I'm not trying to stop you from the date itself. However, him picking you up at your house, that is not going to happen. You will call him back and tell him you will meet him at the restaurant. That's final."

I drop myself into my purple velvet tufted wingback office chair in resignation. "I'll tell him tonight. He's coming in to see me." His facial features don't change much, but I saw the concern and the twitch in his jaw that he didn't want me to see.

"Did you know the back-door alarm isn't working again?"

Well, that's a change of subject if I ever heard one. "No, I didn't know. Let me go ask Jess." I find her hanging the new, black, open-back mini dresses. Hmmmm I may have to steal one of these for dinner with Johnathan tomorrow night. "Hey, when you came in this morning was the back door alarm working?"

"No. I called the electrician this morning to come and fix it."

"When did it stop working?" Giovanni inquires.

"It worked yesterday when we left, but this morning when we came in, it didn't."

Giovanni nods. "I'm going out back to make some more calls."

As I'm walking back into my office, I yell over my shoulder to Jess "You have one of those in my size?"

"Sure do. You thinking what I'm thinking?" She raises her brow. "Tomorrow's dinner?"

"Yup." I smirk.

"Perfect. I'll bring one back to you."

My office is quiet for once. I reach over and flip on my music. Ellie Goulding~ *Don't Need Nobody* comes on. While humming to the song I finish paying all the invoices. I drift off looking around my posh office. Smiling, I remember back to the day Caelan and I argued over my office. He's put so much money into the boutique that when he asked me how I wanted to design my office I told him a plain jane room was just fine. He insisted I needed to feel like a queen when I was paying all the big bills that were going to come across my desk. Looking around I somberly chuckle realizing how much he really knows me and my style. The office was a surprise for me. He wouldn't let me see it 'til it was done and he wouldn't even tell me how much everything cost when I demanded to know. Which I know was a pretty steep penny.

'It's my gift to you, beautiful. You deserve it.'

From the white washed Queen Anne style desk, to the deep grey, almost black, Venetian plaster walls with an intricate damask stencil in a gloss black to my very comfortable, special order, velvet, purple wingback tufted chair and sofa, he gave me luxury at its finest, nailing me and my style to a tee. I was so shocked and happy the day it was finally finished, and he revealed it to me. When he opened the door to my office that day, I gasped because I was so shocked at all the detail he put into it.

Sadness comes over me. I start remembering the day we were sitting by the pool at my parent's house talking about our hopes and dreams while we enjoyed the sun. Caelan had already had his business up and running and doing very well, too. When I told him I wanted to open my own boutique, he was all for it.

'Sofia, I will back you in anything you do. You find the place, and I'll back you with the capital and the workers.'

He hated that I worked at Ice. Still does. He expected me to quit Ice when Hearts Desire opened. When I didn't, he asked me why. When I explained to him that I wanted to pay him back as fast as I could, and Ice would be able to provide me to do that, he was not a happy man.

'I don't fucking care about the money! What I care about is your happiness.'

Those were his exact words. I sigh...

I miss my best friend.

The knock on the door startles me. "Come in."

"Here's the dress."

"Thanks. Just hang it on the hook for me."

"I'm so excited for you."

"Me too. Jess? Do you think I'm doing the right thing?" Her delay in answering me only confirms that she too isn't so sure that me going on this date is the right thing to do.

"I think you have to do what's right for you. I want you to be happy. That's what we all want for you. If going out on a date with Johnathan tomorrow is what makes you happy and it leads into more and you're happy, that's all that matters Sof."

twenty-nine

WHILE HELPING ME INTO THE SUV, Giovanni's cell phone rings. He slides into the front seat answering.

"Yea? No. She has work tonight. I got it. Nope, I'm good man. I heard you were looking for me yesterday? Nah, I'm good. I'll let you know. You take care of Antonio. I'll take care of her," he snaps abruptly, dropping the call.

"Can you put on the radio?"

"Yea, where are we going?" he asks as he turns on the radio. His cell phone rings again. After looking at it, he denies the call.

"Home." His eyes flip to me in the review mirror. "I need some stuff, and I'll shower there and get ready for work."

His cell phone goes off again. Annoyance clearly shown on his face and through his clenching jaw but when he looks at the screen the tension leaves him. "Yea? What? What the fuck are you talking about? What? When? You call anyone else? Don't! I'll call. We're on our way there now. Do not talk to anyone."

"Giovanni what's the matter? I stammer as he's dialing on his cell.

"It's me. Your sister's house, now! Keep it fucking quiet."

Click.

"Giovanni you're scaring me. Is Caelan okay? Tell me what's going on."

"That was Caelan. He just opened the mail at his office. There was a large manila envelope addressed and delivered to him this morning. He thought it was the contracts for the new developments, but it wasn't. When he opened it this afternoon there were photos of you in there."

"W-What?" I whisper.

Silence

"Sofia we're almost to the house. Stay calm and breathe. We'll know more when we get there. Just try to stay calm. I promise I will not let anything happen to you."

The ride felt like it was forever, but in reality, it was only another five minutes. We rushed into the house finding Luke, Chris, and a livid Caelan standing at the kitchen island with the photos in his hand. Caelan throws the photos down onto the counter then embraces me in a breathtaking hold. When he releases me, he grabs my face with both his hands. "I will not let anyone hurt you again. I promise you," he whispers into my ear.

Antonio comes through the door two minutes later like a bull with a red flag dangling in his face. Giovanni grabs the photos and starts flipping through them. Caelan releases me, and now I'm practically hanging on Giovanni's arm so I can see the pictures.

"Motherfucker!" Giovanni hisses in a deep threatening timbre. "First off, why the fuck are these two here?" Giovanni demands drilling Chris and Luke with his raging eyes.

I grab the photos from him and with one glance, my stomach drops as I suck in a deep breath.

It's happening again.

Giovanni's large arm goes around my shoulders, pulling me into him. I watch as Caelan's body stiffens. A look of pure anger reflecting in his handsome eyes. Then, I feel my brother at my back. He's looking over my shoulder at the pictures that my shaking hands are holding. All of these pictures are suggestive that Giovanni and I are intimate. I look up to him in silent question.

He slightly shakes his head, telling me not to say my thoughts out loud. There's a photo of him carrying me in his arms. It's at night. My head resting on his shoulder. The dress I have on in the photo tells me it's from last night. The next photo is of us the day we went to the coffee shop the day the women were drooling all over Giovanni. It's him letting me out of the SUV. My hand is laying tenderly against his chest. While I look up at him, he's looking down at me. It looks like we are gazing into each other's eyes but in actuality it was when I patted him on the chest.

Oh my God. This is bad.

Another photo is of Giovanni and I the first afternoon we walked to the coffee shop from the boutique. We're standing pretty close, having what looks like an intimate conversation. Which, we were. It was about Caelan and the baby. In the picture though, it looks like were having a lover's heart to heart.

Ohhh this is really, really bad.

As I'm flipping through the pictures, Antonio is grabbing them from my grip.

"Chris was already here when I got home. Luke was in my office when I opened the envelope," Caelan explains.

"I'm gonna kill this fucker!" I hear Antonio roar behind me. The hatred radiating from his body is penetrating into mine. I hand him the rest of the pictures, then unwrap myself from Giovanni's arm taking a few steps way, trying to collect myself.

"Why was Chris here before you got home?" Giovanni questions.

I watch Caelan's eyes flash to Christopher's quickly. Then back to Giovanni's. "He was taking care of something for me, and besides, it's my fucking house. He can be here anytime he wants. He has a key."

Giovanni's eyes narrow on Caelan. "What's that?" he asks grabbing another envelope on the counter.

"That's another envelope of pictures addressed to Sofia. It was in the mailbox when I got home."

I grab the envelope. Pulling out the pictures, I notice that these are different. These are of me doing just mundane things. There's one of me standing at the front desk of HD. One of me coming out of the bathroom at the coffee shop. There's also another one of me by the back door of HD with boxes in my hands. This is just this sick fucker's way of letting me know I'm being watched. That I'm not... untouchable. That he's right there, so close, and I didn't even know it. He wants me to know he can get to me at any time. There's a picture of me wearing the red halter maxi dress walking out the front door last Monday morning. The first time I was outside after being drugged Thursday night.

"He was right there waiting for me," I disbelievingly whisper.

"What?" Caelan questions.

"He was right here the whole time, waiting for me. Right outside our door. This picture is from the Monday morning after I was drugged. Look at my dress. I wore that dress on Monday when I went into HD. He's been right here the whole time." I grab the other set of pictures. I grab the one picture I'm looking for and hand it to Giovanni. His eyes zero in on what I'm showing him. It's the one of him carrying me into his penthouse building last night. "Whoever this is knows where I've been this whole time."

"Well, that's just fucking awesome!" Caelan roars. "I didn't even know where you were! I fucking searched the city for you, but yet, this crazy sick motherfucker has been right at your back!" he thunders. "Where the fuck were you in all this?" he roars at Giovanni. "You're supposed to be watching her! I can see by the pictures you're watching her real fucking close, aren't you!" he bellows, provoking him.

Giovanni's already taut body goes even more rigid. I watch as Caelan throws his hands in the air, turning his back on me. Well, hell that hurt, he just turned his back on me.

"Don't you fucking dare tell me how to do my job!" Giovanni's enraged body starts towards Caelan.

Antonio jumps in the middle. "Stop! Calm the fuck down! Everyone's on edge here! Fucking relax!" he yells shoving Giovanni back. "Come on, he doesn't need another busted lip." I look from Antonio to Caelan realizing that, yes, yes he does have a busted lip and a bruised jaw. Looking back to Giovanni, I see him smirking at Antonio in complete utter satisfaction.

"What happened to your face?" I question.

"Nothing," he snaps at me.

Walking towards him, I see it more clearly now. "Tell me what happened to your face?" I demand cupping his jaw softly.

"Nothing. Leave it alone, Sof." He tries to twist away from my hand, but I hold on.

Turning to Antonio. "Did you do this?"

"Sofia, leave it alone," he repeats jerking his jaw from my hand, then focuses on Giovanni. "Do your fucking job and make sure she's protected." His enraged body heads towards Giovanni. Yet again, walking away from me.

Turning, I watch three grown men, the same three grown men that are supposed to be protecting me, argue with each other. Chris and Luke are just standing there, listening to the chaos filling the room. I take a deep breath and turn towards the stairs. At my back are the men that are supposed to be protecting me, but they don't even realize I'm walking away. I reach the top of the stairs and look down to see Luke's sad eyes watching me. I give him a despairing half smile at the scene still unraveling and then walk to my room.

After a few minutes of silence, I turn my music on, then hear a slight knock on my door. When I open it, Luke is on the other side, looking irritated. I open the door wider for him to enter. Then slightly close the door to drown out the yelling of three men.

"You okay?"

"Are you asking just to be nice, or do you really want the answer? Tell me, Luke, do you want me to lie to you or tell you exactly how I'm feeling?"

"I want the truth, sweetheart."

Hmmm, am I holding it together?

I huff some breath from my nostrils and answer as honestly as I can. "Well, let's see, the man that abducted me, violated me and took away parts of me that I will never get back, who, I thought was dead, but in my heart knew wasn't, has come back to finish the job he started. He's been only a few feet from me for days and days and not one of the men in my life who say they're going to protect me have even noticed him. Now, they're standing in my kitchen arguing with each other. So much so that they didn't even notice that I walked away. Tell me, Luke, when you came up here just now did they even realize that you came up here, or that I even came up here?"

His sad eyes answer for him, but still the words sting. "No, no they didn't, but Sofia, listen to me, you are safe. They are trying to protect you. They are protecting you. If it weren't for them, he might have succeeded in abducting you already. Those photos may show that he's close, but they also show he can't get any closer. You're going to be okay. You not only have Caelan, Giovanni, and Antonio protecting you, but you have Chris, Sage, and me as well. We will not let anything happen to you."

"I know you don't know what happened to me that night, Luke, but... but he told me when he let me go that he would come back to get me. Now he has."

"Look at me," he demands grabbing my shoulders. "He. Will. Not. Get. To. You. Do you hear me?"

Before I can answer, I hear someone by my bedroom door. When I look over, I see Chris standing there. He smiles at me, but it's with tight white lips. He's just as pissed off.

"Well, did they even notice you're missing?"

He snorts. "No. They're ready to kill each other down there." The usual happy go lucky, ball busting, Christopher O'Reily is now somber. "Sofia, they're all just worried about you and trying to figure out the best way to protect you."

"Well, that's kind of funny because to protect me they'd have to stop whipping their dicks out to see which one's bigger and take notice that the person you're trying to protect just walked away."

"I agree, honey. I don't think it's so much Giovanni whipping his dick out as it is Caelan whipping his out trying to hold on to you."

"He hasn't lost me."

"He doesn't have you like he wants you either, Sof." Chris raises his brows tilting his head a little.

"If he wanted me so bad he could have had me, Chris. He chose someone else to fill that need."

"Look," he says grimacing. "I'm not going to make excuses for him. What he did is fucked up. It is. I understand you're hurt, I do. But right now, we all have to think about you and your safety. How about we go back downstairs, show them what assholes they're being?"

I look over to Luke who's smiling and nodding. "Show them some of that feisty Sofia we all know and love." He stands from sitting on my bed, holding out his hand for me.

As we approach the top of the stairs, holding Luke's hand, I see Giovanni and Caelan glaring at each other. Antonio is talking, but I can't hear what he's saying until the tail end of his conversation.

"If you would put your dick away for one fucking minute, you would realize he is protecting her, asshole. We are all trying to protect her."

"If he kept his dick in his pants, I wouldn't be flipping the fuck out, but it doesn't look like he can. Where's she been the past few fucking days, huh? With you? In your bed? Fucking you? These pictures say an awful lot."

WACK!

The echoing sound of my hand slapping Caelan's face stops everyone and everything. "You son of a bitch! How dare you!" Caelan's hand goes to his red now starting to swell cheek. I see the shock, then anger, then pure sadness flicker in his gleaming blue eyes. "How dare you stand there accusing him of sleeping with me when you purposely set out to fuck another woman so that I would see you doing it! You have some pair of balls Caelan O'Reily! I don't even know who you are right now. You are not the same guy that cried with me on that couch right there on Saturday," I scream pointing at the couch. "The same exact couch you were fucking that woman on three days after we finally talked about me losing our baby. Who are you? Where did that guy go? Because I want him b-back!" I stammer through my tears. "I want him back!" He stands there with shock, guilt, and shame on his face. Chills flush my skin. I realize at this very moment that I just let everyone know I was pregnant with his baby. I look around the room, all eyes are plastered on me. Giovanni has a sad, but relieved look on his face. Chris and Luke are just standing there in shock. Then I look at Antonio. My tears are like hot knives slicing through my cheeks. Anger crosses his face, then confusion... then sorrow. I feel someone gently touch my arm, but he's not the person I need nor want touching me right now. I slowly walk towards my brother's open arms and sink into his warmth. I break, my body wracked with sobs. When my knees give, he lifts me in his arms and carries me into Caelan's office kicking the door closed.

HE LAYS ME ON Caelan's leather couch, shock still clearly etched into his handsome features. "You lost a baby? Caelan's baby?" he tenderly asks.

"Yes, I lost a baby. Actually, babies. I was pregnant with twins."

"What?" he stammers. His words quiet with disbelief. "When? Recently? Are you two together?"

"No," I huff. "No, we're definitely not together. We are so far apart right now I'm not even sure we can get back to what we once were." I take a minute before I begin. "I was eighteen. Caelan and I... well, we were close as you know. We made the decision together. The night was totally planned. It wasn't just something that happened. Although, he was pretty experienced, I was not. I chose him, Antonio. I'm not going to get into all of the details with you, but just know that he was... perfect for me. I wound up getting pregnant. I lost the baby when I was a little over four months."

Realization now hitting him. "That's when you went into that deep depression, isn't it?"

I nod. "I had never talked to Caelan about losing the baby until this past Saturday. I pushed him away after I lost the baby. He started dating Kate, and

I started going to therapy. It wasn't until Saturday that I found out he's the one who's been paying for all my therapy." His incredulous face is searching mine to see if I am telling the truth. I shook my head. "I wouldn't- I couldn't, talk about it Antonio. He tried, but I couldn't bring myself to do it, but this past Saturday, I told him everything about that life-altering day."

"No one knew? Mommy didn't know?"

"No.

"Wait, even Nikki? She didn't know?"

"No."

His warm arms surround me. "I'm sorry, sis. I'm so sorry you had to go through that alone."

"I wasn't alone, but it's okay. I still hurt from it. I think I always will, but I'm going to be fine," I whisper, hugging him tightly. "Come on." I tug on his hand. "Before they kill each other out there."

WHEN WE WALK out of C's office, everyone stops talking and stares at us. Caelan's standing off to the side by himself leaning against the counter with his head hung. Luke's not too far away from him. If there's one thing I can say about Luke, he's as loyal to Caelan as any blood brother would be. As we both approach the kitchen island, I stop. Antonio keeps walking towards Caelan.

Wham!

I gasp, yelling, "Antonio are you crazy? What the hell is wrong with you?" I scream. He points at Caelan who is now rubbing his jaw, licking the blood trickling from his lip. Anger and retaliation festering in his blue eyes. He doesn't move to retaliate though, but Luke and Chris both step up. C holds up his hand to the both of them.

"That, you son of a bitch," A harshly growls poking him in the chest, "is for getting my sister pregnant!" I watch C's anger dissipate as he nods in confirmation. Then I watch Antonio grab Caelan in a man hug, telling him he's sorry for his loss. C's arms grip A tightly, reciprocating the hug. Just watching the two men I love most in my life have this moment with each other makes me profoundly sad.

After some hard back slaps between the two, I hear Caelan mutter, "That's three hits to the left side of my face by two Heart family members in twelve hours. I'm not saying I don't deserve it, but if one more person fucking hits me, shit's going down!"

After a quick look from Antonio to Caelan, I look back to Antonio and his cheeky smile lands back on Caelan. "Then stop fuckin' up, brother. Now, let's get our heads together, come up with a plan on how we are going to keep my sister safe. I will not let this motherfucker get to her." Everyone nods in agreement. A does all the talking with Giovanni standing at his side. "No one except for the five of us in this room knows about what is going on." He looks at each one of us. "*No One!*" he reiterates. "It stays right here with us. Even my father doesn't know," he clarifies examining me. "Giovanni is going to be her permanent bodyguard. Wherever she goes, he goes. If she stays here, he stays here." He cocks his brow at Caelan. "If she chooses to go back where she's been the last few nights, then he'll be there. No one, and I mean no one, but us can know about this. Don't say anything to any of the girls. The only reason you two know," he adds pointing back and forth between Chris and Luke, "is because you were here when it all went down today." He raises his brow. Then turns to me. "You have work tonight, right?" I nod. "What part?"

"Fire."

"Giovanni is going to be there just like he was the other night. I'm going to give Alex a call and let him know I want access up in The Devil's Lair. It looks down on Fire. I can keep watch from up there, see if there's anyone shady hanging around taking an interest in you. C, I need you to pretend that those pictures really affected you. He sent those specific set of pictures to you for a reason. He wants them to bother you, or it could just simply be that he was trying to lure her home."

"Well, that won't be hard," he murmurs in a low growl leering at Giovanni.

"Dude, I don't know what's going on between you two," he roars looking back and forth between them, "but get the fuck over it, C! We need to keep my sister safe."

Crossing his muscular arms over his large chest, C looks at Antonio then to Giovanni. "At least we can agree on that."

"Sofia, I need you, and I know this is going to be hard, but I need you to pretend that these pictures didn't affect you at all. You need to live your life like you normally would."

My eyes widen in disbelief. "I don't know if I can, Antonio," I exclaim.

"You have to. We're going to piss this motherfucker off, so he makes a mistake. I need everyone else here to act normal. Saturday night's Chris's birthday party, we're all going to be there partying like we always do. Everyone is going to go on just like it's any other day in our 'crazy eight' lives. Just like growing up, you fuck with one, you fuck with us all. We will get this son of a bitch and when we do..."

"He's mine," I growl digging my nails into my palms. "He's all mine."

thirty

I<small>T'S BUSY AS ALL HELL TONIGHT</small>. I'm running my ass off behind the bar, but the tips are rolling in, so that's a good thing. Still in the back of my mind though, there's that eerie feeling, that some sick son of a bitch could be watching me right now. I can feel it. I glance over to the corner of the bar where G-man has been nursing a scotch all night. My eyes quickly flick up to Antonio leaning against the railin in The Devils Lair.

"Excuse me, sexy girl, can I get a scotch? Macallan, please." I pull my eyes away from my brother and take a glimpse in the direction the request came from. Johnathan is standing there with the sexiest panty dropping smile on his face.

Damn he's good looking.

I'm taken aback a little. In all the chaos today, I forgot he was coming in.

Act normal, Sof.

He raises a brow in question because I'm standing here like an idiot, so I plaster the sexiest smile I can conjure up on my face and try to act normal. Heading his way, I grab a rocks glass and the bottle of Macallan as I smile and sashay my ass towards him. "You made it," I enthusiastically say with flirty eyes.

"I did." He grins. "Did you think I wouldn't?" His brow raises and he tilts his head a little.

"Well, I thought maybe one of your other chicks sidetracked you." I shrug my shoulder still smiling.

"Ahhh, Sofia, there's only one thing I have my eyes set on right now, and no one can side track me once I set my sight on something that I want." He pinpoints his eyes on mine.

"Sit." I jerk my chin towards the barstool. "So, tell me, where are you taking me to dinner tomorrow night?" I lick my lips waiting for his answer.

"You are one sexy girl. Do you know that?" He shakes his head as if he can't believe it.

"Mr. Reznor, are you trying to get into my pants? Because if you are... you will not succeed."

"Baby," he growls leaning forward, "if I were trying to get into your pants, trust me I would succeed, but, no, you are a beautiful, sexy woman, and right now, I feel like a pretty lucky guy because you accepted my dinner invitation."

This guy is friggin' good. He stumped me. I don't know what to say. What the hell is that? Oh, wait, yes those are my panties that are now at my ankles because they just fell off. Seriously? I need space.

I shake my head at him smiling. With a flushed face, I turn my back on him and walk away. I place the bottle of scotch back in its spot and do a walk around the bar filling patrons' drinks, but every so often I peek over my shoulder at Johnathan. He looks good tonight. Really good. He has on dark jeans and a tight black V-neck tee shirt. With his dark shirt and dark hair, his green eyes sparkle like the sun shining on a pure gem. He has money. You can tell just by his clothes and the way he carries himself. But, the calluses on his hands tell me he doesn't work in an office. He's a confident man, that much I'm sure of and I'm pretty sure it's a safe bet to say he gets what he wants, when he wants it. Well, Mr. Panty-Dropper meet Miss. Hard-to-Get.

When I make my rounds, I stop in front of him and refill his glass.

When I flick my eyes up to flirt with him I notice Uncle Carmine walking through Fire. I nonchalantly look over to Giovanni, who is no longer sitting at the bar. I quietly panic for a few seconds and quickly glance up to Antonio who has some blonde snuggled up to him. I watch as he lifts his phone to his ear then puts is back in his pocket while he walks down the long staircase from the Devil's Lair. I quickly look away because if I am being watched, I don't want to give away my protection by watching them.

"Am I boring you, Sofia?"

Huh?

"What? Oh, I'm sorry. No, I thought I saw someone I knew." I smile turning on my flirt. "What did you just ask me?"

"What's your favorite food?"

"Ahhh, that's easy." I grin biting my bottom lip. "Steak. Give me a big, fat, juicy piece of steak that I can sink my teeth into and feel the juices oozing around my mouth and down my throat, and I'm a very happy girl." I wink.

"Christ!" His eyes look heavenward and he readjusts himself on the stool. "You're killing me."

"Hey, honey." I hear from the side of the bar. When I look over, Uncle Carmine is standing there smiling.

"Hey, you." I look back to Johnathan. "Be right back," I say throwing the bottle of rum from my last customer back into the Speedwell as I walk over to Uncle Carmine. "What are you doing here? You looking to pick up some women?" I joke.

Laughing, he leans over the bar giving me a kiss on my cheek. "Honey, I know for an older man I look good, but these girls around here, they have no substance. I need quiet walks on the beach and lots of affection."

I burst out with laughter. "Yeah, yeah, 'cause that's what you're really looking for Uncle Carmine! You've never been the one-woman kind."

"Ahhh that's where you're wrong, honey." He pats my hand. "At one time, I had a woman. I was very much in love with her and would have given her the world." He stops talking for a minute. I can see him reminiscing before he shakes his head of his thoughts. "Nahhh, had some business tonight. A was supposed to be there. He decided it was more important to snuggle up to the blonde than back his uncle." He jerks his head towards Antonio. "I needed to have a little chat with him."

Damn. A was supposed to work tonight, and he's here. This makes him look bad. Carmine will tell my father, and my father will freak on Antonio.

"Oh. Well, think of it this way," I pacify waving my hand at the dance floor. "At least you get to survey all the flesh being revealed." I smile trying to lighten the situation.

"I'm too old for this shit. Goddamn music is too loud," he yells over the beat. "Gotta go, honey," he says leaning over the bar to give me a kiss goodbye.

"Be safe," I tell him because the jobs he and my brother do for my father are extremely dangerous. Even though I don't know the details of them, we all know that both of them are my father's go-to men when it come to the most crucial jobs.

Johnathan hung around until almost closing. When I told him I had to meet him at the restaurant, that my bodyguard would also be with me, he was a little taken aback, but quickly complied.

I just started to clean the speed rack when Jake danced up behind me. I smile at him while we both enjoy the music and each other's company. When the song ends, he gives me a hug and asked me to go for coffee with him after our shift is over. I know Jake is attracted to me, he has never hidden it, but I let him down easy telling him I'm exhausted and in desperate need of my bed. When he looks like he doesn't believe me, I go on to explain that a large shipment of inventory had come into HD that afternoon. He looked aggravated that I was blowing him off again, but made me promise that one day this week I would go for coffee with him, which I agreed to.

My thoughts wander to C. I want to go home tonight and sleep in my own bed. I wonder if he will be waiting up for me like he usually does? Probably not. He doesn't even know if I'm coming home or not. Besides, he royally pissed me off yet again today, to the point where I smacked him. Sadness overwhelms me because never in my life have I been so mad at C that I would lay my hands on him. He's always been my rock. I feel like we are so far apart from each other, when, right now, with everything going on, I would think we would be so much closer. When I saw the pain on his face today after Antonio punched him, then said he was sorry for his loss, there was a piece of Caelan that I saw and felt, break in him.

I need to go home tonight.

WHEN WE REACH the front door, I hesitate to open it with the memories from a few nights ago rushing back to me. The feeling that someone after me had hurt him at that moment had torn my heart out. Then, realizing that the same person I was just devastated over being hurt, was trying to hurt me, was more than I could bear. I shake my head of the thoughts while I open the door. C's sitting at the kitchen island with a beer. He's shirtless with disheveled dirty blond locks. The look on his face tells me he's a million miles away.

Or someone had their hands running through it.

I brush that thought off when he stands realizing it's me. His black cotton pajama pants fall below his waist, dipping low on his hips. My eyes are drawn to the V defining his stomach and the drawstring that is dangling back and forth between his legs make my eyes glance lower. My blood starts pumping faster as I look at him in all his manliness.

"You came home," he gruffly says surprised.

I'm nodding before my eyes leave the sight of his curly hair just under his belly button "You waited up."

"I always wait up for you, beautiful." We stare at each other like we're the only two in the room, but we're not.

I turn to Giovanni. "Bedroom or couch?"

"Couch."

"You sure?"

"Yup, lower level. Can keep an eye on things better. Go to bed. Get some rest. I'll make sure we're out the door on time tomorrow."

I head towards the stairs and turn back to Giovanni. "There's blankets and pillows in the large armoire. Help yourself," I tell him while I hear Caelan setting the security alarm.

Stopping at the bottom of the steps. I glance up at the long set of steps. I'm exhausted, physically and emotionally, and just looking at that climb weakens me more. I feel defeated standing at the bottom of the steps and I'm seriously contemplating sleeping on the other couch.

I feel myself being lifted. C cradles me in his strong arms so I lay my head on the soft flesh of his chest while he carries me up to my room and gently sets me down on my bed. He kisses my forehead and quietly walks away. I start to change before I hear my door softly close. I grab for my red spaghetti strap tank top and a red pair of boy shorts panties. I brush my teeth, wash my face and head back to my heavenly bed, but I stop just before laying down. I look at my bedroom door longing for the man on the other side. So, I grab my phone and send him a song that I interpret can mean anything to anyone, in any situation in their lives. For C and I, we have made choices- some good, some bad. Some have been made for us, but in the end, I will always be there for him, and he will always be there for me.

I wait a minute, then walk across the hallway. His door is slightly open so I knock softly and push the door open slowly. He's lying on his bed, eyes closed, legs crossed at the ankles and both arms behind his head. His phone's resting on his very defined muscular stomach with the beautiful, meaningful lyrics of Mumford and Sons~ *Timshel* filling his room.

He opens his eyes slowly, but he doesn't move. A small unsure smile lifts my lips. I stand still, gripping the door handle tightly, silently asking permission to curl up into his warm arms. I'm hesitant because after today I'm not sure he wants me in here with him.

He slides off the bed placing his phone down on his nightstand. He yanks the covers back, then climbs into his bed and holds the blankets up for me. I close his door and quickly pad across the floor and slide in next to him, putting my back to his warm front. He wraps his arm around my waist tightly pulling me into his safe body. He kisses the crown of my head and at the same time I kiss his bicep that my head is resting on. My hand is resting on his other one, resting across my belly. He kisses my head again, lingering there for a minute. I turn my head towards him and gently place a warm kiss to the bruises on his jaw. When I pull away, our eyes meet. I kiss him again. This time, on his full, warm lips. He reciprocates, but I can feel him holding back. I'm not sure what I'm doing, but I know that I feel this crushing need to be with him. To be as close to him as two people can be, to feel that connection. I'm not thinking about tomorrow, or even the other night. I'm thinking about right now and how I feel right now, at this very moment. So, I press my lips to his again and hold them there. When he pulls away silently questioning me if this is what I want, I grab his hand that's resting on my belly and slide it lower. His eyes flicker back and forth over mine. I see the reluctance in his eyes, so I kiss him again moving his large hand even lower, until it's under the rim of my panties. He pulls back from my lips again. I can feel his erection against my hip. I brace myself, knowing the next few moments between us will change our lives and intertwine us in an even stronger, more intimate journey.

"Are you sure?" his husky voice shakes asking.

I'm not sure of anything right now, but yes, I'm sure I want this with him right here, right now. "Yes," I whisper back.

He hesitates for just a second longer, then presses his lips on top of mine in a kiss that is so soft, so gentle, and so full of love, it takes my breath away and brings a tear to my eye.

"I'm so sorry I hurt you," he whispers with his forehead resting against mine.

"I know." It's all I can say because I know he's sorry, and right now I don't want to think about it or him with someone else.

He lifts himself from the bed holding his weight up with his forearm and pulls me under him before lowering himself on top of me. As he lowers himself, I can see the head of his cock protruding out from the top of his black pajama pants. Just the feel of his body dropping down against mine makes my skin tingle. Just the feeling of his hardness pressed against my mound is making me wetter than I have ever been in my life. That dick in his pants is not the same dick I saw and felt when I was eighteen. No no, this one is... this one is making me a little nervous, but in a good way. He lifts my tank top, pulling it over my head. Then slides my boy short panties down my legs. I lay before him completely bare. I watch him skim over my body in complete reverence. Then I watch his eyes land on the small pink and purple butterfly tattoo that he's never seen before. It sits slightly above and to the right of my mound. One's just a little higher than the other. Two beautiful butterflies tattooed in a way that makes them look like they're in carefree flight up my body. His eyes connect with mine. I can see the questions, so I close mine and take a deep breath pulling him into me. I slide my hands under his pants and over his amazing ass. He helps me get the rest of them down then kicks them off under the covers. He lays his naked, hot body against my tingling, burning, willing one. He lowers his head, kissing my breast, then takes my nipple into his mouth as he kneads the other one. I moan, and when I do, I hear a deep rumble come from within his chest. He raises his head to suck on the soft skin just under my ear. My teeth sink into his shoulder, moaning louder as my hands run through his dirty blond hair.

This is not the same animalistic, lust-filled, hot almost sex from the other night on the pool table. This is two people making love. He's making love to me. This is two people with a deep connection to each other filling their emptiness for each other with each other. His hand sweeps down the side of my body, grabbing my hip pulling me into him as he pushes his erection into my core harder. I wrap my legs around his waist, locking my ankles. His warm, wet tongue slides over my nipples, making them so erect they hurt. He slides his hand between us, pressing and rubbing small circles onto my sensitive ball of nerves. My legs uncross from around his waist, falling open to him, for him. His mouth lands on mine again in a deep kiss. Cupping his jaw, I devour his lips and warm tongue. I feel his two-day old stubble beneath my palms, and it's the sexiest damn thing I've ever felt.

Our breathing is heavy, so heavy that it's all you can hear besides *Timshel* softly playing on repeat. There have been no words between us since his apology. No more words needed to be said. We both need this, and I've never been surer of anything in my life.

He lifts himself from me. The cold air hits my body from the loss of his heat. He kisses his way down my belly, to just under my belly button, slightly tugging my diamond piercing with his teeth.

I watch his eyes wander to the two butterflies again in wonder. He slowly lifts his head to look at me, and at that moment, I know he's starting to realize why I have them and why there's two. He places a lingering tender kiss on both of them causing a tear to slide down my temple, only to get lost in the darkness of my hair. He places his forehead against my stomach taking a moment and a deep breath before he looks back up to me. His eyes are flooded with tears as he kisses the butterflies again, then sliding down my body. Kneeling between my thighs, he looks down at my bareness with a tender smile. With his strong hands, he bends my knees, spreading my thighs wide and holding them open. I am completely open to him. I see him quickly glance over my thighs, looking for bruising. They're there, but only slightly. He lowers his head, kissing each bruise that's left then moves up towards my glistening folds. He licks me in one long slow torturous swipe. When he reaches the top of my mound, he closes his eyes and savors my taste on his tongue, which causes his breathing to become heavier and rougher, with low and long groans.

The feeling of his tongue on me sends lighting through my body. Moaning louder and louder I grab at his dirty blond locks between my legs. That long-overdue feeling hits me, deep and hard in my lower belly. As he sucks on my clit, the tingling starts, causing me to whimper and tense, before lifting my hips off his bed moaning his name. His fingertips dig into the flesh of my hips, pushing them down so he can slide his tongue deep inside me. I come, and I come harder than I ever have in my life. He rests his tongue inside of me, feeling my pulsating waves as he continues to hold down my thrusting hips.

When there's nothing but small aftershocks left, he flattens his tongue at the lowest part of my pussy, slowly licking from the bottom all the way up past my clit, almost sending me over the edge again, to my mound leaving a gentle lingering kiss.

I want him so badly. I want him inside me, but I want him in my mouth first. I want to give him the same releasing pleasure he has just given me. Breathing heavy, he kisses his way back up my belly to my waiting lips. I can taste myself on him, which drives me crazy.

I reach down between us, grabbing ahold of his enormous cock. Slightly pushing him back he rolls off me, lying flat on his back. I take one of his nipples into my mouth and hear the rumble in his chest. I work my way down and up, kissing and nipping at the flesh of his neck. Then work my way down to an extraordinarily large, swollen, straining masterpiece of a cock. I look back up to him with a raised brow letting him know this is a little intimidating.

He grins lovingly at me, showing me that dimple that always gets to me. I lower my head to lick the tip of the beast, then drop even more, holding my warm, flat, tongue against his sac, letting it rest there for a few seconds before I lick him from the bottom of his heavy sac to the tip of his cock. He lets out a guttural groan. Loud enough that I think the neighbors heard him, and if so, good, because right now, knowing that I am making him feel the pleasure as good as he gave me, is all I care about. I lick him, leaving as much saliva as I can behind because this is going to be a challenge. Opening my mouth wide, I lower down onto him. His thighs tense then tremble, which only spurs me on. I slowly lower my head, taking in as much as I possibly can. I pull back up, take a deep breath, then lower again. As I do, I moan at the full feeling in my mouth. I try to hum to give him vibration, but he's just too large. I feel his hands grabbing at my hair trying to pull me up. I look up into his concerned eyes.

"I'm gonna come, baby."

I grin. "Good. I want to feel you slide down my throat." I drop my head back down engulfing his cock into my mouth sucking even harder.

"Beautiful," he gruffly murmurs a warning. I slide up, then dip down, up, then down, before he tenses and explodes. His moaning growl is so deep, so fierce, that I feel the vibrations in my body. His shaking hands grip my hair so tight, it's on the verge of pain, but I don't care. When I look up at his face, I see his abs rapidly contracting from his heavy breathing. I wait until he stops coming before I slowly work my way down, then up, until I suck his cock clean. Right before I get to the tip, his hands land on my shoulders. In one swift swoop, I'm under him with his still semi-hard cock pressing into my throbbing, waiting, wet folds. He takes my breath away with a kiss I can only explain as floating through the soft clouds of heaven on a rainy day. There's love, sadness, and hope mixed into this kiss. Breathing heavy, he lowers his forehead to mine before reaching towards his nightstand drawer.

I place my hand on his arm and shake my head. "I'm... I'm on the pill but..." I quietly plead not able to finish what needs to be said. But, he knows exactly what I'm asking.

"I've never been with anyone without a condom except for you. Never. I promise you, beautiful."

He kisses me again working his way to my neck as I feel him start to enter me. I wrap my arms around his neck and my legs around his waist and hold on for dear life. After tonight, I may not be able to walk. Tomorrow morning could be a challenge. He pushes a little more, pulling a long deep moan from me. I unwrap my arms and grasp the sheets, sinking my nails into the soft fabric.

"No, beautiful. Put those arms back around me, I want to feel those nails clawing at my back when I slide into you." He pushes into me a little more with a growl. I whimper, sinking my teeth into his shoulder before he slides back out. He pushes forward again, then pulls back. "Open up for me, beautiful. Open up to me," he whispers into my ear. "I want every bit of me feeling every bit of you, my beautiful girl." I unlock my ankles letting my thighs fall open to him. His left hand hooks under the back of my knee pushing my leg up higher, spreading me open further. When he slides in a little farther, I moan louder. "Look at us, baby," his husky whisper fills my ears with glazed over eyes. I follow his orders and look at where him and I are joined. The site sends a zing through my body. "Look at us, beautiful.

Look at our bodies together." When I see him sliding in and out of my body... it sets me on fire. Then I realize, he's not even half way in. He pumps his hips forward, then pulls back. I screw my eyes shut at the beautiful pain he's causing within my shivering walls with that beast of a cock he has. The feelings, the sensations, the overwhelming reverence between us, brings tears to my eyes. "Look at me, baby. I wanna see your beautiful green eyes." I open my eyes and gaze deeply into his longing blues. "You okay?" he asks with worry in his eyes. I'm speechless so my answer is to dig my nails into his back. "Don't take your eyes off mine," he demands leaning forward, kissing me through a long, deep, groan.

"Caelan... Oh God, Caelan," I whimper biting my lip. He pushes, surging forward, and I swear he just hit my belly button. He stills for a moment and kisses the tip of my nose. His eyes bore into mine. Sweat trickles down his forehead onto my breast. He pulls back. His groaning is getting louder and louder with each thrust forward. There is so much being said with no words being spoken. His one arm that's holding him up starts to shake. His other hand still holding the back of my thigh has such a grip on it I'm sure I will have his delicious finger prints there come morning. I love every second of every minute of what is happening between us right now. His eyes are locked on mine as he rocks his hips back and forth. I can tell he's close. His trembling arm is starting to give way, and both our bodies are covered in our sweat. He lowers his head, kissing me again, and when he does, he changes his angle, hitting me in a spot that sends me into another world. A world of pure, painful, bliss. An orgasm so strong, so powerful, I feel like I won't survive it. My eyes flutter, then roll into the back of my head. My skin prickles just as my eyes tear and my breath gets taken completely away. I open my mouth to scream, but nothing comes out.

"God, baby, that was the sexiest thing I've ever seen." He groans loudly moving at a rapid pace. His body stiffens then jerks and with a moan so long and loud, I feel like his orgasm has now become mine. I open my eyes to his glazed over blues gazing down at me. I feel his cock throbbing inside of me and his hot release filling my body. When I look at him, I see nothing but ecstasy and unconditional love shining through his eyes.

We lay there together in comfortable silence with him on top of me. I'm softly kissing his face, neck, cheeks and shoulder before he reluctantly lifts himself from my body and kisses his way back down to just above my pelvis bone. He rests his forehead against my belly again. Holding it there before I felt his lips touch my tattoos. He lifts his eyes to look at me, silently seeking answers; are those two butterflies etched into your skin for the loss of our child?

"Yes," I whisper.

"There's two?" he mummers, frowning with more sadness in his knowing eyes.

I nod again, lowering my hand to cup his jaw line. "Yes, one pink, one purple, both mixed with yellow and one antenna from each wrapped around each other to keep them connected." His brow furrows as he tilts his head to the side. He knows what I'm saying, but what he wants… no, what he needs, is to hear the words. "Two baby girls," I whisper. "Twins," I confirm through my sorrowful tears.

His whole face changes from a rugged dominant man into a father who now understands he not only lost one baby, but two. Two baby girls… his two baby girls… *our* twin baby girls.

His head lowers to my belly again, kissing each butterfly reverently. I can feel his mournful tears softly hitting my belly right where the remembrance tattoo lays. I run my fingers gently through his hair as his anguish takes hold of him. After a few minutes, he rises, lying next to me. I rest my head on his chest as he pulls me into him and curls his arm around my back, resting his hand on my waist making me feel warm, safe, protected, and completely… satisfied.

This is just where I needed to be.

thirty-one

My eyes flutter open to a delicious soreness between my legs. A smile takes over my face just thinking about the night before. A peaceful feeling invades my body with Caelan's heavy arm draped over the top of me with his large hand spread across my ribs. Images of him flash in my head.

What in the hell? Do they have steroids for penises? If so, he needs to cut back on his dosage. My Lord, that is not the same penis I saw when I was younger.

"I hope that grin I see on your face has to do with me and last night," he teases, smiling as he pulls me into him giving me a kiss on my forehead.

"I, ahhh... was... ahhh... thinking about last night." I chuckle majorly, stumbling over my words with what I am sure are rosy, red cheeks. He looks at me quizzically. "I was just, ummm, thinking about the size of that beast in your pants. It's not normal, C!" I burst out. He busts out laughing along with me. "No." I wave my finger at him. "Really, C that is not the same dick I saw years ago."

"Did you just admit my dick is a beast?"

"Yep." I pout, holding back a smile. He rightfully has his own name now-'The Beast.'"

"Sofia, you fuckin' kill me." He jokes shaking his head. "You have seen me before, cutting through the house or when you're barging in on me in the shower."

"Yes! Yes, I have. Few and far in-between, but he wasn't saluting the Gods either. I mean, I... he has made his presence known from time to time on my hip while we've slept in the same bed, but never full eye contact while he was a happy camper ready to do work!"

His kisses my forehead again laughing, but he turns very serious when he asks, "You okay?"

"No!" I burst with a giggle. "You suck! It's going to be a long day."

Concern reflects in his eyes. "Sof..."

"I'm fine, just sore-in a good way." I wrinkle my nose trying not to grin, but I can't help myself and fail. I start to slide out of his bed, but he grabs me. His mood has gone from happy to very serious in a matter of seconds.

"We need to talk, Sof. I want to talk to you about the other night."

"No, C. We don't. I don't want to." I slide out of bed heading towards the door, butt ass naked.

I hear him growl at my nakedness, but when he calls my name he's serious. "Sofia?" I feel him behind me as I'm now peering out the door to make sure Giovanni isn't upstairs so I can cut across to my room. I feel his hand on my shoulder, and when he turns me around, I see that he too is standing there in all his glory. I just can't help myself, so I do the twice over.

Damn, he's sexy!

When I finally reach his eyes, they're beaming with uncertainty. I know he's not going to let it go. Then his eyes flicker down my body and when he looks back into my eyes his pupils have taken over his irises.

"Whether it's now or later, we will talk, beautiful." His dominance now exuding from his body.

I shiver with lust over his powerful being but my answer to him is by turning, cracking the door even more, giving the hallway a quick glance again then say, "I have to go shower and get ready for work." I slip out his door and cross the hallway to mine. When I get to my door, I look back at him. He's still standing there staring at me with a very unhappy face.

Sorry, C. Can't do it, hurts too much.

WHILE I'M IN the shower, I hear the song on the overhead speakers change. Coldplay's ~*Hymn for The Weekend* starts playing. I listen to the words. I know C is the one who put this on for me to hear. As I wash his delectable smell from my exquisitely sore body, I start reminiscing about the night before. The biggest most uncontrollable smile takes over my face.

Last night was... last night was amazing.

Then sadness finds its way into my chest. Real sadness, the kind that stops your breathing. Did I screw things up between us? I never want to hurt him. I never want to lose our friendship. It's part of the reason why I never pursued anything with him. I know he needs to talk about things, but right now with everything going on, I just wanna live and not dwell on all the bad. I know I'm pushing things off. I know I am, it one of my biggest faults. Don't talk about it. Don't even think about it, and it will all just go away, right? No, I know it won't, but I'll just keep pushing things deeper and deeper hoping they will just go away and I won't have to deal with them until I break.

We went from the night I was drugged, to us finally talking about the baby, then to a few nights after with him and bad-fake-tits, to finding out my rapist is now stalking me again and then to Caelan finally knowing I lost two babies and not just one on that dreadful day. It's all just too much for me.

Then... last night, which was beautiful. I needed him, and I believe he needed me. We needed that connection. He made love to me. There was no fucking. It wasn't just sex. It was love making, that much I am sure. The talk this morning would have been about the babies and the other night, and having that conversation would have ruined what we had just shared. I just want to keep the dreamy thoughts of him making love to me and the sweet sting from that beast of his between my legs, and just forget everything else.

Just keep pushing it all way down deep, and it will go away...

STANDING IN MY extremely oversized, more than a walk-in closet that Caelan built for me, I think about lunch with Momma today.

I can't wait.

I scan the vast amounts of clothing I have, trying to decide what to wear. I grab a high neck, sleeveless, white, daisy lace, mid-thigh dress, and paired a thin, brown belt and pink and white, jeweled, wedged sandals. I put on the pearl bracelet and earrings momma gave me a few years back, then threw my hair up into a messy, but put together bun. I slathered on some pink lip gloss, light shadow, and mascara. Giving myself a once over in the full-length mirror I grant myself a thumbs up.

When I reach the top of the stairs, I see both men in the kitchen. G-man is getting a cup of coffee, while Caelan is already enjoying his along with his cell phone, most likely checking his emails. He's dressed in his office clothes, so I'm assuming he's not going to the site today. When I enter the kitchen and he greets me with a cocky, happy, relaxed smile. I shake my head at him smirking. As I turn, I see Giovanni smirk, but he quickly covers it up.

What the hell?

I glance back to Caelan. He shrugs his shoulders, but he has an all-knowing look on his face. Turning from him, I smile when I see my coffee cup is set out for me.

It's the little things.

Grabbing it, I make myself a well-needed cup of coffee and an English muffin. When I sit at the kitchen island, a feeling that things are just not quite right hits me. It's way too quiet, and there's an air of humor in the kitchen. Plus, the animosity between the two men seems to be gone.

"You look beautiful today."

"Thank you." I look from C to Giovanni again. "Okay, what fuckin' gives? Someone tell me what's going on." I look at C, but he looks at G-man. Then I look at G-man. He looks at me, then to C. "What the fuck? Someone better say somethin'! Like. Right. Now!"

"Beautiful, trust me, you should probably just let this go." He smirks, kissing my forehead as he walks past me to get another cup of coffee.

"Ohhh no! One of you better spill it!" I demand, flipping my butter knife back and forth between the two."

"Sof, trust me, baby. Let it go," he encourages me, now walking his plate to the sink. When he turns around, he leans against the counter crossing his arms over his broad chest and looks at me with the cockiest smile across his face. I watch him give Giovanni a look-not one that he wants to kill him either. Ohhhh noooo, something is going on between these two. Yesterday they were ready to kill each other, this morning they're grinning at each other and...

Ohohhhh shit NOOOOO!

I look at Giovanni again, then back to Caelan, and by the looks on both their faces, they both know that I know, that he knows.

BALLS!

Caelan lifts his large frame from casually leaning against the counter top and walks over giving me a kiss on the crown of my head with a chuckle on his way back to his seat. My face turns bright red.

"It's okay, beautiful. He's a grown man, he knows what great sex sounds like."

My eyes flick to Giovanni. He throws up his hands up in surrender grinning. "I heard moaning. Thought something was wrong. I came upstairs to check on you. Then... I came right back downstairs." He smirks. "I swear," he says, still holding his hands in the air. "Although, coming back downstairs didn't help." He shakes his head. "I think I could have gone back home and still heard you two."

My face is bright red. Caelan is trying not to smile when I look at him.

"Yeah, well, I was hurt!" I yell laughing. "Some bodyguard you are!" I point at him. "I was being attacked by a beast!" I burst out laughing shaking my head, my cheeks now on fire. I look at the man with the steroid induced rod between his legs and he busts up laughing too.

He sits back down next to me once all of us, well mainly me, settle down, and my cheeks don't feel like you could grill hamburgers on them. Giovanni's finishing his coffee when I get up and bring my stuff over to the sink.

"Sof, before we walk out the door today, we need to talk." His now stern, deadly serious bodyguard demeanor taking over from the light, airy mood we were all just in. "No chances. You need to stick close by me today. Don't just walk off. We'll be at HD most of the day, right?" I nod confirming. "When the security guy gets there to fix the alarm. I want you in your office. If you need to sign anything, I will bring it to you. *Do Not* come out of the office. You need to listen to my orders, Sofia. No arguments."

"Okay," I comply. He raises his brow in disbelief. "I promise!" I squeal. "No shenanigans."

"Good. Now let's go see if I can protect you today," he said walking towards the door. "I don't know how well I'll be able to perform my job," he complains, smirking. "I'm exhausted from the lack of sleep I got because of the two rabid animals that kept me awake all last night."

I turn to him. "Yeah, well me too, buddy!" I laugh sarcastically. "At least you can walk normal today," I mumble more to myself than to him as I turn away to grab my purse.

I peek out from the corner of my eye and see Giovanni trying to hold back his laugh and then I hear Caelan crack up behind me.

Well, I guess that was louder than I thought.

Caelan wraps his arms around my waist, leans down and kisses my shoulder. "Me too." He grins. "Why do you think I'm going into the office today and not to the site?" He huffs. "I have no energy left." I throw my elbow back into his hard abs.

"Ouch!" he whimpers acting as if he's in pain. I throw him a- "yeah right like I can hurt you" look. He leans down next to my ear. "Do you remember that day in your bathroom when you said I was small and I corrected you and told you I was a beast?" I squint my eyes at him. "I told you, beautiful. I would never lie to you." He winks along with his cocky smile. "What about lunch today?" he inquires.

I look at Giovanni then to C still over my shoulder. "I can't I am having lunch with mom today."

"Sof, we need to talk." His deep disbelieving husky tone whispers into my ear.

He thinks I'm blowing him off. I lean back and to the side a little, turning towards him so he can see my eyes. "I know you think I'm blowing you off, but I'm really not. Mom asked me to have lunch with her today."

"Then dinner, we'll go to O'Brien's. It's quiet and private. I'll call Pat, tell her to save the back booth for us. Giovanni can sit at the bar again."

Ohhh no, no, no, no. This is bad. No! I don't know what to say. Why do I feel so bad? I shouldn't feel bad. Should I? Oh, no this is not going to be good.

"Sof?" he calls, looking down at me with confusion.

I look to Giovanni, who looks disappointed in me. I falter a bit when I glance back up at Caelan. "I'm sorry, I can't," I say taking a step away from him, in turn making him release me from his arms. He looks pissed.

"Why, Sofia? You are blowing me off, aren't you?"

"No. God no, C. I would never blow you off. It's just…" I look at Giovanni who is slightly shaking his head in disbelief.

"I'll be right outside the door, Sofia," he says, already moving in that direction.

Damn! I have to do what I feel is right for me. Right? Am I doing the wrong thing?

"I… I have a date tonight."

He takes a step back from me. "The fuck?" Confusion and anger flashes over his face. "Did you just say you have a date tonight? No. No, there is no way I heard you correctly. I did not just hear you correctly, right, Sofia?"

"I di… did," I falter. "I do. I'm sorry, but why are you so mad? You go out all…"

"Who?" he demands as he crosses his arms over his puffed-up chest, cutting me off.

"I met him the other night at work. We talked a couple of times this week, and he came in last night to see me."

"Name! Now!" he orders.

"Why?"

"Name, Sofia. I won't ask again."

"Johnathan Reznor."

"So," he gruffly says, tilting his head to the side, "you fucked me last night, and tonight you're going out with someone else? You going to fuck him too?"

Yup, that hurt.

I get that I just hurt him, so he's lashing out to hurt me. I try to keep my hurt temper under control and correct him on how I saw us being together last night. "We didn't fuck last night, C and you know it. Please don't tarnish what happened between us. Last night was speci-"

"Real fucking special." He cuts me off. "Right? So special that you're going out with someone else tonight," he admonishes, cutting me off again.

"What happened between us last night… I would never change that," I whisper. "And yes, it was special, to me at least it was."

"Oh, excuse me, let me clarify. You're right, beautiful, I didn't fuck you last night, like I do every other fucking girl I bring home. No, I made love to you last night, Sofia. Do you know why I made love to you?"

I barely shake my head. Tears now burning the back of my eyes. "No," I whisper.

"No?" he questions raising his voice and his left brow, tilting his head in disbelief. "Really?" he huffs, shaking his head back and forth in anger. "I'm here, Sofia. Standing in front of you. I want you! Only you! I want you in my life. I want you in my fucking bed! Under my fucking body! Against my fucking skin! I want to feel your body trembling beneath me while I make love to you. My God, beautiful, when are you going to get it through your stubborn head? How much more time do you need because quite honestly, I been waiting fucking years for you to come to me and see that I want you!"

he roars. "It's because I love you, beautiful! I'm in love with you, Sofia! But, that means nothing to you, does it?" he yells. "You came to me last night. You came to my fuckin' room!" he booms, poking himself in his broad chest. "Then, because you came to me last night, I finally find out I had twin baby girls. Something you neglected to tell me about the other day when you *FINALLY* fucking decided to talk to me about the miscarriage. This is fuckin' unbelievable!" he huffs again throwing his arms in the air turning his back to me. "How many more, Sofia?" he roars. I shake my head at his back not understanding what he's asking. When he looks over his shoulder at me, he asks the one question that guts me. "How many more secrets do you have?"

I suck in a quick gust of guilty air. That, right there, just knocked the wind from my sails. He knows there's more. He knows me so very well. Fuck, I screwed this up. I keep screwing things up. I keep hurting him.

"That's what I thought," he spits the disgusted words from his mouth.

"I have to go, I'm sorry."

"Yeah, I'm sure you are," he hisses with outrage walking away from me.

thirty-two

SITTING IN MY QUIET OFFICE, ALL I can do is think about last night, the argument between C and I this morning, and my date with Johnathan tonight. I'm not getting any work done, that's for sure. I royally screwed this up. I needed him last night. I did. And what I needed, he fulfilled for me. More than fulfilled. But it was selfish. This is twice now, that in the heat of an argument, he has told me he's in love with me. What he feels right now is nothing more than two people feeling the emotions of something tragic that's happened between them. Him finding out about the miscarriage just brings up a lot of old emotions. Maybe what I did last night was wrong Maybe I shouldn't have gone to him, but in all honesty, I don't feel like it was. It wasn't like I intentionally went to him to sleep with him, but in that of itself, we had an unforgettable night together.

Today is a new day. Tomorrow, he will probably be with someone else. Tonight, I am going to dinner with Jonathan. The man I never gave a second thought to last night while I was making love to Caelan. Am I excited to be going out with him tonight? Yes, yes I am. He's funny. He's sexy as all hell.

He's new. There's no painful past between us. It's a fresh new start for me. He's someone I can laugh with who won't see the sadness in my eyes.

Knock, knock

I hear the rapping of knuckles on my office door. "Come in."

Jess pokes her head through my door. "You're quiet today. Hiding out?"

"Just doing some thinking." I start to tear up. "Jess?" I give my head a quick shake to rid my eyes of the stinging tears, then change my mind about asking her opinion. "What's up gorgeous? You need something from me?" I ask, trying to chase away the sadness.

She stares at me for a minute. "Yeah, I need my bestie to tell me what's wrong."

"I slept with Caelan last night," I blurt. I couldn't help it I had to get it off my chest.

Silence.

Her face is blank. Then I see the corner of her mouth start to lift.

"It was the most... beautiful, powerful, sensual, incredible, sexual act I have ever experienced in my life, Jess. Then I screwed it all up this morning."

Her smile wavers and confusion crosses her gorgeous, soft features. "One sec." She holds up her perfectly manicured finger. "Did you just tell me you slept with C last night and that it was incredible?"

Nodding. "I did. We did. And it was incredible, Jess. Words can't even describe what happened between the two of us last night," I whisper.

"Why so sad then, Sof?"

"I don't want to lose him, Jess. Now, this morning, after an unbelievable night, he's so mad at me." She listens, quietly waiting for the rest. "He asked me to go to lunch today. I told him I couldn't because I have plans with mom. Then he asked me to go to our place for dinner so we could talk."

She's quiet trying to figure out what the big deal is and then it hits her. "Ohhh, shit! Johnathan... you're going to dinner with Johnathan tonight. Oh, hell. Did you tell him? Did he flip? Oh, I don't even have to ask. He flipped. I know he did."

"You could say that. Especially, after last night. I went to him last night because I needed him, Jess. I thought after everything that's happened, he would need me too. I thought it would just be us reconnecting with each other, forgetting all the shit that has happened over the past few weeks. But, what it was, what happened between us, it was so beyond that, Jess. I don't know what to do. I think about Caelan, and he's my home. My safety. My strength. My best friend. Then I think of Johnathan, there's no attachment there. No hurt feelings. No horrible past between us. It's fresh. It's new. I'm just so screwed up in my head. I wish I could just run away from it all."

"What are you going to do?"

A few minutes of silence slips by. "I'm going to go to dinner with Johnathan tonight."

I SEE HER GORGEOUS face beaming at me from the covered outdoor eating area. The water behind her reflecting on her beautiful skin. I hope when I'm her age I look as good as her.

"Fia, baby. You look gorgeous," she compliments, standing to hug me. "You're glowing today. How come?" She smiles at me with a little twist of her head.

Quickly I dodge the question. "Look at you, momma. You look beautiful as always."

"Sit, sit I ordered you a Pinot Grigio."

"Perfect." I smile. "It's gorgeous out here today," I say looking around and taking notice that there are no other tables occupied outside other than ours. "Your doing?" I wave my finger around at the empty tables.

She smiles. "Giovanni's just doing his job, keeping you safe, sweetheart." She smiles again. "So, tell me," she says over the top of her menu as she pretends she's reading it. "Who has you glowing today?" I look up with what I think is good acting confusion on my face. "Fia, honey, don't think I didn't catch the blow off when I said it before. Now spill."

Well, there's no sense in skirting around this. It's momma, and momma already knows. Mother's intuition and all. "Caelan." I watch her as she slowly lowers the menu locking eyes with me.

"So, this is the first time you have been with him since you were teenagers?"

Total Silence.

"Mom?"

"Fia, sweetheart. I'm your mother. If you think that I didn't know that you and Caelan snuck away to the cabin upstate to be together, you are sadly mistaken. Who do you think called off the guards when the silent alarms went off?" She smiles raising her perfectly waxed brows.

Balls!

My mouth drops. Is she serious? Silent alarms? She knew? What the hell? Then it hits me. Wait, oh no, no, no does that mean... does she know...

"I can tell by the look on your face what you're thinking. The answer is yes, Fia. I know what happened. However, I didn't know 'til it was too late. I'm sorry for that." She looks at me sadly. "How do you think you and Giovanni got off the grounds that day without anyone noticing or stopping you at the front gates?"

I'm speechless. Utterly speechless. The waiter places our drinks on the table, and before he even releases his hand I'm grabbing it and guzzling half of it down. We order our food and mom orders me another glass of wine. I glance over to the bar at Giovanni who has a concerned look on his face. "Mom?" I ask trembling, turning back to her.

"Yes, sweetheart?"

"Why didn't... Why? Daddy? Mom, daddy?" I cry.

"Oh no, sweetheart your father knows nothing." She reassures me by reaching across the table to hold my trembling hand.

I exhale, dropping heavily into the seat. I grab and gulp the rest of my wine with a shaking hand. "Why mom?" I ask after setting down my empty glass. "If you knew, why didn't you come with me."

"I knew you were in good hands and had I left so quickly, your father would have gotten suspicious." She tilts her head slightly towards the bar. "He's a good man and very protective of you. I knew he would take care of you. I needed to stay home and make sure things looked as normal as possible because if I hadn't, and your father found out that Caelan got you pregnant... that boy would not be alive today, Fia." She nods her head, and I mimic her, knowing she is absolutely right. "Every fifteen minutes Giovanni texted me to make sure I knew what was going on. And honey, I can tell you, when they kicked him out of that hospital room, I am the one that talked him off the ledge of taking the whole place down. I'm sorry I couldn't be there with you, for you, but what I did, I did to save you from more heartache."

I can't believe my mother has known about this all these years. Ohhh no, does that means she knows about... No, she can't know about that too. Could she? I think to myself as I look into her revealing eyes. She does know. My hand flies to my mouth covering my quivering chin and trembling lips. I'm not sure I can take too much more right now. "M- M- Mom...?" I stutter.

I see her slightly shake her head. I follow her eyes to the bar where Giovanni in now standing looking like the stone-cold killer he is, but he's following my mother's orders by staying put.

"It's alright, baby," she consoles me squeezing my hand. "I understand." She winks at me. "Caelan deserved to know first anyway, and since you haven't told him yet, I will keep this one inside 'til you do."

Swallowing deeply, I stand, following her actions. She embraces me in a long-overdue, sorrowful hug.

After we both sit, and taking a long swallow of our wine, she smiles at me. "Now, tell me Fia, baby, how good was it? Compared to all those years ago?"

Of course, after all this, she will make me laugh by changing the subject. Only my mom could get me to laugh after that gut revealing tell all. "Oh mom," I say shaking my head in disbelief. "It was amazing."

"Amazing?" Her brows lift.

"No, like... mom amazing is not even a good enough word to describe what happened between us. I tried to explain it to Jess this morning and I...

I really can't. It was nothing short of ethereal. We didn't just sleep together we..."

"Made love," she expresses smiling with a slight shake of her head.

"Ya, we did." I glow, smiling back at her.

"Then why did I see sadness in those beautiful, green eyes behind that glow."

What the? How does she see all this? "Because I pretty much took the most beautiful moment that has ever happen to me and stomped on it this morning. Caelan asked me to lunch today so we could talk. I told him I was meeting you. He then asked for dinner..." I say turning my head to stare off into space.

"So you're running?"

"Running? No." I defend myself.

"No?"

"No. I told him I couldn't because I have a date."

"With Mr. Scotch man. Right?" she asked, but already knows the answer. "So you are running."

"Mom you're starting to creep me out now! Can you read minds?"

She laughs. "No, Fia I'm just a mom and a woman. So, now let me put this together for you. You made mad passionate love with Caelan last night. Pretty much all night by the looks of the slight stiffness you carried yourself in here with and..."

"MOM!" I whisper-scream.

"Oh, honey, do you think you're the only woman on this earth that screwed someone all night and couldn't walk properly the next day? Please." She snorts. Been there, done that, and still doing it!" She deviously smiles.

"Oh God, mom please stop. You're talking about daddy!"

"Sweetheart, your father's still a tiger in bed!"

"Oh hell, mom, please. I can hear you talk about your sex life, but when you start putting daddy's name in there, I just can't!"

She laughs at me. "Let me get this straight, you and Caelan spent the night together, he woke up happy as can be and so did you, until he asked you to lunch/dinner so that he can talk to you about things that should have been discussed a long time ago. When you told him you couldn't, and he asked you why, he exploded when you told him you were going on a date. Now you feel like shit because last night was unexpected and the feelings you're having have been buried for years because you buried them in fear of losing him altogether if it doesn't work out. So now you're confused because Mr. Scotch man is sexy and mysterious and new. You have no history with him, and he doesn't know any of your past. You can become someone new with him. Am I correct?"

This woman is incredible.

"Maybe just a little too much." I stare at her incredulously. "Seriously we need to have your head checked." I laughed. "What do I do mom?" I beg this stunning, smart, years beyond my experience woman, who I am proud to call my mother.

"You go on that date tonight, Fia. That's what you do. If you don't, you'll always wonder what if, and that's not a good thing to have in your head the rest of your life. As long as Giovanni is there, and you're safe, you go. You might finish the date tonight and think he's the biggest ass, or you could end the date tonight in his bed thinking he hung the moon, but you'll never know if you don't go."

"Mom, I would never sleep with him tonight after sleeping with Caelan last night."

"Sweetheart... never say never."

thirty-three

THE RIDE BACK TO HD IS QUIET. I'VE SEEN Giovanni glance back at me a few times through the review mirror. At the moment, I'm reflecting on the conversation my mother and I just had. My heart breaks knowing that my mom knew all these years. If I put myself in her shoes, it breaks my heart even more to know that she could have had two grandchildren running around, happy and carefree. She would be an unbelievable grandmother: caring, loving and protective, just like she was as a mother.

Then I think about her betrayal to my father, by not telling him. My father lives his life by truth and loyalty. Without truth and loyalty, he's a dead man. It's the reason why only certain men are as close to him as they are and it is also the reason why in the world that he lives in, his men don't stray. He's just as loyal to them as they are to him. So, for my mother to keep this from him, she has put an invisible barrier between them to protect her child. When he finds out, if he ever finds out… I shake my head. No, he can never find out. I don't ever want to see what he would do if he ever did find out.

Caelan, my mother, Giovanni. I put them all in danger.

The pressure I feel right now in my chest is crushing. Because of me, my mother lied to my father, therefore, breaking his trust which will only end badly for them both. Plus, Caelan and Giovanni. Ughhh. I rub at the tightness in my chest with the heel of my hand. My breathing starts to become heavy. The pressure I feel right now weighing me down is like never before. I inhale slowly and deeply. I try to think of good happy times. I exhale slowly and deeply. The tension is not going away. I have screwed up my own life so very badly and to think now I may have screwed up my father and mother's marriage as well.

No, no, no. Caelan and Giovanni.

I hear my name, but I can't make out what is being said. I try to focus on Giovanni, but I'm too dazed, too confused. All of these feelings, emotions, and thoughts are flooding my body. I ruined so many people's lives.

There are so many secrets.

I hear more talking, but I still can't make out what is being said. I feel myself pulling my knees to my chest in a protectant manor.

Flash

"I will always be watching you, little Ms. Perfect."

Flash

"You will never be perfect again after I'm done with you."

Flash

"I'm going to rip your world apart."

Flash

"Blood."

Flash

"Daddy's perfect, little girl."

Flash

"Chains."

Flash

"Menthol."

Flash

"Whiskey."

Flash

"The repulsive smell of weeks old, dead fish."

"Sofia, look at me. Breathe, baby." I feel strong hands wrapped around me.

Where am I?

"Look at me." I turn towards the voice still lost in a haze. "That's it, baby. Breathe me in." I do. "Now out slowly through your mouth." I follow his actions. "Again, breathe in my air as I breathe out." He exhales. I inhale. He inhales I exhale. "Good girl."

"Where am I?"

"Look around, baby. You're safe. I got you. Breathe me in again."

He exhales.

I inhale.

I take everything in. The fog is lifting. I'm in my office. Panic sets in. "How did I get here? How did you get here? What happened?" I asked with rapid fire.

"Slow down, just breathe we'll answer all your questions in a few minutes, once you calm down."

I look around the room. Jess, Sage, Giovanni, even Nikki and Antonio are standing there watching me. In my office. I'm cradled in Caelan's arms, on his lap, on my sofa in my office.

"Tell me what brought this on?"

"I don't know." I look to Giovanni. The last thing I remember is getting into the SUV after lunch with mom.

"I called Caelan. I was watching you in the review mirror, saw that your breathing was starting to pick up. When I tried to reach out to you, you didn't react to my voice. I called him because he is the only one that calms you."

I looked to Antonio and Nikki for answers as to why they're here.

"I just stopped by to see you on my lunch hour," Nikki explains.

"I came to check out the security system."

My eyes flash to Caelan. "You came here from your office?"

"I was already on my way over. I wanted to talk to you. You weren't answering my calls." He frowns. "Tell me what caused it this time?"

I look around the room. I can't. These people. All these people love me, but I can't talk about this in front of all of them. He notices my hesitation.

"Everyone out!" he demands. "Close the door behind you."

"Wait! Giovanni and Antonio stay." They both look at me. "I remembered more," I whisper looking at Giovanni.

Confusion crosses over Antonio's and Caelan's faces, while sadness washes over Giovanni's. I slide off Caelan's lap and sit next to him. I grab his hand, not sure if it's for him or me, but I need his hand in mine.

Giovanni crouches down right in front of me, placing his hands on my legs. I feel Caelan stiffen next to me. "You sure you want to do this in front of both of them?"

"No, but, I have to, G." I shake my head. After I scan over Caelan and Antonio I begin. I have to.

"My anxiety attack the other night was the worst I have ever had. It was more than an anxiety attack, A."

"No shit!" he snaps.

My eyes widen at his outburst.

"Explain!" he demands. "Now!"

"It was a panic attack. On top of that, some of the memories from the night I was abducted came back to me. Stuff I... stuff I really wish I never remembered."

"Sofia? I thought you told us everything? What else happened?" my brother demands answers.

Giovanni grabs my free hand. "He knows nothing. I promised you I wouldn't say anything and I never will."

I drop my head. I hear a growl come from Caelan. When I lift my head to look at him, I see Antonio pacing back and forth ready to explode. I swallow trying to relieve the lump from my throat. I love my brother. I do. And I trust him, but I never wanted my family to know what happened to me. I didn't tell my mother or father because I didn't want them to hurt. I don't want to tell Caelan either, in fear he would never look at me the same again, but I have to. I have no choice. Antonio though, he could help. If he knew some of the details, he could help me find my attacker. I know whoever did this to me is still out there. I just know it. "I don't want to tell you, A. I don't want you or Caelan to know." I squeeze his hand that I'm still holding. "I have never told anyone until recently. I have been holding this in for so long. I've been okay for the last few years." I look to Caelan for reassurance. "I was living as normal a life as I could. My attacks have lessened over the years, but this thing... what happened to me Thursday night, being drugged, brought back a lot of memories." I peek back over to Antonio, who's still pacing. "If I talk to you about this... if I tell you," I say then stopping for a second to catch my breath, trying to get a read on him, "you have to promise me, Antonio, you have to swear to me you will never tell anyone. Especially mommy and daddy."

His assessing eyes are determining how serious I am or how serious what I'm about to say is. "Tell me," he hisses through clenched teeth.

"You have to make me that promise first, A."

"Sofia... man, I can't believe I'm going to make this promise," he mumbles pacing back and forth running his hands though his hair. "You have my word, Sofia."

"I don't even know where to begin." I rub my hand over my forehead. "I did tell you everything I could remember at the time except what actually happened to me. I'm sure you all probably assumed, even though I denied it over and over again."

"Motherfucker." My brother's jaw clenches and his breathing becomes a rapid pace.

"Son of a bitch," C mutters under his breath, dropping his head and squeezing my hand.

"A, let me get through this," I plead reaching for his hand trying to calm him down. Giovanni stands to let Antonio kneel in front of me. "Whoever it was that took me... this was personal." Both their heads jerk rapidly towards me.

"What?" They say simultaneously.

"He," I hesitate and falter closing my eyes, "he raped me, repeatedly," I spit out with disgust. Antonio shoots to his feet. "Please, let me just finish. This is not easy for me." He stands there above me with his hands on his hips and fire in his eyes, not for me though, but for whoever my captor was.

He crouches down in front of me again. "Sofia, you should have been in the hospital." His voice becomes soft and filled with genuine concern.

"I was. I spent most of the night there. After I had found out I was going to be okay and there was no permanent damage, I walked out. It wasn't easy, but there was a cab at the entrance waiting for another couple. He saw I was in pain and helped me into the cab and gave me a ride to Caelan's. When we got there, he helped me out of the cab and walked me to the front door, but I couldn't bring myself to go inside, so I sat on the steps and laid back against the door. That's where C… well, he found me." I huff air just thinking about the poor cab driver. "He didn't even charge me," I mutter as an afterthought.

"Motherfucker! Fuck! Fuck! FUCK!" he yells as he shoots to his feet again, starting a fast pace back and forth. I give him a minute to calm down. I look over to Caelan and his head is still hung. "Antonio, I… this person whoever it was…"

He stops in his tracks. "We know who it was! If he weren't already fucking dead, I would fucking torture the son of a bitch with my bare hands right now!"

I shake my head at him. He starts pacing again. His back is to me. "The person you kil… the person you thought… it wasn't him. The person that did this is still alive. I know he is. The details I remembered the other night… they were personal." He flips around to me again.

"Explain."

I nod. "I know it sounds like I'm crazy, but I swear to you, I'm not. He's alive. The guy that you guys thought it was had blond hair. The guy that… he had black hair. The guy you 'took care of' lived in an apartment and the guy that did this had me in a basement with blacked out windows."

"Are you fucking serious?"

"Whoever this was Antonio, he said things to me. This was personal, A. When he dumped me, his last words to me were that he would be back for me. That he would always come back for me."

"Tell me what the personal stuff was."

"A... I don't know if I can."

He crouches in front of me again grabbing my trembling hands. "Sof. I know it's hard. I know you don't want to talk about it, but you have to tell me. If you think this was personal and this guy is alive, you have to tell me." He finishes with a rush and then his head drops. "Sofia, I'm so sorry," he apologizes embracing me tightly. "I'm so sorry," he repeats still holding me for a few minutes.

I lean back from our embrace. "Thursday night... I think it's him again. He's come back for me."

"Sofia, liste-" His phone rings cutting him off. He declines the call. "Listen to me he's not going to get to you. I promise you that. We will figure this out." His phone starts ringing again. He stands taking a step back as he grabs for his phone again. "What the fuck man? It's Carmine again," he complains, declining the call again. He bends over, grabbing both my shoulders. "Listen to me. I need you to tell me everything you remember." His phone starts ringing again. "What the fuck!" he roars. "*WHAT!*" he snaps, answering the phone, then becomes silent and turns away from me. His shoulders drop. I look at Caelan who now lets go of my hand and stands. Giovanni sits next to me and puts his arm around me. "What the fuck? You serious, Unc? When?" Antonio yells. Then looks at his watch. He turns around, looking at Giovanni giving me a hug. Confusion and anger flood his face. "I'll be there in forty. Unc, it's gonna take me that long to get to the shipping yard," he argues then hangs up. He flips his head up at Giovanni with a manly chin jerk. "What the fuck is this?" he questions flickering his eyes back and forth between us. "How long has he known?"

"I told him a few days ago. He watched the surveillance tapes with me."

He stares at me for a minute. "You trusted your bodyguard, but not your brother?" He jerks his head and purses his lips in disbelief. When I open my mouth to answer him, he cuts me off. He looks at Giovanni. "We have a situation," he snaps running his hand through his already disheveled hair. "Christ, Sofia, I wish I never made you that promise."

My mouth drops. "Antonio, you promis-"

"I won't say a fucking word." He cuts me off. "Did you make him promise too?" he hollers flipping his hand and eyes to Giovanni.

"Yes, she did, and I won't break her trust either. And honestly, like we talked about the other day, the least amount of people that know about this situation, the better."

Antonio's eyes started flicking back and forth between the two of us again. I can tell something's running around in his brain. "Somethin' going on between you two?" he snaps. I watch an unusually quiet Caelan jerk his head up, waiting for the answer.

"No!" We both indignantly say in unison. I'm not sure he believes us, but he takes a few steps towards us.

I stiffen. Giovanni whispers, "It's fine."

"Someone better tell me what's going on. How is it that you two are so close?" he shouts looking at Giovanni then back to me. "Sof?" he demands.

"Give her a minute. She'll tell you what she wants you to know."

"A, that's not something I'm willing to talk about," I tell him, but I'm staring at Caelan, who's watching Giovanni and I. I can see the hurt in his eyes now that he's starting to realize that Giovanni not only knew about the baby and that night, but he also knows about everything that happened to me the night I was abducted. I close my eyes, when I do, I remember I need to tell them what I just remembered today. "Fish," I say. "Overwhelming, nasty, smelly, weeks old, dead fish. The smell that I kept blocking... it's dead fish."

"The fuck?" I look over to Caelan who's just staring at me in confusion.

"Fucking fish, Sof?" A questions.

"A, sit your ass down and calm down so your sister can talk to you and Caelan." He grabs one of the chairs pulling it over to the couch I'm sitting on.

"I was in a basement with blacked out windows. They were spray painted black. All I could smell was dead fish. There was a bed in the basement with a spindled footboard and headboard. I was chained to them.

Flash.

The wall.

Flash

You were chained to a wall too.

I tilt my head to the side trying to remember.

"Tell me what else you just remembered," Giovanni asks, squeezing my hand softly.

"I was chained to the bed, but... but I was also chained up to the cement wall. There were really big hooks in the cinder block." I hear Caelan mutter something, but I keep going. "There were mirrors on the ceiling. The whole ceiling. I thought it was just over the bed, but it's the whole ceiling. He wanted me to watch what he was doing to me. I was in and out of it the whole time because of the drugs. I remember the basement had a long staircase. When he released me, he dragged me up them, I couldn't walk. I think that's why my memories are so jumbled, from the drugs. I do know the man had black hair though. He wasn't young, but he wasn't old either. I'm not sure. It's hard to tell because I only remember seeing the back of him... on top of me. He smelled like menthol, whiskey and he had a tattoo on his back." I squint my eyes trying to remember what it was. "I can't see it though, I just remember the color red." I shake my head in frustration.

"That's good, Sofia. You'll remember the rest when you're ready," Giovanni reassured me.

"A knife. His knife! It wasn't just a razor. There was a knife too. The one he used to cut my thighs. It had initials or letters or a picture on it. I can't remember."

"Oh, what the fuck!" Caelan exclaims, running his hands through his dirty blond hair.

"This motherfucker." A jumps out of his chair.

"Both of you two, calm the fuck down!" Giovanni demands. "Now!"

"Keep going, Sofia. You're doing good. You remembered more today than you did the other day. Go on," he says soothingly.

I look to Caelan who's standing there expressionless, staring at me. That breaks me inside. I knew it. I knew he would look at me differently. I whimper like a hurt animal at the pain that slices through my insides.

Giovanni's hand comes to my face. "Sweetheart, look at me. It's going to be alright. I promise. Keep going. You're doing great."

"His knife had something carved into the handle. I can't see it, though." I sniffle shaking my head.

"It's okay."

"I can't remember anymore." I exhale with a weary breath.

The next thing I know, Antonio explodes. "The fucking guy, we slaughtered had blond hair, G. What the fuck? He lived in an apartment! That wasn't the right fucking guy! We got the wrong fucking guy!" he bellows. "Her life has been in danger this whole fucking time! FUCK!" he thunders!

"Antonio calm down she has more to tell you."

I look at Giovanni confused. "You need to tell them what he said to you."

I look at Caelan. He has both his hands braced against the wall, his head hanging between his shoulders. He looks sick. Giovanni follows my line of sight, then looks back at me. I tilt my head to the side, slowly raising my shoulders and slowly dropping them in defeat. My lips and chin trembling. "See, I told you," I mouthed.

He shakes his head. "Everything is going to be fine. Finish telling them what he said to you."

So, I spit it all out so I could get away from this situation as fast as I could. "He promised he would come back to get me again. He called me 'Little Ms. Perfect.' He said he was going to rip me apart. He told me I would never be perfect again after he was through with me. He said he would always be watching me. That he was the only man that would want me. Giovanni, I can't do anymore." I push up off the couch.

He stands with me and wraps his hand around the back of my head pulling me to him. "You did good. I know it hurts, but you did good. I made you a promise, and I intend to keep it. Do you remember what that was?"

"Yes."

"Good. Keep that in your head, let it fester inside you. Your day will come, Sofia." He kisses my forehead before separating from me. "You two get your shit together so we can figure out who did this to her."

thirty-four

THE RIDE HOME IS QUIET. AFTER THE four of us talked for a little bit, I excused myself from the office and spent some time alone hiding in the warehouse bathroom. The three of them talked for a while, while Sage, Nikki, and Jess demanded to know what was going on. I hate to hurt my friends and family, but at this point I really just need to be alone. When I finally left the bathroom and made my way back to my office, I asked Giovanni to drive me home. Caelan offered, said he wanted to talk to me in private, but I just couldn't bear the thought of sitting next to him knowing that, I hurt him again, and I didn't want to hear him say last night was a mistake. I couldn't bear to hear it. I wanted nothing more than to jump into his arms and have him hold me, but I understand how he feels because I feel the same way about myself. There was a long period of time when the memories and feelings that came with the violation had subsided, but right now, every feeling of self-loathing and disgust I ever had for myself, is hitting me hard.

I really need to make an appointment with Katherine.

I know what I'm feeling right now is not how I truly see myself, but at the moment it's hard to see myself any other way. My therapist, Katherine, has helped me tremendously with my self-esteem. I was doing so good, but now with everything that's going on, it's hard to be that strong and keep my old mental weaknesses at bay.

When Giovanni parks the SUV in front of the house, I jump out, not waiting for him to open my door. He's not too happy about it, but right now, I don't care. I need a hot shower and some sleep. I need to disappear for the next few hours into dream world and then... I need to shake this off and keep moving.

Just keep moving.

When we get inside, I throw my purse on the island, walk to the refrigerator, grab a large bottle of wine, and pour myself a glass to the very tippy top. I can feel Giovanni's eyes on me. Two minutes later, I hear the front door open and close. When I turn, both Giovanni and Caelan are both eyeing me cautiously.

"Beautiful, you don't need that," he says stepping towards me.

I snort at the term of endearment. "You can still call me that, huh? After what I just told you? That's pretty impressive." I snort again, sarcastically. My anger now unfolding on him. "I'm sure you're now regretting what happened between us last night, huh? I saw your face when I was telling you and Antonio. I saw the disgust on your face."

"Beautiful, what you saw on my face was disgust but-" he expresses stepping towards me.

I throw my hands in the air forcefully to stop him from getting any closer- which he does anyway, just short of touching me. "I can't do this right now. I need to drink this glass of wine, I need to shower, and I need to lie down." I step around him. When I do, I look directly into Giovanni's concerned sorrowful green eyes. "I'll be ready to leave at seven." He reluctantly nods with shock in his eyes.

Just keep moving.

I take large gulps from my glass of wine as I walk up the stairs to my bathroom.

Just keep moving.

I turn on the water for the claw foot tub. Strip my body of my clothes and lose myself to the warmth and solitude of the water.

I should have brought the bottle up with me.

Just keep moving.

THE DING FROM my cell phone pulls me from my sleep. When I look at the message, I notice the time. Shit! It's a little after six. I jump out from under the covers while reading the text.

> **Jess: Honey, I'm not sure you're still going tonight, but you forgot your dress. I'm on the way over just in case. xoxo**

> **Me: xoxo I'm in my room, just come up.**

I quickly run to the bathroom, grabbing my blow dryer, and started drying my hair. I went to bed with it wet, not too smart. I look like I just got out of the crazy ward. I plug in my hot curlers because right now I do not have time to curl it one strand at a time, plus I think I want a nice sexy wave. With my hair being so long and thick, the hot curlers will be perfect. With a curled head, I start on my face. Hmmm, how do I want to look tonight? Fresh and simple or a little smoky, sexy eye. Yip, I'm going for the sexy. Especially with that dress. A black, high neck, open shoulder, mini dress that flairs slightly out at the waist, along with a smoky eye, and nude lip here I come.

A knock at the door grabs my attention. Jess is quiet and unsure when she walks in. After today I'm sure she's skeptical of how my mood will be, but my music is blasting right now, and I feel good. Plus, I am looking damn hot if I do say so myself. Well, I will sans the hot curlers. I turn to Jess to say hi and thank you when her mouth falls open.

"Dammmmmmmmmn your makeup looks good! Once you put this mini dress on and take out those dreadful hot curlers, you will blow him away!" She gleams.

"Thanks. What time is it?"

"Six forty-five," she says taking a glimpse at her watch. A watch I have never seen before.

"New?" I nod towards her wrist. She smiles. "Luke?"

"Ya. Gave it to me last night."

"It's beautiful."

"Thanks. You ready?" she inquirers, quickly changing the subject, but I let it go. If anyone knows about deflecting, it's me.

"As I'll ever be." I chuckle slipping into my dress. I turn, letting her zip me up.

"Sof?" she softly says my name.

Ughh not now. Please not now.

"Not now, Jess. Please. I have an amazing-looking, sexy man waiting for me, and I really want to just enjoy my night. Please," I beg.

Just keep moving

"What do you think, my black satin four-inch heels with the rhinestone heel?"

"Ab-so-lute-ly!" she sings walking into the closet to grab my heels, as I unload a dozen hot curlers from my head. I flip my head forward giving my head a quick shake out, then flip it back upright running my fingers through to tame the curls down. Give it fifteen minutes, and the curls will be under control. Jess walks back out with my heels, handing them to me as I sit in front of my vanity applying some nude gloss. Standing I give myself a once over.

Not too bad, Sof. Not too bad at all.

Out of nowhere my mantra runs through my head by its own volition. "You are not a victim. Never a victim. You are a strong, beautiful, woman," I whisper staring at myself in the mirror.

"You ready? You look gorgeous."

I take a deep breath thinking about her question. "Not too sure I'm ready, but as far as I can see, I look good," I say glancing at her through the mirrors reflection.

"You do, but appearances can be deceiving to how we truly feel. Trust me, I know."

Just keep moving.

I stand after throwing on my heels and do a little twirl for her. She claps excitedly. "Ohhh I wish I could be a fly on the wall tonight when he first sees you." She flashes a huge grin giving me a big hug.

We're chatting away as we leave my room. I can hear the sounds of male wisecracking from downstairs. When I reach the top of the stairs, I see all the boys standing around the island laughing. Well, all but Giovanni, Caelan and Antonio. They're smiling, but it's more passive.

I hear a loud drawn out whistle. Then Sage's bellowing voice. "Woooohooooo. Hot. Pants! You look gooooood!"

Everyone's heads whip in my direction. Sage makes me laugh every single day of my life. "What the hell?" I scold jokingly. "You all having a party without me while I'm gone?" I bellow with a burst of laughter.

"Just a warm up for tomorrow night." Luke mischievously smirks as he gives me a long-lasting bear hug. "Where you going tonight, sexy girl? 'Cause wherever you're going, you're going to need a bodyguard with that dress on."

"I have one." I chuckle pointing at Giovanni as I pull away from him. Then I see it. It hits me square in the chest, Caelan's face. His arms are tightly crossed over his broad chest. The black ribbed A-shirt he's wearing looks a little tight at the moment on his two-hundred-and-forty-pound frame. His puffed-up chest, if at all possible, is broader and heaving with heavy breaths. He lifts himself abruptly and with ease from leaning against the kitchen counter with an incredulous, furious look on his face. "Oh shit," I mutter, letting go of Luke completely waiting for the force of Caelan O'Reily's anger to hit me.

"What's the matter?" Luke's concerned face turns towards whatever threat has me completely stiff.

"Oh fuck," I hear mumbled from behind me, knowing damn well it's Jess. Being that she and Giovanni are the only ones that know about us, everyone else in the room is going to be a little stunned at what transpires in the next few minutes.

Luke looks back to Jess, confused. Then back to Caelan, who's full steam heading my way. He stops directly in front of Luke who has now placed his large frame in front of me, protectively.

"What's going on?" Luke asks. Neither one of us answer him. "C, tell me what's going on," he demands.

I swear I just saw smoke billowing out of his nostrils. I watch him as he gets himself under control to answer Luke's question. His very dominant, alpha male side is coming through in spades with controlled smoothness when he opens his mouth and demands that Luke move.

"Move." He scowls.

"Nah, dude. Not moving until you tell me what's going on."

"I. Said. Move."

"Luke, it's fine. He would never hurt me." I swallow, wishing the butterflies I feel in my stomach would take flight and bring me with them. He hasn't moved his eyes from mine yet. They're like laser beams shooting through my very soul. I see the pain flicker through his gorgeous blues. Then they shudder over with anger again. Luke looks back at me to make sure. I brace myself for whatever he has to say when Luke takes a small step to the side to stand by Giovanni and Antonio. Caelan steps forward to within an inch of me. My nose meets his chest. Then my head is tilted up gently by his large, shaking hand. I look into his blue eyes. I can tell he's stunned and very upset that I'm still going on this date. My guess is after this afternoon he didn't think I would still be going.

In a low, deep tone, he hisses, "Less than fourteen hours ago, I was inside you. Now you're going out with another man?"

"Last night was..." I go to lay my hand on his chest but he jerks away from me, dropping his hand from my quivering chin.

"What? What, Sofia? What was last night? Huh?"

I can't do this right now. I am barely hanging on.

"Tell me, beautiful, when I was inside you, were you thinking about him?"

"No," I state promptly staring directly into his eyes. Because it's the truth. "I was thinking of only us." From the corner of my eye, I see Antonio take a few steps away. I'm assuming this is a conversation he doesn't want to listen to about his sister.

"Then tell me, when are you going to stop running?"

"I'm not running," I stammer quietly.

Am I running? No, I'm not running.

"Beautiful, you're running so fast you can't even keep up with yourself. This person," he says looking me over, "is not you. Last night, last night meant something, and you know it did. Not just for me, for both of us. You spent last night in my bed, fucking me, all night. Now tonight, you're going out with another guy? As a man, who's in love with you, what am I supposed to do with that?"

Gasping and mumbling are heard from all directions around the kitchen. My eyes become as big as saucers, but I don't say anything. I want to say a whole hell of a lot of something. I do, but I am not going to degrade what happened between us last night with an argument. He's mad. I get it. I would be too, but we are not a couple, and I have to do what is right for me. We shared a night that was beautiful. Actually, it was more than beautiful. It was the best night of my entire life. I will not let him ruin that because he's pissed off. I take a deep breath trying to rid the hurt that I know is visible in my eyes. He got what he wanted. He wanted everyone to know we'd slept together and he wanted to know if it meant anything to me. Well, he got his answer just by seeing the hurt in my eyes. I take a step back from him, leaving him with just that, the lingering hurt in my eyes.

"You ready to go?" I ask Giovanni. Luke, who is still standing next to him, is baffled. Giovanni nods. I lean up, giving Luke a kiss on the cheek. "Thank you," I say. Mainly for stepping in front of me to protect me from his best friend who he knows would never hurt me, but also for just being a friend. "You all have a good night. Chris, I'll see you tomorrow. Happy early Birthday." I smile at him, taking a step towards the door. He says thank you, but it's as quiet as a mouse. You could hear a pin drop in the room. I take another step when I hear his growl.

"Sofia-" he hisses in warning, grabbing a hold of my wrist.

"Caelan," Antonio warns as Giovanni takes a step toward him.

I swing back to him, but I'm staring at his hand grasping my wrist. He lets go immediately. My eyes slowly rise to the fire of his determined ones. He takes a step towards me, closing in the space again. His big, bold, powerful body hovering above mine. "I told you before, beautiful, you are mine. You have always been mine. I was just waiting for you to come to me. You came to me last night, Sofia. Do not think for one second I am going to back off from something I have wanted and waited for, for so fucking long."

Just keep moving.

"We need to talk, Sofia."

Just keep moving.

"No. We don't."

"We do, about today, and we will." He fumes. Then gently and reverently runs his knuckles down my cheek to my jaw with his glazed over eyes locked on my soft, dewy skin.

I'm not sure what to say, or even do. The powerful force between us is crushing. Stepping back from him, I turn and walk towards the front door.

"Sofia," his commanding voice demands for me to turn around. I turn, looking back to his handsome face. "you look beautiful," he professes with afflicted sorrowful eyes.

I'm sorry, C.

thirty-five

Bella Maria is a quaint, Italian restaurant. It's romantic, cozy, and sophisticated, right down to the fresh, red roses encased in elegant, etched glass vases. The room is dark with candles flickering warm light across the white cloth covering the tables.

Oh, I love this place already.

My gaze floats through the room, waiting for the hostess to help me, when I hear his familiar, sexy voice.

"My God, you're breathtaking."

I swing my head in the direction of his voice. When I do, I see utter appreciation, heat, and what looks like conflict in his eyes.

I smile, stepping towards him and blushing from his compliment. "Hi, this place is incredible."

He places his hand on my elbow and leans down to kiss my cheek. "Good, I'm glad you like it. Come on." He jerks his head. "I have a table for us out back. It's quiet and private." He turns to the hostess. "Sara please show Mr. Moretti to the back corner of the bar. I left a table reserved for him there.

Whatever he wants is on the house tonight." He looks back to Giovanni, who is just about to complain. "The table is right by the door to the veranda, where we will be sitting, alone. No other guests will be permitted out there with us." After a minute, he gives a slight nod confirming it's okay, but then I watch as the two of them have a full conversation without saying a word. What the hell did I just miss? And ummm hello, does Johnathan own this place? He leads me to the veranda while Giovanni, who's right behind me follows the hostess to the table that is right by the door overlooking the veranda just like Johnathan said it would be. He's well within fifteen feet of me, with just the glass window separating us, giving us some privacy.

The atmosphere out here is so surreal it's, magical. It's a mild summer night in the city with a slight breeze. There are white lights draped from the top of the structure in a zig-zagging pattern through the open dark wood planks of the veranda. Sheer, white curtains are hanging at each post, billowing from the breeze. The table is perfectly set for two, right down to the flowers and candles. Instead of roses like the inside tables have, our table has full-bodied, white, Peonies with a blush pink center. He pulls out my chair and as I take my seat the familiar sounds of Rob Thomas is playing softly in the background. I watch Johnathan as he goes to take his seat and he looks at Giovanni to confirm his seating arrangements are okay. After he nods, Johnathan finally sits.

"Okay gorgeous what will it be, red or white?"

"I'm a white girl, and you need to explain," I say floating my hand through the air. His grin is contagious.

"Yes, I own this restaurant. This one and two more just like it. Plus, a night club. Although this place," he mutters reverently gazing around. "This one I hold close to my heart. This one's the original."

"It's truly stunning." I gleam at him. I see something flicker in his eyes. Sadness, I think it is, but it's gone just as quick as it came.

"No, as I said before, you are truly stunning. You're absolutely breathtaking this evening, Sofia."

I blush again. That's twice tonight he has made me blush. "Mr. Reznor, are you trying to sweet talk me to get into my pants?"

His deep chuckle vibrates his chest while he shakes his head in disbelief. "Well, Sofia I wouldn't be a man with eyes if I say I didn't at least think about it. Especially after seeing you in that dress, but I can assure you it wouldn't be that hard to get in your pants being you're not wearing any."

I bust out laughing. "Okay, Okay, touché, Mr. Reznor. But, I can assure you that what's under this dress has double locks."

His sexy grin illuminates his gorgeous face. His eyes sparkle at our banter. "Well, I can assure you Ms. Heart, I specialize in lock picking," he jokes. "A woman with a sense of humor, spunky, and sexy as all hell, I like it."

I giggle like a school girl. "Well, that's good because I like what I see as well. Now tell me, what made you open three restaurants and a club?"

We sat there for a while, enjoying a couple glasses of wine. Our conversation went from one thing to another fluidly. No awkward moments of silence, just good conversation. Until...

"So, tell me," he inquires, halting his question until the server placed our appetizers onto the table and left the veranda before he continued. "Why does a girl like you need a bodyguard?"

Damn.

I knew at some point he was going to ask. I'm assuming because of the 'almost' altercation between him and Giovanni the other night at the club, his curiosity is even more peaked. The question for me is how much do I tell him? I contemplate it for a moment while I look into his eyes. Wondering if he's the kind of man that runs or stay when things get tough.

"I'm sorry. The question wasn't meant to make you uncomfortable, and I can see that it has. Too heavy for a first date?"

I sit back in my chair, grabbing my glass of wine. Taking another moment before I answer. "Someone from my past has come back into my life. So, until we can make sure I'm safe, Giovanni will be my sidekick." There that should be good enough explanation. His body stiffens and the alpha protectant male comes to the surface.

"This person from your past, was violent towards you?"

You can say that.

"Yes, yes he was. Hurt me very badly," I admit. Taking a deep breath, I lean forward analyzing him as my words sink in.

His jaw tightens and clenches. The muscle's flexing back and forth. "Well, if you ever see this person while we're out together, you point him out to me."

I blow off his comment, trying to lighten the mood. "So does that mean there will be more nights together?"

He grins. "That's exactly what I'm hoping for, Sofia."

Well, hot damn, he's not a runner. Check

"Oysters huh?" I say, squinting my eyes at him after finally glancing down at the appetizers. "Known to be an aphrodisiac. Is this you still trying to get through the double locks beneath this dress?" I laugh.

"Tell me you're the typical woman who doesn't eat oysters? I really thought I had you pegged differently." His grin highlights his tanned face. And what a face it is. His jet-black hair draws your eyes down to his strong jaw line. His thick eyelashes encase his deep, deep green eyes which pull you in.

Hot damn! Did I just hear the drummer being called to play?

When my eye fucking comes back into focus, I realize he is staring at me just the same way. So, that confirms it, we're both very attracted to each other.

Check Please!

I lick my bottom lip unintentionally before taking a sip of my glass of wine. When I do, I watch as Johnathan's eyes flair with want. "Well, Johnathan." I grab an oyster spreading some cocktail sauce on it. "I'll have you know that you are not wrong." I raise my brow slightly, looking him dead in his eyes as I slowly suck the oyster from its shell, letting it slide down my throat, then lick my lips of the leftover juice. "I can suck with the best of them, and I can appreciate the feel of it slowly sliding down my throat." I watch as his sophisticated, in control, well-built body jerks at my comment. His glass of wine stopping midair and he readjusts himself in his seat. I'm sure that erection I just gave him is a bit uncomfortable. We gaze into each other's lustful eyes. He clears his throat, giving a slight shake to his head.

"So, how 'bout those Yankees?" he gruffly chuckles.

I burst into laughter, as does he. "I'm sorry I just had to. You were being all cocky about the oysters, so I had to."

In amusement, he shakes his head. "You are definitely a feisty one."

DINNER WAS TO die for. We both had steak with a sautéed spinach that melted in your mouth. The conversation between us was still continuing flawlessly. We joked, and the banter between us was endless. A couple of times, I thought I saw something in his eyes. Conflict maybe, but it passed quickly. Maybe he is confused at how well we are getting along, just as I am. He asked about Hearts Desire. I told him how it was a shell when I first saw the building. How it's been built up to what it is today. How I wanted to open many of them in different locations around the country.

While in return, I asked about him opening and redoing his places. He said, for now, the three restaurants and club take up his time and that at times he has to travel a lot. In his twenty-eight years, he has accomplished a lot as he had told me in my twenty-four, I have as well. Dessert came to the table, and it was an array of mouthwatering, creamy goodness.

"I am soooo a dessert girl. Although, I never eat it," I inform him with my eyes as big as dinner plates drooling over the desserts the server put in front of us.

"You love it, but you never eat it?" he laughs.

Mirroring his laugh, I tell him, "I would love to eat every morsel on this plate, but my ass wouldn't like it."

He grabs his fork slicing through a thick creamy piece of cheesecake.

Hmmmm My favorite.

Then holds it up to my mouth. When I take the bite, my eyes are locked on his, but when the cheesecake hits my palate, my eyes flutter closed as my vocal cords 'Mmmmmmmm' their appreciation. I roll my eyes in the back of my head over the dessert-gasm I'm having. "This right here," I point to the plate after opening my eyes "It's the reason why I spend an hour at kickboxing four to five times a week."

Although I haven't been there in two weeks.

We take a few more bites of dessert. Rob Thomas~ *My, My, My* is softly playing. "Dance with me?" he says, standing, holding out his hand. We take a few steps from the table. His left hand wraps around to the small of my back, while his right hand cradles mine against his chest. I rest my other hand on his chest as well. The feel of his strong, well-formed, chest muscle flexing back and forth as we sway to the slow music is doing very naughty things to my body. This is so different than the other night at the club. That was fun, flirty, and sexy. Tonight though, this is intimate. He pulls my body into him more. You couldn't slide a piece of paper between us right now we're so close and to be honest, it feels good. Really good. He lets go of my hand, lifting my chin to look up at him. When I do, the butterflies hit my stomach in masses. He lowers his head, gently laying a kiss on my lips. When I reciprocate, his kiss becomes deeper. All the while, still rocking our bodies to the melody of the music. His warm tongue slides slowly over mine. His left hand presses into my lower back pulling me deeper into his hips. My left hand curls around his shoulder, while my right hand lays on the back of his neck. My fingers curling through his hair at the nape of his neck. I can feel his erection growing rapidly on my belly. It's doing crazy, wild things to my insides. The kiss itself leaves me breathless. When he pulls away, the same fire I have in my eyes is radiating through his.

"Sorry." He winks, then kisses my cheek. He's still rocking me back and forth to the beat of Dave Matthew's Band~ *Crash Into Me.*

"For what, the kiss?" I question. Really hoping he doesn't say yes because that would mean the kiss sucked for him, but I'm thinking the kiss didn't suck being that his erection is still laying against my stomach.

"No, not the kiss." He grins with a twinkle in his eye.

"Ahhh, that's okay. That only means you appreciated the kiss as much as I did." I blush thinking about how much I affect his body.

His eyes flutter back and forth over mine. "You're a beautiful woman, Sofia," he sweetly compliments, and I see it again, the indecision, the hesitation in his eyes. And for me, a bucket of cold water just poured over my head, infiltrating my body.

Caelan.

"Did I say something wrong?"

I smile and huff a little. "No, not at all. I ahhh, just remembered Giovanni is watching and as much as I enjoyed every second of it, having him behind me, watching, is a little weird."

I watch his eyes flick over my shoulder. "Well, I'll have you know, he's not looking our way. However, he's a good bodyguard. Knows how to be discrete. I get the impression he's more than just a bodyguard, though?" He tilts his head in question.

Does he think we're more than friends? Hmmm, how do I answer this without going into too much detail or having him ask more?

"We've known each other for a long time."

Confusion crosses his face. "He's not that much older than you?"

"No."

His lips press against mine again, lightly. When he pulls back, he smiles. "Well, we can do a couple of things. We can stay here on the veranda dancing and talking, or we can go to my club, or we can stay here and sit at the bar inside."

Hmmm, that's a hard one. Stay here in the quiet in the arms of a very sexy man and talk. That's a no-brainer. But, on the other hand, I'm curious as to what a Johnathan Reznor's club looks like, and the lure of the beating music and dancing with him sings to my soul. "What do you want to do?" I ask, just to see where his thoughts are at.

"Sweetheart, as long as this night doesn't end right now, I will do whatever you want." His eyes sparkle.

As much as I love being here with him right now in the quiet, I also want to dance the night away with him until the early morning hours. "Club then," I say, my eyes sparkling back at his.

We break apart, and he excuses himself. I watch as he glides smoothly, with confidence and control, to where Giovanni is sitting inside the restaurant. Their conversation lasts a few minutes before Johnathan is back standing at my side with an open hand, waiting for mine.

thirty-six

CLUB ABYSS IS JUST THAT, an endless club. As big as Ice, Fire, and The Devils Lair is tall, Club Abyss is wide and long. There are so many different sections of this club that it's hard to explain. The atmosphere itself is dark, sexy, naughty, and mysterious. The main room is a typical club bar with a large dance floor and dark alcoves hidden throughout the club.

Jess, Nikki, and I have always wanted to come here, but usually the line to get in is around the city block. Walking in, Johnathan is immediately greeted by a very attractive, tanned, and toned blonde. She has legs, that from where I'm standing, don't fucking end, under a short white dress that is as sexy as it is sophisticated.

Maybe we should have stayed at the restaurant.

She kisses him on both cheeks. Then ends those lingering kisses with a sexy smile and a once over of me that lets me know her claws are out.

Oh, joy!

I look over my shoulder to Giovanni who is a solid stature of power and protection. He raises his left brow quickly letting me know he saw the cat claws. Then, he slightly leans over and whispers quietly into my ear, "You're much more beautiful than her." I snort my disbelief, rolling my eyes with a slight smile.

But, thank you Giovanni, for being sweet.

Johnathan looks back at both of us, giving me a curious once over. He wraps his arm around my side, guiding me forward. "Tatiana, this is Sofia. Sofia, Tatiana.

Of course it is.

"Hi, nice to meet you," I respectfully greet her. She nods with no verbal greeting. Then turns to Johnathan.

"Johnny, your VIP booth is waiting. Max is waiting to serve you."

Johnny huh? Ok, she wants me to know they're on a personal level, not just employee-employer. Note taken.

Grabbing my hand, he walks through the crowd to an empty, dark, long hallway. At the end, it's either a left or right. We make a left, but I definitely look to the right to see what's down there. As far as I can see, nothing but two security guards blocking the door and erotic music streaming through the opening to the room. When we get to the end of the hallway he's leading us down, it opens to an extremely large, energetic club. As large as it is though, it's just as intimate. This section is more private then the front part of the club. He guides us through to the back where the VIP area is and I can already tell by the VIP section he's bringing us to that it's his spot and no one else gets to use it.

So, Mr. Reznor is a partier.

I'm assuming the server who asked for my drink order is Max. When he leaves, I settle into Johnathan's private booth and observe my date talking to my bodyguard. He's pointing to the exit doors in his club and a few other areas. Giovanni's eyes scan the entire place from top to bottom like a well-built machine. While waiting on them to finish their conversation, I survey the dance floor. Within two minutes of people watching, the hairs on the back of my neck rise at a furious pace. An uneasy feeling washes over me and my heart rate picks up.

This doesn't feel normal. Am I having an anxiety attack?

Giovanni catches my eyes, noticing my discomfort. Johnathan follows Giovanni's concerned eyes and starts to step towards me only to have Giovanni halt him in his spot. I take a deep breath trying to calm myself. Giovanni crouches down in front of me.

"Tell me what's going on?"

How do I explain it when I'm not sure what's wrong?

"Yeah, yeah I'm good." I blow it off.

"No, you're not. Take a deep breath, tell me what you're feeling."

So, I lie. I know I shouldn't. He's here to protect me. But if I don't, he'll snatch me up and whisk me out of here so fast my head will spin. I want to enjoy the rest of my evening. It's been perfect so far.

"I'm just tired that's all. But, I don't want the night to end. I'm having too good of a time." I smile, patting his comforting hands resting on my knees.

He knows I'm lying. I can tell just by the change in his eyes. "Sweetheart, if you see anything or feel uncomfortable again, you let me know right away." He rubs my leg with a slight comforting pat. Johnathan steps up behind a kneeling Giovanni, asking if everything is okay. Giovanni immediately stands to his full height, ignoring Johnathan's question and proceeds to stand by the column and survey the club.

"What was that about?" Johnathan asks taking a seat next to me. He wraps his arm around the back of the booth behind me waiting for my answer.

Before I can answer, Max is back with our drinks. So, I quickly deflect. "So how long have you owned this club?"

He doesn't answer for a minute. I can see the bewilderment in his deep green eyes over the subject change. "Three years," he accepts the change in subject. "Well, four with a year of construction."

"Wow, that's pretty impressive for a guy as young as you. Especially being that you have three restaurants as well. I thought opening my own boutique was hard, and I had Caelan's help."

"I had help too," he explains. "I have two silent partners."

I laugh. He looks at me confused. So, I explain. "So, basically, it's three young guys who opened a bangin', sexy club to get all the booty they want! It's an open playing field. Especially with a good-looking guy such as yourself," I joked. "I mean look at all these beautiful women in here," I say with an exaggerated wave of my hand.

His hand comes to my face as his body turns in more towards me. "I am looking at a beautiful woman, and I don't need to own a club to get what I want. I always get what I want, Sofia."

Okay two things just happened, heat from inside my loins radiate through me like lightning at his very cocky, dominant statement. Then cold water doused it out because he called me beautiful, *again*. Which to any other woman in the world, would be an awesome thing to hear. For me it brings me right back to... Caelan. His term of endearment for me. He started using it when we were teens. I will never be able to hear it again without thinking of him.

He notices and by the look on his face he isn't too happy. "That's twice tonight you went stiff on me when I told you, you were beautiful."

Okay, need to change this subject. Can't keep doing this.

I grab my drink taking a generous sized gulp as lady like as I can be, being that it's a gulp. As I'm placing my drink down I can see, for him, that this conversation isn't over. For me... it's done. Grabbing his hand, I ask him if he wants to dance. His agreement is him standing, taking me into his arms and kissing me with such fever that I feel like I am going to melt. When he ends the kiss, he says nothing and I just stand there in shock with a slack jaw. Grabbing my hand, he leads me to the dance floor and before I can even start to move, he whips my body around so my back is to his front. His left hand spreads across my belly pulling me back into him as he grinds himself into me.

"Well this is not the same dancing as the other night at Ice."

The deep beat of *Tell Me* by Dru Hill is thumping through my body. I feel his lips touch the side of my neck as he moves my pliable body. When he turns me around I see the look in his eyes, which I'm sure mine are reflecting the same thing right back at him. I am very much attracted to him. With his black hair, green eyes, strong and confident body, and the way he moves my body, it all does crazy, crazy things to me. He leans down and kisses me softly while holding my face. A slower sultry song hits the air waves just as he pulls me closer to him, wrapping his arm around my back. He gazes into my eyes with a sexy grin gracing his handsome face, which causes my heart rate to pick up. My tanned skin tingles, raising my flesh to maximum levels. My lower belly tightens while my legs become weak. One song morphs into another then another. I don't know how long we're on the dance floor when he leans down next to my ear and whispers, "I have a suite upstairs. You want to go have a drink?"

Hell, yeah, I do! Hell, I wanna do more than have a drink. I wanna drink him in. Eat him up. Lick him from head toe! Hmmmmm yes, I do but, but... I can't.

"Just a drink," I agree, with a reprimanding sexy smile. Letting him know this is not going any further than a drink.

Okay, Okay. Who am I kidding? Maybe a little making out.

GIOVANNI'S NOT TOO happy at the moment. After some persuasion, he's waiting outside the suite door, but only after checking out the entire suite from top to bottom. Johnathan was pretty laid back about him searching his private area. Actually, he's been more than accommodating the whole night. It could be a little awkward when it comes to a situation like this, but to me, Johnathan has been more than a gentleman when it comes to helping in my safety. Before he closes the door, Giovanni's commanding eyes connect with mine. It's his way of letting me know he'll be right outside the door if I need him.

Johnathan walks to the bar, asking what I would like to drink just as I drop my purse on the coffee table and walk over to the large picture window.

There's not much scenery being we are right in the middle of the city, but the building across the street is one of stunning architecture.

A creepy feeling comes over me and for the second time tonight the hairs on the back of neck rise and my skin prickles. Whoever is watching me, could be watching me right now. He's out there, somewhere.

I calm myself down, taking a few deep breaths. When I start to turn away from the window, the room fills with soft music. A warm body lightly presses against my back while a glass of white wine finds its way in front of me. He slides my hair to the side, kissing the back of my neck. His warm hands run up and down my arms giving me chills for a whole other reason. I turn my cheek into him grinning. His scotch laced breath flutters into my nose as his lips land on my ear. My mouth parts, my eyes close and for just a few brief moments, I'm just another girl standing with just a guy. It's a moment I cherish. In all the craziness surrounding my life, this quiet moment between him and I is what makes me wish I was someone else.

But, I am not a normal girl and Johnathan is definitely not a normal guy. There's an element about him I can't quite figure out. The looks of confusion I've seen flicker in his eyes, the way he holds himself with confidence and power and commands a room without trying... he's a mystery to me and that, well that turns me on and frightens me all the same. If I hadn't slept with Caelan last night, I would probably sleep with him tonight, but when I think about last night with Caelan… I see the beauty in it, in *us*. The pure honesty of two people making love to each other. Secrets revealed. The closeness it creates between two people. If I had sex with Johnathan tonight, it would be just that- sex. Hot sex, yes, but just sex. The chemistry is off the charts between us, but there wouldn't be that connection I share with C.

Am I looking for a connection? Or am I just looking to forget, to let go of the hurt for a mere hour or two.

I turn in his arms gently cradling the glass of wine and start kissing his neck. Leaving soft love bites along the way. I feel the vibration of his groan on my lips. I work my way to his lips, kissing him passionately. Both his hands hold the back of my head as he takes over the kiss. His warm, tantalizing, tongue glides slowly over my lower lip. Our heavy breathing echoing through the air as we devour one another. His left hand releases its hold on my head, sliding down the curve of my body to my ass, squeezing.

Hmmmm…

I'm losing myself in him, in this force of sexual tension. My thoughts are becoming bits and pieces of yes and no. I need to think clearly. I have no doubt that what would happen between us would be amazing, but this has to slow down. This cannot happen, but before I can pull away he pulls his lips from mine slowly.

"We have to stop." He breaths heavily with a sexy grin, but then I see the flicker in his eyes again. "We have to stop," he repeats again trying to cover his uncertainty.

My eyes glitter at him with a smirk, but my confusion over his confusion has me on alert. "Yeah, yeah we do," I agree breathing just as heavily, licking my lower lip.

"Shit, don't do that again, gorgeous or I might not be able to hold myself back." He smirks taking a step away from me to grab his glass of amber liquor off the bar.

Time to slow this down.

"So, this is your fuck pad, huh? Not too shabby," I joke. He damn near chokes on his scotch. Wiping his lip from the remaining scotch that escaped his full lips, his unsettled look makes me chuckle inside. He's quiet while he contemplates what to say. There's no need. It is what it is. I'm fine with that.

"Sofia, I didn't…"

I throw my palm up, giggling at his discomfort. "It's fine. No biggie. If you think for one second that I didn't know down stairs when you asked me to come up here, that this was your fuck pad, you have a lot to learn about me. It's all good. You can breathe now." I assure him with a chuckle.

"I guess I do," he agrees, looking at me with questioning uncertainty. I quirk my brow at him. "Get to know you better. I guess I need to get to know you better."

"Trust me, I have four very good guy friends and a brother who play the field like no other. We're all very close. So, all your guy shenanigans, I already know about."

"Have dinner with me tomorrow?" he says abruptly cutting me off walking toward me slowly.

"Sorry, I can't."

His eyes narrow, thinking I'm blowing him off. "Lunch then."

"Lunch it is." I nod slightly.

I hear my phone ding and vibrate. I head towards my purse to check it, while he heads to the bar to refill our glasses. It's either Jess or Nikki. Oh, wait could definitely be Sagie boy wondering how my night's going. As I swipe the screen to unlock the phone, pictures of me and Johnathan start popping up. In the club dancing. The club right downstairs. There are close up pictures of him kissing me. Giovanni comes bursting through the door as I gasp throwing my hand over my mouth and dropping to the couch. Johnathan rushes over to me, clearly baffled at what is transpiring. Giovanni is crouching at my feet within seconds, grabbing my phone. He looks at the picture then stands with determined force. He grabs his phone, hits a button and impatiently waits for the other person to pick up.

"The Abyss. NOW! Suite upstairs." He turns to Johnathan waiting for directions.

"I'll have someone meet him down at the back entrance. South side."

Giovanni repeats what Johnathan just said. "Close man, real fucking close! This motherfucker's going down and soon," he barks into the phone then hangs up. He turns to Johnathan and starts barking orders. "I want the security tapes! Like now! Fucking yesterday! You understand what I'm saying?" I hear him order but his voice is slowly becoming miles away.

Overwhelming Darkness Consumes Me.

WHEN I WAKE, I'm in a vehicle with my head resting on someone's lap. Antonio. "Hey, sis. How do you feel?"

"How long have I been out?" I ask instead of answering his question.

"Not long, but we have a doctor coming to the house to check you over."

A doctor? Who gets a doctor to make a house call at this time of night?

"A doctor?" I question. Then it hits me. "A, no! Absolutely not! I do not want daddy's doctor looking after me." The panic's starting to rise yet again.

"Sis, listen to me. You hit your head when you fainted. You're getting checked out. Period! Don't worry about dad finding out. Doc gets paid to be quiet. Trust me, sis. I have used him and so has Giovanni. Dad knows nothing. It's what he's there for, total confidentiality."

I'm quiet the rest of the ride. It's late and I'm tired and worried. When we get to the house, C is pacing the floors. When the door opens, he rushes to me, enveloping me into his strong arms.

Best feeling in the world.

There's a man standing behind him, waiting patiently. Antonio approaches him, along with Giovanni, talking in hushed tones. When Caelan lets me go, he roars at Giovanni.

"What the fuck happened?"

"I need a private room to look her over." The doctor says clearing his throat to interrupt the festering battle that's going to happen between C and Giovanni.

"Use my office." Caelan points in that direction without moving his furious eyes from Giovanni.

Antonio and I walk to his office with the doctor. When we reach the door, Antonio properly introduces me to him. "Sof, this is Dr. Bianconi. We call him Dr. B to keep his name anonymous. The only reason I just told you, is so you feel comfortable with him. His name can never leave your lips." I nod in acknowledgment. Before the good ol' doctor and I enter the office, closing the door behind us. He's not old, maybe late forties early fifties. He checks me over. I'm exhausted. I need sleep. He asks me questions. I answer as best I can. I don't remember fainting so I don't remember hitting my head, but I can tell you I have a knot on the back of my head the size of an egg. I feel a little dizzy and nauseous, but not too bad. Dr. B informs me I have a slight concussion. I should be fine by tomorrow. If the symptoms get worse, have Antonio contact him.

There's something about Dr. B. I can't quite put my finger on. I can't stop staring at him. I have seen him before. Probably at my father's house in passing. So, I blow it off. After a few minutes, it dawns on me. The hospital, weeks ago when I was drugged. He was not the main doctor who took care of me, but he was the doctor that came in and checked on me in-between. He must notice I put two and two together. A friendly smile graces his face and he nods, as do I in conformation. Now I know how I got a private room when I was in the hospital. He finishes his exam. Tells me to get rest, hydrate and ice my head.

When we leave the office, all three of them stop their conversation turning their attention to me. The doctor explains I'm okay, just needing some rest. Informs them to keep an eye on me and if symptoms get worse to call him. With that, Antonio thanks him and he walks out with no questions asked.

I need answers. How did Giovanni know what was going on? I swear if he has me bugged, I'll kill him. That's one of the things after the rape that I need most- control. If I don't have control, I feel out of control, and that's not a good thing for me. After him hearing my conversation that night in the bar with Johnathan because of his supersonic ear piece, he should know that won't cut it for me. The three of them are around the kitchen island with beers in their hands. Giovanni has now taken off his suit jacket and his tie is hanging loosely around his neck. Caelan is in a pair of navy blue loose pajama bottoms, shirtless. And A is still in his black tee and dark pants. I would think I was the luckiest girl in the world right now if I didn't have all this shit going on. I approach the island. The three of them watch me cautiously. All eyes are on me waiting for me to start this conversation.

"I wanna know how you knew to come into the suite?" I direct my question to Giovanni. "How is it that at the same time I got the texts you were already bursting through the door? Were you listening? Do you have me bugged?" I sneer with fire in my eyes.

"You're not bugged. I will not do that to you again without telling you. When I closed that door everything between you two was private."

I hear Caelan suck in a breath and mutter something, but I can't worry about that now. "Then how? I want an answer right now, Giovanni. I'm supposed to trust you, right? You said I could. Right now- I don't."

"Sis, it's okay."

I throw my hand up to Antonio. Shutting him up, all the while never losing eye contact with Giovanni. "Answer my question."

"It was me, Sof. He knew because of me."

My head snaps to Caelan. "Excuse me?"

"Whoever is stalking you sent the pictures of you and him to me first. I sent them to Giovanni then called him." His face looks pained.

It takes me a moment to process. I think back to the pictures that were sent to me. Now I know why his face seems pained. I apologized to Giovanni for not trusting him. Which he accepts immediately. I turn to Caelan apologizing for the fact that some sick fuck who's after me wants to hurt him too. Which, it clearly has, his face says it all. Those pictures of me embraced with someone else has truly hurt him. I turn to Antonio who is right next to me. I kiss him on the cheek thanking him for helping me tonight. Then I walk to my room. Ignoring my name being called by all three.

WHEN I GET upstairs, I open my purse and grab my phone. I want to see these photos again. I scroll through. I have to say, they're pretty hot. Then guilt hits me, hard. Caelan saw these. I feel like every part of my life is an open book. I have no privacy. Then panic starts to set in. These pictures were taken from not too far away. Whoever this is, whoever is after me, my stalker, my rapist, was only a few feet away from me tonight. I breathe through the anxiety building in my body, dropping my phone to my bed and take a few deep cleansing breaths.

Now I know why the hairs on the back of my neck kept rising tonight. I may not know who this person is or what he looks like, but my body sure does.

I strip my clothes heading for the shower. I'm only in there for a few minutes when I hear a knock on the open bathroom door.

"Can I come in?" I hear C ask from outside the door.

Well, might as well, it's not like he didn't see me naked beneath him last night. As a matter of fact, he had me so spread wide open I don't even think I've seen that much of myself. "Yea," I answer.

The bathroom is quiet. Normally I have my music blasting. Right now, though, I just need the solitude of the quietness. He enters the bathroom, leaning against the vanity. He crosses his legs and cups his hands, while I give him a once over noticing his erection beneath his cupped hands. The one he's trying so hard to hide.

Sorry buddy, but there's no hiding the beast.

I watch him close the toilet lid and sit. I chuckle because I guess he thinks that will help, but nothing is going to help. "It's okay."

"Sorry," he apologizes clearing his throat.

"It's fine." I smile trying to lighten up the situation. I can see he feels bad. "I don't know how you do it. How do you hide it when you're out in a club and see a beautiful woman?"

He squints his eyes. "Beautiful, there is only one woman that gets me this fucking hard and she's standing in front of me naked and wet with soap sliding down her amazing curves. So, yeah, I'm sorry, but no matter how much control I have over myself, when it comes to you, I'm defenseless."

Well, Damn!

I rinse off. Turn off the shower and open the glass door. He grabs a towel from the towel warmer, handing it to me. I stay inside the shower and dry off. I know why he's in here. To check on me because the last time I had a freak out I scrubbed my thighs to a bloody mess. "So, why did you come in here? To watch me? Check up on me to make sure I didn't damage my thighs again?"

"Not at all." His anger evident in his tone. "I came in here to make sure you were alright."

"I'm as good as I can be," I admitted, wrapping the towel around myself as I walk into my bedroom to get dressed. I drop the towel, grabbing for one of C's t-shirts that's laying on the back of my chair. On him, it fits tight. On me, it's huge. I throw my dark wet hair into a messy knot on top of my head then slide on some panties. When I turn around I see the desire on his face, desire that's so strong, but he's trying desperately to hide.

He drops his head, clearing his throat. "If you need me, I'm right across the hall." He kisses my forehead. "Good night, beautiful." And with those three words, he walks out.

I climb into my bed. I lie there, staring at the ceiling. I'm so tired, but I can't sleep. I feel alone. I have all these people around me, protecting me, watching me, making sure I'm safe, but I feel so alone. I toss and turn and after thirty minutes I find myself getting out of bed and wandering across the hallway. I knock softly in case he's sleeping. I hear his deep voice telling me to come in. I crack the door slowly. He's lying in bed on his side, under the covers. Neither one of us says anything. He lifts the covers for me to climb in, then wraps his arms around me pulling me into him. He gives me the peace I need to fall asleep. But, before I do...

"I didn't sleep with him," I whisper sleepy truths.

"I don't care. I don't want another man's lips or hands on what's mine."

thirty-seven

I WAKE IN ALMOST THE SAME position I went to sleep. He never let go of me all night. I turn my head to see what time it is, when a knock at the door has Caelan stirring, but not moving. "Go away," he grumbles in a grouchy bark, still not moving. I chuckle. The door swings open anyway.

"We're ordering breakfast sandwiches from the diner. You want- oh Shit."

Balls! Awkward.

I burrow down more into Caelan's body, hiding. He chuckles. "You want something?" he whispers with a sexy gruff into my ear.

"Yup, I'm starving," I whisper back.

"I'm sure you are," I hear Antonio murmur with a chuckle behind it.

Great!

"Two pork roll, egg, and cheese on a hard roll and a large caramel white mocha with coconut milk from the coffee shop next door," C tells him, "and close the door on your way out," he demands still not moving to acknowledge he's there, but squeezing me tighter into him.

I hear Antonio's laugh. "You fucker," he mutters under his breath closing the door.

Mmmmm he hums pulling me into him even more. "Mornin.'"

"Morning."

"You feeling better?" he asks, finally opening his eyes lifting himself onto one elbow looking down at me.

"Yeah."

"You're lying," he reprimands, frowning at me.

"No, I do feel better. I feel better than I did last night. I just... I just feel like everything is out of my control. I feel like I'm on the edge of a very thin, fragile line that I'm teetering on," I admit, looking up into his eyes.

"Everything is going to be okay. I promise you that. He may be out there, and he may have gotten close, but not close enough that he can get to you. Giovanni is good at what he does, and Antonio is now going to be there as well when we all go out."

"You say that he's good, which he is, but last night I heard you yelling at him. You have a problem with Giovanni. Caelan, I can't have the two people in my life that are trying to keep me safe, fighting with each other."

"We're not fighting. Yes, I do have a problem with him. It's my problem. He knows what it's about and if it were vice versa, he would have an issue too."

"What is it?"

"Just something I need to work out on my own."

"C," I frown. "Just tell-"

"No, Sof. Not now. I will, but not now," he says sitting up and leaning against the headboard. "I want to ask you some questions okay?"

Oh boy. I do not want to do this.

I start sliding out of bed. He pulls me back into him. "I don't want to talk." I groan.

"You're running. I've seen it before. The signs are all there. You just got done telling me you feel like you're teetering on a thin line. You do crazy, reckless shit when you feel out of control, just to prove you can control what you do, but in the end, it only proves you're out of control. I see it, Sof. I see it in your glittering, anxious, wild, green eyes. I see it more and more every day."

"I'm fine. Really, I'm-"

He tilts my chin up to meet his concerned eyes. "You are not fine, but trust me, I will be there to catch you when you fall."

I know you will, C.

"I need to ask you something." I nod, waiting for the question-not that I want to answer it. "Do you regret what happened between us the other night?"

"No." I immediately answer with a clear, concise answer.

I will never regret it.

An intoxicating smile adorns his handsome face, then a frown washes it all away. "If you don't regret it, then why did you go out with him last night?"

Shit! What do I say?

"I don't know." I go to speak again, but I'm tongue-tied. "What happened between us was... it was the best night of my life, but we aren't together. We can both date anyone we want. I know this will hurt you, b-but I am attracted to him, C." He growls deep in his broad chest. "And not for anything, this is really fucking awkward to sit here talking to you about this. Especially me being in your arms. I want to be honest with you, but I don't want to hurt you, so this conversation needs to end." I go to move, and he pulls me back with a smirk on his face.

"Do you think that maybe this conversation is only awkward because you no longer see me just as a good friend? Because... quite honestly, beautiful, we have in fact talked about our partners in the past."

Ohhhh, please, how do I get out of this conversation.

"So, you're telling me, if I started dating someone or bring home a random chick, you would be okay with that?"

Hell NO! I would not be OKAY with that! Wait what? What the hell? Where did that come from?

My stomach flips. I'm green with jealousy, but I control my reaction. The fact that this conversation is getting way too close to the situation with bad-fake-tits… I just can't go there because it hurts too much. I need to end this. "You have the right to date whoever you want." He smiles, kissing my forehead with a look on his face I don't understand.

Why is he smiling? I'm boiling inside!

He's smiling like he just won the damn lottery. "Come on, breakfast should be here by now," he says smirking. "I'm sure your brother won't want to come back up here knowing you're lying in my bed with my t-shirt on."

"Well, at least I wasn't naked, riding you." I laugh. "He wouldn't be too pleased about that, I'm sure."

"No, but, I would." His husky voice rumbles with a smug look and that damn dimple gleaming like a shooting star.

AFTER THROWING ON some shorts, I grab my phone and we head downstairs together. My mouth salivates because I can smell my coffee from the top of the staircase. We grab our sandwiches and devour them. After a few minutes, I ask the question that's been burning me. Looking up from my coffee, I say, "I need some answers." Giovanni is the first one to look at me, frowning. He knows right where I'm going with this. "Tell me how this guy got that close to me and why we didn't know it?"

"I don't know," he deadpans, "but, what I can say is this, he may have been farther away from you than it appears, using the zoom on a camera to seem closer, but I will agree that, even so, it's disturbing that he was even there and I didn't know. So much so that I called in a buddy of mine that does private security. He's going to be by my side. His eyes will be on the floor, while mine will be on you. I will do everything in my power to make sure you're kept safe."

I look over at C who is nodding his head in agreement. He must have already known about this.

"Okay," I agree. "You've known this person for a long time? You trust him?"

"Yes, sweetheart. I would never put you in harm's way. Dax is Ex-military, Special Forces. He owns his own very successful security business now protecting very wealthy people from all around the world. He has left his security detail in another country to come back to the states to help me with this situation. His training is extensive. You will be safe with him."

"Okay. I trust you," I concede, walking over to throw away the wrapper from my sandwich and wash my hands. My phone beeps with a text. "Caelan can you grab that. It's probably Sage about the big order that came in this morning." He grabs my phone, and I watch as his face becomes a red beacon of light, making my stomach do flips.

Oh, no, no, no!

The three of us are now watching him. Antonio demands to know who it is. Caelan just stares at me with painful penetrating eyes. "Loverboy wants to know if you're still up to having lunch today. He misses your mouth. Says he still feels your ass in his hands. Oh, and he had a great time last night, but more importantly he wants to know if you're okay," he hisses, flipping my phone back and forth in his right hand.

I hear the mutters of "fuck" come from Antonio and Giovanni.

Shit!

Two things happen. The first is that it dawns on me that when I told Caelan that I didn't sleep with him, he didn't believe me. I can tell by the look of disbelief on his face. The second is that yesterday, when Johnathan texted me, and I didn't answer back right away, he called me. Right now, my phone is still in Caelan's hands like a bomb waiting to go off. If Johnathan calls, he will answer it. I know he will. "Give me my phone," I demand. And right on cue, my phone starts ringing.

B.A.L.L.S! Big, Sweaty, Hairy, Monkey Balls!!

My body stills as I watch in slow motion as he answers the phone with the most devious, pissed off glare I've ever seen on his face.

This is not going to be good.

I lunge for him, grabbing at my phone. "Don't You Dare!" I scream, grabbing at his arms. It's no use though, he's too tall and too strong for me.

I look at the two other males in the kitchen for help. They both just stand there, watching in cautious amusement.

"Hello?" Gasping, I whip my head back to him realizing he connected the call with Johnathan. "Who's this?" he demands with gruff manly attitude. "No, I asked you first, fucker. You're calling my girl's number, so I think I have the right to know who's calling. Don't you?" My heart sinks. "Yeah, my girl, motherfucker," he barks as his eyes survey my body. "About five foot six, wavy brunette hair, amazing green eyes that you can get lost in, bangin' body, unbelievably soft full lips, and her ass, her ass is every man's fantasy to sink his-"

"Caelan O'Reily I swear to the almighty God if you do not give me that phone right now!" I scream pointing at the sky. He drops the phone onto the island still staring at me. Then turns and walks away.

"Don't you fucking move," I shout, pointing at him. I turn my attention to the phone grabbing it. "Johnathan, I'm so sorry. I will call you back. I need to take care of this. I will call you back when I'm done." *Click.* I hang up on him, not waiting for an answer. My blood is boiling! My legs are trembling with anger. How dare he do that? Tears of anger spring to my eyes. My lip is snarling like a rabid dog. I have never done that to him. I have always been very kind to all the girls, even the skanky whores, who have called or have walked these floors. He just stepped way over the line. "How dare you do that? How dare you! You son of a bitch! What the hell was that?"

"That was me letting another man know not to put his hands on *my girl*. He had his hands on you last night, Sofia. I don't fucking like it!"

"You bastard!" I shout with incredulity flooding my voice. "You have women's hands on you all the time. You're constantly parading women around here in front of me. Have I ever, ever said anything to them? *EVER?* I didn't even say anything to blondie when I saw you fucking her on the couch! I saw that with my own eyes Caelan O'Reily. You read a text message!" I scream. "A text message! How do you think I felt, or even still feel, when I replay that night in my head?" My stomach rolls again. "*HUH?*"

Damn, just the thought of it hurts.

My eyes surge with tears. I see the guilt on his face. Before he can answer I whisper, "You didn't believe me last night when I told you I didn't sleep with him, did you? You didn't believe me?" I repeat wearily.

And why this bothers me? I have no clue, but it does.

Turning his head slightly, he squints his eyes. "I believed you. But trust me, that does not mean I will stand by and watch some fucker put his hands on my girl."

"But it's just fucking fine for you to fuck someone in front of me? Deliberately?" I hiss. "How about I bring him back here and fuck him in front of you!" I hear the mutter from the two grown men behind me as I watch his face change from angry to pure rage. The main vein in his neck is pounding like a wild, raging, angry river as his skin starts to glisten with heated perspiration. I hear the concerned mumbling of Antonio and Giovanni from behind me again.

He takes two steps closer to me. He's intimidating as all hell, but I stand my ground, staring him dead in his crystal blue, frenzied eyes. He leans down, almost nose to nose with me. His breath cascading over my cheeks in hot, enraged puffs. In contrast, his knuckles softly caress my cheek. "Don't you ever play a game like that with me, beautiful. The game will not end well for the partner you choose to play with."

"Well, what's good for the goose is good for the gander. Right, Caelan? Isn't that the old saying?" I sneer. "Excuse me. I have a phone call to return." I hastily step around him, grabbing my phone from the counter.

I would say you could hear a pin drop, but that wouldn't be the truth. What I hear is a raging, snarling bull's breath behind me as I walk away.

Game On!

thirty-eight

After calling Johnathan back, apologizing to him, and reassuring him that I did not have a boyfriend, we set up lunch at The Surf. It's the same place momma and I had lunch the other day, which I thought was a strange coincidence. I shower, blow my hair straight, give myself some light summer makeup, and put on a pair of high-waisted black shorts with a silk halter leopard top. A couple of gold bangles on my wrist, some small drop earrings, and a gold, delicate, open heart necklace that my mother gave me a few years back for my birthday.

When I get downstairs the three of them are at the island talking in hushed tones. I know it's about me. I try to listen as best I can, but my phone dings with a text, alerting them of my presence. They stop talking as soon as they see me. So, I stop to check the message.

Sage: Sugar Britches, I miss you. I feel like it's been forever. You coming to the shop today? Not that we need you, I just want Sofia time.

My smile becomes as big as a rainbow. He always makes me smile.

Me: I love you. xoxo. I'm on my way now. Then I have a lunch date with Johnathan at two. See you in a few, stud.

Sage: Deets, baby girl! I need the deets on last night! You looked fabulous btw! Jess showed me a picture. Be ready, you're getting the Sage twenty questions. Lol. xoxo

More like a hundred!

When I lift my head after putting my phone in my purse, all three men are watching me. I can tell they all want to say something, but not one of them does until I do. "You guys done talking about me? If so, you ready to go?" I direct the question at Giovanni.

Antonio steps around the island. "Sofia we weren't talking about you, sweetheart." He holds his hands up in surrender.

"Sure you were, A. I heard my name," I snap like a rattlesnake with pissed off, stubborn hurt in my eyes. "And anyways, why wouldn't my brother, my bodyguard/friend, and my best friend want to let the person that's being stalked into their conversation? I mean it's only her life, right? No biggie," I sarcastically hiss. I can feel my emotions getting the best of me, so I walk towards the door, grabbing the handle. I look back to Giovanni with raised brows. "You coming? You got five seconds, or I'm taking myself." Shock and anger cross his face, before I can even open the door, he's right behind me. I hear Caelan call my name, but I keep going.

The ride to Hearts Desire is quiet. Giovanni tried to talk to me, but I cut him off, giving him one-word answers. The three men in my life that are supposed to be protecting me are talking and planning around me and my life like I'm not even there. How am I expected to trust that, or even trust them?

My emotions have been all over the last couple of days. I was happy last night, feeling free with Johnathan. Well, that is, until all hell broke loose. But just being with him in general, made me feel... alive. There's just so much going on in my head that I can't seem to sort it all out. I just need a minute, just a moment by myself, alone, with no one around. A place that's peaceful and quiet where I can do some thinking. I'll never get that, though, not until we find *him*.

Giovanni turns on the radio, but I immediately asked him to turn it off. I know he was only turning it on for me and right now, there's so much clogging my head that I can't even enjoy something that has always made me happy. I just need the peacefulness of everything being quiet.

"Sofia, are you alright?" His voice full of concern.

"I'm fine," I simply answer without looking at him.

Pulling up in the back alley of HD, I jump out of the SUV heading for the back door. I hear Giovanni's disapproval murmured in the winds, but with the anger festering in me right now, I just don't care. When I enter, I see him with the brightest smile on his face.

"Sugar Britchesssssss! Get your sweet ass over here and give me a hug." I watch his eyes recognize the hurt and sadness in mine, but he doesn't falter. He keeps that big smile on his face as he wraps me in the biggest, best, Sage hug. "My girl needs some alone time, huh?" I glance up, giving him a somber half smile. "Come on girl, let's chat about that hot date last night," he deflects, leading me into the office closing the door on Giovanni.

Thank. You. Sage.

"Give up the deets, baby girl. How hot was this date last night? You sleep with him? How was he? Any good? Big dick? Come on, start moving that tongue and give me details!"

I'm in a fit of giggles, all because of this uncomplicated, beautiful man in front of me. I hug him again. "Thank you," I gratefully tell him. "You just made me laugh when I feel so lost and alone."

He nods, smiling knowingly. "Now seriously, get on with the details, sugar britches!"

So I tell him all about my night. From the beautiful veranda dinner, to the sexy dark, sultry club, the way Johnathan had my body moving on the dance floor, to the fuck pad, and the pictures that were sent to me. I even told him about Antonio finding me in bed with C this morning and then my confusion over all of it.

"So, in all that," he circles his finger. "We still don't know scotch man's dick size?"

"Sage!" I crack up laughing and yell at the same time.

"What? And, Miss. Sex on Legs, we need to chat anyways! You did not tell me you slept with Caelan O'Reily, and that my sexy girlfriend, is a big no-no for Sage here," he playfully chastises me wagging his finger back and forth pointing to himself with raised brows and a smile. "I feel so out of the loop!" He sighs with extreme exaggeration. "I have been waiting for this, my girl. It's like momma waiting for her baby girl's prom day and then she misses it. That's just not right of you!"

"No, I do not know his dick size. I can tell you, though, that he's a decent size from what I felt through clothing, but it's nothing compared to *the beast* in Caelan's pants."

"I fuckin' knew that man was hanging long and wide!" he blurts with a flourish.

I have the biggest smile but also concerned look on my face. "Long and wide," I repeat his description shaking my head. "Ahh so much so that my va-j was sore as shit the next day! But, Sage, if you tell him I told you about his dick size I will kill you!" I threatened pointing at him.

He mimics zipping up his lips and throwing away the key. "Mums the word, sugar! Mums the word! Damn skippy if you didn't just give me so many good spank thoughts, though."

"Oh My GOD, Sage! I. Do. Not. Need. To. Think. About. You. AND. Your. Spank. Bank. Sessions!" I bellow, laughing so hard tears flow from my eyes.

After we settle down, he looks at me earnestly. "What are you going to do about C and Scotch Man?"

I shrug my shoulders. "I don't know," I answer honestly. "I love, Caelan. I do. He's my home. He has always been my home. We have history together, serious history, and I think because of that, I fear what could happen. I lost him once, Sage. Even though it was my fault, I still lost him. I don't ever want to lose him again. Say we get into a real relationship, and it doesn't work out, then what? Where do we go from there? Nowhere. I lose him again. I don't know if I can handle that this time." I stop to think about it for a second. "No, I know I wouldn't be able to handle it. I barely made it out of my darkness last time," I admit. "And Johnathan," I mutter, glancing up at the ceiling thinking about how I feel, "he's funny, he's sexy, and I'm attracted to him. Plus, there's something mysteriously intriguing about him. Although, I've seen concern or uncertainty quickly flicker through his eyes at times. So, who knows if it will even last more than a few dates, but while it does, why can't I enjoy, Mr. Playboy? On top of that, I feel free with him. I don't have a history with him. It's new, and it's exciting. He doesn't know about my past. I can be whoever I want to be with him."

"Sofia," he sighs. "You just said you loved Caelan. Do you love him or are you in love with him and just afraid to be? Because I can tell you right now Caelan is, in love with you, sweetheart. Has been for a very long time."

Shaking my head. "If he's in love with me, he wouldn't have done what he did with bad-fake-tits that night, Sage. That hurt. I can't get it out of my head. As much as I try to push it to the side, I can't stop seeing them together."

"Okay, so now ask yourself this, are you dating Johnathan to get back at him? Or are you dating Johnathan because you truly want to start something with him?" he questions skeptically.

"Sage, why do you have to get all analytical on me?"

"Do you know the answer?" He raises his brow waiting. I shake my head. "You do, sugar. The answer is inside here." He taps my chest over my heart. "When you're ready, ask yourself the same question and then answer yourself honestly. Get rid of all the bullshit, the past, the history, the troubles, the tears, and the futures that are yet to be seen. Just answer the question honestly with what's in here." He lays his hand on his own heart. "When you do, you will see your life will have much more joy then sorrow. Things will fall into place if you would just stop fighting them."

I stand with outstretched arms, tackling him while he sits on the arm of the couch in my office. "I have so much love for you, Sage. Best damn day of my life is when I met you."

"I love you too, sunshine." He embraces me tightly.

"But on a serious note, I like happy, gay Sage better than serious, alpha, deep thinking, male, Sage. He makes my brain hurt." I chuckle.

"You love all of me, sunshine," he boasts, winking.

AFTER GOING OVER the inventory orders with Sage and snagging a gorgeous, black, lace romper from said inventory for Christopher's birthday party tonight at Club 9, I thank Sage for the talk before Giovanni and I head to the restaurant for my lunch date with Johnathan. Giovanni doesn't say much, but I do notice him checking on me in the review mirror a few times. His phone rings and I hear my father's voice filter over the SUV's speaker system.

"Mr. Heart, you're on speaker. I'm in the car with Sofia."

There's silence for a moment. "Hello, angel face. How you doing today? You still pissed off at me? Your mother chewed me a new asshole after you left the other day."

Well, hell. Yes. Yes, I am pissed off and not in the mood for his crap today. But, I'll play nice. "Hi, Daddy. I'm good. Yes, I am still pissed at you, and you deserved momma's ass chewing, but, I still love you."

There's silence for a moment on my father's part. I look to Giovanni with confusion. This is not my father. He's a get to the point, get it done, don't ask questions kind of guy. So, this hesitation confuses and concerns me.

"Angel, you know I love you, right? I would do anything for you, you know that, right?" He somberly declares.

Where's this coming from? This is not my dad. Momma must have really chewed his ass up.

"Yes, Daddy, I do. Sometimes, though, sometimes you go about it in the wrong way. Your temper sometimes gets the best of you, and it hurts people-mostly me. Sometimes it can be forgiven, and sometimes it can't, but with change, we can move forward."

"What have I always told you about family?" He deflects. I don't think the man is capable of change. Which makes me feel crestfallen.

I smile sadly while I stare out the window into the New York City streets whipping past my window, repeating my father's family mantra, the one that he has drilled into us all throughout our childhood:

"Family is everything.
Family protects you.
Without family, you have nothing.
If you betray one, you betray all.
If you betray, you will pay."

"Yes angel, and I live by that every day of my life." He sighs.

Okay, this is starting to make me worry. "Daddy, are you okay?" The somber speaking father is one I don't know, but is quickly replaced by the superior hard man I do know.

"Yes. Stay out of trouble. Don't make Giovanni's job any harder than it is. He's a good man, a good bodyguard, and he's family, Sofia." Then I hear the click. He's gone.

"What in the hell was that all about?" I stare at Giovanni. Waiting for... an answer... something. What? I don't know, but something. He just shrugs his shoulders.

thirty-nine

W HEN WE ARRIVE AT THE SURF, I'm still baffled over the phone call with my father. I choose to push it down, stuffing it away for another day to analyze his words. I take a deep breath so I can try to calm myself and get ready for the conversation that I know, and dread, is waiting for me when Johnathan and I sit to have lunch-that conversation being the phone call from this morning. Even though I apologized already, I know in my heart that no man would just let it go at that. There will be some questions during lunch today. Of that, I'm positive.

Johnathan's waiting for me when Giovanni and I walk through the front doors. His smile is sexy, warm, and calming. He looks good in his dark gray dress pants that he paired with a lavender dress shirt. The first few buttons of his shirt are open with his sleeves rolled up to his elbows, giving him more of a relaxed, sexy, and clean look. But under that clean, sexy look, I can see something else. There's a mysterious air to Johnathan Reznor; one that attracts me to him and also makes me take a step back. I watch his eyes as he gives me a once over as I have just done to him. We embrace in a quick hug before I follow him to a secluded table out back. It's right next to the one my mother and I had lunch at the other day and Giovanni is sitting in the same spot at the bar. When we sit, I notice there's already water and a glass of wine waiting for me.

"You look beautiful today, Sofia."

Awwwwww hell!

"Thank you," I smile, ridding my thoughts of Caelan. "As do you. Well, not beautiful, but very handsome. You must work out a lot to have a body in such good shape."

He smiles. "I train a lot. I need to, to keep up with three restaurants and a club."

"Where do you find the time?" I laugh. "My ass hasn't been to the gym in weeks." Which, on a side note, I really need to get my ass in gear before it becomes as big as the state of New York.

"Well, I can tell you, from what I've seen of it, your ass looks good to me."

I blush. And for someone who always has a comeback- I have nothing. I take a sip of my wine trying to hide the fact that I'm blushing and my tongue is tied.

"Did I just make you blush?" he jokes leaning back into his seat. I blush even more now because he just called me out on it. "This from the same girl that was grinding into me last night on the dance floor?" He reminds me, looking surprised.

"Ummm I think that's the other way around." I laugh taking another sip of my wine, smirking.

"Ahh, I feel the need to say that when I was, let's say, close to you, I definitely felt the resistance of your very sexy ass pushing back against me." He smirks cocking a brow.

He really has me tongue tied. Come on, Sofia. Get it together.

"Okay, Okay I give!" I surrender setting my wine glass down, then throwing my hands in the air. "I'm waving the white flag. There may have been a little bit of a grind on my part but..."

"But nothing! You were rubbing that fine, little ass of yours against me, and you enjoyed it just as I very much did." He smiles with pinched brows. He looks like he wants to say something, but doesn't. He waits a few quiet seconds, thinking about what he is going to say. "You're different than what I thought you would be," he says with speculation and what looks like unease in his eyes.

I need to change the subject. And not for anything, but what did he think I would be like?

"What did you think I would be like?" I ask, surprised that I'm not able to hold back my question. It takes him another minute to answer, like he has to think about what he's going to say.

"A party girl," he quickly admitted. "A wild child with daddy issues."

Ohhhh, what the ever-loving fuck?!

I feel my face become stone.

"You work in a bar like Ice. Most of your shifts are in The Devil's Lair. Which, we all know what happens up there. But, yet, you own your own very successful boutique and still choose to work there. You have a mouth that most men dream about. But, yet drive them crazy with your flirty, wise-cracking challenging remarks. Which, only makes them want you more and you don't even see that. You have no problem putting someone in their spot when they overstep your boundaries. You project self-confidence, but when I look deeper into your eyes, I see the insecurities. You were grinding your delectable ass against me last night, but yet today you blushed like a school girl at my comment. You are surrounded by men who adore you and would do anything for you, yet you don't take advantage of that. You're absolutely stunning, but, last night when Tatiana was being catty towards you, you blew her off when clearly you outshine her and could have torn her a new ass with that mouth of yours." He inhales, shaking his head contemplating his next words. "They say don't judge a book by its cover. I can honestly say, in your case, it's the truth. I think the pages in-between have a lot to tell."

Well, that just went pretty deep, now didn't it? What the hell do I say to all that? Because these pages have too much to tell and he is not the person I'm willing to tell them to. Wait, did he just say I was absolutely stunning? Ha! He did! He just said I was absolutely stunning! Woooo! Well, dip me in a vat of glorious, decadent chocolate and let me swim naked!

"So, basically what you're saying is, when you saw me that night at Ice you thought, 'Party girl with daddy issues. She'll be an easy lay,'" I inquire and accuse with disappointment. More disappointment than I actually feel, being he just called me stunning, but I need to know where his head's at. "Because what I'm thinking right now, is all you were looking for was a quick fuck in the alley. Which, is fine if that's what you're into, but it's not for me. I'm not a whore," I clarify with a gust of frustrated venom getting myself worked up.

Who the hell does he think he is?

I try to settle myself, knowing it's only because of my father calling me a whore in the past, but right now he's got me pissed. Just the thought that Johnathan thought that of me, just by looking at me, burns me. He looks mad. No, he looks infuriated by my spewed words.

Leaning forward, his strong body is overshadowing mine. In a controlled, timbre he asks, "Did I say I wanted to fuck you in an alley? Have I treated you like a whore that I wanted to fuck in the alley?" I shake my head. "No, I have not," he hissed. "Out of all the good I just said to you, you only heard the bad. That being 'the party girl' and 'whore,' and for the record, 'whore' never came out of my mouth. So, you tell me, Sofia, who made you feel this way? Tell me, so that I can make sure they never make you feel this way again."

Oh, holy hell. Not going there. Nope, nada, nothing.

He reaches across the table, seizing my hand in his. When I look down at our joined hands, a flicker of uneasiness flashes through my lust-filled angry body. I feel safe, but there's an edge of threat to his voice that only makes my insecurities flare. When I look back up into his eyes, I see kindness and determination, but also something else too. I can't put my finger on it, which totally agitates me with bewilderment.

Well, this is one story I will not be telling him.

Clearing my throat, I whisper, "Johnathan," looking anywhere but at him. "We all have pasts. Some good, some not so good, and some... bad. Mine is a little bit of all three. I apologize for snapping at you, and for misinterpreting your words. That insecurity you say you see in my eyes, I will tell you, comes from my past. As far as my past, I would like to leave it at that, my past. At least for the time being. I would really like to just enjoy lunch with you."

His eyes search mine. Seeking answers, ones he'll never get through my words. He holds his hand up to the waiter, calling him over, but never losing eye contact with me. "Two more drinks please, then we'll be ready to order," he says still staring into my soul. I squirm slightly trying to hold my ground. When the server leaves, he smiles at me. "So, what are your thoughts on getting a huge plate of messy nachos?"

I chuckle and exhale a deeply held breath at his question because it is so not what I thought was going to come out of his mouth. He just took a very serious deep conversation that could have ended lunch and turned it around. Just like that. I smile at him, relieved, and release another breath I didn't realize I was holding. "Nachos it is," I agree.

The rest of lunch is easy flowing, except for the small talk about last night which he didn't go that much into being that he already knew I was being stalked. Although, as we dug our greasy fingers into the huge platter of nachos, I could sense he wanted to say something about the phone call this morning. So, I might as well bite the preverbal bullet and get it over with. I lift my eyes to see him staring at me with a sexy, shit-eating grin. "What?" I say with puzzlement.

"You ahh," he mutters with a raspy breath as he leans forward slowly running his thumb across my lower lip. Then pulls his thumb away licking it, which does crazy things to my belly. "You had some cheese on your lip. I couldn't resist," he says, leaning forward and giving me a gentle, lingering kiss. When he pulls away, I see the desire burning in his eyes.

This man wants me.

"Well, if all I had to do was leave a little cheese on my lip to get you to kiss me..." I declared, licking my lip slowly with a breathy, blushing smile.

"Sweetheart, you don't have to do anything for me to want to kiss you."

Ummm, okay, so the talk about the phone call this morning... out the window.

We finish up the nachos and order another scotch and wine. I sense he wants to ask me something. I know pretty much what it is already, but I wait for him to start the conversation. After the waiter places the check on the table, Johnathan lands serious, fact finding eyes on mine.

Well, here it comes.

"Sofia, I want to ask you a question. I want your honesty, no matter what the answer is."

"Well, Johnathan, you're in luck, because that's all you'll ever get from me, whether you like it or not. So, ask away."

A perplexed and yet amused smirk graces his handsome face. His body is relaxed, but looks troubled at the same time. His breathing is shallow, but controlled. "This morning, the man that answered your phone, who is he to you?"

Subtlety I inhale a large breath of air. "As easy as this question is, it's also extremely complicated," I confidently confess. Taking another deep breath, I begin trying to describe the dynamics of Caelan and Sofia. "Caelan is many things to me, so when I start to tell you, please give me the opportunity to finish before jumping to conclusions or asking questions."

He acknowledges with the slightest head shake in agreement.

"First and foremost, Caelan is my best friend. He has been since we were little. He grew up next door to me. He's always been there for me and always will be, as I will be for him. He's extremely protective over me, with good reason. But I won't get into that right now," I state matter of factly, staring straight into his eyes. "To answer the question bouncing around in your head right now, yes, yes we do have history together, a history that is as beautiful as it is painful. Which, I also will not get into. Those memories are private between him and I," I say exhaling sadly. "We live together. In separate rooms." I smile playfully. "And our circle of friends is just that, *our* circle of friends, ones that we are very close with. The eight of us are like one big, dysfunctional, happy, crazy, family. We call ourselves the crazy eight. So, he will always be in my life. I know for some, not so secure men, it would be hard to date someone living with someone they have a past with, but I'm thinking you, Mr. Reznor, can handle that. If you cannot, I also understand that as well." I smile with knots of nerves tangling in my stomach.

"You finished?" He quirks his brow at me with a cocky expression. I nod. He continues "This morning on the phone he referred to you as, 'his girl.' I can assure you that any man that says, "my girl" to another man believes she is his girl. So, tell me is this a one-sided love or do you have feelings for him as well?"

Oh. Fuck. Me.

"This kind of falls into the private category, but what I can say is… yes, yes I have love for him, as he does for me. Like I said before, we have a history. Part of that is painful, very painful, and not something I would wish on anyone. It was years ago, but we just very recently talked about the events of that painful time for the first time. It has brought on heavy emotions between the two of us. It is something we're both working through right now." I shrug my shoulder unforgivingly. "So, you tell me, Johnathan, can you handle it?"

Leaning forward he grabs my hand. "I can assure you I can handle it. Are you sure you can?" he questions with a sexy smirk.

I lean into him, batting my eyes and playfully flirting while pushing my chest out further. "It's good to know you have a set of balls." I snicker at him.

"Oh, Sofia, I can assure you I have balls, and if you lean any farther into me showing me more of your gorgeous, ample tits, I can also assure you, you will see my balls sooner rather than later."

I crack up laughing, then provocatively moan while running my finger up and down his arm. "Sooner might be better, rather than later." I wink at him.

"Fuck me!" he beams with flushed sexual desire. "Sofia." He groans. "You definitely have a way about you that makes me question my willpower to do the right thing," he says with dismayed frustration.

Do the right thing?

"Well, if you're up to it, you can start doing the right thing tonight, if you're not busy." I giggle noticing the lust in his eyes that he's trying desperately to get under control. "Get your thoughts out from between my legs, Mr. Reznor. I'm talking about going clubbing with me. Today's a friend's birthday. We're all going out tonight to celebrate. It's a good way for you to meet the crazy, dysfunctional, happy family I was just talking about."

He shifts slightly in his chair, leaning into me more. "Well, I guess we'll see by the end of tonight who has the most willpower. I can promise you, Sofia, I will not make it easy on you," he whispers with a cocky, seductive smirk.

"Well, Mr. Reznor neither will I on you."

forty

L UNCH WAS PRETTY MUCH A SUCCESS except for the lingering feeling I
can't shake. It's not a bad feeling, it's just a feeling. Both of us left with
frustrated sexual desires steam rolling through us. When he kissed me
goodbye, he promised me a night to remember. The chemistry between us is
undeniable, but there's also apprehension on my part that's pulling me back.
There's this feeling inside me, telling me something's not quite what it seems,
and I can't figure it out. I think maybe it's because of the uneasiness between
Caelan and I. My phone dings with a text and then dings again with another
before I can answer the first one.

C: Puddle of Mudd ~ Blurry

*Luke: Hey, I need to talk to you, tonight. It's important. If you can give
me a few minutes in private, I would appreciate it.*

I text Luke back first, knowing this has to do with Caelan. Especially after the song he just sent me.

Me: Yeah, I need to talk to you too.

Then I text C back with a song that I feel like describes how I'm feeling right now at this very moment.

Me: Creed~ Weathered

The emotions between him and I are confusing right now. Us talking about the loss of our babies, then us sleeping together the other night. We've kinda crossed a line that friends shouldn't cross, but... C and I are more than friends. I have admitted that to myself at least. The love we made a few nights ago can only be made by two people who love each other. But, how deep does my love go for him and how deep does his love go for me? He's said he loves me, but is that love in the sense of loving someone more than a friend or loving someone mind, body, and soul? What if we start something and we blow it? I'll lose him as a lover, but most importantly, a friend. Plus, how can I be this attracted to Johnathan if I have love for C? Besides the fact, he likes to play the field. I've only ever seen him in one long-term relationship, and that was with Kate.

Uggggghhh Kate. The girl was the total opposite of me. Tall, blonde, model thin, and the only one to capture his heart. She was totally in love with Caelan. Speaking of blondes, that's all I've ever seen him with. I'm a brunette. Well, now that I think about it, Tatiana is also a blonde. Does that mean Johnathan is into blondes, as well? The two of them are so different, yet, so, so similar. Ohhhhh, I'm so damn confused.

My phone beeps again.

C: Keith Urban~ Break on Me.

I close my eyes, letting the words to the song sink into my soul. This is him letting me know he will always be there for me. I feel overwhelmed, and he knows it. He always knows what I'm thinking or feeling. I feel the need to tell him how I feel.

Me: I love you. There's no one in my life that I can count on more than you, I love you for that. I miss you. I don't want to fight with you anymore. I hate fighting with you.

C: I love you too, Sofia. You have no idea. Stop running. Ditch the boy-toy, and we'll be okay.

Ohhhhhh C, Why?

Me: C... don't be like this.

C: Not gonna share, baby.

Me: He'll be there tonight. Are you going to be okay with that? If not, I'll just stay home.

C: It'll be fine.

Well, that short answer doesn't make me feel any better. I look down at the vibrating phone in my hand. Nikki's smiling face flashes on the screen. I feel like I haven't talked to her in so long. "Hey, you. How are you? I feel like I haven't talked to you in forever."

"No shit. I've been so busy with contracts and paperwork. This new job Caelan contracted with these luxury estate homes is really taking C's company to a whole new level."

Wow. I feel guilty as hell now. I haven't even talked to him about this, at all. We always talked business in the morning before work and late at night when all is quiet. I feel like such a selfish bitch right now.

"Stop. He knows you have a lot going on, sis. I know what you're thinking. Stop right now. He knows you care."

"Ya," I murmur with no energy behind it. "So, tell me why is my very talented well-organized sister calling me? Is it just because you miss me?"

"That too." She laughs. "I wanna know something way more earth-shattering."

"Lay it on me, sis."

"What are you wearing tonight?"

I burst out with laughter. "That's so serious, Nikki!" I laugh again. "I stole a black lace V-neck romper from HD. I'm pairing that with the black, knee high, strappy heels I wore the other night. Actually, wait you know those red heels I got last month when we went shopping? How 'bout those?"

"Those would work. Especially if you're putting out the fuck me vibes."

"Johnathan's coming tonight," I hesitantly confess.

"Well, there you go, sis. I'll bring some condoms."

I giggle. "I'm not going to sleep with him, Nik."

"What? Why? He's fucking hot!"

"I haven't talked to you. A lot has happened over the last few days," I reveal, staring out the SUV window watching the hustle and bustle of the New York City life pass me by as we sit in a traffic jam. "I'm," I falter sighing, "to say the very least, I'm confused," I confess without a care that Giovanni can hear my every word.

"Why? Is he a dick? He turned out to be a douche, didn't he? All the good looking ones prove themselves to be."

I love my sister. "No, sis, he's not a dick. I just think it might be bad timing."

"Bad timing?" She's quiet for a moment "You slept with someone! Oh. My. God. You slept with someone! Who? Give it up! Tell me! Tell me!" she demands, screaming into the phone.

"C," I whisper. So quietly that I almost didn't hear myself say it, but she sure as hell heard me.

"Did you just say, C? Like in Caelan, my boss? Your best friend? The man you live with? Oh. My. God! When? Wait, you don't even have to tell me. A few nights ago, right?"

I'm shocked to all hell. "How did you know that?"

"Because he came into work in the best mood. I figured he got laid the night before, but you know C, he's always getting laid. But, then I thought it must have been a really good night because he was in a really good mood." I chuckle with the biggest smile on my face hearing her say that, but then she ruins my high when she keeps talking. "But, wait you two had a fight right 'cause he came into work this afternoon like a bear. He wasn't even supposed to come into the office today. So, when he showed up and I caught his mood I asked if he was okay. He just blew it off. What did you do, sis?"

"What do you mean what did I do? Maybe he did something."

"Did he?"

"No."

"Well, what happened then?"

"I went to lunch with Johnathan today."

"Oh."

"Oh? That's it? Just, oh?"

"What do you want me to say, Sof? That it's kinda fucked up? 'Cause it kinda really is, sis. I mean this is Caelan we're talking about, not some Joe-shmoe you banged the night before and was never going to see again. This is Caelan, the man that has had feelings for you, for like fuckin' ever. I'm sorry, sis, but that's fucked up."

"Fuck me. And you," I mumble. "I don't know what I want, Nik."

"Well, I guess you better figure it out 'cause tonight could get real interesting if you don't."

JESS AND NIKKI wound up coming over and getting ready with me. Cheesy girl-power pop music is playing throughout my room, and I feel good. We did each other's hair and makeup, and now Jess and Nikki are both in my closet looking through my vast array of dresses. Nikki and I share clothes all the time, but Jess, with her long legs and thin frame, may have a problem being that I'm all ass and tits. My dresses on her might be too short and have her showing off her va-j tonight if she's not careful. Although, Luke may love and hate that.

I walk over, grabbing my red, four-inch heels from the shelf then sit on my velvet, tufted, round ottoman. Nikki sits next to me, putting on a great pair of red soled beauties. She stands in front of the floor to ceiling beveled mirror. "You look hot," I praise. "Those shoes with that blue and turquoise sequined dresses looks so good. If you're looking to get lucky, you're headed in the right direction."

"Good 'cause it's been awhile," she jokes. When Jess laughs, I look at her; she looks like a goddess in the white dress she has on. "Damn girl, look at those legs! Well, one thing's for sure he won't have to lift that dress too much tonight to get some." She shoots me a look. I roll my eyes, basically tell her to shut it and that I won't blow her and Luke's little, secret, sexual twist going on.

I changed my mind on my outfit. The black lace romper was replaced with a black dress. The deep v in the front goes to just above my belly button. Boob tape will help the girls from popping out. The back of this dress, well basically there is no back to this dress. The shoulder straps go around my shoulders and connect to the front material under my arms. The back is open all the way to just above the crack of my ass. It's short, but not too short. I mean hell, I gotta have some kind of modesty here. I throw on the red heels I got with Nikki and some small, drop diamond earrings. I take a deep breath giving myself a once over in the mirror. Nikki and Jess are both staring at me when I turn around. "Well?"

"Well, if you're looking to make him come in his pants, you're going to succeed," Jess bust out.

"Too much? Should I change?"

"Ummmmm, absolutely not! You look gorgeous!" Nikki boasts.

"No," Jess blurts.

I smile, feeling pretty good about myself. I feel confident. Actually, I'm feeling kinda spicy tonight. The sexy, evil, jokester in me is making her presence known. "Tonight's going to be fun," I say.

Jess's phone rings. She answers. I can tell it's Luke just by the way her face lights up. She hangs up looking at us with a mischievous smirk. "Change of plans. We're meeting the guys at Blu Ballz first for a couple of drinks."

"Oh good. I hope Chrissy's working. It's been so long since we've been there."

"That would be so much fun," Nikki chimes.

"Yeah, it would. Gosh, I haven't seen her in so long," Jess says.

Chrissy used to work for me before she decided to move on to sow some wild oats. Great girl, just a wild child. So much fun to hang with. We all became close with her over the past year, but recently she started dating the love of her life and spends most of her time with him now.

We finish getting ready and head downstairs. Giovanni is waiting for us along with a mountain of a man. When he takes us all in, he shakes his head.

"You okay, big man?" I ask patting him on the shoulder.

He just shakes his head looking heavenward. "I have a feeling tonight is going to be a long night," he huffs. The three of us laugh confirming his suspicions.

"Sofia, this is Dax. Dax, Sofia."

I give him a once over. He's a good looking man with an enormous build. Caelan is the biggest of all our friends. He's got inches on all the guys, and his build is extremely large, but this guy is like an elephant. He's tall with a powerful build. He has extremely short blond hair with hazel eyes. Intimidation to the max is exuding from him. I put my hand out in gesture to shake his and when he connects with me, I thank him for dropping everything to come help.

forty-one

THE RIDE OVER TO BLU BALLZ IS LIGHT and fun. Even Giovanni is smiling at the crazy antics in the car between us girls. It's been a hard few days, but I feel good. Shit, who am I kidding? It's been a hard few weeks. I just wanna let go, be free, and have some fun tonight.

When we walk into Blu Ballz, we're greeted with Nickelback's~ *Something in Your Mouth* blasting through the sound system into the dark, smoky, sexy room. A gorgeous red head is dancing on the center stage that's surrounded by the bar under the ever-changing neon lights.

We spot the guys by the bar throwing back some shots. The butterflies that took action in my belly as we walk through the door have become more restless as we walk towards them. Not knowing what it will be like between C and I is what is making me nervous. I watch him as he sets down his empty shot glass on the bar. I hear the thunder of Chris's voice piercing my ears, which is then followed by Caelan's stunned blue gaze taking me in from head to toe. He mutters something under his breath, but I can't make it out.

"What the fuck? Look at the chicks accompanying us tonight fellaaaaas!" Chris bellows.

Oh, yea, he's already torqued up.

Caelan and my eyes haven't faltered from one another's. He looks good, really good. Like, really, really good. His black V-neck tee and dark jeans along with his black boots make him look lethal. The ink on his chest is peeking out from the V-neck of his shirt and the tattoos on his arms are becoming three dimensional with every twist and turn of his muscles. His dirty blond hair is in an array of messy waves and with that gleam in his eyes, my butterflies take flight.

Balls! He's hot, sexy, and holy hot damn, I just had that man inside me a few nights ago. Okay, Sof, get your shit together and wipe the drool from your chin. Did you forget you're meeting Johnathan in a few hours? Get it together.

I groan to myself just as arms wrap around me in a tight hug. "Hey, sexy girl. You look hot. You wear this dress just for me?" Chris mischievously jokes.

"Of course I did!" I laugh.

"Well, happy birthday to me. I'm going to have fun staring at you all night." I know he's only saying it to rib his brother, but right now, I could do without the ribbing between two brothers.

I hear the clearing of a throat then his deep timber, letting Chris know to back off. "Birthday or no birthday brother, I'll whoop your ass," he advises, warning him with two hard unforgiving slaps to his back.

Chris chuckles in my ear. "Well, that got him going, now didn't it?"

"I don't think he needs anything to get him going."

"No, definitely not, especially when it comes to you, but it's nice to fuck with him. It's my birthday, so I've got some leeway," he reasons, pulling away from me. I laugh, giving Sage and Luke a hug hello. When I turn back around, C is casually leaning against the bar watching the dancer.

He didn't even say hello to me.

A twang of jealousy erupts in my belly, catching me off guard. We have been here many times with the guys before, but never once have I been jealous of him watching the dancers. Maybe it's the fact that she's gorgeous and moving her very healthy, thin body around the stage with grace. Plus, the fact that her eyes are plastered on his as he intently gazes over her.

Relax, Sofia. Tonight's supposed to be fun.

I turn to the bartender ordering a round of drinks and a round of BJ shots for the girls and I. Then I hear Luke's calm voice behind me.

"He's only doing it to get a reaction from you. And by the looks of it, it's affecting you more than you want to admit."

"Yeah, well, if he wants a real reaction, I'll jump up on that stage myself and show him how it's done."

"Sofia, if you get on that stage, I'll throw you hundreds, but you don't have enough balls to do it, so my wallet's safe," Chris chimes into our conversation.

Oh. No. He. Did. Not. Just. Challenge. Me! Did he?

I look at Luke in surprised question. "Did he just challenge me?" Before he can answer, the bartender hands us our drinks. When the girls and I throw back our shots, Sage chimes in.

"Girls, did we not learn our lesson from the BJ shots the other night?"

I laugh, watching Sage turn green as I pass the shot glass under his nose for him to smell before placing the shot glass back on the bar. The bartender makes eye contact with me and smiles.

"I heard the challenge your friend made, gorgeous. Just so you know, it's open amateur night so if you want to take a crack at it, feel free."

I smile at Scott, the bartender. "He doesn't know who he challenged, although Chris should. He's known me long enough."

"Well, maybe that's why he challenged you. He wants to see you up there." He smirks.

"Ahhhh it's more to piss off his brother," I say, tilting my head to the left towards Caelan.

"Well, gorgeous if you take that challenge I will be more than happy to take a five-minute break to watch."

"Scott, are you're behaving?" I hear the soft voice of a crazy, wild girl I know behind me. "She's not the one you should challenge," Chrissy says slapping my ass.

"I didn't challenge her, her friend did." He nodded his head towards Chris. "I was just letting her know it was amateur night if she wanted to take a whirl."

"Ya ya, I'm sure you were," she says to him while turning to me throwing her arms around me. "How the hell are you? I haven't seen you in so long."

"Not my fault, you're the one that had to go and fall in love," I bust her chops, laughing.

She laughs right along with me. Gushing with the biggest smile. "I did. I did. I know it's so bad of me. I couldn't help myself. He's hot, great in bed, and well, hell he treats me nice."

"Treats you nice?" I crack up laughing. "He adores you and treats you like a princess."

Crinkling her nose, she smiles. "I know, he does, doesn't he." She giggles.

We chat for a bit, catching up with each other before she goes off to work the room. It's dead in here tonight, especially for a Saturday night. There's a group of women in the corner enjoying drinks and having fun. There's a dozen men sitting around the stage and some stragglers throughout the place. All in all, though it's pretty dead. But, it is still relatively early.

All of us are enjoying each other laughing and joking. A couple more shots down and were dancing on the side of the bar. There's a blonde on the stage dancing to a song I've never heard before, but it's got a great, sexy beat. She's pretty with huge boobs, but they're definitely fake. At least they're done well. She's good, but I can work a pole just as good, if not better, than her.

I should ask her for her doctor's number so C can give it to bad-fake-tits.

My eyes peer over to, C. He's watching her dance as well. His eyes are attached to her, taking all of her in. She's eating up his undivided attention. The jealousy from before flares again, hitting me square in the chest. His eyes are filled with lust when he winks at her. She sways her way over to him, dropping down in front of him and spreads her legs. He doesn't take his eyes off her. The guys all stop joking with each other and watch the scene unfold before us. I feel a hand touch my lower back in calm reassurance.

"Let it go, sunshine. He's only doing it to piss you off." Sage's warm irritated timbre fills my ears. I nod in sad, jealous, agitated acknowledgment, but I don't turn my head because my eyes are glued to what is transpiring in front of me. He slowly slides money into the side of her G-string and then slowly glides the back of his index finger down her thigh. I swallow the bile that's rising in my burning throat and excuse myself.

I need to get my emotions under control.

Once I hit the privacy of the restroom, I take a deep breath. Trying to rid the feelings that are drowning me right now. I am ready to rip someone's head off. The door opens and Jess walks through with a concerned face.

"You okay?" She frowns.

"Mmmhmmm."

Her anxious look tells me I don't even look close to being okay. "Sof, he's only doing it to make you jealous. As many times as we've been here with them, he's never acted this way. He's going out of his way to make you jealous. You know that, right?"

"Mmmmhmmm."

"Sof, you're scaring me. Stop saying Mhmmm 'cause Mmmmhmmm from you is nothing but trouble."

At that, Chrissy walks into the bathroom. "Hey, girls. Everything okay? Sage just sent me in here to check on you."

I smile. "Yeah, yeah we're good, just freshening up. Jess, can you do me a favor?" She reluctantly agrees. "Can you go let Sage know I'm alright?"

"Sof? I can see it in your eyes. What are you planning?"

I smile mischievously. "What's good for the goose and all..." I wiggle my brows. "Just let Sage know... I'm fucking spectacular! Then tell Chris, birthday or not, he's going to be a couple hundred lighter in the next fifteen minutes."

Once Jess leaves, I explain the plan to Chrissy. She helps me figure out a way to get around Giovanni and Dax. Which wasn't all that hard being she told them she was showing me the new dressing area in the back with the girls and he wasn't allowed back there. We head to the dressing room where she goes in search of her costumes. Some of the regular girls come over, sharing tips and giving me advice. Which I take, gladly, but little do they know, I have danced my entire life. Starting with the typical ballet as a five-year-old, then tap, jazz, and hip-hop as a teen. Now, I work a pole at my gym to keep in shape as well as kickboxing. I won't get naked, but I damn sure will show Caelan that if he wants something to lust after, he can stare at me.

What are you doing? Don't do this, Sof. Screw that! I'm doing this!

Chrissy leaves to tell the DJ what music I want. It's a combination of *You Can Leave Your Hat On* by Joe Cocker, then morphing into *Animal* by Nickelback. My outfits coincide with the music. I have a trench coat and hat on to hide my identity at first. It covers a soft, white, innocent, virginal teddy. Then, once the fast lyrics of Animal start, the easy-to-remove, white, flowing teddy comes off to reveal an S & M, black, leather, nothing-but-straps outfit underneath. Basically, it's a very skimpy bikini with black leather straps everywhere.

Thank. God. I. shaved.

Chrissy enters the stage while the beginning beats of the music start. She grabs the microphone from the DJ and directs everyone's attention to her. Whistles and hollers can be heard from all around the club. Her sexy smile lights up her face. "Ladies and gentlemen, I have a special dancer here tonight. This girl has been dancing her whole life and tonight she's going to show you what she's got. Give a warm round of applause and your money to the one and the only... Heart-breakerrrrrrrr!"

Joe Cocker bellows his chords as I strut my stuff out onto the stage. My hair is pulled up into the hat concealing it. The hat itself is pulled low covering my face, and the trench coat is tied closed. As I strut down the stage, all eyes are on me. I can see our group watching me, but none of them realize it's me until Jess gets the biggest smile on her face. She shakes her head in amusement and starts howling. Sage quickly glances at her then back to me and gets the biggest smile on his face. He throws his fingers in his mouth and starts whistling. When Nikki realizes what's going on, she jumps on a bar stool and starts hooting and hollering as well. Chris is the funniest though. He turns to Nikki in confusion, and when he turns back to me. I give a slow whirl around the pole blasting him with a sexy smile. When realization hits him, his face is priceless.

I walk back up the stage, turning my back to them as I untie my trench coat. I teasingly slide it over my shoulder and pull it back up. With the whistling getting louder, I slowly let it slide down my body, ending with a gust, to reveal the innocent, white, flowing teddy. My face is still covered with the hat and my hair is still tucked safety inside. I twist my head over my shoulder grabbing the brim of the hat and give them all a naughty smile.

I turn, dropping low, moving my hips to the sultry beat of the music. I'm trying to conserve energy for my routine when *Animal* starts playing. I turn back and walk towards the end of the stage. Luke now realizes why everyone is carrying on the way they are. He cracks up laughing, then instantly gets a concerned look on his face muttering the word "fuck." The song is ready to change over, and I'm getting ready to burst into the next song when I see realization cross Caelan's face. His laid back, relaxed, Mister Cool demeanor goes from leaning casually against the bar talking to Scott, the bartender to stiff and erect. Within seconds, tension's filling his face and body. Chris slaps him on the back and laughs his ass off until Caelan forcefully shrugs him off. Sage is right behind them, still whistling. When we connect eyes, he mischievously smiles and starts howling, just rubbing it in.

The beginning beats of *Animal* start. I tip the hat back slightly, then forward again to tease. Swaying my hips in a very seductive move, I throw the hat on a hard bass beat to the music at Caelan and swing my hair as Animal starts playing full-force. I grab the hook on the white teddy, teasing the crowd with it as I keep opening and closing it quickly to the beat of the music. Everyone in the club is screaming for me to take it off. I shoot Caelan a sexy grin. He shakes his head no, in warning. He stands there with his legs spread and arms crossed, directly at the end of the stage, watching my every move. He's mad, but I can see the hint of amusement in his eye. That is, until I drop the white teddy. The fast beat of the song carries me through the routine. I hit the pole with force, swinging around like I've been doing this for years, which I have. I slide down the pole upside down, opening my legs right in front of Caelan. When my ass hits the stage floor in a split, I wink at him and then twist pulling myself up. When my fingers once again start to release the hook to the white teddy, Caelan shakes his head no in slow motion again and the amusement in his eye that was there a few seconds ago is gone.

"Don't do it," he mouths in warning, clenching his jaw.

Damn, he looks good standing there with his arms crossed, looking all dominant and sexy.

Oh, he's gonna be really mad in about two seconds. I release the hook on the teddy throwing it at his head with a burst of energy to reveal the black strappy outfit. Shock and anger take over his handsome face when he sees the new, very S & M outfit I revealed.

The white teddy slides down his body, hitting the floor. I hit the pole and work it hard. When I slide down again and my heels hit the stage, he's crooking his finger at me in a come here motion. I playfully shake my head no, biting my lip.

"Now," he mouths with furrowed brows. So, I whip my hair around in defiance and make my way to the other side of the stage. Hands filled with money are waving in the air, but I don't take it. That's not why I'm up here.

The place is loud. The music is blasting. And my heart is pumping. It's exhilarating. When I turn back, he's now standing right up against the stage. He's pissed. When two of the club bouncers start heading his way, I decided to end the routine early. There's less than a minute left of the song and before a brawl breaks out, I head towards him at the end of the stage. Chrissy cuts off the two bouncers, letting them know it's okay.

He crooks his finger at me again with a little more edge to it. This time I decided to listen. I sashay my ass on down to the end of the stage as sexy as I can. When I get to the end, I stare down at him with a crooked grin. He reaches up and wraps both of his strong hands around my waist, lifting me off the stage. Without losing eye contact he slowly lets me slowly slide down the front of his body until we're almost eye level. My feet dangle as I look into his eyes. He's pissed, but I'm basking in the heated animal I created. His nostrils flare with the deep breath he takes as his pupils become laser beams staring into the souls of my eyes. After what seems like an eternity, his jaw clenches and he grits out words that shock me.

"If you ever do that again, I promise you, I will put you over my knee and make sure your ass is so red you won't be able to sit for a month."

Even though he just shocked me with his seriousness, I try holding back the smile fighting with my cheek muscles, but the rush of energy flowing through me makes it really hard.

"You think I'm kidding, beautiful, but what you don't realize is I'm very serious. I've fantasized about my hand on your ass for a very long time. Don't push me."

"Well, then don't push me," I counter having the stare-off of the century with unspoken words until I feel Chrissy cover my back with a satin robe.

"If you needed my attention all you had to do was ask."

"Really? Because you couldn't even say hello to me when I came in. You were too busy watching the redhead and then your favorite, the blonde." I quickly look away so he doesn't notice the hurt in my eyes. He lets go of me so I can tie the robe before everyone bombards me with cheers and hugs. That's when I look up at Chris. He's holding two hundred dollar bills in his hands. I snatch them both quickly. "Don't ever challenge me, Christopher O'Reily. You should know better. Birthday or not I'm taking your cash!"

"Well worth the two hundred bucks!" He high fives me with a howl.

That's the moment Caelan realizes his brother was the instigator in all of this. His brow furrows and he stares at Chris who starts laughing uncontrollably. He grabs his shirt and clenches his jaw. "Do it again, and I'll fucking beat your ass to a bloody pulp!" he promises, waffling Chris upside the head.

Chris is on his own for this one. I start to walk away to go change, but my wrist is grabbed and I'm jerked back into his vibrating body. "I'm serious, beautiful. Lose the boy toy."

"Why? So I can be with a man that will never be satisfied with just one woman. You proved that tonight. No, thank you." I turn away quickly and abruptly stop with faltering steps when I see Giovanni's face. He's livid. I take another step but that one falters too. "I'm sorry," I blurt, but really, I'm not.

"Sofia!" Caelan growls from behind me.

"No, you're not. Now go, get changed," Giovanni orders. "I'll be right outside the door." I take a step towards the dressing room. "Sofia!" he hisses. I turn back. "No more fucking games!" he demands. "You understand me?"

I nod, then I look at Dax who's standing there like a stone statue. So, I walk through the dressing room doors and take a deep, cleansing breath. Then the biggest smile erupts on my face because, hot damn, I just ruled that stage! "Damn, that was fun!" I bust out laughing right along with Chrissy who's now helping me out of my outfit and back into my own dress minus the boob tape.

The girls from the club congratulated me, and the owner came in after I was done changing and offered me a job. Which, I politely decline explaining it was just a dare. I had fun, and for just a few short minutes I was someone else and it felt... so... freeing.

forty-two

CLUB 9 IS HOPPIN'. IT'S PACKED. The music is cranking, but it feels weird when I walk in. I feel a little uncomfortable. I haven't been back here since the night I was drugged. Tension fills my shoulders. We find our way to our VIP booth and order drinks. Everyone is buzzing with happiness around me. I can't seem to bring myself out of the inner turmoil I'm in. When I look up, Caelan is watching me. The server places all our drinks on the table. Everyone grabs for theirs and starts taking much needed sips. However, I don't. Mine sits there while I stare at it. I excuse myself from the group and find my way to the ladies room. Giovanni and Dax, not far behind. I turn on the water and cup my hands, drinking from the faucet.

At least I know I won't be drugged this way.

I lock myself in a bathroom stall, giving myself a few minutes to collect myself. I hear heels walking the tiled floor. Then my sister's voice. "Sis, open the door."

"I'll be out in minute, Nik."

"No, you won't, you're hiding."

She knows me to well.

"Come on open the door," she pleads.

I do, but I'm not happy about it. "I just needed a minute."

"Well, while you're taking your minute, stud muffin showed up looking for you. Sage and I introduced him to everyone, but I'm thinking you might not want to let Caelan and Johnathan hang out together for too long without you being there. On top of that, Caelan sent me in here to check on you."

She's right on that, I don't want them hanging out together. I have no idea what C will do. We make our way back to the table. Johnathan's at the bar getting a drink, so I make my way towards him. As I approach him, I notice a beautiful brunette standing next to him. Her body is turned in towards him, lightly rubbing up against his arm.

Hmmm let's see how he handles this.

He orders his drink. As he does, the brunette lays her hand on his arm, giving him a sexy smile. He pulls his arm away from her. Her smile fades. Mine becomes wider. She tries again and he puts her in her place letting her knows he's here with someone. His back is to me so he doesn't know I'm there, until Jimmy, the bartender, gets the biggest smile on his face and calls out to me.

"How are you doing, sweetheart? I haven't seen you in weeks," he greets me, reaching over the crowded bar to give me a hug and a kiss.

"I'm good." I smile. Not wanting to give up too much information being that Johnathan is now watching us from inches away. He knows nothing about what happened to me and I would like to keep it that way.

"I'm assuming they didn't catch that fucker yet being that I saw Giovanni here with you guys?"

"No, not yet. They will though, I'm sure of it."

"You need anything, you let me know, sweetheart."

"Well, you could give this very attractive man his drink so I can get him out on the dance floor," I say smiling at Johnathan.

He smiles back. "Hi." He embraces me, kissing my cheek lightly.

"Hi, back."

"You okay? You don't seem like your happy-go-lucky, sexy self."

"I'm good," I assure him, laying my hand on his forearm. Jimmy hands him his drink while the brunette gives me a once over.

Yup I'm the one he's here with. Back off chick.

We head back to the table. We chat, joke, and laugh with everyone for a while. Well, almost everyone. Everyone except Caelan, who is just staring both of us down. Yup this might be a really long, uncomfortable night. He throws back a shot with Chris and Luke then says something to Luke, who then quickly looks my way.

Yep this is going to get awkward.

Johnathan, noticing the tension asks me if I want to dance. Calvin Harris's *How Deep Is Your Love* is playing. I feel myself starting to loosen up when we start dancing. We stay on the dance floor when the song morphs into an oldie, but goodie. *Slow Motion* by Juvenile croons through the speakers. At this point, pretty much all of us are on the dance floor. I notice Caelan dancing with Jess. Instantly, a pang of jealousy grips my insides again.

What the hell? It's just Jess. Get it together, Sof.

I ignore the feeling and keep dancing with Johnathan. He's being innocent tonight compared to the other night at his club, which I appreciate. We dance to a couple more songs and decide to take a break. When we get back to the table, Luke and Chris are sitting there. Chris throws his drunk arms around me smiling down at me. "You're the best. You know that?"

"And you're drunk, my friend." I state the obvious. "But, it's your birthday, you deserve it. Now we just gotta find you a hot chick to go home with you." I wink. Johnathan grins at me

"I love you, Heart-Breakerrrrrrrrrrrr!" he bellows throwing his head back.

Oh, my God, he did not just do that.

He turns to Johnathan. "I'm two hundred bucks short tonight, but it was well worth the show!"

I hear Luke bellow in laughter. Johnathan studies me with curiosity. I shake my head at him in a "never mind" fashion. Then I look to Chris "And you, my very good friend, might get cut off if you do that again." I lean forward, whispering into his ear, "You fucker, you will pay for that."

"What's the matter, sweetheart? You don't want boy toy to know you just worked that pole like a professional? I would be glad to give him a blow by blow," he mischievously teases, whispering into my ear.

"Christopher O'Reily, I will kick your ass."

"Not on your best day, babe. But, I will gladly give you a brother's go around if that's what you're into!" He wickedly grins.

I slap him on the chest "You're done!" I laugh. "Someone cut him off!"

"The night has just begun HEART-BREAKERRRRRRRR!" he yells, walking towards the dance floor, grabbing Nikki along the way.

Johnathan's eyes are searching mine for answers when I see him reach into his pocket for his phone. He holds his finger up to me, connecting the call. Then he excuses himself to hear better.

Luke walks over to me smiling. It's just him and I. I'm assuming, being that were finally alone, that talk he wanted to have with me is about to happen.

"You happy, Sof?" he asks over the blasting music.

That sets me back a second. I wasn't expecting that at all. "As far as?"

"You know what I am asking."

I do. Actually, he wants to know if I'm happy with Jonathan. My eyes linger across the dance floor trying to find Caelan who is no longer dancing with Jess, but instead has a gorgeous blonde in his arms that he's grinding into as she holds onto him tightly, grinding back. I look back to Luke and snort my answer "What is happy, Luke? Do you know?" I yell over the loud music. "Tell me, 'cause I don't." I glance back to Caelan. "I thought I knew what happiness was once, Luke, but it got ripped away from me. Now when I thought I could move on, I can't because of a choice I made a few nights ago. A choice which has now made me feel all these feelings that I don't quite understand. So, tell me... what is happiness? Is it being with someone who knows nothing about you so you can be whoever you want? Or, is it being with the person who knows everything about you and can hurt you so badly that you won't be able to come back from it if it fails?"

Sadness reflects in his eyes and with a frown he steps closer to me and leans into my ear. "Sweetheart, he loves you. He will do everything in his power to make you happy."

"Really? What I see right now is not making me too happy, Luke."

"He's just doing it to make you jealous, Sof."

"Well, while he's trying to make me jealous he's pushing me in the opposite direction, Luke." At that, I hear the deep rumble of Johnathan asking me if I need a drink, which, I say yes to.

Yes, I need that damn drink!

As a matter of fact, I need a shot of tequila and a drink. We head to the bar so I can watch my drink being made. Sage and Jess meet us at the bar and we all do a round of tequila shots. Sage is pretty torqued up and when I give Jess a good once over, I realize she is too. Damn I am so out of the loop tonight. I throw back my shot, thanking Jimmy for the drinks, paying him with the money I won from Chris's dare.

Sage sees the hundred I pass to Jimmy and cracks up. "Free drinks tonight!" he bellows.

Johnathan looks at him confused. "I think I missed something here tonight," he says curiously.

"Yes, yes you did buddy, but my lips are sealed. My loyalty is to her."

Jess cracks up swaying a bit. "But it was fucking hot!" she bellows.

I groan. "Come on, let's dance." I grab Johnathan's hand pulling him to the dance floor. Sage and Jess are right behind us. Johnathan stops mid-stride. It's his phone again. He answers, giving me an unhappy look. He apologizes once again, saying he has to step out. Sage doesn't miss a beat, grabbing my hand pulling me towards the dance floor. Jess follows, as does Luke. An energetic beat hits the air waves and we all go crazy. Sage wraps me in his arms swaying our bodies to the music. My eyes are closed, enjoying the music and the freedom it gives me. I feel Sage release me when the song changes over to *Tell Me* by Diddy featuring Christina Aguilera and a new set of hands land on my hips from behind.

Johnathan... shit! Not Johnathan! Caelan.

I know just by his touch. My heart rate picks up. With eyes still closed he moves my body around the floor. His hands are all over me and I'm enjoying every minute of it. I lose myself in this vortex of Caelan and Sofia. With my back to his front I raise my arms wrapping them around the back of his neck. My bare middle is open to him. His head is resting over my shoulder. I feel his breath panting on my collarbone. His left hand is spread, holding tightly to my lower belly while the tips of his fingers on his right hand lightly skim down from my collar bone to my navel, caressing the exposed bare skin between my breasts. The deep beat of the music carries me away. His massive erection digs into the crevice of my ass. I grind into him, moaning at the feel of him. The rumble from his chest vibrates my aroused skin when he growls. When the song comes to the end, my eyes spring open. Reality hitting me...

You're here with someone else. What the hell did I just do?

Panic hits me. I frantically look around the dance floor and outer perimeter searching for Johnathan. Not there. I look over to the table we're all sitting at. Not there. I look to Giovanni standing on the perimeter of the dance floor. Nonchalantly, he shakes his head, letting me know Johnathan's still not back. Well, at least I have a little luck on my side. Caelan must sense my tension.

"Stop fighting this, beautiful." I break from him, missing his touch instantly. I head for the bathroom. "Fuck!" I hear him thunder behind me.

Once I hit the bathroom, I suck in huge gulps of air. First, to calm my ass down. Second, to calm down my hormones. And third, to get these raging emotions under control. Jess walks in, looking a little more drunk than she did just fifteen minutes ago.

"Honey, are you alright?" I reach out touching her arm, trying to keep her steady.

"Yeah I'm good. I wasps just coming to check on youuuu." She tried to say.

I chuckle. "Honey, you're drunk."

"Imabe fine. I stopped drinking howers ago," she slurs, waving her hand like it's no big deal.

I pull out my phone. "I'm gonna text Luke and have him meet us outside the bathroom. He should take you home."

"Fuccckk herm. Heezzzz dancing with some wretched britch out there." She points at the toilets with a wobbly arm.

"Oh boy." Yeah, no. She's done for the night.

"Oh, bozzz you go thwaat right. Cuz I'm pizzzesed. I jazz sucs his dick."

Yeah, ummm on that note... we're on level five and a half of five levels of drunkenness. She's gonna be feeling this tomorrow. I divert from the original plan and text Sage to come to the lady's bathroom. I wait a few minutes and lead the way for my drunkin' friend. When I step into the private hallway from the women's bathroom, Caelan is leaning against the wall with his arms crossed and his foot resting against the wall. Sage is standing beside him. He catches my eyes and I watch the lust in his eyes turn to concern for Jess. He straightens up, looking at Sage.

"What the fuck? How much has she had to drink?" Caelan's words laced with concern.

"Juzzz a wittle, C." She tries to hold up her two fingers. "You know your bozzz a d-dick hehead."

"Oh boy," I mutter staring at Sage, desperately begging him to take her home. "Jess, honey, it's time to go home." I motion her along.

"Come on gorgeous you're staying at my place tonight." Sage wraps his arms around her waist. "I have a feeling it's going to be a long night."

"Sag I can'tttt I too drunk, bezides yourrrrzz gay," she slurs with confusion.

"Holy shit. How much did she have to drink?" Caelan yells in frustration. "I've never seen her like this."

"Itzzzz allww yourz faults boyz faultzzzz."

"Oh hell. Sage get her out of her before she starts really babbling and letting things out she might not want put out there," I mutter leaning towards him as he nudges her to walk.

"Yur boyzz a fuc. Whyyy youzz boyzz gottaaa play gamzz," she rants.

Thank God, this hallway is empty. Wait, why is it empty? It should be packed.

"I wuv yozz," she gushes, leaning in to give me a kiss. I quickly turn my face dodging her lips and wrapping her up into a tight hug. I'm not really feeling like I should let her kiss me being she divulged she just gave Luke a hummer. We say good night with promises to call in the morning, but considering how drunk she is, I'll give her 'til late afternoon.

When I go to walk away, Caelan grabs onto my arm, pulling me back, flush to his body. He quickly turns, pushing my back up against the wall. His large hand circles around to the small of my back holding me in place as he lays a kiss on me that takes my breath away. His warm tongue slides over my lower lip so slow I damn near come right there. When his tongue enters my mouth, I take him in, all of him. It's a sensual, hard, and demanding kiss. When he pulls away, he nips my lower lip, teasing the plump skin with his teeth as he tugs my bottom lip from my mouth. His eyes drop down to my bare heaving chest. He runs the back of his index knuckle over my glistening skin. His finger slides underneath the barrier of my dress, stimulating my skin and giving me goose bumps. I shiver with passion and his eyes ignite with fire when he notices my nipples harden through the rippled, black silk. His finger slides in more, grazing over my nipple and back up again. His thumb meets his index finger, pinching me to the point of erotic pain. I moan, making him growl.

"You wear this dress tonight to drive me crazy? 'Cause that's exactly what you've been doing to me since the moment I laid eyes on you tonight, beautiful." He pinches my nipple again, watching my glazed over, lust-filled eyes become hooded.

Johnathan. I'm here with Johnathan.

I place my hands on his strong, broad, masculine chest. His other hand traces a line up my outer thigh. When he gets to the hem line of my dress he slowly inches the satin up my quivering thighs. When his thumb brushes across my panties, I shiver. My head falls to his shoulder. "C."

"Feel me, baby. Feel us. Feel the undeniable force that surrounds us. Stop denying what is right in front of you. We have something most people never get to feel," he confesses, caressing his thumb lightly over my clit, sending sparks to my lower belly. I'm lost in a sea of emotions. My breathing picks up to a steady panting. My fingers twist into the front of his shirt. He caresses a little faster while he whispers in my ear. "Give it to me, beautiful. I want to see you come. I want to watch your eyes glaze over as your body tenses and falls into sexual nirvana."

I do. Right there, in the private empty hallway to the ladies bathroom. The back of my head rolling back and forth along the wall. My orgasm takes over, my head drops, burrowing into his chest.

"Christ," I hear his strained mummer. "There's nothing in this entire world like watching you come, beautiful."

And with those words, I snap back into reality. Guilt rides the tail end of my orgasm.

Johnathan.

I break away from his arms, straightening myself as best I can.

"Don't do it, Sof," he warns. "Don't run." His voice and words change to a plea. I step away from him, straightening my dress again, then start to walk away. He catches up with me in two long strides, grabbing my arm and pulling me around to face him. "I love you. Don't do this."

"Ha! Me? Don't do this?" I snap.

He was the one just grinding up on some random girl. If he really loved me he wouldn't have been.

"You love me?" I point at myself. "You. Love. Me?" I huff a rush of disbelieving air through my flared nostrils. "Are you sure about that? Because, when you love someone you show them respect. If you loved me, you wouldn't have been dancing with your dick up that girl's ass. So much so you probably should have had a condom on!" I hiss. "Pretty sure you just had anal sex with her on the dance floor. But you love me. Right, Caelan?"

"Fuck me, man!" he roars, smacking the wall with the palm of his hand.

"No, I won't, but blondie out there," I hiss throw my thumb over my shoulder, "with the blown-out asshole will! I'm sure of it. Go find her," I sneer. "Oh, and don't forget the stripper you eye fucked and fondled in front of me tonight. Fuck you, Caelan O'Reily. Fuck You!" I scream, walking away from him down the *still,* empty hallway.

"Don't believe everything you see, Sofia," he thunders.

"I hope you enjoy the rest of your night, C." I yell over my shoulder.

"Sofia, don't go home with him tonight," he roars with warning.

I didn't plan too, but I keep walking because it's none of his business. When I get to the end of the hallway, Giovanni and Dax are both standing guard.

Now I know why no one was in the hallway.

"Johnathan's looking for you. He's at the bar. Told him you were in the ladies."

"How longs he been waiting?"

"Not long," he confirms with a straight face.

"Did Jess and Sage..."

"I called a car service to pick them up." I nod, silently thanking him. "You okay?" he asked with genuine concern in his eyes.

"No," I answer honestly, then head towards the bar. Jimmy is handing Johnathan his drink. "Hey, I'm sorry." I smile placing my hand on his back. "Everything alright?"

"Don't be sorry. I'm the one that should be sorry. I keep having to step out, which isn't fair to you." He wraps his arms around my waist leaning down to give me a light kiss.

I'm so damn confused. It's a nice kiss. I mean, it's more than a nice kiss, but it's not the flames I feel when kissing C.

"Jimmy, can I get a shot of tequila please?"

"Sure thing." He pours and hands me the shot. "That, by my counting, is number five. It's on the house, but it's your last one from me, sweetheart."

I smile, winking at him. Johnathan and I head to the dance floor. There's a slow song playing which I'm so grateful for.

He wraps me up in his arms. "You're a pretty amazing girl, you know that?"

Oh hell. Guilt just became an avalanche through my core. He wouldn't be saying that if you knew what just happened in the hallway.

"You're pretty amazing yourself."

"No seriously, most women wouldn't be so tolerant about me stepping out to take phone calls. You didn't complain, just asked me if everything was okay."

"You have business to attend to." I shrug. "I know how that is. I mean it's not like we were in the middle of having sex and you left me hanging," I tease.

His face turns serious. "Trust me, that would never happen."

"The sex or you leaving me hangin'?" I laugh.

"Gorgeous, I can assure you, if I had the privilege of having you in my bed, you can bet your sexy ass I would not leave you hangin.'"

Damn!

It's LATE. THE club is closing soon. SG Lewis's song *Warm* starts to play, so we stay on the dance floor. I feel emotionally, physically, and mentally drained from the highs and lows of this whole night. I think about Johnathan and how nice he is. Then I think about Caelan and what happened between us tonight. My heart is torn.

The song comes to an end. Johnathan leans down, holding my face in his hands. His green eyes sparkling as they burrow down deep inside of mine. He leans in closer, holding himself just centimeters from my lips. I tilt my head slightly, giving him permission. His lips touch mine. It's passionately slow, like he's savoring me. Our mouths open simultaneously to what becomes a very slow, sensual kiss.

Yup that kiss got me going.

He excuses himself to use the restroom and I head back to our table. I want to check on my sister. I feel like I haven't seen her all night. On my way back, I notice her and Chris on the dance floor making out.

Ummmm that's a shock. When I said we needed to find him a girl to go home with I didn't mean my sister.

I keep heading for our table. There's a crowd of people standing around, mostly women. Luke's with some girl with his arm around her waist. Her lips are attached to his neck. "Fucking Asshole!" I mumble loud enough that Luke looks at me. After a few minutes of eye contact, I just shake my head in disappointment at him and turn away.

It's then in that very moment that my world drops out from underneath me. My heart shatters. The oppressive pain is paralyzing me. I'm frozen. My eyes slam shut, my head drops. Tears stab the back of my eyes. I can't believe what I just saw. I open my eyes, making eye contact with Luke who is now standing directly in front of me. I look back to the scene unfolding on the dance floor behind Luke.

"Caelan," I whisper with incredible sadness. My hand finds my mouth, stopping the sounds of my gasping.

A tear flows over my waterline, to my lash, and then falls onto my cheek.

Caelan.

My Caelan.

He's kissing someone, but it's not just any someone.

Caelan's kissing... Kate.

Kate, the only girl he has ever dated seriously. The same girl that took my place after my miscarriage of his babies. Another tear spills over my lashes to my cheek.

Get yourself together, Sofia.

"Sofia," Luke softly whispers, rubbing my arm.

I turn abruptly stepping away from Luke's hold and straight into the brick wall of Giovanni's chest. I try to collect myself, quickly wiping away my tears and giving my head a quick shake, trying to rid myself of the pain. I hold my head high, ignoring Luke and side-stepping Giovanni. I walk straight towards the bathrooms, trying to escape the scene ripping my insides apart, praying I make it to the privacy of a bathroom stall before the dam breaks and the flood comes and I lose the contents of my stomach.

There's commotion behind me but I know Giovanni is one step away from me. He's yelling something in his dictated tone, but I can't hear him, nor do I want to hear him. My ears are ringing from the lack of blood flow that's rushed from my head. Johnathan exits the men's room. When he sees me walking towards him, he gets a big smile on his face. I smile back with the biggest, most fakest smile I can conjure up. "You ready to go?" I ask cheerfully.

"Yeah. You want to go have a drink at my place or do you want to just call it a night?"

Without hesitation, I answer, "Your place is good."

forty-three

Everyone makes mistakes.
Some fueled by anger, some by jealousy.
Some... are just plain bad decisions.
Mine was a combination of all three.

THE RIDE OVER TO JOHNATHAN'S PLACE IS quiet. I can feel Giovanni's eyes on me through the review mirror. Johnathan's holding my hand, softly caressing my knuckle with his thumb. Dax is nowhere around. Confusion hits me when we pull up in front of a building I've never seen before. I thought when Johnathan asked me if I wanted to go back to his place he meant his fuck pad, but this is not it. I look to him for answers.

"It's my home."

So instead of the fuck pad, he brought me to his home? Hmmm.

I'm not sure what to think of that. We exit the SUV. He holds my hand as I follow him through the spectacular building to the back elevators, Giovanni in tow. The ride up is quiet. I can feel Giovanni's eyes on me. When we reach the top floor, the doors open into an enclosed vestibule with a table and two chairs. The doors on the opposite side of the vestibule swoosh open. I walk through with Johnathan as he tells me to make myself at home so he can go back and talk to Giovanni for a moment. I'm looking around the expansive penthouse when I feel Johnathan at my back.

"This place is amazing," I mutter, more to myself than to him.

"Thank you. I bought it a few years ago. You want a glass of wine or some water."

"Wine's good."

Maybe it will help me numb the pain.

I feel like I'm in a dream of thick fog I can't wade through. I feel like nothing in my life is real. I feel like what I just saw with my own eyes didn't happen, but it did. Caelan was kissing Kate. Kate, of all people. After he told me he loved me, he was kissing Kate.

When I saw him with the girl the other night, that hurt. It hurt badly. This, though, I just... I can't...

Just keep moving.

I feel his hand on my lower back when a glass of wine appears in front of me. His lips caress my neck. I lean my head to the side opening up to him. He kisses his way down my shoulder leaving goosebumps as a trail. My phone starts ringing, which jolts me from the kiss. He stops so I can answer. Caelan's handsome face flashes across the screen. It's a picture I've had for years. It's of me and him on a park bench under a tall Oak Tree enjoying the rain shower. I decline the call. Then I notice that I have ten missed calls. Eight from Caelan, two from Luke. The sound of music filters through his surround sound. My phone rings again. I hit decline. His text comes through almost immediately. I go to delete it, but curiosity gets the best of me. I slide the screen and read his message.

C: Sofia, please talk to me. Let me explain.

There's nothing to explain. You had your lips on the one girl that could destroy me.

So, I say the only thing I can to him, with a song.

Me: Adele~ Love in The Dark

Then I turn off my phone...

I WALK TOWARDS Johnathan's open hand that he has held out for me. I take it with somewhat of a forced smile. He pulls me into his arms and slowly moves me to the beat of the music.

He smiles down at me. "You okay being here? I didn't want to bring you to the club."

"Yeah, I'm good, but why? Why didn't you want to bring me to the club? That's where I figured we were going."

"Because I realized something this afternoon. Actually, last night after you left, but today at lunch confirmed it for me." He grins. "You're a pretty special girl, Sofia. You'd have to be to have so many people around you that cherish and want to protect you. It tells me that you're someone I have never encountered before in my life. Most women want me for what I have or what I can give them, and that's fine, because honestly, all I want from them is a few hours of their time, but you, you're different. You were pissed and ready to walk away from me today when you misunderstood what I said, and you weren't even going to look back." He shakes his head like he's fighting something in his own thoughts. "Three weeks ago, I can honestly say I never thought I would be standing in my living room with a woman like you. A place I have never brought any woman," he admits with a disbelieving tone. He breaks our contact, walking to the bar, which confuses me. How do you say something like that then walk away? I can see the indecision in his eyes. I hear the uncertainty in his voice. But why? He pours himself a hefty drink and takes a large mouthful. "I gotta do the right thing here, Sofia."

"And what is the right thing, Johnathan? Do you want me to leave?"

"Fuck No! No, I do not want you to leave." He grabs the back of my neck with his strong hand, pulling me close to his lips. When he looks into my eyes, I see hesitation again, but then he kisses me. Which only confuses me more. The kiss at first, was slow and unsure, then rapidly became a compulsion. His hand comes around to the small of my back, pulling me into him, then suddenly breaks the kiss. "Sofia, I think maybe we should-"

I anchor my lips to his. He reluctantly falls into the kiss again. I feel his erection growing against my body, and I quickly think... *Caelan.* I shut him out of my thoughts again. He pulls me into him harder. His hand leaves the small of my back, working its way to my thigh. He breaks the kiss for a mere second, only to work his lips down my neck to my shoulder. I close my eyes, feeling what he's giving to me. I'm turned on, there's no doubt of that, but this is not Caelan's lips on me. I can feel the fire, but it's not the blaze.

Stop thinking about him.

His fingers tickle at the hem of my dress, inching it up. He breaks the kiss, searching my eyes. I kiss him again, giving him the permission I think he's searching for. His kiss becomes hungry. He slides my dress up to just above the crease of my upper thighs and butt. His fingers caress the tender skin. With a surge of strength, he grabs my upper thighs and lifts me from the floor. I wrap my legs around his hips, locking them.

He breaks the kiss. "You sure?" he stammers with broken, heavy panting.

"Yes," I consent, kissing his neck. "Are you sure?" I ask with concern, feeling like there's something holding him back.

"More than sure."

He walks us towards a long hallway, kissing me the whole way. We reach a room I assume is his. I notice a chest of drawers with cologne on it as he glides by. He sets me down on his oversized, manly bed. Kneeling in front of me, he removes my heels one at a time, running his hand up my legs to my slightly open thighs. His fingers gently grip my inner flesh opening me to him. His eyes still haven't left mine. His hands caress their way higher until he's tracing the outer edges of my panties. His thumbs run over my clit through my lace panties. His fingers attach to the thin string holding the material together. He tugs them tenderly telling me to lift my bottom from his navy blue comforter. I do, and when I do, he trails them down my legs to the floor, leaving them there. His hands return to my inner thighs again, spreading me wide open to him. He finally breaks our eye contact and takes all of me in.

"Jesus, you're stunning," he professes with admiration. I bite my lip, trying to mask the blush on my cheeks. He tilts forward. His lips find the skin of my inner thighs kissing, sucking, and caressing his way to the meaty flesh above my clit. He kisses me again, then looks up at me with hooded eyes. "Lay back, sweetheart."

I do, and when I do, he lifts my legs-one over his shoulder and one raised and bent onto the edge of his bed. His thumb finds my clit and gently massages. When, his tongue finds my swollen eager nub with a long, warm, savoring lick. I moan and squirm. He devours me until I climax with a broken cry of release.

God that felt good.

He pulls me up from the bed to stand in front of him. His hands find the side zipper to my dress. It drops to the floor. I stand before him naked while his roaming eyes take me in. He runs his hands down the curves of my body, holding steady onto my hips. I reach forward, grabbing his shirt, pulling it over his head, and dropping it to the carpet. I run my hands through the light smattering of chest hair, then lay a soft kiss in the center. I drop my hands to his pants releasing his button and zipper. I hear the rush of air leaving his lungs. When I look up at him, he has the sexiest look in his eyes. His pants drop to the floor. I kneel, removing his pants from his thick, strong calves. His eyes burn with desire as I pull down his boxers, uncovering his erection. I tilt forward, sliding my tongue along the thick vein leading to the head of his cock. He hisses, grabbing my chin pulling back from me.

"I won't last if you do that again." He grins, pulling me up to kiss him. He lifts me, laying me on his bed, then drops and covers me with his body. He kisses me again working his way down to my nipples. He sucks, pulls, and twists them. My moaning stops him. Drawing his eyes to mine. His hard length lays between my folds. "You sure?" he questions again.

I lift my hips rubbing his cock against my clit. "Yes. You need to wear a condom."

He lifts from my body. Reaching for his pants he pulls a condom from his pocket. He rips it open, rolling it down his shaft. The moment he does I see his control let go. He crawls over the top of me, grabbing my legs as he does. Pushing them back as he surges inside of me. His eyes close as he stills for a moment.

I close mine. A moment of guilt hits me. When I open my eyes, he's looking down at me. He starts to move. Slowly at first. His lips find my neck as his pace picks up rapidly. My mind goes blank. My body takes over.

The soft tender caressing is gone, being consumed by lust from both of us. The clawing need to come fills me again. His rapid movements jilting my body up his bed. Our bodies glisten in this soft lighting. I clutch onto him digging my nails into his back causing him to groan low and long.

My orgasm hits me. Whimpering as I clench my teeth. Johnathan growls, and after a few powerful, heavenly thrust, he stills, coming with a growl. He releases his weight from his arms laying his full body onto mine kissing my chest. He lifts his head, looking down at me with a grin. "You okay?" he asks affectionately.

"Yeah, I'm good."

No, I'm fucking dying inside right now. What did I just do?

He kisses me again, then rolls off me and the bed to take care of the condom. He's in the bathroom a few minutes before coming back out with a facial expression I can't read. His jaw is tight and pulsing.

"What's the matter?" I sit up with concern. He's silent for a second, staring at me with sorrowful eyes.

"The condom broke."

What the fuck? Did he just say the condom broke? The. Condom. Broke?

"I'm clean, Sofia. I promise you, I'm clean," he stresses with sincerity.

It's gonna be okay.

"I'm clean too," I quietly assure him. "And I'm on the pill, so we're fine."

He sits back down next to me. "I'm sorry, sweetheart."

"Why? It's not your fault."

He searches my eyes, looking for... what? I don't know. Anger, fear, regret... If he looks hard enough, all three are right there, simmering under the guilty surface. "I'm alright."

He leans down, kissing my cheek, then my lips. He pulls me down to lay with him. His hand wraps around my waist. I lay still as he falls off into a relaxed, sexual released slumber.

With Jonathan's arms still wrapped around me, I lie there wide awake. The guilt is eating me alive. It's a funny thing, this thing they call life. It waits until you make a mistake before it smacks you hard in the proverbial face. I just had sex with Johnathan because I'm hurt and pissed at Caelan. It hurts because ... well, there's only one reason why it could hurt me.

You're in love with him. I am in love with him. If you weren't, you wouldn't feel the way you do right now, Sofia. You can't deny this anymore. You can't fight these feelings anymore. You can't go through the steps of everyday fooling yourself anymore. What the hell did I just do? I blew it. I fucking blew it. I waited too long. He gave up. He moved on. He was kissing Kate tonight. Kate, of all people. I pushed him away one too many times. The only girl he has ever seriously dated. She's the only girl that would be able to hurt me as much as I am hurting. It took seeing him kissing Kate to realize I'm in love with him. I'm sure he's in bed with her right now. I can't. I can't think about it.

My stomach wants to hurl. My eyes swim in tears. I'm so stupid. I was so afraid to lose him, but because of my stubbornness and fears, I lost him anyway. All my fears have come to fruition, and I didn't even get to show him my love.

I SLIDE OUT FROM underneath Johnathan's arm. Quietly grabbing my dress and shoes. I tiptoe to the living room. Shit, where are my damn underwear? I dress quickly as I scan the room looking for my purse. I zip myself up while looking for my underwear again.

Damn, they're in his room still.

I decided it's best not to go back into his room. So, I head for the elevator doors. Before hitting the button to open them, I take a deep breath removing the tears from my burning eyes.

"You just made the biggest mistake of your life," I whisper to myself, rubbing my forehead with tense fingers, hanging my head. I turn back, looking toward the hall that leads to Johnathan's room. "I'm sorry," I mutter. Feeling guilty that I was walking out after what really was a good night between two people. Well, that is until one of those people finally realized that they're in love with someone else. "Damn, you screwed this all up." I chastise myself.

I hit the elevator button. The doors swoosh open to reveal Giovanni, along with Dax, standing in the vestibule. There's nothing worse than doing the walk of shame. But, this walk of shame is seriously fucked up because I'm standing in front of my bodyguard who has also become a close dear friend. He takes one look at me when intense concern floods his face. I look to Dax, noticing he has a busted lip, a bruised jaw, and some serious swelling around his eye. I look to Giovanni for answers.

He shakes his head. "What's the matter?" he demands taking forceful steps towards me.

I cautiously shake my head glancing towards Dax, letting him know I don't want to talk about it in front of him, who at the moment is wiping his bleeding lip. The door behind me closes while the opposite door opens. We enter the elevator. The doors close, shutting out the worst decision of my life. It wasn't fair to Johnathan. It wasn't fair to Caelan, and I damn sure wasn't being true and genuine to myself.

I realize I never picked up my purse from the couch. I tell Giovanni and head back inside. I grab my phone from inside my purse and turn it back on. When I do, I hear his deep, resentful voice.

"So, you were just going to leave?"

My head snaps up in shock that he's awake. "I'm sorry," I say as my phone starts beeping with text messages and missed calls from earlier. Out of habit, I look down at my phone quickly. I see a picture pop up on the screen that holds my attention.

Johnathan's phone still sitting on the bar from earlier dings with a text message. He goes to grab his phone when mine beeps again. I hear his confused mumble.

"What the fuck?"

When I look at my phone again, it's a picture of Johnathan and me in front of the window in a very passionate kiss from last night at his fuck pad. His hands are on my ass. Another picture comes through, this one of us in the club tonight. Another of us walking into this building just a few hours ago. The last picture that comes through breaks my heart all over again. It's Caelan kissing Kate at the club tonight. Her arms are wrapped around his neck. His hands on her hips. My phone dings again from the same unknown number. It's a link. I press it, and when I do Giovanni grabs my phone from my hands. As he does, the words that splatter across the screen... I just can't comprehend. My body goes weak and starts to tingle. My hearing starts to buzz. The room around me starts to become darker and spin. My body becoming heavier and heavier by every sickening moment. I hear my name being called, but I can't focus. I feel hands on my shoulders.

Then it all goes black. I fall into the black abyss of safety.

forty-four

I WAKE TO GIOVANNI'S CONCERNED WORDS. "Everything's going to be okay. Please wake up," he whispers into my ear. Someone's holding my hand and there's a wet washcloth on my face. I'm disoriented at best. The doors to the vestibule burst open in a swoosh. Antonio, Caelan, and Luke are rushing through the door, guns blazing.

Johnathan, who is holding my hand, grips me harder before letting go and standing. I notice that he's still only in his boxer briefs. Giovanni's already moving across the room to the three of them. Three set of eyes are giving Johnathan a very close inspection.

Antonio slams his hand against the button to close the elevator doors, while Caelan rushes to my side. I hear a lot of orders being barked out. An unknown male voice comes over what sounds like an intercom. Everyone goes silent.

Giovanni rushes to the doors of the vestibule, raising his gun to cover Antonio who is already hitting the button for the doors to open.

Johnathan goes to step towards the door when Luke stops him.

The doors slide open. Antonio takes a step through to the other side, opening those doors.

A nervous man is standing there, dressed in all black. He's holding two things in his hands. In one hand he has a tape, and in the other, a piece of paper.

Giovanni rounds the elevator door, forcefully grabbing the man by his shirt and shoving him to marble of the vestibule floor with force.

Dax slams his foot onto the man's back holding him down as he points the barrel of the gun at his head.

"He works for me," Johnathan starts yelling.

After patting him down, Giovanni jerks him to his feet. The guy looks like he wants to throw up.

Johnathan apologizes to him. The guy hands him the tape, but hesitates when Johnathan asks about the piece of folded paper he has in his hands. After he finally does hand the paper over to Johnathan, I watch as his face becomes stone. He hands the letter off to Giovanni.

"Who fucking gave that to you?" he demands. The man doesn't answer. Johnathan's ferocious sneer vibrates through the room asking him again. "Who. Gave. That. To. You?"

"Some guy, maybe thirties, dark hair, about six foot. Stopped me on the back staircase, told me to make sure I gave it to her," he points to me.

Caelan jumps up from the couch, grabbing the letter that is now in Antonio's shaking hands. "Fuck!" he thunders.

With unsteady feet, I walk to Caelan, holding out my hand. "Give it to me."

"No, beautiful. Let us take care of this," he says holding onto my shoulders.

"Caelan give me the note!" I demand.

"Sis, you shouldn't read it. It's his sick, twisted way of getting into your head."

"Give. Me. The. Note!" I hiss.

I hear Giovanni exhaling a breath of resignation. "Fuck."

"Sis, really, you don't..."

"NOW!" I scream at Caelan.

"Sofia, when you read this note there is no coming back from it. You can't unread what's on that paper. It's going to get into your head and fuck with you. I'm going to give it to you, but please, please take this for the mind fuck that it is. Okay?" He slowly hands me the note, looking behind me to Luke.

I feel Luke step closer to me from behind. He lays the folded paper in my open hand. Taking a deep breath, I open it slowly. Before I finish reading the last word, I hear Luke's deep rumble of curses in my ear. Then vomit hits the back of my throat. It's the same sick words that were texted to me. My knees give out. Arms wrap around my waist from behind. I look to Johnathan with tears burning in my eyes from trying to hold back the vomit. I fight until Luke releases me. I run to the only bathroom I know. His master bedroom en-suite. I barely make it to the toilet before vomit rises at a vicious pace, burning through my throat and mouth. I throw the lid open just in time. Caelan's right behind me, holding my hair. Johnathan's at the door. I wretch again and again, bringing up the contents of my evening. I can hear Antonio yelling from the other room.

"Tell me how the fuck he got this close and you didn't see it? Tell me how he knew where she would be last night and tonight?"

Silence.

"Someone say fucking something!" he thunders. "That's my baby sister in there, throwing her guts up! There's a sick fuck out there that has balls bigger than an ox to get that close to her. Especially when she had a date with her, two fucking bodyguards, and friends surrounding her all night."

"Better?" I hear Caelan ask.

I look up to him. He's not looking at me. He's now staring at Johnathan in his boxers. I don't even fret that because I think I'm in shock. Nothing seems real right now. "He h... h he has video, C? I swallow the copious amount of saliva that's meeting the bile rising in my throat. He has video of me?"

"Out!" he bellows at Johnathan.

Babbling in shock. "C-C, he v-videotaped himself raping me?" I ask in question. Not believing it. "No, no, no, no, no, no, no."

"Baby, stop talking," he whispers, running this hand over my hair, consoling me. "Get The fuck Out!" he thunders at Johnathan with such force I swear the walls rattled. "And close the fucking door!"

forty-five

I DON'T KNOW HOW MUCH TIME HAS PASSED. The next thing I remember is Caelan carrying me in his arms through the vestibule to the elevator, with all the men surrounding me. Everyone except for Johnathan. When we reached the ground floor and started circling through the spinning doors, a flash of Caelan kissing Kate hits me. That pain penetrates my heart. I am in the arms of the man that said he loved me and was kissing someone else tonight. Not just someone else… Kate.

"Put me down, Caelan."

He stops. Concern hitting his tense face. "You okay? You going to be sick again?"

I shake my head. "Put me down."

Confusion flickers through his sad eyes. "What's the matter?"

"Nothing. I just want to walk."

"Sofia, I got you. I'm going to drive you home."

I stiffen. "No." My face starts to involuntarily scrunch from the ugly cry that is ready to burst through the locked gates. I wiggle trying to get him to release me. He does. My feet hit the pavement.

"Tell me what's the matter."

"Kate." Is all I can bring myself to say.

Anger and hurt flash across his face. Dax is standing in front of me. Giovanni on one side and Antonio on the other. I walk directly towards the SUV. Dax opens the door for me to enter. When he closes the door, Giovanni say something to him. He stands by the passenger side door without entering. Giovanni comes around the driver's side then slides behind the wheel. He starts the car, then turns in his seat when Antonio opens the front door.

"I'll follow you," he tells Giovanni. Who acknowledges with a quick nod.

Outside my window, I hear Caelan's deep, broken voice. "Sofia, open the window, baby."

I ignore him.

Antonio leans back from the SUV. "Caelan leave it alone for tonight." I hear him say.

Dax is standing there, protectively watching our surroundings. Caelan steps towards the open front door where Antonio is now standing. Dax puts his hand up to his chest stopping him. Antonio steps in-between them when he sees the fury on Caelan's face. He looks past Antonio, asking if Dax wants another bloody lip.

C gave Dax his bloody lip? Why?

"Get in the vehicle, Dax," Antonio orders with a harsh roar.

He does, shutting the door to the yelling going on outside the car.

"Baby, open the window. Talk to me," he pleads.

Baby, huh? Baby? Was I his baby when his lips were on her tonight? No, I don't think I was.

The SUV starts pulling away from the curb. Caelan's desperately yanking on the locked door handle, yelling at the truck. I have no idea what he's even saying, but I yell at Giovanni to stop. I open my blacked-out window to a relieved-looking Caelan. "Do not call me baby when your lips have been on someone else tonight."

"Sofia, don't do this. Let me explain."

"No!"

"No?" His brows pinch. "Seriously? You fucked him tonight! Didn't you, Sofia?" he accuses, pointing at me. Antonio grabs him, reprimanding him as his pushes him back farther from the SUV.

Well that just pissed me off even more, if at all possible.

"You know what? At least I didn't tell my best friend I loved her and then had my lips on my ex-girlfriend!" I yell, thrusting myself back into my seat, hitting the window closed, separating us with the blacked-out window again.

"Go," I demand, hitting the back of the seat.

He pulls out and drives for two blocks before pulling over and stopping again. He tells Dax to step out of the vehicle. He does it, no questions asked.

With concerned determination, he turns and asks. "Are you okay?"

I stumble on my words, not knowing how to answer this, but know I have to say something. Is he asking because of the turn of events tonight with my stalker, or Johnathan, or Caelan? "Which part are you asking about?" I say rambling sarcastically. "Physically, yes, I'm okay. Emotionally, no. I'm all fucked up in the head. My stalker is always within ten feet of where I am in this big ass city that we can't seem to get lost in and we have no idea who the fuck he is. Caelan professed his love to me twice, then I see him with some girl on the dance floor tonight with his dick so far up her ass he should be tested. And as for Johnathan, well, that poor guy did nothing wrong except choose to fuck a girl that's fucked up beyond all recognition in the head. He was a pure gentleman. I just realized a little too late that I was making the biggest mistake of my life. So, you tell me, am I okay?"

Sadness fills his eyes as tension filled his jaw line. He reaches back, grabbing ahold of my hand and squeezing. "Tomorrow's a new day. Don't fall part, sweetheart. Tomorrow's a new day."

I nodded my agreement. "Giovanni?" His sorrowful eyes tell me to ask my question. "Can I sleep at your place tonight?"

"You can sleep at my place anytime you want, sweetheart."

He yells for Dax to get back into the SUV. The ride to Giovanni's was long and quiet. When we reach the penthouse, Dax disappears immediately. I head towards the room I slept in a few nights ago when Giovanni calls me back. When I turn to see what he wants, he's already right behind me. He wraps his arms around me in a hug I would consider brotherly.

He pulls away slightly, looking down at me. "Sometimes our biggest mistakes lead us to the realization of what we truly want in life. Those mistakes are not mistakes, they're bumps in the road we called life, telling us to get it together."

I scrunched up my face trying not to cry. "Well, I made one of the biggest mistakes of my life tonight. One that fills me with guilt."

Frowning he says, "Sweetheart, trust me things will be okay."

I squeeze my eyes shut tightly, my shoulders dropping in defeat. With total surrender in my voice, I say "I don't think they will." When I open them, I watch his expression harden.

"Don't you give up. You're a strong girl, Sofia. Don't you dare give up."

forty-six

I take a hot shower, washing Johnathan from my weary body. Leaving the bathroom, I make my way to the bed. I notice a large white t-shirt laying across the bed along with some gray, drawstring sweat pants. I change into the clothes left for me and lie on the bed, staring off into the dark ceiling. I can't sleep. I hear my phone ding from inside my purse, which is laying at the end of the bed. I know it's going to be Caelan. I stretch for my purse because I simply don't have enough energy to get up and grab it. The song he sent in the text brings the flood of tears that I have so desperately tried to hold back.

C: Lifehouse~All That I'm Asking For.

Me: Lifehouse~Broken.

C: I love you, Sofia. Don't you ever doubt that.

Me: Why her C? Why?

C: Baby, answer your phone.

Me: Just tell me.

C: Answer.

My phone instantly starts vibrating in my hand, but I decline the call.

C: Answer the damn phone and I'll explain.

It starts vibrating again.

Me: Tell me why.

C: Beautiful you're scaring me now. I can't lose you. If you don't answer your phone, I'll come over there.

Me: Why her?

C: Answer your phone. I'll explain.

Me: No. Hearing your voice will be too hard. This is all too hard. It's too much for me. I can't do it. Why did it have to be her?

C: I'm coming over there.

Me: Don't!

C: Don't do this Sofia!!! Answer your fucking phone!!!

Me: I didn't do this, C. You did. Don't come here.

Because I won't be here.

I roll out of bed grab my heels and head to the kitchen. I grab a pen and paper telling Giovanni not to worry, that I'll be okay. That I just need time to myself, that I need to be alone. I tip toe with bare feet holding my heels to the elevator enclosing myself inside. I need space. I need time. I need quiet time. I need to turn off the pain. I need to turn off the noise in my head. The elevator quickly descends to the ground floor. I walk the lobby quickly in case Giovanni heard the elevator.

The night air washes over my face. I hail a taxi and disappear into the city night. I give the cabbie my home address, knowing Caelan would be true to his word and go to Giovanni's. It's early morning, almost 5:00 AM. After telling the cabbie to wait, I open our front door and enter an empty home. I need to do this fast. I pack a bag, grabbing only the essentials and quickly change out of Giovanni's massively oversized clothes. When I get back downstairs, I notice the keys to Caelan's Ducati are missing, which means his keys to his blacked-out Ford Raptor are all mine because his car is in the shop. I grab the keys off the counter and head out the back door, leaving the cabbie waiting out front. I hop into his truck, adjust the seat to my small frame and head to who knows where.

I drive around for hours. My cell keeps going off. Without looking, I finally just turn it off. There is one more thing I need to do before I leave town. I need to apologize to Johnathan for last night. I feel bad for the way things went down. I feel bad that while he peacefully slept in sexual weariness, I was too weak of a human being and tiptoed out of his room to leave him to wake up alone. I was wrong for that, and for so many other things that I can't forgive myself for.

I turn my phone back on. I text Sage and Jess, letting them know I won't be around for a while, basically telling them to do what needs to be done at the shop and that, I trust them and love them.

I turn my phone back off and drive around for what feels like hours. When I turn my phone back on, a call from Johnathan comes through. I decline. He leaves a voice mail telling me he wants to see me today so we can talk. I hear the clatter of dishes and glasses in the background. I assume he's at his restaurant. So, I take my chances, heading that way. What I need to say should be said to his face. He's only ever been a gentleman to me and he deserves at least that much respect back.

Pulling up in front of the restaurant, I jump out, letting the valet know I'm not staying, to hold the truck there. I make my way inside, asking the hostess if Johnathan's in. Being that it's the same girl from the other night, she recognizes me and brings me around to a private table off in the back of the bar. What I see takes what little I had left in me, out of me.

"No, it can't be," I mutter in disbelief. "This cannot be happening."

My world breaks. There are no words. I don't think there is one man in my life that has not let me down, except for Giovanni. Everything is always a lie. The air is sucked from my burning lungs. My world stands still. My vision blurs. I feel a hand on my arm asking if I'm alright. My vision returns and focuses on the two men standing in front of me. Johnathan and Mr. Robert Heart. My father. The man who is always supposed to be there for me. The man that is supposed to protect me. The strange phone call from yesterday starts replaying in my head.

Johnathan works for my father. This was all a game. This is just his way of keeping tabs on me. This is his sick, twisted way of having control over me.

Oh God, I knew something wasn't right. I felt Jonathan's hesitation. I knew there was something I was missing. My female intuition kept screaming at me, but I didn't listen. I never listen. He slept with me while he worked for my father. That's more than low. That's why, last night, he looked hesitant to do anything.

I kept kissing him. I pushed it. This is my fault. I'm gonna be sick. I'm so stupid.

I swallow deeply, glaring at my father. So much anger radiates from within me. Then I look to Johnathan with even more anger. I trusted him. "You work for my father. I trusted you." It was a statement, not a question. He shakes his head in denial. "Don't you lie to me, you piece of shit! You put your dick in me last night, and you work for my father. He's paying you to watch me, isn't he?" I scream, not caring that I just said it in front of my father. I just don't care anymore. I'm done. He goes to lay his hand on my arm. I rip it away screaming at him not to touch me. My father tries to calm me, but I wrench away from his touch as well. "I came here this morning to apologize for my behavior last night, feeling so guilty. I guess I'm the fool, huh? I was doing you a favor by leaving, wasn't I?" I shake my head, biting my own lip so hard out of frustration that I taste my own blood. "God, I'm so fucking stupid," I mumble to myself.

"Angel Face, listen to me."

"No!" I scream. "You listen to me, you piece of shit. You wouldn't know how to be a good father if the Lord himself came down here and held your hand and showed you how."

"Sofia," Johnathan tried to intervene. "I'm sorry."

"Yeah, you are sorry! The worst mistake of my life!" I scream at him again as I turn, bursting through the doors, running to Caelan's waiting truck. The truck that is going to take me far, far away from all this. When I look back to the restaurant, I see both my father and Jonathan rushing out the restaurant doors, both with faces of shock, anger, disbelief-and remorse on Johnathan's.

I hit the gas with force squealing the tires and race towards the freeing highway.

Without.

Looking.

Back.

forty-seven
Caelan

SMASH!

The resounding noise echoes through the dreary room as the empty bottle of beer whips across the room, colliding against our brick fireplace.

"Son, calm down. We'll find her."

"Calm down? Calm down?" I holler in astonishment. "You want me to calm the fuck down when she is out there?" I thunder, pointing to the outside world. "She's out there on her own right now, in danger! Why? Because every single fucking one of us has let her down! To the point that she felt safer by herself!" I bellow with such force the veins in my neck hurt from their pulsating. "Don't you dare tell me to calm the fuck down! You can go fuck yourself, Mr. Heart!" I roar pointing at him.

"C." I feel Antonio's hand of warning on the back of my shoulder, giving a slight squeeze, letting me know I stepped over the line.

I don't care.

"C, what?" I rip my shoulder away from him. "What? Say it, motherfucker! Say it! You know what? I already know what you're going to say! I don't fucking care. He's the reason why she feels the way she does about herself. He's the reason she's not here right now! And you and you." I point at Giovanni and Antonio. "Are the reason why she doesn't trust me! I should have never gone along with the two of you. I should have been there with her, by her side, protecting her all along! So, fuck you all!" I thunder striding towards my front door. "I'll find my girl myself!" I roar slamming the front door.

forty-eight

Evil eyes lurking
It was me who kissed her cheek
A sinister sneer
It was me who she gave the embrace
Obsession burning
It was me watching through the lens
Her fear
It was me who fed it
I hide in the open
Peering through my lens
I hide in the night
It is me who she feels in her nightmares
My rose
She knows I am coming
and I am coming...

Sofia and Caelan's journey continues in book
two of The Heart Series,

B R E A T H I N G
together

Excerpt

DINNER WAS EXCELLENT. IT FELT GOOD to eat some real food. My stomach is doing flips though. I thought coming up here would be relaxing, but here I am again with nervous knots in my belly.

"What's the matter?" he questions. "You don't look so good."

"Yea, I'm good. It's just my nerves making my stomach flip. Either that, or it was your cooking." I smirk, busting his chops.

"No, it's probably because you have been eating shit for the last couple of days and now your stomach's protesting the real stuff it just consumed. Was that a vegetable? Oh God, no!" We both laugh as he pulls his cell phone out. I'm going to text everyone and invite them up.

"It will be so good to have everyone together." I smile with excitement.

Me: Hey everyone it's Sofia and I. We're spending a few days up at the cabin for the holiday weekend. We want you all to come up here and spend the weekend with us. Sage and Jess, Sofia said close the store tonight and reopen Tuesday morning. Luke, Chris, and Nikki, I know you all have off this weekend, being that I was the one who gave you the time off, so get your asses up here. Antonio and Giovanni are on their way up already. Everyone grab a tray of food and some bags of chips and stuff. Chris, can you grab me some jeans and tees from the house? Everyone, we're keeping this weekend on the low. Keep it to yourselves, we don't want anyone to know and make sure when you leave the city you're not being followed.

We chat for a few minutes while the texts start coming in.

Chris: My ass will be there! I wanna see my favorite stripper, HEART-BREAKERRRRRRR!!!! I miss her!

Sage: "Heart-breakerrrr in da house!!!!!!!

Nikki: Bahahahahaha

Luke: I'm in as long as she does a dance for us all. Did Mr. Heart install a pole yet?

I crack up laughing. Caelan's red face right now is priceless.
Keep on smiling because your ass is going to be as red as my face.

Me: Guys!

Chris: Hell no big bro! Just cause you're now tapping that ass doesn't mean we all can't still love on her!

Me: Chris when you get up here, I'm going to beat your ass!

Nikki: She did have some moves, though.

Sage: OMG! The pink sausage wallet finally got some action? Like some real honest to goodness action?! Heart-breakerrrr, baby, you're holding out on me!

Luke: I'm rolling right now! Who says that . . . pink sausage wallet?! WTF man? Dude, you're not right in the head!

Sage: Don't be hatin'

Jess: Pink sausage wallet? Ewww! Sage, I'm riding up with you.

Nikki: Ewww!

Chris: First off, dude, I'm not into men. No spankings for me (no offense Sage). And not for anything, you're my brother that's just plain, gross, dude. And not for nothing, she was a stripper for a night, and there was a lot of money being thrown at her, so the wallet came in good use.

Me: CHRIS!

Chris: What bro? She did have a lot of money being thrown at her.

Sage: none taken

Sage: That she did!

Luke: Yup!

Nikki: Oh, yeah, she did!

Jess: Oh, she worked it!

A: Guys! That's my fucking sister you're talking about!

Chris: Oh, yes it was!

A: C, I'm gonna kill your brother!

Me: You're all fucking fired! I'll help you, A.

Chris: Fellas, fellas... No need to beat on a guy for simply stating the fact that she is a fine piece of ass and made A LOT of money that night! Never mind the catcalls from the guys!

Me: You're done, dude!

A: Agreed!

Sage: Meet me at my house, hot lips. We'll take off first thing.

Jess: See you then.

Chris: Nikki and Luke meet me at Caelan and Sof's place. We'll leave from there.

Chris: No scratch that. Everyone just meet up at Caelan's first thing in the morning. I'll grab one of the trucks from the office. This way it's only one vehicle driving up. Less chances of being followed. Is that okay boss?

Me: I'm not your boss anymore, I just fucking fired your ass!

"Wait, what did I miss?" I question looking at Caelan through my tears of laughter.

"What?" he barks.

"Give me the phone why are they calling Jess hot lips?" I stop and suck in a breath "Oh no!"

"What?"

Me: It's me Sof. Why are we now calling Jess hot lips!

Chris: HEART-BREAKERRR!!!!!!!! WHERE HAVE YOU BEEN?

Sage: You know why!

Me: Ya, take one of the trucks with no business logo on it.

Chris: Wait what did I miss? Guys tell me!

Luke: Sage! Shut the fuck up!

Sage: One cannot forget the sputtering of a drunkin' woman!

Jess: Sage Rhinehouse! Shut it!

Sage: Yes, love.

Chris: Oh snap! Shut down hard!

Sage: Kiss my ass!

Chris: You would love it too much!

Me: *Everyone shut it! Meet Chris at our house tomorrow morning. You can all drive up together. Make sure you keep checking all the way up here that you're not being followed! Especially when you leave the city!*

Chris: Got it!

Caelan throws his phone down on the counter as he rounds the island like he's stalking prey. I start taking steps back in preparation for the sprint I know I might have to do.

"So, you think this shit is funny, all the joking about you stripping?" His irate words pass through his gritted teeth.

Oh no, he's not happy. I try so hard not to laugh. I really do, but my smile morphs into a smirk because I'm trying desperately to hold it back. I shake my head rapidly.

"No? Because I can clearly see a smirk on your face. You're amused that I am burning up inside because they all got to see you naked?"

"I wasn't naked," I correct, pointing at him, still stepping back and doing circles around the kitchen island.

"Close enough. What would possess you to do something like that?"

"Two hundred bucks!" I yelp incredulously like he should have already known.

"No other reason?"

"Maybe." I shrug my shoulders, trying to look innocent.

"Maybe?" he questions, raising his left brows, tilting his head slightly. "What would that reason be?"

"Maybe, maybe I was trying to make you jealous."

"Why were you trying to make me jealous, Sofia?"

He totally knows why and he's enjoying every minute of me being uncomfortable right now.

"Maybe because you didn't even acknowledge I was in the same bar with you. You didn't even say hello to me that night." I tear up, remembering the hurt I felt. "Maybe because your eyes were glued to that blonde that spread her legs in front of you, for you, and you tipped her." I stopped moving because now all the hurt I felt that night come rushing back.

He steps right up in front of me so close our bodies are brushing against each other. He looks down locking eyes with me. "Did you ever thinking I was doing that for a reason?"

"Yea because you like blondes. All you have ever dated is blondes. They're your thing." I spit with disgust.

"You're my thing, beautiful. Do you want to know why I only dated blondes?"

I shake my head no. Because honestly, "I don't want to know."

"Oh, but I'm going to tell you. It's because they weren't you. The only reason you have ever seen me with blondes is because they weren't you. The only brunette I ever wanted and will ever want in my bed, in my life, is you."

Bullshit.

"You are seriously trying to tell me you only dated blondes because if you dated a brunette, you wanted it to be me?"

"That is exactly what I'm telling you. There's no one else for me. I told you, those women to me were just me passing time, waiting on you. Now, ask me why I wasn't paying attention to you and I was paying close attention to her."

I shake my head no again and drop my head, leaving our eye contact because again I don't want to know, but I have a feeling I'm going to find out regardless.

His index finger and thumb find my chin, lifting my head back up to meet my eyes. His blues sparkle with determination and pain.

"I didn't say hello to you that night and I didn't pay attention to you because, number one, that fucking dress you had on made me so fuckin' hard I couldn't see straight, and two, Antonio, Giovanni, and I decided that we needed to show some separation between you and I. Whoever is stalking you thinks we're together. We were trying to show separation to piss him off, make him believe he doesn't know everything about your life like he thinks he does. We were trying to get him frustrated, so he would mess up. So, my interest in the blonde on the stage, had to do with that, not that I was attracted to her, because if I had had my own choice, I would have been deep inside you."

Gulp.

"So, do you still think it's funny that you burned me up with jealousy that everyone got to see you on that stage?"

I start to smirk again

"Think carefully, beautiful, because that promise I made you when I removed you from that stage is still a standing warning.

Ohhh hell, the spanking. His fantasy of slappin' my ass. Or is it my fantasy? Hmmmm. Well, now I might have to do something to piss him off.

"I was trying to protect you, and you deliberately set out to piss me off what should I do about that?"

"Love me?" I shrug, smiling with an unsure smile.

"Ohhh, I'm gonna love you all right." He smirks, slapping and grabbing my ass. Now, go finish what you were doing so I can give you my surprise," he orders, kissing me roughly then strides away.

Acknowledgements

Where do I even begin?

First and foremost, to my husband who didn't think I was crazy when I said, "Hey, babe I think I'm going to write a book."

His words, spoken with a smile were "Go ahead. You can do it."

Months passed, and with a road trip up to the mountains later, a story that had been festering was born. It wasn't until four months later, on a cold February day, that I started typing away. Five months later, *Breathe With Me* was finished. So, I thank my husband from the bottom of my heart for letting me be me and supporting me in this crazy time-consuming ride. You are my rock, my strength when needed, and the person that encouraged me the most on the days I had tears rolling down my cheeks because I thought I sucked. Thank you for the shoulder you provided, and most of all... your love. I love you more, baby. ☺

To my children who drive me crazy. You two are the most stubborn, bullheaded, driven, loving human beings, but, I guess I know where you got that from. I love and cherish you and always will, even when you drive me batty! May your dreams and aspirations take you to heights you never thought possible. May love fill and overflow in your hearts for eternity.

To my beautiful niece, Sabrina. You are the epitome of strength and determination. I admire you more than you could ever know. Thank You from the bottom of my heart for all of your help.

From those late night random texts asking you what sounds better, or should I put a semicolon here or there, or is it than or then? lol I thank you for answering them all. I wish you nothing but the best in a future that is brighter than a star. You rock my sweet, gorgeous, girl. You rock!!

To my book bestie- Megan: Girl, we have read some books, haven't we? Some good, some bad, some that have ripped our hearts out, and some that have made us laugh like crazy. You are my 1:00 am text message - "Are you serious? How far are you? I can't believe he did that! What a loser!" -girlfriend. You were the first person that read *Breathe With Me* outside my hubby and I thank you for all your praises. Little do you know, but it is your words that excited me most because if anyone knows, it's only an avid reader that can tell you if the book is truly bad, good, or great. When I asked your honest opinion and your eyes lit up… I knew I had something good going.

To the women who have read *Breathe With Me* and were hunting me down for book two when it was finished… Peggy, Pat, Ellen, Betty Jean, Maryann, Toni Lynn, Heather, Mary, Judy, Nicole, Michelle, and Jen, thank you for your kind words, enthusiasm, encouragement, and for the love of this couple and their heartbreak and shenanigans. There is way more to come, trust me! I promise you all by the end of book three you will stop calling me names!

To John and Tony Lynn: Thank you for putting me in contact with someone who knows this crazy book world. She was a wealth of information that was priceless. Also, thank you to Theresa for giving me the information/ facts on the stomping grounds of New York. I may only be one state down but if you dropped me in the middle of Manhattan and told me to find my way home… I'd be a lost girl. So, thank you for that.

To Faith Andrews for giving this new girl a wealth of information in the book world. You have made this road easier for me and I truly thank you for that.

And to my sister-in-law, Ellen, if it were not for you forcing me to read *Fifty Shades of Grey*, I would not be sitting here writing this acknowledgement page. When I said, "I'll just watch the movie when it comes out." And you said, "No way, you have to read it. I'm telling you, you will be glued." I then said, "Ellen, I don't read books. I'm not a book person. I'm a movie girl." You then said, "I'm bringing them over and you're going to read them." Well, you were right. It is from those three books that started my journey of reading viciously and then a year and half later, writing. I truly feel like I have found my home in writing and I strive to be better every day as I sit down and start to type. I thank you for being so persistent.

To the readers: Thank you for taking the chance on an unknown author. I hope you enjoyed this journey with Caelan and Sofia as much as I have. There is so much more to come with this couple and the crazy eight. Trust me, when their journey ends, you will no longer hate me for leaving you hanging. Their story is finished and there will be healing and a HEA. *I promise.*

If you enjoyed Caelan and Sofia's story in *Breathe With Me*, please take a moment and give a new author a review/rating on Amazon and Goodreads. Without you, the reader, giving us a rating, it is hard for an independent author to get their name and story out there for the world to enjoy.

I would love to hear from you!

Goodreads:https://www.goodreads.com/book/show/35965024-breathe-with-me?from_search=true

Email: michelle.b.author@gmail.com

Facebook: https://www.facebook.com/michelle.b.author501

Twitter: https://twitter.com/MichelleBAuthor

Instagram: michelle_b_author

55375502R00266

Made in the USA
San Bernardino,
CA